ARMORICA IN THE FIFTH AND SIXTH CENTURIES

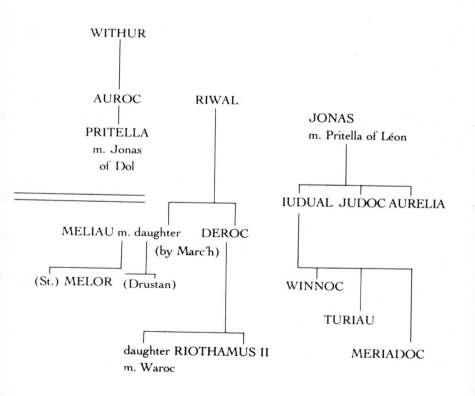

LÉON AND ACHM

W. DOMNONIA
(St. Brieuc)

E. DOMNONIA
(Dol)

WITHUR

AUROC

RIWAL

PRITELLA
m. Jonas
of Dol

JONAS
m. Pritella of Léon

MELIAU m. daughter   DEROC
(by Marc'h)

IUDUAL JUDOC AURELIA

(St.) MELOR (Drustan)

WINNOC

TURIAU

daughter RIOTHAMUS II
m. Waroc

MERIADOC

THE
WHITE
RAVEN

Novels by Diana L. Paxson

THE CHRONICLES OF WESTRIA:

Lady of Light
Lady of Darkness
Silverhair, the Wanderer
The Earthstone
The Sea Star
The Wind Crystal
The Jewel of Fire

DEL EDEN BOOKS:

Brisingamen
The Paradise Tree

HISTORICAL FANTASIES:

White Mare, Red Stallion

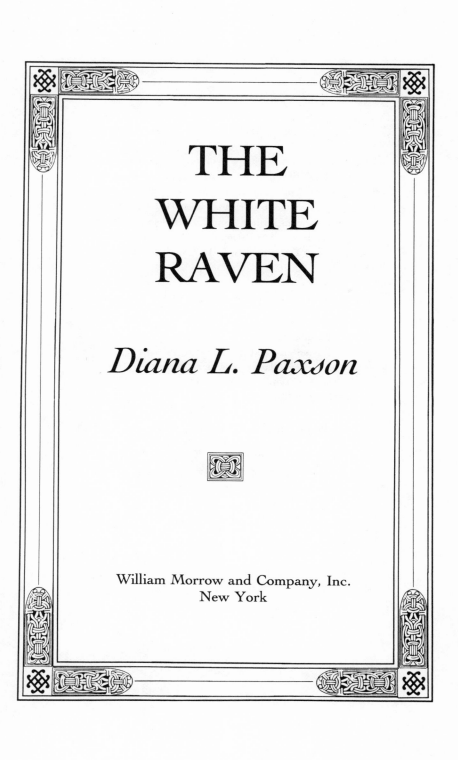

THE WHITE RAVEN

Diana L. Paxson

William Morrow and Company, Inc.
New York

Library of Congress Cataloging-in-Publication Data

Paxson, Diana L.
    The white raven.
    1. Tristan (Legendary character) — Fiction.
2. Iseult (Legendary character) — Fiction. I. Title.
PS3566.A897W47 1988   813'.54   88-1795
ISBN 0-688-07496-0

Printed in the United States of America

First Edition

1 2 3 4 5 6 7 8 9 10

BOOK DESIGN BY MICHAEL MENDELSOHN

MAPS BY VIKKI LEIB

To Marion,
more than a sister,
for showing me the way

ACKNOWLEDGMENTS

In writing this book, my intention has been not only to place the Tristan and Iseult legend in the context of the history of the sixth century, but also to attempt to harmonize my interpretation (wherever possible) with those of the major works of fantasy which have dealt with this period already. In particular I have attempted to reconcile genealogies and placenames with those used by others, mainly Rosemary Sutcliff in her classic series of books on Roman Britain, especially *Sword at Sunset*, Marion Zimmer Bradley in *The Mists of Avalon*, and Poul and Karen Anderson in *The King of Ys*. Thank you all for the inspiration, as well as the information!

I would also like to acknowledge my debt to those whose expertise has contributed to the book's authenticity. My thanks to Sharon Morton for checking my herb-lore and suggesting more ancient names for the herbs in Queen Mairenn's potion. Please note that this recipe is based on early beliefs about herbal properties, not our current knowledge of pharmacology. Many of these herbs are poisonous if the wrong amount or part of the plant is used. *Do not attempt* to prepare the potion — at the very least, it would probably make you as sick as it did Branwen!

My appreciation goes also to Paul Edwin Zimmer, whose collection of materials on Irish legend and prosody was an invaluable resource, and whose success in using those poetic forms in English inspired me to attempt them in my adaptations and original verses.

Above all, I am grateful to Alexei Kondratiev, Celtic linguist and scholar, for providing me with the correct sixth-century forms for names and titles, suggesting resources, and checking the book for inaccuracies. At times the demands of the story or my own interpretation of sources may have led me to make other choices, but any mistakes are my own!

I would like to offer special thanks to Chris Miller, my editor at Avon, whose interest gave me the courage to tackle this project at last, and whose enthusiasm and faith kept me going until I finished it.

My gratitude finally to Brigid Herself, patroness of bards and of the British Isles, who insisted on becoming part of this story. . . .

CONTENTS

THE BRITISH ISLES

PICTS

Iona

GODDODIN

CLYDE

B R I T A I N

THE ULAID

CONNACHTA

E R I U

RHEGED

DEIRA

MAN

Inber Colptha

Temair

MIDHE

Mona

Cill Dara

LAIGIN

GWYNEDD

MIDDLE ANGLES

EAST ANGLES

MUMU

Porth Mawr

DEMETIA

GLEVISSIG

GWENT

Londinium

Sabrina Sea

KENT
(JUTES/FRISIANS)

DYFNEINT

Ker-Esk

KERNOW

N

A R M O R I C A

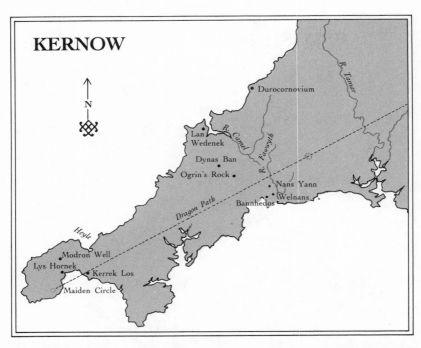

KERNOW

N

Durocornovium

R. Camel

Lan
Wedenek

Dynas Ban

Ogrin's Rock

R. Fawwyth

Nans Yann

Welnans

Bannhedos

Dragon Path

Heyle

Modron Well

Lys Hornek

Kerrek Los

Maiden Circle

R. Tamar

Barsa

DOMNONIA

LEON

Dol

Ker-haes

BROCELIANDE

Redon

Inis-Sun

Plebs Marci

Kemper

CORNOVIA

VENETIA

Venetorum

N

Namnet

ARMORICA

PROLOGUE

On Samhain, the doorways open between the worlds.

In the lands of men folk watch and ward and keep the Festival, for although the Christos rules in Heaven, on Earth there are older powers that do not obey the priests' law. I know this, for I have felt them throbbing beneath my feet and heard their whisper in my soul. Men celebrate the great Festivals that they may live in harmony with those powers, and for that purpose also they consecrate their Kings.

Diarmait McCearbhaill was such a King—Diarmait the great High King of Eriu, in whose house I was born. Marc'h of Kernow, last heir of Artor the Conqueror, is another. And the marriage of the King with the Queen is one with his serving of the Land—that is the Mystery.

But what is the Queen?

If I am ever to know how Esseilte's fate and my own have been twined with those of Drustan and Marc'h the King, that is what I must understand. Many a thread has gone into the weaving, and who can say that without this one or that the pattern would have been the same?

One strand—when Mairenn of Mumu came to the House of Diarmait MacCearbhaill as a bride her brother came also. For his strength they called him the Morholt, and he was the Champion of Eriu.

Another strand—before the King forbade his warriors foreign raiding, the Morholt brought home a proud brown-haired woman as his captive from Kernow. When he took her he bedded her, as men do in war. But he had no use for her afterward, so they put her to grinding grain in the house of the King.

A third strand—after the Queen had given her lord two sons there

15

were no more living children. Folk thought Mairenn past bearing, and then came a last daughter with hair like the sunlight. That same day the British woman bore a daughter to the Morholt, and named her Branwen — White Raven — and died, and the father gave the infant to his sister to be raised as a servant to the little Esseilte. And I was that child, and if the tale of Esseilte has since become a legend to rival the tale of Grainne, then my own story is the warp upon which all the bright weaving has been bound.

The Queen gave us both to one nurse to be suckled, and together we played and quarreled through all the years of our growing — Esseilte and Branwen, like sunlight and shadow, so that if one of us were looked for, then the other was surely to be found. We heard rarely of events in the Isle of Britain across the water, where the heir of Artor sought strength in Armorica to withstand the Saxon wolves. Even if we had known, we would have cared little. How could these things concern us, weaving wildflower crowns in Laigin while Diarmait fought for his throne? But we grew older and our lives were strung upon the loom.

That one strand in the pattern was love is something all men know, but maybe hate was in it also, for the one is often the other's shade. The love of man for woman was part of it certainly, and the blood love between kin, the need of a child for a mother, and running through all of them, the compulsion of the eternal cycle of Sovereignty.

It is the Feast of Samhain, when the doorways open between the worlds. The pattern is almost completed now, and soon I will understand. . . .

One

SAMHAIN EVE

Earlier in the day it had been raining, but the sky had begun to clear and in the sunset the tattered clouds glowed like the embers of the old gods' sacred fire. Esseilte and I waited for the Samhain procession by Carnait's mill, where the road from Tlachtga curved up the slope toward the hill of Temair, watching for the glitter of torches that would herald the king.

Behind us, Eithne of Mumu and one of the princesses of the Ulaid were discussing men. I had no need to turn to know them — they had spoken of little else for the first three days of the festival.

" — and Curnan of Connachta will win the great race tomorrow." Eithne's voice carried like that of a crow among blackbirds. "He has the gray horse, and a beauty like Diarmait who was the darling of every woman in Eriu!"

"Have you no eye for anyone but the Connachta lad?" asked her companion. "There's Aillel of Dal Raida, and Fergus Mac-Ciaran to consider, both of them fine riders and well-mounted too. You'll not be forgetting that it's the horses that will be running, not the men?"

Eithne laughed, but I felt Esseilte stiffen beside me as the girl from Mumu went on. "I saw the footracing yesterday, and a fair sight it was, but it is the horses who bring the greatest glory to a man."

"Then my uncle the Morholt will be the first!" Esseilte flung back her bright braids and whirled to face them.

17

The princess of the Ulaid stared at her, but Eithne smiled like a bear sighting a honey tree.

"For sure he was a fair man — six years ago, when your father took Tuathal's throne. But there's silver now in his beard, and he limps when the rain is coming on!"

"— From a wound got when Tuathal sent men to kill us all!" retorted Esseilte. "And doesn't that give him a better claim to the hero's portion than any deed of those pretty boys with their virgin swords?"

Eithne raised one dark eyebrow. "Such a fierce defense — is it your uncle or your sweetheart you're praising now? I will marry an old man if my father requires it, and so will you, but surely a maid can dream of strong arms and a smooth brow?"

I stood silent, torn between amusement and exasperation, for the Morholt was my own father, though his only paternal act had been to take me from beside the body of the little British woman who had died bearing me and give me to his sister the queen to raise with her own newborn child. But that was hardly a thing worth remarking, and the princesses paid no more mind than if I had been Esseilte's shadow, standing there.

"I know who the Morholt is, and who I am" — Esseilte pulled dignity around her like the rich folds of the subtly checkered blue and purple cloak she wore — "and I swear that no man who is not the Morholt's master will win a pledge of love from me!"

Suddenly the wind seemed colder. It was an east wind that came from beyond the dim veil dusk had cast across the British sea. I drew my own gray brat more closely around me, glad of the warmth of the thick wool, for I fancied I heard in Esseilte's defiant words the echo of a geas from one of the old tales. The princesses were laughing, and I tried to smile too, for I had heard Esseilte make just such pronouncements after the death of a pet sparrow, or the time her golden arm-ring was lost.

But on Samhain Eve, the earth itself has ears to witness the oaths of men.

Someone motioned from the hilltop — a long white hand whose gesture commanded attention even before one realised that it belonged to the queen. The princesses' chatter abruptly stilled. Esseilte lifted her hand in acknowledgment and without farewell turned and began to climb the hill. I watched her go, her fair head shining even after her cloak became one with the shadowed grass, wondering if I should follow. But if she were attending the lady, she would have no need of me.

In the silence I could hear the voice of water chuckling against the mill wheel. Slowly I made my way down the hill. Fed by the welling waters of the hidden spring, the millpond was mirror-dark in the fading light. I leaned over it, and for a moment thought I saw Esseilte's face reflected there. Then I realized it was my own — thinner, with eyes more gray than blue and hair the pale brown of a shadowed wheatfield where hers was like the same field shining in the sun.

It does not matter who I am, I thought then. *I share Esseilte's fate now.*

And as if my thought had summoned her, I looked up and saw Esseilte waving to me from the hill.

"Branwen, come quickly! We can see the Tlachtga fire! They'll be bringing the torches — Branwen, come and see!"

I waved back at her, then swept a few fallen grains from the path and tossed them into the dark waters in offering to the spirit who lived there. Then I got to my feet and hurried up the hill.

Seven miles away rose the mound of Tlachtga where they kindled the sacred fires. In the old days they had burnt sacrifices there as well. A spark of light shone there now, tiny, but brighter than the rosy glow that faded in the western sky, and I knew it for the needfire that could keep the hosts of earth and air at bay.

And even as we watched, the fire exploded into myriad points of light. Esseilte clutched at my arm and we stared as they grew larger — a swarm of sparks that danced above the mass of shadow thundering toward us along the road. So came the hosts of Faerie when they moved to their winter fortresses on Samhain Eve, and I felt the hair rise on my arms even though I knew this riding was of human men.

"Ard-Righ, Ard-Righ!" Queen Mairenn raised the cry and the fierce ullulation of the other women echoed her. I could see the white glimmer of two horses and a gleam of gold from the king's chariot behind them, trailed by the other riders with the Samhain torches burning furiously in their hands. Around the curve and up the gentle eastern slope of the hill they swept, sparkling with a terrible beauty.

"He is there!" Esseilte's voice shrilled through the shouting. "You see, Branwen — the Morholt is leading them!"

I saw my father then, reining back his big bay lest he outrun the king, and shouldering Prince Curnan's gray aside. In the torchlight his hair and beard shone like unmixed gold. And I could see also the glitter of Esseilte's eyes, and I knew then that there had been some truth in Eithne of Mumu's words. Esseilte had worshipped the Morholt with a child's adoration, but she was grown woman-high now. And at that moment, though we were of an age exactly, I felt immeasurably older than she.

I should warn her, I thought. *The queen fostered me to take care of her.* But as easy to rule Esseilte as to govern the wild wind, that no matter how the sailor trims his sails will back and blow. And so I sighed instead, and kept still.

Then the riders were all around us. Hoofbeats thundered in our ears and the torches showered sparks like falling stars. The king's charioteer pulled up the white horses and men sprang to hold them. Rearing white shapes filled all my vision, like great birds that lifted, crying, into the dark. Diarmait balanced on the heaving platform of the chariot, holding his streaming torch high. His scarlet cloak was thrown back. The fitful light flared from the gold-work in the embroidery of his white tunic and the golden boars' masks on his belt, on his arm-rings and neck torque, and the golden circlet that held his auburn hair.

He was grinning, still flushed from the breathless rush of the ride and the heat of the fire, and men gave way from the sheer pressure of power that pulsed around him as he stood above us. In that moment the praises of the poets who called him the greatest of the kings of Temair — Cormac MacArt's true heir — seemed no flattery.

Then the tumult quieted a little, for the queen was coming. The red and gold serpents that spiraled across the dark stuff of her cloak writhed in the light of the fires. She was a tall woman, her body thickening now from the children she had borne, with strongly marked features that took on an austere splendor as she reached to take the burning torch from the hand of the king.

"The year's wheel turns, summer to winter passing — behold, the sacred fire is lit anew!" The king's voice rang out over the shouting, and the pipers echoed his cry with a dissonant sweet skirling that was somehow more pleasing than any harmony.

The queen grasped the torch and whirled, her cloak flaring around her as if the scarlet gown she wore beneath it had taken fire.

"At home they say she is a sorceress," came the princess of the Ulaid's whisper. "They say she gave her golden hair in exchange for her powers, and that is why she always wears a headdress.

Well, with that horse face, she must have used some magic to hold the king! And as to the kingship, they say—"

"Hush!" Eithne silenced her. It did not surprise me. Eithne was a gossip, but Queen Mairenn had been a princess of Mumu, and Eithne had her share of family loyalty.

Esseilte was already running across the grass ahead of us, and I was glad she had not heard, because, though we did not speak of it, at least some of the stories about the queen were true. Our old nurse had told us how the king had had a second wife who was jealous of Mairenn and hired a woman-jester to pull off her headdress before all the people at the Lughnasa Fair. Messach said that Mairenn had cursed her rival to a series of miscarriages, and only the prayers of Abbot Ciaran had enabled Mughain to bear her first living son.

I hurried to catch up with Esseilte, for they were nearing the mound where King Loegaire had been buried armed and standing to defend Temair against the men of Laigin. The libations for the spirits were allowed to sink into the earth that housed them, but the offerings for the ancestors were set out in cups of clay with candles left burning beside them. The priests disliked it, though without the fervor with which they had condemned the blood sacrifices. I could never see why, for they shared with the wise ones of the old faith a belief in the spirit's immortality, and what harm can there be in enlisting the protection of the dead for their descendants? The world of men and the hidden realm are like sunlight and shadow, and the power comes from within.

Then we were swinging out around the great earthen rampart that surrounded the king's house, our feet moving in rhythm to the piping and the swift rattle of the bodhran drums, so that I no longer cared that my thin leather slippers were soaked through from the wet grass.

The procession had become a meandering line of fire, passing among the Druids' stones and between the mounds of Dall and Dorcha. Then we moved downward, circling the women's houses where the hillside fell steeply away toward the plain. We stopped again below them, and the queen took extra time with the offering, for it was here that all the women of Temair had been slaughtered by warriors of Laigin at Samhain three centuries before. Some of the girls took advantage of the stop to slip away into the women's house where they could get warm, but Esseilte stayed at her mother's heels, and where she went, I must go too.

Finally we were on our way again, swinging outward away
from the buildings to make the sacred right-hand turn around
the circle of tumbled stones. Northward the valley of the Boinne
curved away toward the Ulaid, dim and peaceful beneath scattered stars. If I looked hard I could make out the hills of the Old
Ones humped against the darkness, and it seemed to me that
they held a veiled glow.

Holding my breath, I touched the nearest standing stone. Despite the chill of the air it was warm, and as I pressed my hand
against it I seemed to feel a throbbing, or perhaps I heard it — a
deep, vibrating hum. In a moment I would recognize it — in a
moment I would understand —

"Branwen, what are you doing? They are making the prayers
at the triple mound already — come along!" Esseilte's face was a
dim blur in the darkness, but I knew her voice better than my
own.

"Put your hand here, Esseilte — can you feel it?" I felt for her
hand and guided it to the stone. For a moment we waited, listening to our own breathing and the fading murmur of the procession. Lights shimmered on the plain below us; I stilled, and
glimpsed movement — rushing chariots and the flash of weapons,
bright hair blown back by the speed of their passing, laughter
sparkling in bright, unhuman eyes. . . . Then an owl swept overhead, calling almost too softly to hear. Esseilte jumped and
jerked her hand away, and I saw only a glimmer of mist upon
the plain.

"Oh, Branwen — there's nothing to feel but hard stone! Did
you fancy you heard the Sidhe calling you to the faerie mounds?
Never mind." She slipped her arm through mine and pulled me
along. "I won't let them carry you away."

We came up behind a group of warriors and I heard the Morholt's laugh. I would have drawn Esseilte past them, but she
held me there in the darkness.

"If our lord leashes us back from Laigin, there's always the
British shore — " It was a young, thin voice — one of the princes
of the Ulaid, by the accent. I could not remember his name.

"Unless the Saxons have looted it all already — they've had a
hundred years to pick Britain's bones!" commented another.

"The Saxons never overran the Cymry, or Kernow . . ." the
Morholt spoke again. "Their great King Artor is dead these forty
years, and the fabric of his empire has pulled apart into a patch-
work of kingdoms while the Saxons still lick the wounds he gave

them. King Marc'h is a lord in Armorica, besides reaping the wealth of the tin trade out of Kernow, and no overlord has tithed it for a generation or more!"

"It has been still longer than that since the men of Eriu raided there, though we used to take a tribute as regularly as if our lord were their High King. Do you think our ships can still find the way?"

"As a wolf finds the way to the sheepfold, or the fox to the chicken-run!" answered the Morholt. There was general laughter.

"But what about the High King?" the third man objected. "Will Diarmait let you go?"

I wanted to applaud him. This talk of raiding made the pit of my stomach ache as if someone had hit me there.

"He will let us go." The Morholt's voice was ugly. "He thinks to keep me as his lapdog, but I'll find a way to compel him. I tell you truly I have no mind to sit and watch my white hairs growing by the Ard-Righ's fire!"

Their voices faded as their strides lengthened and they drew away from us. I gripped Esseilte's arm. "We must find a way to warn your father — do you think the queen —"

But her hand was already closing my mouth, and even in the darkness I could see the shake of her fair head.

"The Morholt is a hero! Don't you understand?" she hissed in my ear. "You heard Eithne laughing. I have heard the young warriors taunting him, too. Fergus MacGabran swears he will take the Morholt's place as champion. The Morholt is worth ten of them, but my father gives him no chance to prove it here. They will not laugh when his ship returns, wallowing in the water from the weight of British tribute he has won! All Eriu will know that the Morholt is the champion then!"

I shook my head, but without Esseilte's word to support me who would listen? And perhaps she was right after all. Swallowing my fear, I ran after her.

The procession had moved around and back to the center of the hill, forming an uneven circle surrounding the place where the old shrine had been. A little church stood there now, with the round huts of the priests huddling beside it like chicks around a hen. Through the wickerwork that screened their windows came a glimmer of candlelight, for they were the only folk in Temair who would not wait to light their hearthfires from the sacred flame.

Esseilte and I fell into line and knelt in turn before the red
sandstone pillar at whose base the figure of the little horned god
was carved. The stone glittered in the torchlight, wet with the
mead that had been poured over it. I reached out to touch it and
felt the stone warm as the standing stones had been.

We still honored him, but there were few now who knew the
godling's name. The wind lifted the damp hair from my brow
and I shivered, remembering the silence of the mounds. Were
those who had raised them still living there, transformed into the
Sidhe as our old nurse used to say? Or were they dust like any
other men? Once the whole land of Britain had belonged to
tribes who were our kin, but now half that land lay beneath the
heel of men who spoke a different tongue and worshipped other
gods. And I had heard how wild tribes from the East were
striding across the old empire of Rome. Would Temair itself be
overrun and deserted someday?

I stumbled and clutched at Esseilte, for it felt as if the earth
beneath my feet were tilting, and all certainties were slipping
away.

"Branwen, what's the matter? Are you ill?" Esseilte held me
and I clung to her, shaking, drawing reassurance from her solid
warmth as I willed the dizziness to pass.

"Can't you feel it, Esseilte? The world is changing! Everything we have known will pass away —"

"You've spent too much time listening to old Messach's tales!"
Esseilte put her arm around me and gave me a quick hug. "Do
you want to go inside? We've done most of the circuit. No one
will know if we go back to the women's house now."

I shook my head. "I'm sorry. I'm all right. I want to see them
light the Samhain fire."

We went on, but for a time Esseilte was unusually silent and I
knew that I had troubled her. A fair exchange, I thought, for the
many times her passions had frightened me. But I had scared
myself as well, and I was glad to be beside her, for I shivered
even as the light and excitement of the procession closed around
us, remembering the chill of the wind and my vision of the hill of
Temair silent and overgrown as the mounds of the Sidhe.

We followed the track around the eastern side of the king's
dun and through the southern gate beside the mound of Teá
after whom Temair had been named. It bulged out from the rampart which had been built out to incorporate it, the highest point
of the hill. And there they had built the boar-fire, and as Esseilte

and I thrust through the crowd, the queen touched her torch to the tower of logs and it exploded into flame.

"Samhain! Samhain! The year begins anew!" the people cried, and we were shouting with them. The flames shot a man's height into the air and for a moment I thought I saw the form of a woman among them, extending bright arms to bless the land. Then the young men shouldered past us to touch their new torches to the fire, and raced off in every direction to rekindle dead hearths. Soon light glimmered through windows all over the hill of Temair and from the shelters that people had erected for the Samhain Fair upon the plain of the Boinne below.

Esseilte was shouting with the rest, but I kept silent, watching the little lights spring to life. For a moment I felt the presence of a host of others watching with me — not just the crowd of people, but the spirits of the Old Ones as well, and I knew that however fearful the changes in the land, still something of every race that had ever lived here would remain.

"Praise to the Lady, that's over — now we can get to the feast!" said Esseilte. "I feel as if I could eat the whole boar!"

The roar of male laughter echoed hollowly from the meadhall; for a moment Queen Mairenn lifted her head to listen. In the moment of silence that followed we heard more laughter, and a snatch of raucous song. Then the queen picked up the thread of the conversation like a woman at her embroidery, and the murmur of women's voices closed over the stillness again.

Not for the first time, I was grateful for the privilege that allowed the women of rank to leave the men alone and retire to their own feasting hall after the first flagons of ale had been borne round. We were well supplied with mead and cider, but the men had a hundred vats of different kinds of ale — enough to last a hundred and fifty princes and a mixed bag of craftsmen through a long night's drinking, and they would have been shamed if there had been more than a sip left in the bottom of any one of them when morning came. It was something for the poets to praise when they celebrated the splendor of the king, and if the guests were expected to hear out a recitation of the full genealogy of the Ui Néill, I supposed they would need the wherewithal to toast the ancestors.

The queen's part was to entertain everybody's wives and daughters in the Grianan, but though things occasionally came to hair-pulling, we did not commonly expect to find our guests

with cracked skulls instead of sore heads when morning came. It
had always seemed to me that the men were crazed to set to
drinking with each man's weapons hanging behind him on the
wall, but as well to try and separate a man from his sexual parts
as from his sword. And that reminded me of the Morholt, and
the conversation Esseilte and I had overheard, and I drank
quickly to quell the anxious cramping in my belly.

"Is your cup empty?" whispered Esseilte from her couch. "I
need more cider too." She handed her goblet to me. It was a
precious thing of white bronze banded in chased gold. The Morholt had given it to her.

When I eased back down on my hassock beside Esseilte, the
clarseur was tuning the great harp while that strange woman
Leborcham spoke with the queen. She was stout, red-haired, with
a tongue like a sword when she saw injustice. There were poets
aplenty in Temair, but few were women, and fewer had the gift of
satire. A woman's tongue and a satirist's skill made a formidable
combination. It was said that she had sung warts upon the lord of
Dun Cannon for a breach of hospitality, and there were other
tales which had doubtless lost little in the telling.

But tonight I hoped there would be no need for Leborcham's
particular expertise. Simple entertainment was all that was
wanted now, and I listened to the clarseur's careful tuning and
watched the bronze strings gleam in the firelight as they vibrated
to his touch. Finally he was ready. Leborcham saluted the
queen.

"What do you desire me to sing?"

The queen looked around the circle of women, caught sight of
Esseilte quivering on her couch like a leashed hound bitch, and
smiled.

"Let her chant the tale of Grainne and Diarmuid; Mother —
say that you will!" As the queen nodded, Esseilte sank back on
her couch and squeezed my hand.

The harper struck the first chords, stopped to adjust one last
string, and Leborcham began.

> *"Cormac MacArt was the builder of Temair,*
> *True judge of the men of Eriu, the splendid king.*
> *And Grainne his daughter was long-limbed and gracious,*
> *Her hair like the flower of the iris, or the yellow broom . . ."*

Verse by verse she continued the story of how a marriage had
been arranged between Grainne and the great war-leader Finn

MacCumhail, and how when Grainne saw that Finn was older than her own father she desired a younger man. The bronze harp strings flickered in the firelight as the clarseur's agile fingers moved over them, the strong chords and grace-notes carrying the song.

> *"'Who is that sweet-voiced man who sits by Oisin?*
> *With the ruddy cheeks and the curling dusky-black hair?'*
> *'That man is Diarmuid of the bright countenance,*
> *The best lover of women that is in the world —'"*

Closing my eyes I listened to the story, knowing already how Grainne had put a potion into the honor cup to make Finn and her father sleep while she came herself to Diarmuid and laid upon him the obligation to flee with her across Eriu, for Esseilte had dissected the tale as avidly as yesterday's gossip too many times. I wondered how many other princesses dreamed there might be a way of evading the marriages policy laid upon them. I looked at the empty goblet in Esseilte's hand and thought that perhaps I should not envy her.

It was very warm in the hall, and the procession around the hill of Temair had been more tiring than I expected. I was half asleep by the time the story ended with Grainne's lamentation over the body of Diarmuid. The voice of the singer thinned, whispered to silence, leaving only the sweet notes of the instrument to finish off the tapestry of the old tale with a last thread of harmony.

Esseilte gave a loud sniff and wiped her eyes on the corner of the silk coverlet. I looked at her narrowly — she was one of those fortunate women who can weep at will — but beneath its dusting of freckles her nose was red. And I knew well her fondness for the old love stories. Surely there were a great many of them in the clarseur's harp-bag, and most of them ended badly. I wonder if we are so fond of hearing tragedies because we hope that weeping over other people's sorrows will spare us our own.

But the queen seemed to feel that we had had enough of melancholy, for she asked Leborcham to lead us in a rhyming song which required each one in the circle to add a verse about some other woman in the room. By the time the circle had been completed we were all laughing helplessly, too excited to listen and too breathless to sing anymore, and ready for Eithne's suggestion that it was time for the Samhain divinations.

We would have taken it all more seriously if there had been some question about the fate of the kingdom. The archpoet knew the Druid ways of foretelling the future, though the priests frowned upon the more elaborate ceremonies. But it was not worth their while to criticize the games maidens play to learn who their husbands will be.

The basket of hazelnuts was already sitting by the fire. Laughing, the girls clustered around it.

"Eithne, you should go first!" Esseilte's voice seemed innocent of malice. "If you can decide which of your young men you most desire!"

Blushing furiously, the Mumu princess came down from her couch to kneel by the fire, flinging back her braids of shining dark hair.

"Give to me the maid whose hair is like a raven's wing . . ."

Thus ran the old song, and surely it was not Eithne's rank alone that had the young men fighting over her, but none of us could see the name she scratched into the shell of the second nut before she cast it upon the coals.

The giggling stilled as we watched the two hazelnuts roasting, snug as two dark eggs on a nest of coals. Then there was a loud pop and one nut leaped from its place and landed, smoking, on the hearth.

"Eithne, my poor girl — that's not the lad you'll be marrying. Better try again!" said her friend from the Ulaid, but Eithne shook her head and sat back, forcing a smile.

Everyone was eager for a turn then, carving names into the nutshells and then fighting to keep them hidden while they waited their turn; hovering anxiously as they watched the paired nuts roast quietly or, more often, spring apart to a commentary of lurid predictions and laughter. The system was simple enough — if your hazelnuts remained where you dropped them your love affair would go smoothly, but if they parted, then trouble lay ahead. In truth, any question with a yes/no answer could be answered this way.

Fortunately no one pressed me to participate, for I would not have known what name to write on the nutshell. It was likely enough that I would never marry at all, for even if my father had cared to dower me, his wealth lay in standing, not in goods or land.

But it was just as certain that soon the girls would be at Esseilte to try, though we were scarcely come to the age where we must consider such things. She agreed readily enough when they asked her, but her face had a pinched look that I did not like as she knelt before the fire. I pushed through the others to get next to her. Was she taking this too seriously? She had no lover, nor any thought of one beyond a girl's vague dreams. Surely if she had fixed her mind on any man but the Morholt I would have known.

Then one of the nuts exploded with a pop that split its smooth dark skin all the way round and sent it into the flames. I saw Esseilte's face whiten and knew suddenly that the shell had indeed borne the Morholt's name. Not that she was mad enough to think of him as a lover, but surely she had asked if he would prosper. I gripped her arm hard, afraid she would betray herself, but she shook me off and reached for the tongs.

"It's nothing, Branwen—only two nuts, and what do they know? It's a heathenish thing to be doing anyway." With a deft twitch of the tongs she had the spoilt nut out of the fire, and in a moment the other lay beside it on the gray stone of the hearth. She picked it up and dropped it into my palm, and for a moment I was too busy tossing it from one hand to the other to keep from being burned to worry about her. By the time I got my nut open Esseilte was already peeling the other one, tossing the bits of shell back into the fire. I chewed on the hot sweet mealiness of the meat in silence. The queen was looking at us from across the fire, and I forced myself to answer her faint frown with unconcern.

Fortunately someone had brought in a tub of apples for bobbing, and the other girls were sidetracked by this new amusement like hounds scenting a hare.

"The hour grows late," said Queen Mairenn. "Time for you younger girls to seek your beds."

Esseilte nodded silently. It was clear that for her the joy of the evening had gone. As we walked across the court and through the herb garden separating the women's house from the queen's feasting-hall we could hear men's voices raised in song.

Esseilte stood listening, staring at the open doors of the Mead-Circling Hall. "He is a hero . . ." she said softly. I was not sure if she knew she was speaking aloud. "Heroes have to go into danger, or there will be no new tales. . . ."

Above the low mists the moon was shining, just past the full. The humped mounds of the Old Ones watched silently beneath their offerings. *And is it so necessary to provide more meat for the poets?* I wondered then, for surely there had already been enough blood spilled in the land of Eriu for a century of tale-telling — we did not need any more.

But Esseilte was already moving away from me. In the moonlight her shadow lengthened across the set stones of the path until I followed her.

That night I slept badly. Perhaps it was because the singing from the meadhall had gone on until morning, degenerating into a hoarse bawling punctuated by a rhythmic banging on tables, shields, even on the walls; or perhaps because there were so many strangers with us in the hall. Some hours past midnight I heard Esseilte whimpering. Blinking sleep from my eyes, I saw in the waning moonlight that her face was wet with tears. I hugged her, murmuring some meaningless reassurance, but she did not wake, and after a while I curled back down beside her and slid imperceptibly into unconsciousness again.

And although I had placed no charmed apple beneath my pillow, I dreamed.

There was a stronghold set on slate-gray cliffs above an emerald sea — it was a land I had never seen before, with bare, close-cropped hills whose grass seemed edged with gold. I saw a dark, slim man sitting in the window, looking out over the sea, and he had the eye of a king; and beside him another, younger, as comely as Diarmuid who won Grainne's love, who was playing a small harp. Then the older man touched the other's shoulder and pointed out to sea, and I saw, small but distinct upon the horizon, three ships with painted Irish sails.

Then the scene changed. A bull and a boar were battling on a sandy island in a river-mouth — no — they were two men. . . . It was sunset. The shadows made it hard to see, but I heard the Morholt's battle-cry; and as the other man turned, his lifting sword caught fire from the failing sun and I recognized the harper. I struggled to see better, to beg them to stop, but someone was holding me —

Still struggling, I woke and realized that it was morning. Esseilte was shaking me, and laughing.

Two

THE MORHOLT'S RACE

"Esseilte, sit still! How can I do your hair with you jumping like a hazelnut on the coals?" I pulled taut the gleaming strands and began to braid again, expecting her to protest, but she held her peace. Not that her silence made any difference. The Grianan hummed like a beehive with the voices of the women preparing for the fair—giving advice on ribbons or brooches, adjusting the drape of a mantle, asking which merchants had the best wares. I finished Esseilte's third braid, fastened the golden apple to its end, and began to comb out the last section of her hair.

It was not fair. Esseilte had spent the hours of darkness fighting nightmares, not I; yet now she was wide awake, quivering with eagerness to be out and away, while my hands were stupid and a dull throbbing at my temples promised a headache later in the day. If I had been suspicious, I would have accused the princess of transferring her pains to me, but her mother had not yet taught her that witchery. It was far more likely that I had absorbed them as I lay beside her, as milk stored with onions will take their sharpness.

I must have jerked harder than usual then, for Esseilte squealed and turned, jerking the braid from my grasp.

"Branwen, take care—you're not carding wool!" Her voice shook, and abruptly I realized that though she might not remember her dreams, still they shadowed the bright morning.

"I am sorry for it," I answered more softly than I had intended. "I think my fingers must be sleeping still."

The women of Mumu left the Grianan like a flock of jack-
daws, and behind them relieved silence eased some of the tension in the room. Through the open door I could hear splashing
and men's laughter. The warriors must be dousing themselves in
the icy horsetroughs to shock away the last fumes of the mead. I
shuddered, almost feeling the cold on my skin.

"Branwen, I understand," said Esseilte, "but *do* hurry now. If
Eithne reaches the raceground first she and her friends will take
the best seats, and I cannot protest, for Mother will say it is their
guestright after all."

I nodded and gathered up the loosening strands of bright hair,
plaiting them with swift twitches of my fingers until the fourth
braid hung with the others a little below Esseilte's waist, the
golden apples clashing sweetly as she moved. I had gathered my
own hair loosely in a single plait down my back, unfashionable
but quick. After all, no one would be looking at me.

Esseilte pinned her mantle over the fine checkered stuff of her
gown, for outside the morning mist still coiled about the hillsides, and the ground would be wet with dew. Quickly I took up
my own brat and followed her out the door.

By the time we reached the foot of the hill, the early sun was
burning the mists away. I took a deep breath of the acrid, aromatic smoke of peat fires that mingled with the disappearing
mists in a blue haze. The air throbbed as if we stood inside a
drum. It was not quite a sound — more a pressure on the skin —
the pulsing excitement of concentrated humanity.

The fair was like some great city of the Tuatha Dé Danann
before they came to Eriu, or perhaps like Rome that the priests
praised, or the British Artor's Caer Leon. The order of it had
been established for centuries, with streets marked out between
the sectors assigned to each trade, and pens for the cattle. For a
moment the wind shifted and I heard their melodious lowing.
The Lughnasa Fair at Tailtin was the place for horses, but the
Samhain Fair did a great business in cattle, for this was the last
Assembly before the autumn slaughtering.

I wondered if perhaps we could look at them when the racing
was done, for though there is a magnificence to a fleet horse that
stirs the soul, the liquid eye and proud haunches of a fine cow,
her udder swollen with milk, have another kind of beauty. Like
the earth itself, the cow is a bearer of bounty, and therefore
holy. Thinking about it I could envision such an animal in my

mind's eye, her smooth hide glowing copper like that of the cow
that nursed the Blessed Brigid when she was a child—

My foot slipped, the world whirled, then Esseilte's hard fingers closed on my arm.

"Holy Mother, Branwen—what were you dreaming of? Come
on now, we're already late."

As Esseilte hauled me forward I looked behind me, saw the
brown smear of the cowpat which had nearly brought me down,
and began to laugh. Would the droppings of a holy cow be sacred too? The idea of some priest venerating such a thing in a
gilded reliquary nearly upset me again, but when Esseilte asked
me why I was laughing I could only shake my head and go on.
She was in no mood to see the humor in it now.

Catching my breath, I followed her past the displays of the
merchants, men from every land, whom we called Greeks out of
habit established when the world was young and only the men of
that country ventured to these shores. Esseilte marched past
stalls where lengths of bright silk shimmered or strings of northern amber glowed in the early sun with never a sigh, and I knew
by that how determined she was to see the racing. We had never
passed through the fair before without stopping to try on neck-
laces or bracelets while Esseilte described the jewels she would
have someday, when she was somebody's queen.

The enclosure they had built for the high-born women was
walled and canopied with woven willow, providing privacy and
a certain amount of protection from the elements. It was
crowded with women, gowned and mantled in every combination of colors and laden with all their best jewelry, clucking like
hens in a yard. The boys' race down the short course to the river
had already been run. Gold flashed as the women traded false
smiles and settled their wagers.

Horns blared and men came forward for the javelin throwing,
followed by boys carrying their weapons. Slaves dragged the
man-shaped straw targets onto the course and hurried to get out
of the way again. One target fell over and the poor fellow scurried back to set it upright, looking apprehensive. I laughed, for
even a slave's life was sacred at the festival.

The first contenders took their places and threw. Three of the
javelins found their mark, and one missed and slid rattling along
the grass while the spectators jeered. The green slope of the hill
of Temair had sprouted cloaks like unseasonable flowers as the
commoners found places there. Their view would probably be as

good as ours, I thought ruefully, pushing between two arguing women and looking for Esseilte.

The next group of spearmen took their places, posturing like Cuchulain and Ferdiad at the ford. But there was no Queen Medbh here to urge them on, and no Princess Finnabair to reward the victory. The renown of having won a contest at the Samhain Fair and a ring of pure gold were reward enough, and one could tell that the boasts of the javelin throwers hid no enmity.

Except for those whose relations were among the contenders, the women seemed mostly uninterested. During the period of the fair there would be many contests — shooting from horseback, chariot races, and footracing for different age-groups as well. But only one race claimed everyone's attention — the long-distance horse race in which brothers and sons from every royal family in Eriu tested mounts and men. Until that was over, the lawgiving and judgments that were the other purpose of the Samhain Fair would have to wait.

On the other side of the track the king's enclosure was as crowded as our own, but more orderly. The king's harpers sat to one side, their sky-blue mantles draped carefully over their white gowns. The other kings who had come to the festival were ranged in state on the other, but it was Amergin MacAlam the Archpoet, robed in white like a Druid, who sat close by the king's right hand. Diarmait himself was half-turned, speaking with the steward of the racing, his white fingers smoothing the two forks of his red beard together and then separating them again. The great golden ring-brooch at his shoulder was Saxon work, a convoluted twisting of golden dragons that glittered when it caught the sun, and the purple silk of his mantle was bright with embroidery.

Again I looked around me, but Esseilte was nowhere visible. Suddenly I felt suffocated by the pressure of so many female bodies, the reek of damp wool and heated bodies and the spicy scent of ambergris. The javelin contest finished, and the winner came forward to receive his prize from the hand of the queen. As the women drew back I saw Esseilte behind her.

The air shivered to a long horn call. I felt the hair on my forearms lifting as the herald lifted the curved cow's horn to his lips again. The noise intensified, and the slaves rushed out to drag the targets back off the course as the rapid drumming of hoofbeats thundered in the air. The murmur of anticipation from the crowd crested suddenly as the horsemen rounded the curve. Then it broke and left silence behind it like an empty shore.

The princesses moved back to their benches, gold glittering on their necks and brows, and Esseilte sat down at her mother's right hand. So, the queen had saved a place for her after all — there was no reason for me to be surprised. If there was anyone who loved the Morholt more than Esseilte, it was his sister the queen. And he was Esseilte's uncle — it was only right that —

And he's your father — what right does that give you? came a treacherous voice from within. But after a moment I realized that was not what had me blinking away sudden tears. I found it hard to care whether my father lost the horse race or won. But after dragging me down the hill in such haste Esseilte had not even told me her mother had a place for her, had not apologized, had simply taken it without a thought for me. I had thought we would sit together — we always sat together — I had been one step behind Esseilte ever since we could walk.

And what right does that give you? I asked myself again, as I shouldered through the women to the front, ignoring their objections. Through a mist of tears I saw horses curvetting toward the starting line: gray horses like swans, blacks and bays like straining hounds, a melée of gleaming flanks and tossing manes and rolling eyes jumbled like figures in a gospel. Then the horn blew again, and the confusion resolved itself into a quivering line of straining horses and taut, focused men, their faces stamped like coins with an identical intensity.

Curnan of Connachta sat his rangy gray as if they were one animal, dark eyes raking the women. I watched Eithne color and pale again, but there was no way to tell which face he was looking for. Knots of red and blue yarn had been woven into the stallion's mane and tail, and gold glittered on his browband as it did on the circlet the young prince wore.

Fergus MacGabran was beside him, red as a fox and burly, sitting his chestnut with a solid assurance, as if he thought that being cousin to the High King would help in the race somehow, and next to him Firtai Iugalach of Damchluain in Connachta who was new at the festival, with the fuzz of manhood just beginning to shadow his cheeks, riding a big brown.

I saw my father coming up on Curnan's other side, splendid as I remembered him from my childhood — a figure limned in gold as the sun broke suddenly through the clouds and flooded the plain. The Morholt's hair, knotted on top of his head to keep it from his eyes, was a helmet of gold. Light glistened on his bare torso as if the swelling muscles of breast and shoulder had been oiled, flared from the metal studs in his broad leather belt, seemed to glisten even on the threads of his checkered trews. The coat of his copper-bay horse glowed like fire.

Curnan reined his gray back beside him, grinning maliciously as his horse lashed sideways at the bay, which leaped aside with a jerk that nearly unseated its rider. I saw a sudden focusing of attention in the Royal Enclosure, and Diarmait leaned forward, watching them.

"If you cannot control your beast perhaps you should go back to footracing with the boys!" growled the Morholt.

Curnan laughed, shaking back his dark hair, with no thread of silver to dim its luster. "At least he has spirit—perhaps it would be fairer to mount you old men on geldings, or mules!"

The bay shook its head angrily at the sudden jerk on the reins. I could see the Morholt's arm muscles tremble, the little betraying quiver of muscle at the jaw, but he controlled his anger.

Curnan was still laughing. He was one of the king's hostages, and well he knew that as long as his father stayed loyal to Diarmait he had little to fear from any man. The king knew it too, though his face remained impassive beneath the gold band on his brow. Even had this not been the High Festival, when it was death to break the King's Peace, he was responsible for the safety of his hostages.

Crimthan MacFergus moved his roan close to the Morholt's side. I heard a low, outraged murmur, but not what he said. The Morholt shook his head, his eyes still on King Diarmait, who had taken the long spear with its golden rivets from his armorbearer and was extending it over the track. It seemed to me that Diarmait was moving with unseemly swiftness—he must want to get the riders started and let them expend their anger on the race instead of each other.

Now the Morholt's attention was all on his horse. He bent low over the shining neck, whispering in the stallion's flicking ear. Even Curnan was finally minding his own business; the excited gray tossed its head and half-reared, and, swearing, the prince brought him down again. For a moment horses and riders were poised in a moment of impossible stillness, as if a falcon had paused in mid-strike.

Then the spear swung down in a blaze of sunfire and the horses were launched like arrows toward their distant goal.

Churning haunches splattered dollops of mud in all directions. None hit me, but I heard shrieks from either side. I turned, saw Eithne wiping mud off her cheek, and struggled to suppress a grin. Oblivious to the commotion around her, Esseilte was on her feet, her eyes fixed on the dwindling figures of the riders.

I turned back to the course. Standing at the rail, I could see at least as far as Esseilte, but by now the horses were moving so fast it was hard even to make out their colors. It seemed to me that a darker horse was leading, with Curnan's gray just behind it, but I could not tell whether the leader was bay or black or brown. The sound of their hooves came ever more faintly, like distant thunder.

The riding was going to demand all the warriors' attention. This was the long race that tested not only the speed of a horse but its endurance, as well as the rider's skill. The Morholt was too big a man to be carried by a sprinter. The distance race had always been his event, and this was where Curnan must challenge him.

I strained to see the Mound of Mag, the first marker. The observer would note each rider as he rounded it and angled south toward the Longstone. From there the route ran south to the ford, then back west through the hazelwood and north and east through a variety of hazards until they had completed the circuit of the Hill of Temair and returned to their starting point.

The women around me settled back and began to chatter again. Bets that had been laid earlier were being altered, odds changed, additions made. Discussion of the words between Curnan and the Morholt added spice to the conversation. As the women speculated on the possible consequences of adding human malice to the dangers of the course I thought they sounded like crows waiting for a warrior to die.

It was a punishing course — Esseilte and I had gone over parts of it on our ponies, and I had heard the rest described in such excruciating detail during so many long evenings around the fire that I could almost have ridden it myself. The turn at the mound was not so bad, except that after last week's rains it would be slippery, and the ground to either side was boggy and could bring a horse down. And then there was the first ford at the lower Nith, where a rider must slow his mount or risk the horse putting a foot through the hurdles and giving them both a wetting, if a leg was not broken when the animal fell. The hazelwood was not too bad — a man had only to get through it without being swept off, not to make the run afoot without tangling his hair or breaking a withered branch or leaving a trembling branch behind him, as the candidates for the Fianna in the old tales had to do.

Both horse and rider needed to have superb judgment of the ground, the direction, their own strength and that of the competition so there would be something left for the final sprint home. If the Morholt's bay possessed half the virtues his rider ascribed to him his chance should be good. I stiffened then, thinking I saw some confusion at the ford, but even from my vantage point I knew I deceived myself if I believed I could see so far. If anything had happened, other senses must have told me of it, but now was no time to wonder.

The course was three miles long. It would be some minutes before we could expect to see them, for no horse could continue to run all-out at the pace at which they had begun. Esseilte had sat down, finally. I shifted from foot to foot, wishing I could do the same, but by the time I settled myself on the grass they would be on the home turn and I would only have to haul myself up again.

Somebody shouted from the top of the hill. Were they coming then? The railing groaned beneath me and I forced my feet to stillness, eyes fixed on the rise.

Yes—yes, now they were on their way home! For a moment the head of a horse with flying mane was silhouetted against the sky, then the shape of his rider, then others, pouring down the hill after him like rocks being rolled along the bed of a flooding stream. But the horse in the lead was gray!

"Connachta!" came the cry from the crowd, for Curnan was in the lead, hand flailing his mount's neck to extract the last bit of speed.

But the Morholt was close behind him. It looked to me as if he were holding back the bay, conserving his speed. In a moment he would have to make his move—yes—his hand moved up and down again on the bay's sweating neck. There was a roar as if the earth itself had opened its throat to cheer.

Onward they came, and closer still. The bay's nose was ahead now; I saw the red flare of nostrils, the agonized gleam of rolling eyes; through the wood of the platform I felt the earth quiver like a beaten drum. Afterward I found my own throat raw, and I suppose I must have been shouting too.

And then the bay horse missed a step, and another. The gray

drove past him and across the line and the shouting resolved itself into the single word "Cashel!"

The gray took five more flashing strides before his rider could pull him up and turn, grinning, to the crowd that had already spilled over the barriers and was swirling around him. The bay had already faltered to a halt a few paces past the finish line. As he turned I saw ocher mud smeared along his side and flank and up his shoulder. The Morholt's leg and left arm were muddy as well — they had fallen then, and that was why the Cashel horse had won. It was a tribute to the bay's heart that he had gone on so valiantly. The horse took another step and stopped, trembling, and I saw a spot of brightness spreading through the dull mud on his shoulder, a red stain that welled through the dirt and rolled sluggishly down his foreleg toward the ground.

A murmur spread through the crowd around him, then stilled. The Morholt unclenched his fist from the dark mane, looked around him, then carefully eased his left leg over the horse's neck and slid stiffly to the ground. Someone began to babble some foolish sympathy — a fall could happen to anybody . . . the horse would recover . . . maybe next year . . .

The Morholt ignored him as he ignored the lad who came to lead the horse away. Limping a little, he took the bridle and gently coaxed the bay forward two steps, then another, and then, when the bay would move no more, drew his head around so that his left side was toward the king. Sound swelled and faded as the two men locked eyes, then the Morholt threw back his head and shouted — I could see his chest swell —

"Justice! I call for justice from the High King!"

King Diarmait had not moved; every hair on his beard seemed carved from unmoving stone. It was the ard-filidh, Amergin MacAlam, who leaned over the railing, with the golden fillet of the archpoet glinting on his brow and his white robe billowing in the wind.

"Speak, then." The deep voice was not loud, but everywhere audible. Those who were still talking ceased, one by one, until all eyes, all attention, was focused on the men before the throne. "What is the crime against you, and what justice do you demand?"

The Morholt took another step forward and raised one hand as if taking oath. " '*The abuse of steeds in their career is not allowed to contending racers* —' Thus the Law of the Fair, my lord, is it not so? And I call foul therefore, for the jostling of my horse that

brought him down at the ford, and it is upon Curnan of Connachta that I lay that crime!"

Curnan himself had dismounted by now. He sauntered toward
the Morholt with his face twisting into its familiar mocking
smile.

"And what is the fine for poor horsemanship?" said the young
man. "For it is your noble steed to whom you should be paying
it, for pushing him too fast through the water with no care for
the ground."

I heard a low growling—after a moment I realized it came
from the Morholt's throat. I could see a vein beginning to pulse
at his brow, and gripped the post till the knuckles whitened on
my hands, wondering if the Morholt's skin would burst and send
a jet of black blood spraying above his head as the poets said
was the way of Cuchulain when he went battle-mad. The look
on his face was terrifying enough to make men give way before
him, leaving only the beaten horse standing beside him, trembling, with the sweat foaming upon him like snow.

"I was winning this race when you were butting at your
mother's breast, boy—will you tell me how to take a horse
through a ford?" the Morholt's voice rasped the silence. "And I
will have justice upon you!"

"Liars get justice in Hell, old man!" Curnan laughed and
turned away.

And the growl that had never ceased in the Morholt's throat
became a roar as he sprang.

The two bodies were a blur of motion, any sounds they might
have made lost in the outraged, avid cry of the crowd. The Morholt had a bear's strength, but the prince was like an eel in his
grip, hooking his leg around the older man's, almost bringing
him down. For a moment they swayed, then the Morholt
twisted, and suddenly Curnan's feet left the ground as he was
slung across his opponent's hip, his head pinioned beneath the
older man's arm.

There was a collective gasp from the crowd as the Morholt
began the classic wrestler's throw, but in the moment when the
Morholt himself began to fall, Curnan stiffened and contracted
suddenly, breaking free and landing in a half-crouch from which
he sprang at his slower enemy. The Morholt regained his footing
just in time to receive him, gripping the front of the prince's
bright tunic to lift him and bringing his left foot forward in a
move that swept his legs out from under him. But as his feet

lifted, Curnan hooked his right leg around the Morholt's and scissored convulsively, unlocking his knee so that the Morholt was beneath him as he fell.

For just a second the two lay breathless. Then the Morholt's arm snaked around Curnan's neck and began to press down. The prince gripped it with both hands, tendons standing out like roots on his arm as he fought to keep it from cutting off his breath.

For a moment there was stillness again, as if some spell had turned the two to stone. The Morholt turned his head to whisper to his foe and Curnan answered with a slight shake of the head and a desperate wriggle that turned him in the older man's iron grip and nearly freed him.

They rolled over once more, skin and clothing dyed to a single brown by the mud that had already been churned by pounding hooves. Now the Morholt's greater weight gave him the advantage. His great arms pinioned the younger man, pushing one arm up behind him while the other closed around his head. The king's officers hastened through the crowd toward the barrier.

And then, shockingly loud in the momentary gap of silence, came the unmistakable snap of breaking bone.

Diarmait's officers scrambled over the barrier, ran toward the Morholt, sliding in the mud, and seized him. He did not resist them, and when they had hauled him upright he stood with mired chest heaving, staring down at the boy who lay motionless in the mud. Whispers stirred around me. I saw Esseilte on her feet, her eyes blazing. The queen's face was like stone. I felt a cold wind on my neck and pulled my brat more closely around me — storm clouds were building in the east, dimming the bright day.

"Judgment! Judgment!" The cry came like thunder, the instinctive, horrified response of the crowd. Now one of the king's leeches had reached the fallen man, and bent over him, gently straightening his twisted limbs.

"Death to the Morholt! He has broken the Law of the Fair!"

"You cry for judgment —" The king's answer was a whipcrack across the tumult. "You shall have it — now be still!"

The concerted gaze of the crowd moved from the Morholt to Diarmait, avid, questioning, as a pack of wolves might look at their leader, assessing his strength and skill. I felt suddenly chilled, knowing that more than the Morholt's fate was at issue here. The faces of the subject chieftains showed no emotion, but their eyes glowed.

How fragile, I thought then — how slight the bonds by which the sovereign united all these warring powers. Chaos licked at the edges of their unity.

The Morholt stood with arms folded, head held as proudly as if he had never heard of danger. But the king seemed abruptly older. I had never realized how much silver his auburn beard showed. And yet he also stood proudly, forcing the others to wait, until the crumpled body in the mud groaned, stirred, and lay back again, gasping, but alive.

The breath we had all been holding was released in one great sigh.

The king leaned forward with an oath that startled even the Morholt to attention.

"By all the gods and saints of heaven, if you had killed him it would have been death for you, kin though you be!"

"It is a just payment for what he did to me!" said the Morholt.

"As for that, when the watchers come to give their evidence we may know the truth of it, but that does not matter now!" said the king. He turned to the leech. "How is it with the lad?"

"A broken arm, my lord," said the old man, "but nothing that cannot heal."

"And well for you if it is so," Diarmait told the Morholt, "for the price even for the maiming of a prince of Connachta will be your patrimony. As for the insult to my law — the punishment is exile from the land of Eriu!"

The wolves around the king eased back, for the moment satisfied, and there was a kind of horrified, admiring murmur from the people. The queen's face still looked like death, and I was not sure it was all the effect of the failing light. What would have happened if Diarmait had condemned the Morholt? Would she have left him, or perhaps used poison? She had the knowledge, and the will. Even now, perhaps, the king was in danger, for was it not a greater punishment for a man to never again set foot in the land of Eriu?

That was the whisper that went through the crowd, but there was something in the line of the Morholt's body that made me wonder, as if his head were bent not in submission but to conceal the expression in his eyes.

"I hear you, my lord, and I will obey," he murmured then. "How long do I have to prepare?"

"The rest of this day and the night that follows it," said the king. "When the sun reaches its zenith tomorrow, you must be gone."

Shivering in the chill darkness, Esseilte and I waited in the shadow of the queen's still-house for the Morholt to come. Queen Mairenn had not spoken at all as we returned to the hill, but when she reached the dun she had stripped off her festival ornaments, wrapped herself in a dark cloak, and come here. No one had dared to question or to stop her. And nobody else had dared to follow. Perhaps the still-house was only a place to dry herbs and make medicines, but rumor spoke of darker purposes. No one knew for sure, for whatever the queen did in this place was done alone.

"Esseilte, the Morholt is busy gathering his friends and his gear. He will not have time to come here, and if your mother discovers we have done so, she'll turn us into toads!" I touched Esseilte's arm, but she shook her head and twitched away.

"He will come," she said in a hoarse whisper. "He will not leave her without a word, and he knows as well as she that only here can they be alone!"

"Well then, he will come, but surely she will know if you try to talk to him." Clouds had hidden the stars and the moon. Light glowed through wicker shutters in the other buildings of Temair, but that was little enough comfort here in the darkness beside the little still-house, with nothing to do but wait and wonder what witchery the queen was up to inside.

"I'll wait until he leaves, and even *she* will not forbid him to say good-bye to me! Now be still, or she will hear us and send us away before he comes!"

I shook my head. Esseilte could not see me, but that was no matter, since it would not have moved her. She and her mother were very much alike in some ways. I eased down on my haunches, huddling into the lee of the wall, and tried to cover myself completely with my shawl. But the wind was still cold, and I could not tell if the whisperings I heard came from the standing stones near the house or the sorceress inside.

And then, when I felt as if I too were turning into stone, I felt Esseilte stiffen beside me and heard a heavy step on the stones of the path. For a moment the dark figure approaching could have been anything, then I recognized my father's arrogant stride and sighed. I could have touched his mantle as he strode past. The opening door of the still-house spilled light across the stones, and for a moment I saw his grim face as he went in.

Esseilte gripped my shoulder. "The back window's not shuttered completely. We'll be able to hear there, and perhaps even see."

"I thought you only wanted to say farewell —" I muttered under my breath, but I followed her around the still-house where a thin line of light edged the window frame. We could see nothing, which relieved me somewhat, for those who see can also be seen, but I found that we could hear.

For a few moments all we could hear was the queen's sobbing, and the Morholt's awkward attempts to comfort her. Then wood scraped, and her voice came clearly.

"Brother, I do not know why I give you kisses. It is blows I should be giving you for this disgrace, and the loss I shall have when you are gone."

"Mairenn, Mairenn," he answered, and I had never heard him speak so gently to anyone. "Surely I thought that *you* would understand! If that cub Curnan had not challenged me I must have found some other way to win Diarmait's wrath. This was the only way I could get free!"

"Free!" She was not troubling to keep her voice low now. "Are you not the Champion of Eriu?"

"Champion of what? In the time of Niall of the Nine Hostages the High King of Eriu ruled the coasts of Britain and challenged Rome! Whom may I challenge now to earn the Champion's portion? Boys like Curnan who can scarcely grow a beard? Diarmait is a peacemaker, and that may be well for the land, but it is not so for me — he will never let me go against Laigin, the ancient enemy. Now his own word has unbound me, and Britain will learn to fear the wolfhounds of Eriu!"

"Niall fought abroad and he died abroad," said Mairenn bitterly, "on an island in the Muir n'Icht that flows between Britain and Gaul. Nath his successor was killed on the way to Rome. Will it cheer you to know that the women of Eriu are reddening their bright eyes with weeping when your bones lie lonely in a foreign land?"

"No matter what I do the mourning women will wail for me one day. I would rather die in battle than dwindle into old age like a hound who is given a place by the fire when his use is past! They will say — 'He died in his bed!' What kind of an ending is that for a hero's tale?"

"You wretched boy—and it is boy I call you, for you've not changed since we were children together, not at all . . ." Her voice was still bitter, but the intensity had passed. "We have achieved so much, and now you will throw it all away!"

"No, sister," the Morholt laughed softly, "I will finish what we began so long ago. Your man means well, but he is too weak with these whining priests who make the word of their God greater than the word of the king. It is not good for priests to rule men's bodies as well as their souls. Diarmait tries to appease them, but a day will come when he will not be able to compromise, and if they put the ban upon him then, whom will the people obey? It is not good, Mairenn. Already the young men murmur because Diarmait keeps them from war. If he bows to the priests, the other kings will know he is weak, and the unity of Eriu will shatter like an egg dropped upon stones!" There was a short silence and I shivered, not entirely from the cold.

"And your death on a foreign shore will change that?" the queen asked tiredly.

"Sister, sister—have you so little faith in me? Good fighting men are sworn already to follow me—it is not death I will gain in Kernow but gold." The Morholt's voice rang out triumphantly. "Once the Britons paid us a tribute—they will learn to know their masters again! When I return, with the gold of Kernow in my hold and the submission of her king in my hand, Diarmait will be glad to forgive me, and who then will be his chiefest counselor? Believe me, Mairenn, this is the final play in our game!"

The final play? He spoke as if life were a game of fidchel. But his words echoed in my hearing like the tolling of the bell that the priest rings for funerals. And surely something was changing—I could feel it as if the earth had shifted beneath me. Whatever came of the Morholt's great ambitions, our lives would never again be the same.

"I will believe you," said the queen. "I must believe you, or my sorrow will be too great to bear. Your sword I have enchanted already. Where you go now my name will be no aid, but maybe there is something else I can do to help you. Hold out your hand—"

I heard a slight sound from within, and then Mairenn's laughter.

"Does a warrior flinch from such a little blow? See, I will not take much blood—just enough to link you to this mannikin."

"What is it?" The Morholt's voice shook just a little, and for the first time I wished that I could see inside.

"Are you afraid? It is only a thing carved of oakwood with a head of crystal. The crystal is clear now — if it stays so I will know that all is well with you, but if it clouds, then you will be in danger and I will put forth my power to bring you home again." She laughed once more, more gently.

"Mairenn, you mothered me when you yourself were little more than a child, and the two of us stood alone against that woman our father took to his bed. I will not begin to doubt you now. Only take care of that thing!"

"My lad, my lad — you have been dearer than the children of my womb, and even death shall not part us!" Her voice shook with a passion I had never known, and I covered my ears as if I had overheard a woman at the confessional. There was a silence, as if they held each other in an embrace beyond words, and then the door creaked as he prepared to go.

Esseilte's breath tickled my ear. "Stay here," she whispered. "He must not suspect that we have heard." Then she slipped lightly around the still-house. By the time the Morholt emerged she was coming toward him down the path from the dun.

Painfully I got to my feet. Esseilte was hugging him now, and I heard the murmur of assurances. He would bring her a brooch of Saxon silver and a cup of gold; he would bring her a dozen British girls to be her handmaidens; he would bring her the world tied up in a silk kerchief if that was what she desired. I had heard his words to his sister, and been afraid, but there was only sorrow for me in listening to what he was saying now.

My mother was a British girl, I remembered with a pain that I hardly ever allowed myself to feel. *Esseilte already has a silver brooch and a British handmaiden. But what will you bring me from Kernow, o my father? What will you bring me?*

Three

THE TRIBUTE OF KERNOW

The Morholt sailed out of Inber Colptha, where the Boinne flowed into the sea, on the morning tide. Folk said that his ship was full of fighting men, and that two other ships had followed him — merchantmen converted to carry warriors, with brightly painted sails. Folk whispered that his departure had more the air of an expedition than an exile, and wondered where he was bound. And Diarmait's enemies spun tales of conspiracy and collusion, while Curnan of Connachta nursed his grievances along with his broken arm.

Grim-faced and uncommunicative, the king presided over the rest of the fair. But the storm that had threatened during the horse race moved in during the night that followed, dampening everyone's enthusiasm for the open air. After the drama of the race, anything else would have been an anticlimax anyway, and the people left early, eager to tell the story to those they had left at home.

For a week, Queen Mairenn remained in the dun as if she were in mourning. Esseilte stayed with her, leaving me to say farewell to the princesses. People seemed to think I would be an easier nut to crack than the queen's women, and I struggled to answer them without actually giving anything away — it was a skill that I became adept at, in later years. Then one morning the queen emerged from her quarters, her headdress draped impeccably as usual, and her face as unreadable as a saint's in one of the holy books the monks made.

"What has happened?" I asked Esseilte as soon as I could.

She grinned and pulled me over to the embankment where we could speak without being overheard. "Do you remember the mannikin my mother showed the Morholt in the still-house? Until now the crystal has been a little cloudy — perhaps because of the storm on the sea. But this morning it was clear again. The Morholt is safe, and my mother thinks that he has reached Kernow!"

For a moment I saw not the peaceful valley of the Boinne and the lovely blue-hazed shapes of the distant mountains, but a rocky coast and thatched roofs blossoming in flame, and I pitied the people of Kernow, about to suffer as my mother's village had suffered when the men of Eriu came; but I was half of that blood too, and by upbringing entirely so, and at that moment what was important was the well-being of the people I had to live with, not the dangers of those I had never seen. I wondered why I felt so happy, and then I realized that it was because Esseilte was happy, and the Morholt was not here to give the love that should have been mine to her, or to steal hers from me.

Good hunting to you, my father, I thought then; *may you be a hero upon all the coasts of the world. But leave us in peace here! Do not try to come home!*

And then the queen came upon us, her headdress fluttering in the chill wind, and I felt myself flushing, wondering if she could read my heart.

"You are both grown now and of an age for marriage," said Mairenn abruptly. "I have neglected your training, and there are things that you should know. Dress yourselves for riding and pack clothing for a journey of several days —"

Esseilte and I stared at each other in astonishment. "Does she mean to tell us about love-making?" I wondered aloud. We had both watched the matings of animals, and seen enough of the grapplings of the maidservants with the men so that the major mystery remaining about sex was why people worried about it so. There was no need for the queen's instruction unless Esseilte were about to be married, and surely we would have had some warning if *that* were planned.

"My mother?" Esseilte giggled. "Sometimes I think she must enchant a mannikin of herself to lie with the king. I cannot imagine them . . ." She broke off, because we were both laughing. "No, it can't be sex," she went on when she could speak again. "She could tell us about that without dragging us along on a pilgrimage. But it might be magic—yesterday she took me with her into the still-house to see the mannikin, and she has never done that before."

I licked dry lips. "Abbot Ruadan would say it is a sin."

"It is not a sin to acquire learning," said Esseilte virtuously, "and besides, if you had your choice of someone to be cursed by, would you choose Abbot Ruadan or the queen?"

"On the slope of that hill there lies a primrose wood," said the queen, shifting both reins to her left hand and pointing. "In the springtime the ground is carpeted with flowers the color of the rich cream just before it begins to turn to butter in the churn—"

Esseilte sighed. I stared at the bare branches netting the pale sky above the hill and longed for the sweet air of springtide, with the sun warm on my back and the green leaves quivering with an ecstasy of birds. For two days we had ridden at an easy pace through the gentle countryside, following the curve of the Boinne south and then crossing it to head west again, and it seemed to me that every mile of it had called forth some lesson from the queen. Indeed I could not be ungrateful—this knowledge was likely to be more useful to us than the reading and writing of Latin that Brother Ambrosius tried to drum into our heads—but we could have learned it just as well at Temair.

"And which of you can tell me the worth of the primrose to the children of men?" came the next question, as inevitable as the tide.

It seemed to me that the beauty of the primrose was itself sufficient reason to value it, but obviously that was not the response Queen Mairenn wanted. I looked at Esseilte helplessly.

"I think the root can be used to relax muscles and soothe the nerves," she said finally. "Doesn't old Messach put it in the tea she gives us for cramps?"

She looked relieved when the queen smiled, and it occurred to me suddenly that in some ways, Esseilte had been deprived of her mother's love too. *"You are dearer than the children of my womb,"* she had said to the Morholt, but in any case the duties of her state would have prevented her from giving much attention to her last-born child.

"And what about those willows down by the stream?" said Mairenn. "What are they good for?"

"A tea made from the bark will ease pain and loosen aching joints," I began.

"Or cleanse wounds or clear the complexion —" Esseilte completed the sentence confidently. We had memorized this one yesterday.

"Name another herb that will also dull pain," said Mairenn.

There was a strained silence; then, a memory of the distinctive smell of a sickroom came to me and I cleared my throat. "Birch oil?"

The queen nodded and gave us a rare smile. "Oil bruised from the twigs or bark of the birch can be very useful for stiff joints, and birch leaf tea will grant a gentle healing sleep without dreams."

"I don't suppose we have any of the oil with us?" asked one of the queen's women, who had been listening with amusement to the instruction. "These old bones are complaining with every step the pony takes. My heart will be glad indeed when we see the holy well."

Herb-lore and holy wells! The queen might as well have been a nun for all the sorcery there was here! I found it hard to remember what Esseilte and I had been worrying about. Of course there was the mannikin, which Esseilte said she had seen, but riding beneath a sky the pale clear blue of a kingfisher's wing, and a sun that deepened the hue of the ripe grasses to tawny gold and found depths of color even in the winter woodland, I could not believe there was such a thing as evil in the world.

On the third day of our riding we came to Tobar Brigid, the holy well.

Rath Mullingar nestled into the lee of the hill beyond it. Thin spirals of smoke from the houses curved across the still air. Between the rath and the well a hazel copse curved in a half circle around a meadow with a little beehive chapel on the north side. A bright stream of water curled away to lose itself in the grass, but I could not see the well.

"There it is —" Esseilte pointed. I squinted, looking along her hand. "On the south side of the field. The well-house is covered over with turf and stones." She smiled with the authority of one who had been on pilgrimage to holy wells before, though it was only the saint's well south of Temair they had taken her to when she was sick with the boils. Now that she had pointed it out I could see the hump of green, like a fairy mound. I suppose I had expected something more imposing.

A little woman in a faded red gown came bustling out of the

church as we rode up to it, still holding a broom in her gnarled hands.

"My lady, God save you, and Blessed Brigid! I did not expect such a company when it is not the time for the festival, but 'tis thrice welcome to the holy shrine you are, and your people, and the princess too, with her bright hair!" The woman's words seemed to flow as freely as the stream, and as we reined in I could see that it had been a long time since a comb had touched her hair, no matter how energetically she used the broom. Perhaps the hair was some kind of a penance. I smoothed my own back and shuddered slightly.

"My thanks for the welcome," said the queen, "and my greeting to the keeper of the well. My daughter and I have come here to petition the Lady. We will return to make the pattern tomorrow when the sun clears the hills. Let all things be ready for us then—"

I could already see people hurrying from the rath. Smoke thickened above the thatched cone of the chieftain's house as if someone had thrown more wood upon the fire. I kicked my pony's sides and reined him after the others toward the welcome that was waiting for us there.

The air was chill in the morning when the queen, Esseilte, and I went to the well. I had wondered if I would be going with them, but Queen Mairenn seemed to have the same conviction that had come to me that my place would always be with Esseilte, or perhaps it was only that she wanted someone to carry the basket with the offerings.

As we came up the path through the hazelwood, birds chirrupped sweetly around us, too many for their presence to serve as an omen, though the queen paused for a moment, listening carefully, before we went on. The woman of the well was waiting for us when we came out into the meadow, a dark shawl drawn over her head so that her features could not be seen. The queen put a piece of gold into her hand and she stepped back to let us pass.

"Folk come here from all about this country to walk the pattern at the Feast of Brigid that begins the spring," said Queen Mairenn. "The priests come then as well, to give the rite their blessing, as if the well depended on them for its holiness." Her strong features smoothed for a moment as she smiled, and I thought of the severe beauty of an unsheathed sword. "But this shrine was sacred before ever holy Padraig reached these shores, and Brigid is older than the Christos in this land."

For a moment the morning seemed very still. A kestrel hung motionless in the sky above us. A dew drop trembled on the edge of a blade of grass, without the power to fall.

"Old Messach told us Brigid was Christ's foster-mother, and nursed him at her own breasts though she was a virgin, through a miracle of God," said Esseilte at last.

"Brother Ambrosius says that the Blessed Brigid was abbess down in Cíll Dara, and that she gave everything she had to the poor," I added. "Which tale is true?"

"Both of them — all of them —" said the queen. "She was here when the Sons of Mil came into this land, and though the men of Eriu forget the language of their fathers and the names of their kings, *She* will remain."

Remembering the dizzying sense of change that had come to me on Samhain Eve, I stared at the queen.

"Who is She?" asked Esseilte in an awed tone. I felt cold, knowing that we had come to something deeper than an old wife's herb-lore now. Again Mairenn's face changed, and it seemed to me that the face I had seen her wear before was only a mask, and for the first time I was seeing the real woman. I was a woman grown, and I had thought I knew my world, but in that moment I realized that I knew nothing at all.

"She is the water and the well, the pattern and the prayer," said Mairenn, and her voice thobbed like the deep note on the great harp in Diarmait's hall. "Walk the path the way of the sun and pray at each of the stones, and when you come to the well, drink of Her waters and make your offering, and you will understand. . . ."

Her face had gone distant, as if she were listening, and I thought I knew why we had come. Not to teach two green girls the ancient learning, though that was part of it. Queen Mairenn never did anything for one reason only. She had come to make prayer to a Power older than the figure on the Cross in the chapel at Temair for the Morholt's safe return. I wondered then if what we did here was a sin, but there was the chapel — whatever the origins of the Lady of the Well, She was the ally of God's sweet Son now. With an easier mind, I picked up the basket and followed Esseilte along the path.

There were fourteen flagstones set into it, nine on the left side of the well, and five on the right. Barefoot we walked the pattern, and three times round, stopping at each one to kneel and pray. The queen followed us, more slowly, and once, as I paused at the stone behind her, I heard her groan.

At first my thoughts flew hither and thither like birds startled from the cornfield when the reaper comes. I forced myself to breathe deeply, tried to empty my mind in prayer as Brother Ambrosius had told us to do. Fragments of prayers came into my mind —

> *"I am bending my knee,*
> *In the eye of the God who made me,*
> *In the eye of the Son who saved me,*
> *In the eye of the Spirit who succors me . . ."*

I went on to the next stone. The familiar prayers helped to steady me, but the power that had seemed so close when Mairenn spoke eluded me now. This was Brigid's well — it was She whom I should be addressing.

> *"Blessed Brigid, to thee I make my prayer —*
> *Fire of burning gold,*
> *Well of sweet wisdom,*
> *Healer of every ill — hear me!"*

I took a deep breath, still kneeling there. Suddenly it seemed warmer, as if the air of autumn had been touched with a breath of spring.

From stone to stone I went onward, uttering the words that came to my lips without intention, and if some of them came from prayers to God's mother, it seemed to me that She who had shared the nursing of the Son of God would understand.

> *"Thou art the Queen-maiden of sweetness,*
> *Thou art the Queen-maiden of faithfulness,*
> *Thou art the Queen-maiden of peacefulness,*
> *And of the peoples."*

That sweet warmth in the air continued, and as I went on, my feet, that had been numb with the chill of the dew on the grasses, began to warm as well. Around the circle I went, and then around once more, moved by some power that was not my own, as one is moved by the music in a dance.

"Thou art the well of compassion,
Thou art the root of consolations,
Thou art the living stream of the virgins,
And of them who bear child."

I completed the third circuit and came to the well. I knelt there on the soft grass, gazing at the glimmer of dark water beneath the arch of the well-house, listening to its gentle gurgling as it welled over the lip of stone and down the channel toward the field. I pulled from around my neck a thong upon which I wore a bronze disc with an incised spiral that I had found in the earth atop one of Temair's mounds and dropped it into the well.

"Thou art the river of grace,
Thou art the wellspring of salvation,
Thou art the garden and paradise
Of the virgins."

Esseilte's voice answered me —

"Thou art the vessel of fullness,
Thou art the cup of wisdom,
Thou art the wellspring of health
Of mankind."

And then a third voice joined ours, and in that moment, I was not surprised to see the face of Mairenn the Queen.

"Thou art the sun of the heavens,
Thou art the moon of the skies
Thou art the star and the path
Of the wanderers."

Perhaps their voices continued after that — I do not know — the sound of the waters grew louder in my ears until all I could hear was its singing. Then a ray of the rising sun shafted across my right shoulder and struck the surface of the well. Light flared in the enclosed space, and I saw in momentary sharp illumination a triple spiral carved into one of the stones. Brightness burned Vision upon vision then, and I saw nothing but a Face which was the old Brigid and the new, the Lady of the Well and the Mother of God. . . .

Faintly, as consciousness returned to me, I heard the voices of Esseilte and her mother blended in supplication:

"Lady of fire and water, Lady of power — stretch out Thy

strong hand across the green sea and bring him back to us! Blessed Brigid, bring back the one we love!"

After we had finished our devotions at the well, everyone seemed more at ease. We guested with the lord of Rath Mullingar for several days before beginning the ride home, and the queen was as blithe as I had ever seen her, going so far as to make an occasional jest which left her daughter staring in wonder. When we started home again, we rode slowly, taking four days to repeat the journey we had made in three.

It was not until we rode into Temair that anything occurred to trouble that cheerful mood, and that was only a wren, singing at us from one of the standing stones. But the queen's face stilled when she saw it, and I remembered abruptly that Messach had told us that such a bird brought tidings of the death of a great man. I stared around me, but the slaves were sweeping the courtyard and two warriors sat dicing against the whitewashed wall of the dun while another mended harness nearby. It could not be the king, then, or any other man of the blood who was here.

The queen slid off her mare and without a word to anyone hurried toward her still-house. Esseilte and I traded glances and scrambled from our ponies. We were halfway across the yard when we heard a great cry. I thought of the cry of the Morrigan, whose shout shattered the souls of men in battle so that their weapons fell from nerveless hands, and stopped short, as men and women were stopping all over the hill.

But Esseilte was still running. After a moment I forced my legs to carry me after her. I found her standing at the door of the still-house, clinging to its frame. I peered over her shoulder and saw the worktable overturned and the queen kneeling on the floor.

"What is it?" I whispered in Esseilte's ear.

Wordless, she moved to let me see. Mairenn had something cradled against her breast. She was swaying from side to side, keening softly. I stepped across the threshold of the still-house, and saw that the queen was holding what looked like a doll. Its head was a lump of crystal, fixed with pitch to the wooden body, but the crystal had a crack through it, and its surface was as dull as building stone.

* * *

A bitter wind was blowing winter across the land when the Morholt's ship sailed into Inber Colptha once more. The Lady of the Well had brought him back over the water as the queen and Esseilte had begged her to, but his flesh was cold, and his eyes stared dully into the dark. The chill had preserved the body, and I helped Esseilte and the queen to ready it for burial while the mourning women wailed by the door.

Mairenn had had a week to prepare herself, by then. She worked as carefully as if she were making her medicines, washing the body, binding her brother's right hand to his arm, and setting the severed head upon its neck again. The queen had forbidden the other women to touch the body. Only Esseilte was allowed to be with her in the still-house. Only Esseilte, and me, for the queen granted me a daughter's right in the Morholt's death which during his life had gone unrecognized. It was as well, for Esseilte huddled in the corner, weeping soundlessly, while I assisted the queen.

As I handed her the cloths to wrap him in I felt as cold as the body before me. I could not believe that this was my father — despite the silver in his beard he had always been more like some natural force than a mere man. He had been more than mortal; he had been Eriu's champion. The body before me seemed shrunken, and its flesh had the clammy chill of the clay that soon would cover it, for on the morrow was the funeral, and they would lay him in the mound.

And then we were done. Leaving the women still mindlessly wailing, Esseilte and I followed the queen to the meadhall where Diarmait and his warriors were drinking the funeral ale. The men grew silent as she entered, for she was robed in black like the Hag, and her eyes were terrible. Mairenn came straight in through the door in the midst of the hall and paused before the high seat, her bleak gaze moving slowly from the king to the archpoet who sat at his right hand, and down the long hall where the warriors watched her from their couches, the mead-horns forgotten in their hands.

Finally her eye fixed upon Fergus MacCiaran, who sat next to Donal MacForgaill, huddled in upon himself like a sick man, staring into his mead.

"You were with him," she said in a still voice that nonetheless carried the length of the hall. "Why do you still live when the Champion of Eriu lies slain? Tell me how such a thing can be?"

Fergus paled, reddened, and then lost color again. He was a young man, from the Ulaid, maybe one of those I had heard talking with the Morholt on Samhain Eve. Certainly he had tried hard enough to form himself into the Morholt's image, being always ready to take up a fight, or a dare. He rose to the queen's challenge now.

"Lady, hear me, and all of you, warriors in this hall—" He got to his feet and gestured around him, and I could see them sobering. "Hear me out, and say then if I did ill, for Christ knows I would have died to save my chieftain, and if I did not, it was because his own will forbade me!"

Queen Mairenn nodded, but she did not move. Esseilte and I drew close behind her. We were robed in black too, and I suppose we must have looked like the triple Babh, raven-cloaked and avenging, standing there.

"Wind struck the sea as soon as we had left Eriu, and in the howling of that storm I thought for certain that this was the greatest danger that men might endure! But the Morholt only laughed at our fears, and held the helmsman to his task, and so we went on. For a week we sailed so, freezing and miserable, beating up and down the sea lest the wind drive us onto the cruel rocks of the British shore." Fergus shivered and took a long draft of mead, as if he were not certain even now of the stability of the floor or the warmth of the fire.

"On the eighth day the wind dropped, and through the disappearing mists we saw a coast like the palisade of a fortress, whose brown rocks rose like tree trunks sheer from the sea. Seabirds screamed around us as we passed the little rocky islands, and once or twice we saw seals. Our captain looked at the sun and the shore and calculated that the storm had driven us south, toward Gaul and the open sea, and so we came about and began to sail northward along the coast of Kernow, though it seemed to me then there would be little profit for us in such a barren land."

"And little profit did you find—" said the queen harshly. "How came the Morholt to his doom?"

"At first it seemed otherwise," Donal MacForgaill spoke up in defense of his friend. Donal was small and dark for a man of the warrior class. Someone had once told him he looked like Cuchulain, and he spent most of his life in hare-brained exploits intended to prove it. "The wall of stone opened out at times, and where the little coves let in the sea we fell upon the villages, taking such treasure as they had there, and provisions, and a few slaves. Four such we set in flames, but they were only poor places, and my lord wanted tribute for the High King."

King Diarmait's face tightened at the words. I suppose that any ruler has a use for more gold, but I could see that he would have paid much from his own treasury to have prevented this. No matter that the Morholt had run after his doom. I did not think that the queen would forgive Diarmait for letting him go.

"We sailed therefore for the town of Lan Wedenek, where our captives had said that their king was visiting, and came upon them when the tide was out and their own boats stranded on the mud of the inner harbor. With fire and sword we came down, for we had heard the king had only a small force with him, and rumor had swelled our own numbers a hundredfold. It was a good fight"—he grinned reminiscently—"and the Morholt raged among them like the brown bull of Cualigne, while they cried out that the devil had come upon them. But it was something worse, it was the Irishmen!"

"It was no good fight if my brother got his death in it," Mairenn said fiercely.

"No—it was not in that battle that his fate came on him, though that was the beginning of it. But on that day there was no man of any nation who could have touched him. Cuchulain himself would have been pressed to stand against the Champion of Eriu on that day!"

He spoke proudly, and the warriors around him murmured in fierce satisfaction. Even I felt something stir in my breast, for the Morholt had been my father, and however unregarded, still it was the blood of a hero that ran in my veins. Then I remembered that there was someone in Kernow who in the end had been better than he.

"The king came out to meet us with his house-guard, and they fought well, but we were getting the best of it; and so they were ready enough to parley when the Morholt called for it, for he would have gotten no tribute from a dead king."

"Of what likeness is King Marc'h of Kernow?" asked Diarmait then. "Does the blood of Artor truly run in his veins?"

"My lord, I cannot say." Fergus had got his composure back now, and took up the tale again. "I have heard that the High King of Britain was like a bear in his rage, but this prince of the Domnonii is a narrow, dark man, good enough with a sword in his hand, but better at the council table than on the battlefield. He told the Morholt that if we proved the stronger he would not let us take him living, but to save both his men and ours he would agree to decide the issue by a fight between champions."

"And my brother agreed to it?" cried the queen.

"He was the Morholt," said Fergus, as if that explained everything. "Do you think he could have refused?"

Slowly she shook her head, and I remembered what he had said to her that last night before he sailed away. No — the Morholt would never have refused a chance to gain glory, to prove his right to the name of champion before them all.

"They settled that the combat should take place in three days on a low island in the estuary, where the champions could fight undisturbed but in full view of the shore. I wondered if their king was planning some trick on us then, but the Morholt laughed, and said that if the king had no better warriors than those we had seen, it was no wonder he wanted time to seek a new defender. And so we went back to our ships to wait." Fergus looked around him, but no one dared to interrupt him now.

"When the day of the combat came, we sailed as far into the estuary as we dared, and the Morholt took one of the ship's boats and paddled across to the island. I think the British were surprised when they saw how few we were, but their king's pledge bound them, as we were bound by our own, that no man of either side should give aid to his champion, and that we should receive the tribute of Kernow if the Morholt won, and if he fell, we should give up all we had taken and go home."

"How did the Morholt go into battle? How did he appear?" asked the warriors.

"He dressed himself carefully for the battle," said Fergus, "with his hair and beard combed so that every separate hair of them shone like red gold from beneath the shining, steel-banded bronze of his helm. His good shirt of white silk was next to his body, and over it he wore a tunic of crimson with its borders worked in gold and a corselet of hardened leather, triple-layered, riveted with bronze. His mantle was woven of many colors that shone like the rainbow in the morning sun, and it was held to his shoulders by two brooches of worked gold . . ."

His listeners nodded approval, for he had fallen into a storyteller's cadence, as if to tell the tale like a poet describing the heroes of old would somehow distance the pain.

"What weapons had he?" said the queen. She knew well enough what the Morholt had worn into battle, for she and her women had embroidered that crimson tunic, and spun the wool of which his mantle was made.

Donal spoke now. "He had his round ash shield, covered with bronze and bound with iron around the rim. And he had his strong, long-bladed spear, and the sword of the champion by his side, with its golden hilt shining in the sun."

"When the Morholt had landed on the island, he drew the boat up on the sand," said Fergus, "and we saw another boat coming out across the water from Lan Wedenek, but when the other man had stepped out of it, he turned and shoved it so that it floated away. The Morholt laughed then, but we could not hear the other man's reply."

I thought that they hardly needed to. The meaning of the deed was clear enough — both the Morholt and the British champion knew that only one of them was going to row away.

"Who was this warrior who dared to stand against the flower of our men?" asked the king.

"We stayed apart from the British while we were waiting for the combat, and there was no one to tell us his name," said Donal. "We saw only that the Kernow champion had a shield with a black boar painted on it, and a sword and a spear. He was wearing a sark of punched and riveted iron rings, and his helm shaded his face so that all we could see was the occasional flash of his eyes. But he did not seem to be a big man, despite the armor. He moved well," Donal added uncertainly, as if he still could not understand how anyone could have beaten his lord.

"For a little while they faced each other, exchanging challenges," he went on. "Then they came together, and the sound of steel on bronze or leather rang across the water. It was hard to know how anyone might withstand such blows as the two of them were dealing. The Morholt drove the British fighter back across the island and I saw him stagger when the Morholt got a blow past his shield, but he did not fall."

"The Morholt drew back a little then, taunting him," added Fergus. "And the other man went hero-mad. He got strength from somewhere and rushed him. There was a flicker of light from his sword, but it moved too fast for us to see." His voice cracked and he swallowed, and Donal gripped his arm to steady him and he went on.

"What we saw was the Morholt's blade wheeling through the air with his hand still gripping it, and his helm bouncing on the sand. The Briton wrenched his sword free from my lord's head and stood with it ready. But instead of attacking him, the Morholt swayed, as a tree sways when its trunk has been cut through, and then he fell."

Fergus covered his face with his hands and slumped over the table, shaken by racking, soundless sobs. Donal looked down at him and then back to the queen.

"Was the British pig wounded?" Her harsh whisper made me shiver. "Was he bleeding at all?"

"We could not see," said Donal heavily. "His back was to us when he put down his shield and took his sword in both hands and struck the Morholt's head from his body with one blow. Then he got into the Morholt's boat and rowed it toward us until we could hear him. It was a message, my lord"—he turned to Diarmait—"from his king to you."

"What did he say?" the Ard-Righ's voice grated like steel scraped over stone. Donal cleared his throat, and when he spoke the words seemed to have a foreign ring, as if another man indeed were speaking in the room.

"*Warriors, the tribute you came for lies waiting for you on the island. Tell your king that the lord and people of Dumnonia send you this present, and if he orders other messengers to collect such tribute here, we shall return them the same way, whatever the cost to us may be!*"

There was a long silence, and I felt the hair stand up all along my arms. I felt Esseilte trembling and pulled her against me, patting her shoulder in mute comfort, for at that moment I could not have spoken a word. But even if the rest of us had been stricken dumb, the queen still had control of her tongue. She took a step forward and held out her arms to the king.

"Ard-Righ, Ard-Righ! I call for justice! I call for justice and revenge. The Morholt went out of the land at your bidding. Give me the honor-price for this loss to me, King of Eriu!"

There was a long silence while the archpoet whispered in the king's ear. At last he answered her.

"I may not give it to you, Queen of Eriu. The Morholt broke the law of the assembly, and his banishment was just. His fate does not lie on me."

I thought she would rail against him then, but Mairenn only nodded slightly, as if this had been expected by her.

"Then I claim the blood-price against his murderer," she cried. "Send your warriors into Kernow. Let the land of the Britons grow red with the blood of their warriors! Let their women weep as I have wept today! Bring me the head of their champion to lay upon the Morholt's mound!"

From the warriors came a rising murmur of eager approbation. Clearly they had been hoping for just this thing. But again the High King shook his head.

"The terms of the Morholt's own oath prevent me," he explained. "The duel of champions was to decide it, was it not, with neither side to pay further indemnity? If we spill the blood of his slayer we dishonor him."

The queen was shaking her head in denial, swaying from side to side. "You yourself dishonored him, King of Eriu. You have lost the bulwark of your kingdom, the sword of your power — do not you understand? Who will stand now between you and your enemies? The world changes, and the glory of Eriu passes away — ill luck will follow you always if you do not avenge the Morholt now!"

A fearful muttering swept through the hall like wind. "Silence her! Make her be still before she curses us all!" Esseilte pulled at her mother's sleeve, and the queen stilled.

"Let the men of Britannia pay for it!" said one of the High King's counselors. "If we may not carry war into their land, at least let the ban fall on any one of them who profanes Irish soil!"

"So may it be," said the king. "Let it be death for any man of Kernow to come into Eriu! But as for seeking the blood of the Morholt's slayer, I cannot do it, Mairenn. My own law binds me! I do not even know his name!"

"Can you not? Do you not?" said the queen. "I can then, and I will! As he brought death to my blood, I and my blood shall bring death on him. In the names of the ancient gods of our people I swear it, and so it shall be!"

In the deeper silence that followed, I heard a raven's harsh crying, and I felt a cold wind sweep through the hall.

Four

THE SORCERY OF MAIRENN

After the warmth and flickering brightness of Diarmait's crowded hall, the chapel seemed very small and still, its air heavy with a smell of damp and incense and the herbs with which they had prepared the body of the Morholt. The warriors on guard to either side of the doorway saluted as we entered, and then the door shut and the scented air closed around us.

The queen bowed to the wooden image of the Christos that hung above the altar, arms outstretched in an eternity of sacrificial blessing, then she moved toward the draped shape of the body that lay on a trestle table before the altar and stood looking down at it.

"What is she doing?" I whispered to Esseilte. "Has she come to pray for the Morholt's soul?"

"What good will that do?" she replied bitterly. "He died as a hero, but his blood still cries out for vengeance. If only he had been able even to wound his foe!"

It was my turn to ask her what use that would be — men healed from wounds, even those dealt by a hero's sword.

"Not from that sword," she answered, with a smile that seemed even stranger in the uneven light. "Don't you remember what my mother said to the Morholt about it? She told me more, later on. It was a very practical enchantment she laid upon it — it is like the sword of Nuada whose wounds were always deathly, for it bears a poison that will sicken a wound in a way no leech in Kernow can heal. If the British pig had even been scratched by that blade he would be wasting with fever by now."

I swallowed sickly at the thought of it. At least the Morholt's death had been quick and clean.

"We do not even know his name, Esseilte. There is nothing we can do now!"

"There is something *she* can do, Branwen," she said fiercely. "Wait, and see . . ."

I stared at her. In that moment Esseilte herself sounded very much like the queen. Then there was a movement before the altar. I clutched at Esseilte's arm as the queen drew back the pall.

"Esseilte, take off your shawl and roll it up," she said in a hoarse whisper. As Esseilte approached her with the folded shawl, the queen loosened the bindings that held the Morholt's severed head to his trunk, wrapped a cloth around it, and hid it under her mantle. "Put the shawl where his head lay and draw the pall over it again," she said then. "Quickly! Now come with me!"

The queen saw me hanging back uncertainly and gestured. "You bear his blood, and that will help us. I want you too."

Trembling, I followed her out of the chapel to the still-house. This surely must be a sin, but Esseilte was gripping my arm as if her hand had frozen there, and I could not bear the thought of not knowing — of not being with her there.

"Branwen, make up the fire, and Esseilte, go to the spring and fill the bucket with fresh water," said the queen. She had set the head of the Morholt, still wrapped in its cloth, in a low niche in the wall next to the hearth. Esseilte hurried to obey her while I bent to the hearth, watching the queen from the corners of my eyes.

Mairenn had removed her dark cloak and laid it aside. She unlocked a small chest in the corner, and from it took three fat candles made from some grayish waxy substance, several small silk bags, and a shallow vessel bound in tarnished silver that looked as if it were made of bone. These she placed on a linen cloth that covered the whitewashed step built out from the wall beside the hearth, below the niche where the featureless shrouded head of the Morholt had been placed.

"Are the coals there still alive?" she asked, and when I nodded, reached past me with the tongs, lifted out several, and set them in a wide stone bowl. From one of the bags she took a handful of mixed herbs and scattered it over the coals. In a few moments heavy curls of smoke began to eddy through the room. My nostrils flared as it reached me and I suppressed a desire to sneeze. The scent was acrid and a little heavy, and it made my nose tingle. I knew that it was not anything I had ever smelled before.

The kindling I had laid across the coals was catching now, and carefully I added short logs from the basket, leaving space for air to reach the wood below. Flames flared and caught and settled again, but their light only seemed to sharpen the shadows, and darkness fluttered black wings in the corners of the room. It painted an unfamiliar mask over the queen's harsh features, and I realized that I was afraid. Then Esseilte came back into the chamber with the bucket of spring water, and the firelight made a nimbus of her bright hair that held the shadows within me at bay.

"Pour the water into the little cauldron until it is halfway filled," said the queen, "then swing the hook out above the flames and hang the cauldron there." One by one she measured out herbs from her packets and crumbled them into the cauldron, singing softly.

> *"Herbs of danger, herbs of power, be my allies in this hour!*
> *Wolfsbane and celery seed, I call upon you in my need.*
> *Banewort and valerian, well may you do your work within.*
> *Cinquefoil and mysteldene, do my bidding as I mean.*
> *Leaf of wormwood seals the spell, now the potion is made well!"*

When all the herbs had been added, she handed the spoon to Esseilte. "Keep stirring — the herbs must be mixed thoroughly." Carefully, she replaced the little bags in the chest.

White-faced, Esseilte was still stirring the cauldron. I glanced fearfully at the queen. I had heard things about some of the herbs that had gone into that pot. Was she going to poison herself, or the king?

As if she had read my thoughts, the queen permitted herself a grim smile. "Many herbs can harm or heal — knowledge of proportion and use is all. The potion I brew now will enable us to walk between the worlds."

I shivered. The smoke from the stone bowl was making me dizzy already, and I realized that there must have been herbs of power in the incense as well.

"Mother—" Esseilte's voice squeaked painfully. "What are you going to do?"

"The Morholt's men did not learn his slayer's name. He cannot be avenged until there is a name on which my curse can fall. But Donal said the two champions spoke, there on the island, before my brother died. The Morholt knows the name we seek, and so we must compel his spirit to speak to us."

The queen spoke calmly, reasonably, as if this were only a matter of hallooing down the hill of Temair to someone on the plain below. But it seemed to me that light pulsed in her eyes, and I wondered if the seeming came from the smoke I had been breathing or only the flickering of the fire.

"Daughter, is the potion brewed?" she asked then.

Esseilte looked at her with wide eyes. "I have been stirring and stirring. The tea grows very strong . . ." The scent of it, bitter and moist, mingled with the harsh reek of smoke from the coals.

Mairenn took a deep breath, and then laughed softly. "Are you afraid? Never fear, my blood runs in you, and I have walked this way many times before. . . ."

I looked at her uneasily, hoping that the inheritance that came through her brother's blood would keep me safe as well.

Abruptly, the queen was on her feet. From a casket she took a curious dagger of bronze hilted with bone. Starting at the doorway, she moved slowly to the right, muttering, the dagger extended in her hand. The cadence of her speech sounded like poetry, but the words were in no language that I knew. When she had finished the circuit, she laid the dagger in the doorway, point outward. I started, for as she set the weapon down I had felt an inner tremor, as if someone had slammed shut a great door.

The queen turned and lit the three strange candles on the hearth bench. Then she moved between me and Esseilte, lifted the cauldron off the fire-hook, and set it steaming upon the floor. She knelt and held her hands over it, closing her eyes.

"May the word-craft of En son of Ethaman be in thee, brew that is in this cauldron, that the lips it touches may speak words of skill!" said the queen. "May the word-craft of the Morrigu, daughter of Ernmas, be in thee, brew that is in this cauldron, that the lips it touches may speak words of prophecy! May the word-craft of Lugh Samildanach be in thee, brew that is in this cauldron, that the lips it touches may speak words of power!"

It seemed to me then that there was a glow in the steam that curled under the palms of Queen Mairenn's hands and around them, though perhaps it was only the light of the fire. The steam shimmered and swirled as her fingers moved in a sign whose shape flowed and faded almost before she was done. Then she took the drinking vessel from the altar, dipped it into the cauldron, and set it to her lips.

I watched her throat muscles constrict as the dark liquid went down. Then she passed the vessel to Esseilte, who imitated her, grimacing. Now the bowl was in my hand, and I felt the shock pebble my skin as I realized that it was made out of a human skull. But they were both watching me, and though my hand trembled, I dipped up a bowlful of the potion and drank.

All other flavors were overwhelmed by rank bitterness. For a moment my throat felt as if its lining had been stripped away, and as the stuff settled into my stomach, I wondered if I was going to spew it up again. Then the pain gave way to a numbness, and a warmth in my belly that gradually spread upward and outward through my limbs. I handed the bowl to the queen, who dipped and drank again.

Three times the bowl went round, and by the time I had swallowed my third portion my ears were ringing and sensation prickled on and off so that at times I seemed to have no body at all. I was vaguely aware of Esseilte giggling softly by my side, and had the distant thought that if this kept on we would be no use to the queen at all. I wondered if she had misjudged the proportions and we would die of it. I wondered if, maddened by her grief, Mairenn had intended this all along, but strangely neither thought inspired any fear.

The queen had set the bowl back in its place and sat with her hands braced on her thighs, swaying, and humming deep in her throat something that was not quite a melody, but wandered up and down the scale. As my body assimilated the potion I found that I was humming too, and so was Esseilte — three voices plaiting odd, endless patterns of pure sound. Louder and louder we sang, and the harmonies changed more and more quickly. Mairenn lifted her hands and slapped them down upon her thighs, beating out a rhythm that steadied us as it drove us deeper into that place to which the drink had opened the way.

Time stretched and squeezed and stretched again. Mairenn's headdress had fallen off in the violence of her swaying and I saw her bare head, cropped gray hair like the stubble of a mown field where even the birds can find no more to glean. But it did not matter. My attention was focused on the flickering of images that never quite resolved itself into vision, fluttering raven-winged into shadow; with a sound like many voices whose words I could not quite understand. Beasts uncoiled from dark waters and subsided again — a white horse, a black boar, a raven with feathers of snow that shrieked despair. . . .

Then the queen fumbled at the niche in the wall and drew forth the Morholt's head. The wrapping fell away. Crooning, she held it against her breast, stroking the lank hair. The skin of the face looked white, waxy, the features already shrunken. It was not like the face of anyone I had ever known, no longer really like the face of a man at all. But Mairenn kissed it as if it had been her lover or her child, kissed the lips, the brow, the blood-stained hair.

And then, abruptly, she stilled. Even in our detachment, Esseilte and I could feel her tension, and our humming faded as we stared at her.

"See — already he speaks to us." The queen's voice seemed to come from very far away. Her fingers probed the great wound in the Morholt's head, and suddenly the candlelight glittered on a jagged piece of steel. "This came from his murderer's sword. I will use it to draw the man himself into our power, as soon as I have his name!"

Carefully she set the fragment down beside one of the candles. Then she took the drinking vessel and dipped up a little of the potion, which she held against the dead man's gray lips. Dark liquid ran from the corners of his mouth and stained the pallid skin; some went into it, and horribly, down his throat to drip from the severed gullet. Mairenn took a little more on her fingertip and marked his forehead with it, and his two closed eyes. Then she placed the head on the hearth-step, with the candles around it. In the uneven light the features seemed to move.

"Now you too shall have the words of power," she whispered. "Now you shall speak to us as we speak to you." She motioned, and Esseilte and I moved around so that the three of us faced the thing on the step.

"Hear me, my brother, my love — I am calling you to come to me now! Do you remember how I comforted you when that woman had you beaten because you were her rival's child? Do you remember how I rejoiced with you when you killed her son, when you began to destroy our enemies?" The queen's voice continued, recounting a hundred anecdotes, the truth of deeds known to all but understood only by these two, the truth of deeds that none but they had known. Her voice hoarsened, cracked, faded finally, but I felt a listening stillness in the room.

"Hear me, my uncle, my champion" — Esseilte echoed her — "I am calling you to come to me now! Do you remember how I took my first steps holding onto your hand? Do you remember how you carried me on your saddlebow and called me your little queen?" Esseilte's tale was shorter, brighter, but it ended in tears. She and her mother both turned to look at me.

"Hear me, my father, my enemy—" I whispered at last. "There is nothing we ever shared for me to recall to your memory, only your blood that runs in my veins and the family you have given me. For Esseilte's sake, I am calling you to come to me now!"

At first in a whisper, and then more loudly, we called his name. Again and again we called it, while the room whirled around us and the potion we had drunk worked in our blood. My pulse beat like a drum through my bones; air rushed through my lungs like a great wind. The features of the face before us flickered dark, light, dark, light, shifting, altering.

The white lids lifted and I stared into the endless depths of empty eyes. The gray lips writhed back from stained teeth. The swollen tongue moved.

"I have heard you," came the whisper from everywhere. *"I have come to you. My spirit wanders homeless between earth and heaven. What do you want of me?"*

"The name of your murderer, so that you may have rest!" cried the queen. We waited while silence pulsed around us and the blood pounded in our veins.

"His name," came the whisper again. *"His name is Drustan . . . now, let me go free!"*

"Yes, my dear one, my beloved — with treasure we shall bury you, and I shall pour out the blood of your enemy upon your mound. Listen to me now, and bear my words to him, and to the lords of the Otherworld who hear all oaths of men!"

The queen picked up the piece of steel that had been in the Morholt's skull and held it so that it glittered darkly in the light of the dying fire.

"Thus I affirm the binding — by the Morholt's blood and Drustan's steel!" the queen's words rang like a gong. "Over land, over sea, I send this summoning — by the ore from which this blade was forged, the blood that is on it, the air that carries my words, and the fire of my passion I summon Drustan. The hand of the king cannot touch him, but my curse shall speed like the harpoon of the fisher to draw him here!"

Mairenn's voice deepened; I felt the words, rather than hearing them, as if the elements themselves had formed the phrases she spoke now. Esseilte reached out and covered her mother's hand so that the piece of steel was held between their two palms.

"When bit and blade lie together, the slain man's kin shall hold the life of his slayer in her hand. Woe to the one who tries to evade this geas, for neither time nor distance shall weaken it, neither love nor hate shall alter it. Thus the shackle of fate is welded, and death alone shall break this bond!"

A cold wind swirled around us, blowing out one of the candles and sending a drift of ash whirling like a ghost across the room. Queen Mairenn began to laugh, exultantly, wildly, and Esseilte's laughter echoed hers. Then she took the fragment of steel and laid it in the casket with her other things and began to put her implements of magic away.

The effects of the potion were beginning to wear off now. I felt sick again, and my temples throbbed as if a headache were coming on. Had the Morholt really spoken? Memory of what exactly had happened was fading like mist dispersed by the day. I could only remember the words of Mairenn's cursing, and I felt as I had on Samhain Eve, as if something had shifted in the pattern of the world.

A cold wind from the east tugged at cloaks and blew out the candles the monks bore. Abbot Ruadan had come from Clonmacnoise to perform the Morholt's funeral mass, claiming the privilege more to honor the Church than the king. I watched him go by in the procession, his face set and proud, and drew my brat over my head lest he should read from my face what we had been doing the night before.

Esseilte and I had wakened wishing that the funeral was our own, and though the queen had brought us another tea to counteract the worst of the sickness, I still felt a dull throbbing at my temples, like a drumbeat of doom. I heard one of Mairenn's women wondering at how Esseilte had loved her uncle, to be so stricken at his death. But it was not the Morholt's absence, but his continued presence, that had laid this sickness on us. Perhaps he would rest easier when head and body were reunited and laid in the mound.

"Kyrie Eleison —" sang the monks who had come with Ruadan. Four warriors of the king's household bore the weight of the body and weapons on the bier with a steady swaying tread. Abbot Ruadan said that to bury a warrior with his sword and shield smacked of heathenry, but I think even the priests feared that if they did otherwise the Morholt's spirit might wander, wanting them. At least this way the queen did not have to explain the poison on the blade of the sword.

The opening in the side of the mound gaped like the great wound in the Morholt's skull. No one knew who had raised the mound first, or for whom, but the Ui Néill had laid their royal dead here when they began to reign at Temair. It was an honor for the Morholt to rest in such a company.

I wondered if the spirits of men were like the Sidhe, and held court in the hollow hills. The thought made me shudder, or perhaps it was the wind whose cold fingers tugged at my garments like a ghostly lover, chilling the flesh within. I remembered how the queen had kissed the Morholt's waxy lips and knew that even if his flesh was at peace it would be long before his image ceased to haunt my memory.

A ripple of music from the great harp quieted the crowd. The archpoet stepped forward as the pallbearers set their burden down in front of the mound, motioning to the singer to take his place before it. The monks were silent now as well, standing with hoods drawn forward for warmth and hands folded in their sleeves.

> *"Bare branches blown by the sea breeze*
> *Release our sorrow; less joyful your landing,*
> *Lord, at Inber Colptha than Amergin's*
> *Arrival when he came to that cold strand."*

The voice of the singer was strong and clear. The archpoet nodded approval of his performer's delivery of the words, and the man went on.

> *"You were true seed of the race of Mil —*
> *Still of that breed of Mumu's kings —*
> *Corcc and Eoganachta among your ancestors,*
> *Boars for battle that glory brings!*
>
> *Not as a sapling were you struck down;*
> *Crown of the forest, true oak tree,*
> *Free-standing, most mighty of limb and girth,*
> *On earth unequalled, felled spitefully."*

The wind stung tears from my eyes—I was sure it was the wind, for why should I want to weep for him? Esseilte was sniffling beside me; I looked away from her. Curnan of Connachta stood with the other hostages beside the High King, his bold features looking even more fine-drawn than usual, though I could not tell whether it was from triumph or frustration that he had not been the one to bring the champion down. Would he be less quarrelsome now that the Morholt was no more, or was the last restraint upon his wildness now gone?

> *"Your sword shone upon the field of*
> *battle;*
> *At the word of your coming your foes*
> *fled.*
> *Red the ground you chose for fighting,*
> *Hero-light around you. Yet you lie*
> *dead!*
>
> *Ochone! Our sorrow—the towering tree,*
> *Restorer of glory, our sheltering shield,*
> *Is felled! What man can protect us,*
> *when*
> *The Champion of Eriu to death doth*
> *yield?"*

The east was growing dark with battlemented clouds. Chill wind whispered in the dead grass on the mound. The warriors of the Ulaid were whispering too, and I realized abruptly that in this case at least the traditional agonies of the poets were simple truth. Fergus MacGabran's stiff features could not quite hide his smug certainty that the sword of the champion would come to him now. But what good would that do? More than Prince Curnan had been controlled by the Morholt's might. Ainmere of Emain Macha must be smiling now.

> *"How could God allow it? Your trunk hewed,*
> *Food for foreign crows, will feed the ground*
> *Of the mound. Generous to poets, your*
> *praise*
> *We raise—where shall your like be found?"*

From the gray sky came a splattering of freezing rain. As the lament ended and the pallbearers eased the Morholt's body into the shelter of the mound I wondered if they were laughing in Kernow.

❀   ❀   ❀

The clouds that had gathered over the Morholt's funeral stayed with us through the Feast of Midwinter and the first month of the year. The rain that had begun on that day turned to alternating snow and sleet that made the roads mudholes and kept men huddling by their smoking fires. But it was not the weather that set new lines in Diarmait's face and new silver in his beard. Word came that men boasted of Curnan's triumph in Connachta, and talked of making war on the Ulaid in the spring. Royal intervention was not likely to be welcomed by either side.

But I paid little attention to such rumors. The queen had grown silent and grim, but she at least had duties to occupy her attention, and perhaps she realized that with her brother gone, she dared not relax her vigilance if she wanted to retain her power. Esseilte had nothing. In the old days I had feared lest her love for her uncle lead to scandal, but a sharper fear ached in my belly as I watched her after his loss. She could not avoid the queen's lessons in herb-lore, but Mairenn had little time for teaching. The tellers of tales did not amuse her. She would embroider a stitch and set the work aside.

Just after midwinter Esseilte took a sore throat that turned to fever, with a rash and pains in the joints that kept her moaning with pain. For a week I sat at her bedside, feeling her pulse gallop between my fingers, holding her when she twitched uncontrollably, dosing her with willow-bark tea. She recovered slowly, and the cough remained with her. I had never before longed so painfully for the lengthening days and new life of spring.

At Imbolc, the priests set the blessing of holy Brigid upon the ships. Almost immediately the weather improved, with days of clear skies between the storms, and the fishermen began to go out again. Merchants, also, dared to send their ships across Ler's plain, and the week after the festival, word came to us that traders had sailed into Inber Colptha and were offering their wares.

I looked at Esseilte, who had lost weight till even in the shadows no one could take her for my twin, and went in search of the queen.

"Is the child still grieving?" said the queen. "She will have to bear it, as I do." There was pain in her voice, but in her face no yielding.

"My lady — have you seen Esseilte's face in full light? There is a transparency to it, as if the Sidhe had put the soul-sickness upon her. I am afraid . . ."

"And what do you suppose I can do?" Mairenn asked bitterly. "My magic has failed. If the tonics I have mixed for the girl do no good I know nothing more to try."

"We've all been cooped up here together for the winter. Even the gossip has been picked as bare as last week's beef bones. But they say the merchants are here. I thought, perhaps, if they had something new, something to distract her —"

The queen lifted one plucked eyebrow. If she thought that I also wanted to get away from Temair, well, perhaps it was true. But what I had said about Esseilte was true also, and it was clear to both of us that anything that might do her some good must be tried.

Esseilte complained weakly that the brisk air would worsen her cough, but she could not withstand the queen's will and mine. We rode out on a bright morning when the sun glittered on rainpools and harness fittings and the blades of our escorts' spears and the air echoed with the harsh cries of returning waterfowl. For the first few hours Esseilte rode slumped, refusing to look on the bright world around us, but by the time we turned off on the road to the Rath where we were to spend that night she was eager enough to be out of the saddle, and she peered ahead. Distracted by our presence, a duck made a splash landing in the pond, and Esseilte laughed.

On the second evening we came to the village at the mouth of the Boinne, and the following morning went down to the landing to see what wonders the merchants had brought from afar.

We never found out. Half the crews of the merchant ships and most of the villagers were standing on the shore, chattering excitedly and pointing out into the bay. Where the white sand shelved toward the beach the water was the clear pale blue of aquamarine, with purple mottlings where the clumped kelp grew. But farther out its color deepened to a rich lace-edged blue that seemed to have leached all the color out of the pale sky. Bobbing like a fisherman's float on the choppy water, and at that distance looking almost as small, a brown coracle was being slowly carried landward by the tide.

Esseilte stared wonderingly as I started to ask one of the old wives what was so remarkable about someone's stray boat, but the old woman hushed me, hand to one ear. Perhaps she was deaf and had not understood me, but I shut my mouth, trying to understand. Gull and skua wheeled and dipped excitedly, scoring the pure air with their harsh calling. I was about to pull Esseilte away in exasperation when I heard another music, thin and delicate as if it were drifting to us from Tír na nÓg across the sea.

Esseilte gripped my arm. "It is harp music . . ." she said softly. "From an enchanted harp that the sea is offering as a gift to the shore."

Tenuous as the breeze that brought it to us came the music, now growing louder, now fading into silence again. Once or twice I thought I heard a voice as well, but I could not tell whether it belonged to a mortal singer or to one of Fand's people, as the fisherfolk were muttering now. Some crossed themselves, and one woman sent her boy running for the priest from the little beehive chapel on the headland.

Esseilte began to move forward through the crowd, still holding my arm so that I was drawn along with her. The coracle was closer now. The hides were worn, and patched here and there — there was no glamor about the craft, but the music was certainly coming from it.

Perhaps Esseilte was right, for if the coracle held a mortal harper, why was he playing lying down? Indeed, why should anyone play the harp while drifting ashore in a small boat at all? It did not seem to me that the thing required exorcism, but it was certainly a wonder, and I did not resist Esseilte's fascinated progress until the cold waves slid up the strand and soaked our shoes and the hems of our gowns.

The shock of the chill water brought both of us to our senses again. I recognized a snatch of melody, then it ceased, and for a moment there were only aimless notes as if the harper had forgotten what he played. Several times it broke off, and each resumption was softer, even though each wave brought the boat nearer to the shore.

The voice of the singer rose, grew harsh, and whispered into silence again. The words to the song were in no language that I knew, but the voice was a man's voice, roughened by pain.

"If he is from Tír na nÓg then they have cast him out from it!" I said aloud, suddenly understanding the meaning of what I heard. "There is a mortal harper in that boat, Esseilte — and I fear that he is likely to prove mortal indeed if we do not get him quickly to shore!"

Esseilte stared at me for a moment, and then, before I could stop her, splashed into the sea. I shouted to the people behind us to help us — that the singer was only a man, and then plunged after her.

The water was shallow, and the coracle very near, but Esseilte and I were both soaked to the waist by the time we laid our hands on its round rim. A man dressed in the clothing of a wandering bard lay curled in the bottom of it, fingers still instinctively plucking at the strings of the small harp that lay against his breast though his skin was stretched tight across the bones of his skull.

As we steadied the boat the man's fingers plucked one last loud chord, and he opened his eyes. They were deep blue, even darkened by pain — the same deep blue as the sea. Esseilte stared back at him as if spelled.

"What shore is this? In what land?" came a harsh whisper, in recognizable Irish.

"Inber Colptha, in the land of Eriu," I said when I realized that Esseilte was incapable of answering him.

The slightest of smiles twisted the mobile lips, thinned now by pain. With an effort he drew breath, and with its exhalation came words:

"I am a wind on the sea . . . I am a wave of the ocean . . . I am the roar of the sea . . . I am . . ." the voice whispered away to silence.

"You are going to be nothing soon if you won't stay still," I finished for him, with a laugh that twisted somewhere in the middle so that it came out as a sob. What he had chanted was the first lines of the song Amergin had made as he set foot on this shore.

"Is he dead?" asked Esseilte in a shocked whisper, letting go of the rim of the coracle. Wordless, he stared at us, his eyes seeming to grow darker in his flushed face.

"Not yet — " Waves swirled around us and I struggled to hold on. Seeing that we had not been blasted or transformed, the villagers were venturing into the water. I shouted to them to come help us, and this time they responded, and in moments we had dragged the coracle out of the water and laid the harper's limp body on the sand.

"He will be, though, if we do not help him." I set my hand for a moment on the pale brow. "He is burning with fever."

"Wound-fever," said Esseilte, recovering herself. "Look — he has a great festering gash on his thigh."

"Is there a healer in the village?" I asked hopelessly. There were murmurs of the skills of some local goodwife, but it did not sound promising.

"We must take him to my mother," Esseilte said, more decisively than I had heard her say anything since the Morholt died.

The harper was struggling to speak. I patted his shoulder soothingly.

"Do not fear. Her mother is the queen, the most knowledgeable herbmistress and healer in Eriu."

The harper's eyes widened, and for a moment wonder and that hint of self-mockery I had seen before warred in his ravaged face. Then, as if the remainder of his strength had left him, the blue eyes closed, and he fainted at last.

Five

THE HEALSONG

"As you can see, this wound has mortified. When an injury is not treated immediately it is a common thing. In such a case the healer has two tasks," said the queen. "First, to fight the poison it releases into the body, and second, to cleanse the wound that caused it so that the natural course of healing can resume."

She spoke as if this had been only another lecture in the still-house, but I knew without looking at it that the harper's wound had gone bad. The stench was almost overpowering in the small room. I eased toward the door, breathing deeply from the cold draft that crept in around the leather hinges.

A hard frost had set in after we returned from Inber Colptha, as if the hint of spring had been only an enchantment to tempt us out where we might find the harper floating in the sea. But if he was a wizard, he had come to the end of his magic.

We huddled in shawls against the chill, but the stranger burned with his own slow fire. I could not help but remember the relapsing fever they called the Yellow Plague that had devastated Eriu when I was a child. Even Mairenn's magics had not been able to save her older son, and I had heard that in some lands whole villages died.

More than the wan light filtering through the oiled parchment in the windows made Esseilte look sallow now, but she did not stir. Her expression reminded me of one of the martyrs in Abbot Ruadan's book of saints, and I wondered which legend she saw herself in now.

The queen replaced the bandage and felt the harper's forehead, drew back his eyelids to peer at the discolored whites of his eyes, then bent to sniff at his breath, all with the brisk detachment of someone buying a horse at a fair.

"To cleanse the blood you must give him a tea of dandelion and burdock with elderberry over which the spells I taught you have been sung. You may add some mint to flavor it, with a little honey," she added grudgingly. The patient grimaced, but he knew better than to make any objection. An infusion of white willow and feverfew had lowered his fever a little, and for the moment he was in his senses again. The queen's pale gaze fixed Esseilte until she nodded, and then moved to me.

"The man is a foreigner with no claim on us — if it amuses you to doctor him, then I will advise you, but the labor must be yours. Do you understand?"

I understood that Esseilte had found something to interest her, and that was all that really mattered, even though I suspected that the late night watches and sessions with the chamber pot would fall to me.

"But what about the wound?" asked Esseilte. "You said that treating it was the second part of the task."

"It must be washed with a solution of rosemary and garlic in vinegar and poulticed thrice daily with freshly bruised comfrey leaves. . . ." She got to her feet and moved toward the door. "I have taught you the herbs and the prayers — it is in your hands now!"

The harper's eyes followed her to the door, then returned, warily, to Esseilte and me.

"Do you fear to be left in these hands?" Esseilte held them out defiantly. "My mother is a Child of the Oak, and I have inherited her power! You *will* get well!"

The tale had shifted. No longer the saintly nurse, now Esseilte was something more ancient — perhaps one such as Artor's sister Morgaine, whom men called mistress of all the old magics. The harper's eyes widened a little, and the twist of his parched lips hinted at a smile.

"When the hands are so fair, how should I dare disbelieve you?" he whispered, "especially when the same penalty attends your failure, as my own. . . ."

The smile faded abruptly when he saw that he had hurt her, but I could not blame him. It was his life we were playing with, after all.

"Yes," she said tightly. I took a last breath of clean air and moved to her side. "First, harper — but I cannot nurse you without a name. What are you called?"

"Call me Dughan," he said, with a bitter twist to his lips that was trying to be a smile. "For surely that has always been my name."

"Well, Dughan, you may soon be sorry indeed, for it is time to wash out that great gash in you again."

It took both of us to do it, for though he made no sound, the man jerked as the vinegar wash touched the raw wound. Both Esseilte and I had to retch into the bushes beside the door before we were done, and when we had cleaned out all the pus and dead matter the flesh was still discolored, like meat that has hung for too long. It was going to take more than poulticing to set this right again, I thought then.

By the time we had finished the dressing and said the prayers and bandaged the leg up again Dughan was unconscious once more.

"We had better brew up some more of the white willow bark," I told Esseilte when we were done. "He'll need it when he wakes up again."

"He will. . . ." She looked down at the harper's closed face, still frowning a little as if even in his faint he could feel the pain.

Beneath the stubble of black beard his face was the faded yellow of an outdoor man deprived of the sun, but his skin was very white where the tunic had covered him. His hands were pale, too, as if he habitually wore gloves. But of course, he was a harper — he would have to take care of his hands. They were shapely hands, with strong nails on slender fingers that suggested an agile strength even now, when they were thinned to the bone. Harper's hands — or those of a swordsman, I thought, noting the breadth of the palm and feeling the calluses there. And he had been wounded just where an enemy would strike a swordsman who was a little late in bringing down his shield.

I noted it, but I thought little of it, except that if this Dughan lived, he must have an interesting story to tell. But as the day wore into darkness, I began to wonder if we would ever hear it, for the fever returned, and his body radiated heat like an oven and dried the wet cloths with which we bathed him as soon as they were laid on.

As the fever grew he began to babble. Most of his words were in a tongue kindred to Irish, but broken so that we would have been hard pressed to understand them even if we had known the language well. But there was sorrow in it, and once he called out, very clearly, for his mother to forgive him.

"It's a bad sign when they cry for their mothers," said old Messach, who had brought our dinners to us in the Strangers' House when we would not return to the Grianan. "You had better go off to your beds, my daughters, and let me watch him now."

"The white horse . . . oh, my lord, don't let me fail you again!" The words disintegrated into more babbling.

"You believe he's going to die, don't you!" Esseilte turned on her. "Do you think that would frighten me? I know what death is! I prepared my uncle's body for the grave! But the earth will not have this one — not this time!"

And then I *was* frightened, for this was the first time she had mentioned the Morholt since he went into the mound, and it seemed to me that if the harper died, it would be as if my father lay newly slain, and Esseilte might not recover from the grief a second time. And despite Esseilte's brave words, it seemed only too likely that Messach had spoken true.

Esseilte bent over Dughan and pressed the cold cloth against his brow as if she would impress her will upon his fevered brain. And somehow her intensity penetrated his delirium, and his eyes opened to meet hers.

She was breathing rather quickly, her eyes bright with angry tears. The harper's whisper came harsh as tearing cloth in that still room.

"Royal woman . . . you must not weep for me . . . I should not have —" He stopped, and she spooned a little of the willow-bark infusion between his lips. "I have brought sorrow to all . . . who cared for me. Better . . . to let it end now." His hand opened in a gesture of defeat, like a warrior laying down his sword before a victorious foe. "Princess, let me go. . . ."

"No! Your life belongs to me!"

He stared at her, eyes clouding as he tried to understand. I did not understand either, but I shivered as if the north wind had clawed open the door. Then the awareness left his gaze once more.

"Quickly, Messach, get more water," I said in an undertone. "If she wants him that much, we must get him through this night."

I had spoken bravely, but I began to think my words meant

no more than Esseilte's as the night wore on. The skin around Dughan's wound was hard and hot. Its angry red grew darker until we saw the black streaks that meant the poison of the wound was invading the body.

"We will not save him, Esseilte," I said softly.

"We will!"

"Why does it matter so much to you? He is only a wandering bard, and a foreigner. Death is stronger than we are, and you are guilty of sinful pride if you think your will can save a man whose time is come. Esseilte —" I added desperately, "if we could stop death do you think the Morholt would have died?"

She sat back on her heels and wiped the sweat from her brow. I tried to catch her gaze, but she kept her eyes stubbornly on the face of the wounded man.

"That's why!" she answered harshly. "Death will not take what I have claimed again!"

I shuddered, for neither the Christos nor the old gods suffered men to speak such words. The stranger did not matter — he was only a test of the power of her will. Until the Morholt died, Esseilte had never lost anything she cared for, and she was challenging the heavens with the fierce abandon of a child who still believes in fortune's favor. I saw defeat ahead of us and accepted it as the way of the world, for I had never had anyone to lose.

Except for Esseilte herself . . .

I looked at her and felt something in my belly twist painfully. Then I got to my feet and went quickly to the door. I do not think Esseilte even saw me go.

When I came back again, the lamplight was dimmed by the pallid light of dawn. I stood aside from the door, and Queen Mairenn swept through, raven-cloaked as if she had come for the harper's soul. The flame flickered wildly in the draft and Esseilte jerked to her feet.

"I told you to deal with this on your own," said the queen.

"*I* did not call you. . . ." Esseilte answered her.

Mairenn looked from her daughter back to me, and I forced myself to meet that dark gaze without flinching.

"Do you love her so much?" she said softly, "or do you only fear?"

I swallowed, staring back at her in wordless appeal.

"Very well," said the queen. "I will do what *you* have asked of me. But you must swear in turn to do what I shall ask of you. . . ."

"By my life I swear it —" I whispered. The wind from the open door behind me was like the breath of the grave.

"Indeed . . ." Mairenn smiled. "Well then, let us begin by closing the door!"

The harper lay still now, his laborious breathing loud in the silence of that early hour. As I took the queen's cloak I saw that she held a casket of age-darkened wood. She bent over the sick man, touching wrist and brow, then she straightened again and turned to Esseilte.

"You are my daughter, the last woman-child of my line. This knowledge is your inheritance. The harper's illness will demonstrate its power. Listen well, and remember what you see!"

Esseilte's eyes widened, and tired as she was, pride straightened her back.

"Lay bare the wound —"

We stripped the bandages away and once more cleansed the gash, so used to the stink now that we never flinched from it. The queen sat down on the three-legged stool beside the bed and opened the casket. A silver bowl lay inside, with several parchment packets. She unfolded one of them and breathed on the gray powder within.

> *"A pinch for thy age, a pinch for thy youth, a pinch for thy past, a pinch for thy future . . ."*

As she spoke, she cast powder from the packet into the bowl.

> *"The three portions of the Secret Three to preserve thee from every envy, evil eye, and death, from all spells and all witchery:*
> *The portion of the God of Life, the portion of the God of Power, the portion of the God of All Good Healing. . . ."*

She passed her hand above the bowl, and the grains of powder within it swirled sunwise as if she had touched them. Then she spat thrice into the bowl and commenced to stir the mixture with her forefinger, whispering:

> *"Sacred seed of the oak, ground beneath the new moon by the sacred stone —*
> *The power is in thee, the power is within thee, in the damp and the darkness the magic mold grew upon thee.*
> *Power of the oak, obedient to my will, where thou dost touch, the flesh shall be whole, and the bone shall be whole, and the blood shall be whole. . . ."*

The light came silver through the morning mists outside, as if we had already passed beyond the circles of the world. The harsh gasping of the man on the bed was the only sound in the room; the air lay motionless and chill. I felt its pressure against my skin and knew that death was with us in the room.

What are we doing? I wondered then. *Is it permitted to lay mortal hands upon a spirit that stands already upon the road to the Otherworld and bring it back again?* The priests would have condemned Mairenn's sorcery over the Morholt's head, and they would have blessed this attempt at healing, but in that moment it seemed to me that both operations challenged heaven equally.

And it was my own word that had brought us to this second sin. What price would Mairenn ask of me? What must I pay to God?

Mairenn finished her stirring and held her hand above the bowl.

"In the name of Slaine son of Partholon and in the name of Diancecht the Physician, and in the name of Miach from whose flesh grew the three hundred and sixty-five herbs of healing, thus do I command thee!"

She handed the bowl to Esseilte. "Spread this upon the wound. . . ."

"What will keep him alive until this stuff has done its work?" I whispered to her as she worked. Except around the wound, the man's skin had gone cold, and his body shuddered with irregular waves of chill.

The queen asked Messach to fill a goblet with wine and mixed in a powder of mistletoe with another charm. As they finished the re-bandaging, Mairenn lifted the harper and forced the edge of the goblet between his slack lips. Dark liquid dribbled from the corners of his mouth, then instinctive responses took over and his throat worked as the potion went down.

In silence we waited as the light grew stronger, watching the tortured landscape of the harper's face as warriors in a beleaguered fortress will watch the plain around them, memorizing every rise and rivulet as they wonder if friend or foe will first win through. Lines of strength and weakness marked that face, lines of humor and pain. But beneath the ravages of illness a fine structuring of bone proclaimed the man's essential quality. Such a one should not be allowed to die before he had made his name in the world.

Esseilte had taken his hand, gripping it until her own knuckles went white as if she could transfer some of her own slender strength to him. I put my arm around her, supporting her.

And then, as the bells were ringing for the priests' mass, Dughan gave a little sigh.

"His hands are warm!" said Esseilte. I listened — he seemed to be breathing more easily now, and the tension had left his face.

"He is asleep," said the queen. "The crisis is past." She bent to whisper first into his left ear, then into his right. Then she placed her hands over his pale forehead.

> *"The healing of dawning be upon thee, the healing of noonday, and the healing of eventide;*
> *The healing of the green meadows, the healing of the heights of heaven, and the healing of the plains of the sea;*
> *The healing of the faerie-mounds, the healing of the blessed angels, the healing of the abode of peace be upon thee,*
> *Child of man; may they be upon thee now. . . ."*

The queen sat back with a sigh. Since I could remember, she had never been beautiful, but now she looked old. Whatever virtue was in her herbs, power had gone out of her tonight as well. She staggered as she stood up and I put my hand beneath her elbow to steady her. For a moment she suffered it, then moved out of my grasp with a bitter smile.

"He needs sleep now to finish the healing, and we must rest as well. I have never felt so drained, as if the battle were within me. It is a chancy thing to go up against death this way, and who knows for what fate we have saved him? I hope that none of us has cause to regret what we have done this day!"

Her words were gloomy, but outside the sun was strengthening, and its golden light gave an illusion of color to the pale face on the pillow, and glowed in Esseilte's bright hair. The queen left the room like a shadow, but it was Messach who opened the door for her. I was at the hearth putting more peats on the fire.

      ✧   ✧   ✧

> *"'— Whence have you come, Bard Merlin, in clothes all torn?*
> *And where are you going, bareheaded and forlorn?*
> *Oh where are you going, barefoot, with oaken staff?'*
> *'— I seek my harp, that maketh the heart to laugh —'"*

The harper's voice had little strength in it, but it was clear, and the harpstrings jangled sweetly, supporting his song. A week had done wonders for the man, I thought as I walked through the wet grass toward the Strangers' House, and for the weather as well. It was still rainy, but the crippling cold had lifted, and perhaps the harper's song would bring the sunshine.

I stopped short when I came through the door, for the queen was there. She had come, not every day, but often, like a farmer watching a new-planted field for the first shoots of green.

"He plays well," she said to me. A little unaccustomed color stained the harper's cheeks, and for a moment I saw a man very different from the gaunt and sallow musician I had been caring for. He must be a bard of some repute in his own land, I thought then, for clearly he was not used to being treated like a piece of furniture.

"I was trained well," he answered proudly. "I know the music of Eriu, that of greater and lesser Britain and of Gaul, and some tales of the Romans also. I can tell you stories of Artor and Ulysses, of Siegfried and the Dragon and Theseus and the Minotaur. I have sailed with the pagan traders of the North and learned their tales. I speak five languages, and in addition to the harp I am proficient upon the creuth and the viol. Though fortune has been unkind to me, I know well the ways of noble houses, Royal Woman, and would gladly repay your care!"

"He speaks well, too," said Mairenn with a faint smile, but she was looking at Dughan now. "But if you are a man of price in your own land, how came you to be floating like a piece of driftwood in the bay?"

He shrugged his thin shoulders. "Not for any lack in my music! As long as I held to my craft I did well — too well — for like the Greek singer Arion, kings rewarded me, and great lords gave me gold. And like Arion, I came to grief upon the cold gray sea." A flicker of his blue eyes assessed our reaction. It jarred a little, but I suppose the bard never lived who could tell a story without elaboration, even when it was his own!

"I thought to increase my wealth by trading, see you," Dughan went on. "And I bought goods in Gaul and found a ship to carry them home for me."

"What goods?" asked Esseilte, setting down the water jug she had just brought in. She was not testing him — her eyes were bright with the wonder of strange seas and unknown strands.

"Ah — gold from Ophir and peacocks, and spices of Arabia Felix —" The bard saw the queen's lifted eyebrow and flushed, then shook his head. "I only wish it had been, and yet the loss was great enough." He thought for a moment. "I had a cargo of painted wares from Burdigala and wine from the banks of the Garumna, with some worked silver from Constantinople that was very fine. Oh yes," he added, "I have been to the Eastern Rome and worshipped in the temple to Holy Wisdom that Justinian has built there. If that cargo had come to port I would have been a wealthy man." He sighed, waiting with a story-teller's sense of timing.

"What happened to it?" I asked quickly, playing the game.

"Just off the coast of Armorica, Herul pirates from the northern seas came upon us, and I was wounded in the fighting. My captain and his sailors were thrown into the sea. . . ."

"But you lived," said the queen. "What ransom did you give them?"

Dughan grinned and lifted the harp. With his hair combed and a fresh gown on him, it was hard to believe that this was the same man for whose life we had been fighting only a week before. He was still painfully thin, but there was a light in his blue eyes, and a grace in his gestures as if he had been much among princely men.

"When they saw I was a bard they wished to keep me for their own entertainment. And yet God punished them. From the time they took me aboard the storms were constant; and also, my wound grew foul as you know, and it was no pleasure to them to be in my company. They began to talk of killing me again. . . ."

In his illness he had babbled of bringing sorrow . . . I felt an odd shiver—but what sorrow could he bring to us here?

"But they couldn't kill a harper," said Esseilte, grinning.

"No, they dared not," Dughan agreed, "so they put me into the coracle and set me adrift, and I consigned my soul to God, my body to the sea, and my last moments to music." An automatic movement brought the instrument back into his arms, and his fingers flickered across the bronze strings.

"And then you found me—" He looked from Esseilte to the queen with a twisted smile. "How shall I repay you for giving me my life again?"

"The obvious recompense would be in music," said the queen, "and yet the bards of Temair will be offended if I set up a foreigner in the king's hall. Also, it is my daughter who has given her strength in your behalf. My lord's musicians are too bound by tradition to teach a girl to play—will you teach her, harper? Instruct her in the ways of the instruments you know, and teach

her how to sing the songs of many lands. It will be an adornment
to her beauty, and add to her worth wherever she may be. . . ."

"Mother! You promised you would tell me if a marriage offer—"

Esseilte fell silent as Mairenn turned. "There is none now,
child, but there will be—as you know. You will marry to serve
the king's need—you cannot change that, nor can I. All that I
can do for you, my daughter, is to teach you so that wherever
you go you shall be a queen. . . ."

That spring we walked surrounded by music that we drew in as
we breathed the soft air. It seemed as if the year and the harper
gained strength together, and harpsong and hawthorn blossom
equally adorned our ways. There were times when I wondered if
in his delirium Dughan had indeed been to the Land of the
Blessed, and brought back with him the silver branch of Niamh
whose bells could banish all sorrow, for each day brought new
delight.

Each morning Esseilte and I joined Dughan for music. We
would meet in the big common chamber of the Strangers' House
when the weather was cloudy, but as the season advanced, more
and more often we sat on the ramparts of Temair, where the
bees hummed contentedly among the golden flowers of the
broom. At first they had to carry him into the sunshine, but by
the time the first month had passed he was hobbling along with a
cane, and by Beltane he could limp out to give us our lesson on
his own.

Our lesson . . . to me that was the greatest wonder, for Dughan said he needed me to keep the rhythm on the bodhran, and
to join in the choruses. Esseilte's voice ranged higher than mine,
but my notes were more consistently true. Dughan himself had a
sweet and resonant voice in the middle range, though he could
sing also in an odd upper register like a boy. After a time Esseilte and I began to tease him to challenge the filidh of the king,
but he seemed quite content to remain with us while the strength
came back into his limbs.

"Hold your hands correctly—Esseilte, what have I taught
you? That's right—to avoid distortion, you must pluck the notes
mid-string!"

The harper's arms came around Esseilte's slight shoulders and
he positioned her hands, then he eased back again. The queen
had cautioned me to see that he took no advantage of a teacher's

necessary familiarity, but it was not needful. Dughan touched Esseilte with the firm friendliness of a man handling a spirited mare. I could not tell whether illness had drained all the sap from him, or whether he simply had superb self-command. It was hard to believe that a man who could play with such power had no passion in him, but for now, at least, it was just as well if he felt no desire.

Esseilte's left hand moved carefully, picking out the first phrase of a new melody, and the fingers of the right supported it with single notes and then, a little late, with a chord. She bit her lip, finished the phrase, and set the harp down.

"A little uneven, but it is coming," Dughan said calmly. "Hear again how it should go." He tipped his own harp back against his shoulder and music rippled from beneath his agile fingers, clean and clear.

Esseilte shook her head. "I am hearing it, Dughan, but my fingers will not move the right way."

"Are you discouraged?" One dark eyebrow lifted quizzically. "Your father's harpers began their training when they were little children, and I myself have been playing since I was twelve years old. You must be patient, lass — you will play very sweetly in time."

"Very *sweetly* . . ." Esseilte rested her chin on her hands. "Yes, I suppose that is all I can hope for, now."

"Did you want to become a famous performer, like the woman-satirist Leborcham?" I laughed. "They would never let you do it, Esseilte, even if you had the skill!" Esseilte had never known restraint, and now she flailed against the bonds that duty was tightening around her. I understood her, but I found it hard to pity, who had never been free.

"But what is it you would wish for, lady, that you do not have here?" Dughan asked gently. His gaze moved from the curling interlace painted on the whitewashed walls of the king's house, bright in the sun, to the green slope of the hill of Temair and the rich valley beyond it grown blue with distance as it reached the hills. "They say that Eriu is the fairest of mortal kingdoms, and Temair is the navel of the land of Eriu."

"A mortal kingdom, it is — no matter how fair," said Esseilte, "and I a mortal woman."

"You are the High King's daughter," said he.

Esseilte laughed bitterly. "And what is a king's daughter, with nothing but a brief beauty to commend her to men's memories before earth shuts it away? My uncle the Morholt gave his life to gain glory. He dwells now with the heroes, may peace gladden his soul and torment twist his murderer!"

The harpstring twanged as if an unwary finger had struck it and was instantly stopped again. Dughan picked up his harp key and began to tune, his face closed as if to pretend he had not heard.

"But where will I be when I am gone—in the priests' milk and honey heaven? Maybe holy Padraig tricked Cuchulain into that place, but I doubt there are many other heroes there!"

"Mad Medbh is dead, Esseilte, and Scathach and Aoife are dust. There are no more warrior queens," I said quickly. I had thought Esseilte's heart was healing, but if she had accepted the fact of the Morholt's death, clearly she had not yet resigned herself to his loss.

"Nor woman harpers, either, except perhaps in Tír na nÓg! There is no way now but Deirdre's for a woman to gain renown. . . ."

"Oh come now, Esseilte—" I began to laugh. "I have heard of warriors who wished to die for glory, but I have never known of a woman who deliberately sought to die for love! Besides, it takes two to tell that tale. Where will you find a man who is willing to play Naoisi to your Deirdre?"

"If the hero-power is in me, he will come. . . ." Esseilte's eyes were pools of shadow. She stared at the haze across the valley as if she saw some vision there, and I shivered as I had shivered when I sensed death in Dughan's room.

But now Dughan had finished his tuning, and he began to coax music sweeter than birdsong from the harpstrings. Sound surrounded us; wave upon wave of melody lifted the spirit beyond sorrow, and Esseilte's words were forgotten as men forget the world when they hear the harpers of the Sidhe.

"The men of the North believe in a wyrd that may not be evaded, and in Rome they argue predestination versus free will. But Pelagius was a man of Britain, and our people hold that folk make their own fates, and give both joy and sorrow their due," said Dughan.

"I have had both in my life, Princess, and dare hope for no good ending. But at this moment the sun is warm, and the hawthorn scents the air. You have your health, and I am getting mine again." He looked from Esseilte to me, and smiled with a painful sweetness. "Let us rejoice in the moment, knowing well it cannot last. Is not the song sweeter because we know it soon must end?"

His fingers caressed the harpstrings, and a whisper of music floated through the air.

"Oh tell me, have you heard —" Softly he began, the harp gaining strength to support the singing, and we echoed him, *"Oh tell me, have you heard —"*

> *"The holy man has given this word —*
> *To King Gradlon in Ys, he has appeared . . .*
> *   If sea fish is your meat, if sea fish is your meat.*
> *Be sure the fish your own flesh will eat —*
> *He who consumes will suffer the same fate."*

Esseilte picked up her own harp again, and began a simple chording against which Dughan could improvise, while I took up the whistle and repeated the melody.

> *"Now King Gradlon has said, now King Gradlon has*
> *   said,*
> *'My good companions, joy we have had,*
> *And I am going up to seek my bed . . .'*
> *   Then sweet the lover's plea, then sweet the lover's plea,*
> *To the king's daughter whispering so gently,*
> *'My sweet Dahut, oh give, give me the key!'"*

It was a song from Dughan's homeland that told how the city of Ys had been drowned, especially poignant in the midst of Temair's verdant splendor. With voices and instruments we began to build the song into something that distilled the beauty he had shown us into something that was a part of us, or perhaps we were a part of it, as it was a part of the spring.

Perhaps the bards of Eriu would have scorned that performance, but for that moment we three were happy, our spirits one in joy as harp and voice and whistle were united into one music. And glancing at Esseilte's bright face, I realized that it was not only Dughan who had been healed.

Six

ISLANDS

The winch creaked as the bucket swayed upward. I threw my weight against the handle, reached out to grab the bucket and pulled it in. A few last drops of water tinkled musically as they rejoined the dark stillness below. The air from the well-shaft was cool against my face, a welcome contrast to the heat of the sun. The softness of spring had given way to a blazing summer in which the grain ripened swiftly. There had been barely enough rain to keep the grass green. I could feel sweat running down my back already. I rested my forearms on the rim of the well, savoring the coolness before I climbed back up the hill.

"Is it heavy? I'll help you if I may —" Arms reached past me and lifted the bucket away, then unwound the winch a little to set it on the ground.

I turned, blinking at the brightness. For a moment the dark shape behind me seemed oddly elongated, and I started, thinking it was the cluricaun that had come to my aid. Then my vision cleared, and I saw it was the harper, Dughan. For a moment we were very close, and I noticed, as if for the first time, the intense blue of his eyes.

"I can carry it —" I began.

"So can I," he smiled. "I was used to be accounted a strong man, and my leg has healed. I need labor to toughen the muscles once more."

I looked at him critically, comparing the wan wreck Esseilte and I had dragged ashore with the man I saw now. Dughan was still too thin, but I thought now that a wiry strength was his natural habit of body. No amount of feeding would give him the massive muscles of a man like my father, but he might be a very effective fighter for all that—I stopped myself—this man was no warrior. And yet the smoothness with which he came up from his bend had made him look for a moment like a fighting man.

"Then it is my duty to help you to exercise—" I laughed and stepped away from the bucket.

"Best of nurses!"

There was almost too much warmth in Dughan's words. I looked at him narrowly. Had I imagined it? His smile deepened, and I knew then that his desires, at least, were fully recovered. Had this happened only now, or was it only now that he had allowed it to show? The queen had warned me to guard Esseilte—it had not occurred to me that I myself might need protection.

"It was Esseilte who healed you," I said stiffly. "Esseilte and the queen—"

"Perhaps," he answered more gravely. "But I know who watched during the long nights, and I know who made the queen come to me."

I stared back at him. That was true, and though Esseilte had claimed his life and the queen had saved it, the responsibility for his survival was also mine. And as those blue eyes held mine I realized also that this was a man whom women would find very easy to love.

"Do you know the story of the first Branwen, whose name you bear?"

I looked at him, curious in spite of myself, for I had known only that it was a British name.

"She was the White Raven—for in our language that is the meaning of the word—the sister of Bran the High King, and Lady of Logres, that is the eternal soul of our land. And they married her to Matholwch the king of Eriu. But one of her brothers had not been consulted, and to Matholwch he did great insult and dishonor. Still, they needed the alliance, and so they smoothed it over, and Branwen went back with them to Eriu."

"These alliances!" I shook my head. "Do you wonder that Esseilte is not eager to be wed?"

"She may have the right of it," he replied, "for the story of the dishonor to Matholwch got out soon enough, and the men of Eriu turned against Branwen and separated her from the king, and made her labor in the kitchens and at grinding the king's corn."

Like my mother, I thought then, and wondered if perhaps that was why she had given me the name.

"But Branwen trained a starling to carry a paper to Britain on which she told her woes. And when they knew of it, Bran summoned his hosts and they came in arms against Eriu. But the Irish threw their slain into the Cauldron of Rebirth, and—"

"Oh, be still!" I turned on him. "I can tell already that the story ends badly! Is not life sorrowful enough without a bard's tragic tales?"

"Perhaps," he answered me, "but it may be also that only by listening to the stories of others' woes can we find the courage to bear our own. . . ."

A jingling of bridles close by made us both turn. A party of riders was trotting up the road to Temair, the gold on their own bodies and on their horses' harnesses glittering blindingly in the sun.

Dughan blinked. "Are we having a festival? Who are they?"

I squinted, trying to make out the design of their embroidery, and recognized a man who had visited Temair before.

"The men of Laigin! Sweet lady, I must get back to Esseilte—"

Dughan picked up the pail and in a few long strides had caught up with me.

"Is it a marriage they're making? For the princess?" His glance was far too keen. But everyone would guess as soon as they saw Esseilte in her finery in the meadhall—

"They're only talking about it," I said quickly, "but it's true that Muiredach of South Laigin has asked for her for his youngest son."

"She said nothing this morning. . . ." He was frowning.

"Of course not, no decision has been made—"

"Oh, Branwen." He took my arm and pulled me around to face him. "You'll not tell me that one would let custom keep her silent if she felt strongly! Does she wish this?"

I shrugged, refusing to meet his eyes. "She has not decided either . . . but she is a daughter of the royal house. She must marry someone. . . ."

"Yes, that is usually the fate of royal children," Dughan said with a touch of bitterness, and sighed. "And what about you?"

I looked up at him then, not understanding the question. He

took my arm and pulled me closer; even if I had willed it, I could not have resisted the grip of that strong hand.

"If this comes to pass, what will you do?"

"I will go with her, of course," I answered him. We began to walk again. My breathing had quickened, and I strove to master it. No one had ever cared what would become of me. . . .

"Of course." He nodded.

For a moment — only one moment then — a vision flickered into consciousness of myself and Dughan wedded and serving Esseilte as a queen. Such a match would not have been impossible. Indeed, some such arrangement would be the only way I could ever marry and still keep faith with her.

"Are you feared for your position?" I asked then. "Surely Esseilte will want a harper for her household — shall I speak to her for you?"

"Do not!"

I stared at him, and perhaps my face showed the death of that moment's dream, for he let go of my arm and tried to laugh.

"I'm . . . a wanderer, Branwen. My father died soon after my birth, and my mother in the bearing. I've never had a home I really belonged in, and now I don't know if I can settle anywhere. If I could, it would be here —" He looked at me and it seemed that his eyes grew brighter, but how could I trust anything I thought I saw in his face now? "But your cure has been too successful, Branwen — I'm not ready to sit down and play harper-by-the-fire!"

He meant it — I could hear it in the tremor beneath the light tone. I knew only too well how it felt not to truly belong in your home. And yet there was something there that sounded wrongly, like a harpstring not quite tuned. Perhaps the vanity I had not thought I possessed was smarting too badly for me to judge what I heard. I must not blame Dughan for rejecting what he had not even known I was offering him.

But still — but still — what he had said was not all true, or perhaps not all of the truth, and I had no way to tell just what was wrong, or how it was that I knew. . . .

"I drink to the bright eyes of the Maiden of Temair!" King Muiredach's envoy lifted his silver-banded drinking horn to Esseilte. "May her beauty never fade!"

Esseilte smiled, eyes downcast so that one could not read them. But it had not been an empty compliment. She was wearing a mantle of deep blue edged in red and gold over a purple silk gown. Gold thread glittered from the embroidered bands at wrists and neck and hem, and bright ribbons had been braided into her shining hair.

When I had helped her to dress she had complained that she felt like a mare being readied for a fair, but now she was all sweet decorum. Perhaps she did not wish this marriage, but she would have been mortified if Laigin had rejected her.

"And I drink to the hope that an alliance between our kindreds will seal the friendship begun so long ago," the envoy went on.

The quick color receded from Esseilte's face and she glanced at her father. One did not lightly refer to the dark days after Muirchetach MacErca died, when his successor exiled Diarmait and only the king of South Laigin had dared to shelter him from the High King's wrath.

"I have not forgotten what I owe Muiredach your lord," said Diarmait. "It needs no tie of blood to remind me. The claims of justice are reinforced by love and memory." He leaned back against the embroidered hanging, framed by the splendor around him like an image of Sovereignty in an illuminated page, and the envoy nodded his understanding. As Esseilte realized that her father's decision was not yet made I felt her relax as well, and her color returned.

For a moment my eyes blurred and I saw them all—king and princess, clerics and warriors too, as figures in the intricate pattern of the hall.

The Mead-Circling Hall was one of the wonders of Eriu. It was at that time newly refurbished according to the teaching of Fintan MacBócra, and was already becoming a pattern of magnificence, so that when the poets wished to praise a dwelling in song or story, they need say only that it was constructed on the plan of Temair's great hall. But I think that it was famed less for its workmanship, though the gilded bronze that covered the pillars and the partitions made a fine show, than because its arrangements and divisions showed the diversity of the world, united by its center, the king.

The hearth where we were sitting was in the center of the raised dais in the midst of the hall, with the royal couch on the northern side of the fire. Tonight, the queen shared it with Diarmait. A lesser seat had been placed for Esseilte nearby, while I sat on a low stool beside her, trying to memorize all I saw. Until

now, Esseilte and I had always been thought too young to participate on those rare occasions when the women of the royal
household joined the men in the hall.

At the great feasts, the kings of the four provinces held court
in their own compartments just below the central dais, but
tonight those couches, and the compartments behind them that
would have been filled with subject kings and warriors, were
occupied by the masters of every profession that were in the
stronghold of Temair, each in his proper direction and degree.

The pattern was preserved even in the placement of the Ard-
Righ's honored guests. Muiredach's envoys were set on the eastern side of the fire, for the east was the direction of Laigin, as it
was also of all those who worked the land. The herdsmen who
looked after the king's cattle and the farmers who tended his
fields had their places in the compartments behind them.

Behind the king were his warriors, for the north was the direction of the Ulaid, the domain of men of war. Just behind
Diarmait sat Fergus MacGabran, who had replaced the Morholt
as Champion. MacGabran was a big red man, with freckles on
his arms beneath the wiry hair. Esseilte scorned him for trying to
take her uncle's place, but not too loudly, for his father was a
kinsman of Tuathal of West Midhe, who had been Diarmait's
predecessor in the high seat of Temair, and his enemy. Just now
he was looking at Esseilte in her finery as if he had never seen
her before.

At Diarmait's right hand several notable churchmen who had
paused at Temair on their travels were already deep in discussion, with the king's men of learning listening intently behind
them. Across the fire sat the officers of the royal household. But
the poets who should have been among them were off that night
at their own conclave, and it was Dughan who sat tuning his
harp on the low stool, scrubbed and combed and looking surprisingly elegant in a new blue robe.

He also looked, I thought, a little apprehensive, and I wondered if he had ever played for such a gathering before. It had
been the queen's idea to call on him. Had she too begun to think
of him as a permanent part of Esseilte's household? Would they
have beamed on him so approvingly if they had known he
wanted to leave them? I shut my lips against the temptation to
tell Esseilte, who was watching the men of Laigin beneath her
lashes and did not notice my frown.

"And think you that it was truly the Land of Promise you found?"

A lull in the other conversations let the words come through clearly, and I turned. It was the younger of the two churchmen who had spoken, and I recognized him at once, for the Abbot of Derry was born a prince of the northern Ui Néill, with the look of a warrior about him despite the coarse robe. I picked at my food, straining to hear as they went on.

"That is what Ternoc called it, and I am certain that this island was the same. For six weeks we explored, and never came to its ending. And all the time we were praising God for the sweet sight of groves of trees that have never known the axe, and flowers and fruits like the meadows of Eden. Ah, Columba my brother — if only I could have remained. From a land unstained by the evils of men surely it would be but a simple step to Paradise!"

The monk who had replied was older, with a bushy beard and dark grizzled hair springing back from his shaven brow. Even in the hall, his gray eyes seemed fixed on some far horizon. Columba smiled a little at his enthusiasm, and then shook his head. Firelight shone from his ruddy hair as he leaned forward.

"But Brendan, could even the groves of Eden compensate for the loss of Eriu? This land that bore us is surely the pearl of the countries of creation, and if it be stained by the sin of men, then it is our duty as servants of God to cleanse it!"

Enthusiasm had loosened the bonds that held his words to the hearing of his immediate companions, and they rang out now so that everyone looked around. Columba acknowledged their attention with a little lift of the head like a royal stag, and I understood that only his own control kept his voice from filling the hall. I wondered what irony had made him choose the name of the dove? His name in the world had been "Crim Thánn," the Wolf! Perhaps God had power over him, but only his own princely will would ever force Columba to obedience in the world of men. Diarmait was looking at him along with the others, but I could not read the glance that passed between them.

"It is the duty of both prince and priest to care for the health of the land," the High King said calmly. "Perhaps we cannot make Eriu into an earthly heaven, but men are free to seek their own salvation when peace and justice are in the land."

"But whose justice?" Columba had lowered his voice, but its

resonance carried it clearly, and by this time, all of those around the king's fire had stopped their own conversations to hear.

"Are there two kinds?" asked one of the men of Laigin. "In the old days, the Druid was the conscience of the king. The kingdom must be served."

"As it is," answered Columba, "when kings obey the will of God. But when they do not, God's wrath destroys them and their lands, as indeed we may see in Britain today. I have recently read a copy of the chronicles of the monk Gildas, who cries out against their tyranny—

> *"Kings Britain has, but they are tyrants; judges, but wicked ones. They terrorize and plunder the innocent; they protect and defend criminals and robbers."*

Columba rolled out the Latin words with relish. Esseilte and I had been taught enough of the language to follow it, although we neither read nor spoke it very well. Seeing the zeal that flamed in the monk's blue eyes, I wished that I had not been able to understand. The queen fixed him with a basilisk glare and Esseilte stirred angrily, but before she could make any outburst Fergus MacGabran stood up behind the king, face purpling with anger.

"If you were a man of the sword you would not dare to speak so in the house of the king!" MacGabran cast a swift sidelong glance, not at the king, but at Esseilte, as if seeking her approval.

Columba's eyes blazed, and I was glad he had no weapon, for I felt the throb of danger shake the air. Then some mighty effort of will mastered the instinctive responses of an Ó Néill, and his features assumed a calm that was in its way more formidable than his rage had been.

"Peace, Fergus." Diarmait held up one hand. "He has but quoted the words of a foreign monk regarding the abuses of foreign rulers. You shame me by defending where none has accused."

Fergus's red beard still bristled, but after a moment he sat down again. An awkward moment had been smoothed over, and yet an ill thought had been planted in the minds of those who had heard, and I shivered suddenly.

"If I were to betray my trust in such fashion he would be right to condemn me," the High King went on. "I have worked to make the land secure and establish the rule of law everywhere. I too am the servant of God, and it is He who must judge my deeds!"

"All the land of Eriu knows the justice of the Ard-Righ, the people and the churches as well, for he has protected all of them!" exclaimed the envoy from South Laigin. "These Saxons may eat up the British, who have no strong king, but our land is secure!"

"May it be so!" came the murmur from all around us.

"In Christ's name, amen!" The churchmen crossed themselves, and everyone addressed themselves to their meat and drink with a self-conscious enthusiasm. Dughan began to play softly, and the sweet ripple of harpsong spread its benediction through the hall.

"Indeed we do have peace now," said the monk Brendan after a little time had passed. "And the land prospers whose king fears God. But all men, even kings, are mortal, and if the people have no other source of justice, who will protect them if the king be an evil man?" Brendan had spoken calmly, and the sense of danger did not return. I could feel them all settling happily to the debate.

"And who would you have as their champion—the Church?" asked the queen. "How has the Church of Britain protected its sheep against these royal wolves?"

"Badly, lady—very badly," answered Columba with a frown. "Gildas tells how the bishops serve as mouthpieces for tyrants. Princes take holy vows to protect themselves against their kinfolk, and when the situation changes, they renounce them as if they meant no more than the promises a sailor gives a maid, and seize power. They say that Constantine of Kernow murdered two of his royal kinsmen in the church before the eyes of their mother, with the robes of an abbot still on his back. The sufferings of the British Church at the hands of the heathen are a well-deserved chastisement, for it cannot protect either itself or the people until it serves God alone!"

"Then Church and kingdom must exercise their separate powers, is it not so?" Diarmait said very quietly. "If it is evil for the kings to rule the bishops, then would you not agree that the bishop must not usurp the rule of the king?"

For a long moment cool gray eyes held hot blue, and we watched with stopped breath as if two wrestlers strove for mastery. Then Columba laughed, on his face a look of such sweetness that I understood suddenly how he drew men to him, and why there were now ten monasteries that followed his rule.

"For my own soul's salvation, may Christ help me to believe it is so!"

I sighed as the mouse in the mown field must sigh when the shadow of the hawk passes by. Columba had understood the warning in the High King's words because he had already struggled with that temptation. I prayed then that his strength would not fail him, for by tradition the sovereignty of Temair fell alternately to the Ui Néill of Midhe and of the North. Save for his tonsure, Columba would have been the next High King.

"Though it go against the grain for a churchman to credit, I believe some of Britain's griefs have other cause," said Queen Mairenn, "when so much of their best blood has migrated overseas to Armorica, and those lords that remain have not the strength to reconquer the half of the land that lies under the Saxon heel."

"My lady, the strength is there!" Everyone turned in surprise, and I realized that it was Dughan who had interrupted her. "It is the rivalry of the princes that has defeated them — cousin against cousin, brother against brother, grandfather against grandson —" his voice cracked painfully. There was an uncomfortable silence, and I wished I had taken the time to instruct the harper on some of the darker aspects of Esseilte's family history. It was by no straight path that King Diarmait had come to his throne. But Dughan was too caught up in his own memories to see. He caught his breath and went on.

"Gildas speaks truth, so far as he goes, but he does not understand the real triumph of Artor, which was to unite the tribes of Britain against their enemies. You men of Eriu, who have a strong Ard-Righ, cannot appreciate the tragedy of a land whose provinces tear at each other's throats like maddened wolves! And yet Artor, who conquered every other foe, was slain at the last by his own son! It was so in Britain, and in Armorica now it is the same, and the Franks sniff round her borders like dogs. A land whose lords betray each other is easy prey to any enemy!"

"You speak as one who has suffered from that plague." The High King's face was watchful as if he sat in judgment. "Those are hot words for a harper. Are you of noble kin?"

Abruptly Dughan seemed to realize that everyone was staring at him, and though it may have been the firelight, it seemed to me that the strange flicker I had seen before came and went in his eyes.

Then he was shaking his head and blushing like a boy. His fingers brushed the harpstrings in a series of minor harmonies.

"Oh, my lord, a bard trades in such tragedies. Singing the deeds of a noble ancestor is the best way to earn a bed in his descendant's hall! The harper who laments the lord's kinfolk and curses his enemies will never want for a place — but what is bread for the bard may be ruin for the kingdom. . . ."

It was an excellent answer, and the king appeared to have been satisfied by it, but I found it hard to believe that Dughan's outburst was merely professional passion. In that moment it occurred to me that it was panic that had come and gone so swiftly in the harper's eyes, and I wondered why.

"Indeed, it is an evil time," said Brendan then. "And I fear that even when the king is just and the land at peace there is no perfection in the world. Men, and women too, come to the monasteries to seek what they can never find at home, and hermits go even farther, building their oratories on every barren rock to find the kingdom of God."

"And you, Father, have gone farther still. Is that what you are seeking in your voyages?" asked the High King.

"In the world or out of it, what other goal can there be?" the monk said simply. "And we have the word of the saints who went before us that the Land of the Blessed lies across the western sea. Even before Christ's coming those islands were known to the men of Eriu, and surely that is no wonder, for our country is the westernmost land in all this sinful world. Did not Bran son of Febal go to the Land of Joy? And did not Oisin return from the Land of Youth to tell Blessed Padraig of the wonders there?"

For a moment everyone was silent, as if Brendan's words had awakened in them the same longing that shone in his eyes. And into that silence fell the sweet shimmer of music, and Dughan's clear voice upraised in song:

> *"I know where is a distant isle,*
> *For miles around sea-horses glimmer;*
> *A fair course run o'er white-swelling wave —*
> *Four posts uphold its rainbow shimmer.*
> *Splendors of every color glisten;*
> *Listen joyful to music's strain.*
> *Throughout the gentle-voicèd meadows,*
> *Spread through the white-silver plain.*
> *Unknown is treachery or wailing*

In the smiling land we plough,
There is nothing harsh or wounding,
Only sweet sounding of music now.
Without death or grief or sorrow,
Without health's thief, debility,
Of Emne fair that is the sign —
Uncommon to find such stability . . ."

As the song continued, all tensions were soothed away, and instead of the human splendor of Diarmait's meadhall we saw the glimmering beauty of that island where the immortal women and their warriors pass eternity in music and play. If Brendan had shown us a ship, I would have gone aboard without a backward look, for the lilt of the sea was in that singing, and the cry of the restless gulls, and the song of birds whose music this earth shall never know. I looked up at Esseilte, and in her blue eyes I saw the glitter of tears.

"There are thrice fifty distant isles,
Miles in the ocean westward, twice
As large they are as Eriu's strand,
The land of each of them, or thrice.
Eagerly then let Bran row,
Not far away, the women's steading,
To Emne of the many welcomes
Thou shalt come before sun's fading . . ."

sang the bard.

We sat in our old place on the lip of the green hill of Temair — Dughan and Esseilte and I. The undulant plain of Brega stretched toward blue hills that seemed distant as a dream. One could imagine the sea that lay beyond them, with islands floating on the horizon like a mirage. It was dusk. The bark of a dog came faint from below us, and the liquid trill of a homing lark blessed the stillness.

The envoys from Laigin had gone back to their master with Diarmait's terms, calculated to prolong the negotiations while the High King considered the value of alternate alliances. With their departure, a weight seemed to have lifted, and so we sat, breathing deeply of the sweet evening air.

"Would you sail with Brendan if you could?" said Esseilte to me.

"At a word—" After the feast, I had dreamed of Brendan's islands, and wept like Oisin when I woke in the dawning and realized that they were gone. "Between the monk's tales and Dughan's singing, I think Brendan could have filled a flotilla. They say that the men who built the ships for his last voyage asked no wage but a place among his crew."

"The sea-longing is strong in the people of Eriu," said Dughan. "As if even the conquest of the island were only a stop on a journey to a fairer land."

"But why go further? Is not Eriu the image of heaven?" Esseilte laughed. "To hear Columba talk you would think it so!"

"Don't speak of him—he frightens me. . . ." It seemed to me that Columba had been in my dream also, journeying across the gray plains of the sea.

Esseilte shook her head. "Without the tonsure he might have been a danger. But he is bound by the Church now. My mother says there is nothing to fear."

"If he stays there—" said Dughan. "Such a man might renounce pleasure, but can he renounce power? He has the bearing of a king. In my experience, the world is divided between those who desire power, and should not have it, and those who are burdened with it, and would just as soon give it away."

"And which are you, Dughan?" Esseilte laughed as the slow color rose from his neck to his brow, then faded away.

"I am only a harper," he said stiffly. "I have nothing to do with power." But I remembered how he had spoken in the hall and wondered. Dughan might be nobody, but last night was certainly not the first time he had played before a king.

"Would *you* go with Brendan?" I asked him then. Slowly he smiled.

"I have told you of the city of Ys that was swallowed by the sea. Sometimes, when the wind is right, they say you can hear the mournful echoes of drowned bells."

"Did you ever hear them?" Esseilte had drawn closer and was looking at him as if she could read in his eyes the wonder he had sought beneath the waves.

"Once, when I walked along the shore, I thought I did. But to me they did not sound sorrowful . . . what I heard was a summoning to all the peace I can never find in this world, and all the beauty, and all the joy. . . . If Niamh should shake her silver branch over me, I would not be so foolish as to return to the world of men!"

"And you are still seeking that country?" she said in a still voice.

Dughan nodded.

"And that is why you want to leave us now?" she added even more softly.

I had not thought she knew.

"That is one of the reasons . . . I have never really had a home. . . ."

The enchantment of the Otherworld was still upon him, and hearing the truth in Dughan's voice, I understood how often it had been absent before.

"I forbid it." Esseilte's voice was still quiet, but the flat denial was like a slap, and Dughan's face closed. "Unless a woman of the Sidhe should invite you to the Otherworld, you shall never go! I did not nurse you back to health to see you waste my labor chasing faerie gold. I care not whether we go in the end to the Christians' heaven or to Tír na nÓg. Abbot Columba was right, though I do not share his reasons. The songs are made in this world! You are a harper! You should know that better than any!"

Still unshielded, he turned, and scorn for once uncontrolled sharpened his reply.

"Is that why you saved me, *Princess*" — he drew out the word scornfully — "so that I could praise your bright eyes and golden hair?"

I felt a sudden prickling as a different man seemed to look out of Dughan's eyes. His bearing was as princely as Columba's, and both Esseilte and I shrank from his wrath. In her case, sheer surprise had overwhelmed her; then she sprang to her feet. For a moment they faced each other like combatant warriors.

There had been truth in Dughan's sickness, but since then, how many men had I seen come and go in him, as a mummer changes his masks? *Who was he really?*

"You are insolent!" Outrage shook Esseilte's voice.

"But am I right?" He seemed to shrink back in upon himself, and irony veiled whatever else had been in his eyes.

Esseilte shrugged disdainfully. "I am a piece on the fidchel board, to be sacrificed or moved as my father's policy requires. I could be as beautiful as Deirdre and never win renown unless someone famous chooses to marry me. But a song may outlive its maker . . . your words will live when I am dust, though you be only a wandering bard and I a princess of Eriu. Will that not reconcile you to the world?"

"Like the beauty of the princess, the words of the poet are made memorable only when they adorn great deeds," Dughan said mockingly. "I am only a servant. Give me the story, lady, and I will make you the song!"

"*Oh!*" Esseilte shook with frustration. "All the heroes are dead!" And with that cry she ran headlong back up the path.

There was desperation in Dughan's face when he turned to me again.

"Kind Branwen, you must help me get away!" He seized my hand, and pressed a kiss into the palm. As if the touch had opened a door to his soul I sensed the relentless pressures of love and pride and loyalty, and beneath them, the endless uncomprehending loneliness of an abandoned child.

I shivered and snatched my hand away.

Suddenly, as much as Dughan desired to go, I wished him gone.

Seven

THE FIRES OF CÍLL DARA

The Feast of St. Michael was just past, and the stubbled patches of the harvested fields gave a moth-eaten look to wood and meadow, when Queen Mairenn announced her intention to make a pilgrimage to the abbey of the Blessed Brigid at Cíll Dara. The queen had never been one for explanations, and now was no exception, but for the first time in months, Esseilte and I truly *looked* at her. Mairenn's long horse-face was gaunt and colorless — was it grief for the Morholt that had aged her, or something more?

The previous winter I had watched Esseilte, and then we had nursed Dughan. Since he had left us, we had both been too busy pretending his absence left no gap in our lives to notice anyone else's pain. Esseilte had never asked me what I knew of the manner of the harper's going. But I knew well that the queen could easily have had the truth from me if she had tried. Had she also understood? Or was she too preoccupied with her own pain to care?

Certainly Mairenn gave orders for the journey with all her old authority. We were still salving our anxieties with such reassurances when we rode out of the carved gateway to the enclosure of Temair and started down the eastern slope of the hill. As we moved southward I thought that Columba had been right to be content with Eriu. What country that Brendan might find across the sea could equal this gentle landscape that ripened into deeper richness with every day? Except for the fenced strips of the grainfields, the rangeland stretched unbroken in mingled swirls of grassy meadow and thick woodland studded with hazel and holm oak and elm.

And every yard of it had been watered by the blood of heroes and given meaning by their stories. If Britain were the Island of the Mighty, as Dughan had boasted, then surely the Isle of Heroes was Eriu. For the first few miles Esseilte and I could tell those tales, for like the folk of any district we knew every inch of our own land. And for the leagues that came after we had the bards, whose business it was to know the history of every spring and standing stone. The sons of Mil had come to Eriu as conquerors, but their descendants had struck roots as deeply as any of the older peoples who had landed here before.

King Diarmait took pride in his justice, and he ruled the kingdoms with the same alert control with which the charioteer had driven his team. But a driver of unruly horses has little leisure to enjoy the country through which he passes. It seemed to me suddenly that it was not Diarmait's royal visitations but Mairenn's pilgrimages that truly linked the sovereigns with the land.

Perhaps this journey was only another of the queen's visits to the holy places, and there was nothing wrong with her at all. . . .

"You are very silent, Princess — are you weary? Take heart, we will be halting soon —"

I turned abruptly and saw Fergus MacGabran, who had left his place with the escort and drawn up beside us. He smiled broadly and Esseilte replied with a stiff nod. Lost in my own speculations, I had not noticed that she had said nothing for nearly an hour. In her face I could see only a thinly veiled distaste for Fergus, whom she had never forgiven for claiming the Morholt's place as Champion.

"You shame us to suppose that we are wearied already," I said quickly. "We will stay in the saddle as long as you!"

Esseilte's lips twitched, and the color in the man's face clashed with the orange of his hair.

"Do I shame you to be concerned?" Fergus forced his voice to gentleness. The result sounded patronizing, and I thought that he would have done better to show his anger, for Esseilte was stiffening again. "You are the kingdom's fairest flower. If I had my will, your father would give me the right to keep you from harm!"

"To cage me, you mean!" Esseilte snapped back at him. "I have no need for that kind of concern!"

"But perhaps your father has need for it — if you care nothing for yourself, perhaps you can summon some concern for him?" Fergus's temper snapped suddenly, and the words came out in a snarl.

Esseilte stared at him. "What do you mean?"

Fergus let out a bark of laughter and a glint of good humor began to come back into his eyes. They were little, piggish eyes; I shuddered, imagining them feasting on the beauty of Esseilte's naked body. But her face stayed like stone.

"Servant of my father, are you threatening me?"

"I am trying to teach you, little flower. . . . Ainmere of the Ulaid would like to see an Ó Néill of the North upon the High King's throne. There may come a time when your father needs an alliance with his southern kin."

Fergus allowed us a moment in which to remember that he too was of the royal kindred and came from the family which had been Diarmait's rivals for the throne. But the speaking of that truth did not recommend him.

"It is the right of the Ui Néill of the North to claim the throne in the next generation. If Aed MacAillel or one of the sons of MacErca should be elected when my father feasts with the heroes, what cause have I to complain?"

"You speak as if this is a thing far in the future, but your own father's path to the throne was none so plain," Fergus said harshly. "The men of the Ulaid have been bloody-handed since the time of King Conchobar, and their descendants have not grown more peaceful. What makes you think that the lord of Emain Macha will wait for age to strike King Diarmait down?" Above the bronze bracelets the short hairs stood out from Fergus's forearms like copper wires. I could see the muscles flexing beneath the skin as he reined his mount closer to ours.

"So you see, my flower, that you might do well to look more kindly when I court you," he added very softly.

Esseilte had gone white — with rage, I thought, though Fergus might suppose it was fear. I kicked my pony to bring me up between them.

"Diarmait is a great king," I said stoutly. "There has never been such peace in the four fifths of Eriu. I suppose that the North will breed men of contention until time's ending, but what makes you suppose them to be more dangerous this year than any other? You will have to give us more than vague fears to recommend this alliance!"

"Does the High King take counsel with maidens?" Fergus asked scornfully. "He knows if the threats I speak of have substance, and by midwinter all Eriu will know it. It is the seventh year of Diarmait's kingship, and the dragon-power must renew the land. Go to the Brugh na Boinne when the year turns and you will see for yourselves — this year the dragon's sacrifice will be more than mummery."

"My father is the true king," said Esseilte. "The earth itself will rise against the Ulaid if they try to pervert the rite." But her voice was uncertain. Diarmait was a just king and a skillful leader of men, but this ritual of the dragon-slaying was a thing of the old magic. Esseilte and I had been children the last time — the year the High King had come to the throne — but we had heard the tales. They said that it was the queen's powers, not the king's, that had given his champion the victory.

Now the dark-cloaked shape of the queen bobbed ahead of us on the road to Cíll Dara. Were her shoulders bowed from pain or from weariness? I stared at Mairenn's bent back as if it could answer me. If Fergus had spoken true, then the queen's health might be more important than any of us knew.

It took us two slow days of travel to reach the village at the ford of Cliath. From there we moved westward up the river, and then south again toward the headwaters of the Bearbra. Mountains rose up on our left hand, mist-veiled in the morning, but before us stretched a wide rich grassland. It was·called the Curragh, a fine place for the breeding of horses, and for racing them as well, but it belonged to the monastery at Cíll Dara. Men said that the king had offered the Blessed Brigid as much land as her mantle could cover, and the power of her prayer extended it across the plain. Perhaps it was so, for even now Cíll Dara was a place of wonders, but the miracle would have been as great if the king had simply been inspired to imitate Brigid's famous generosity.

Brigid's church stood at the edge of the plain, a fine, timbered building with the round stone and turf huts of the monks and nuns and the abbey buildings gathered around it as if a mother hen were sheltering her chicks beneath her wing. The afternoon sunlight was a golden shimmer in the air that lent grass and stone its glow, and gave even the queen's worn features an ephemeral beauty as the abbess embraced her. I smelled wood-smoke, and cattle, and baking bread — the incense of Brigid.

They put the queen and her women in the nuns' guesthouse, but Esseilte and I had a hut to ourselves nearby. By the time we had arranged our things and washed off the journey-dust the bell was ringing for vespers, and we joined the others at the church door.

The sweetness of women's voices chanting the introit soared on the still evening air. We followed the queen around the left side of the screen that divided the building and took our places behind the nuns as the deeper voices of the monks on the other side began to answer them. The last of the daylight blazed through the windows behind us, glowing on the frescoes and embroidered hangings and striking sparks of flame from the goldwork that was everywhere. More screens flanked the altar, and as the priests censed the sanctuary, form and color blurred until ornamentation seemed to coil around the room.

Light and color swirled around me. For a moment consciousness spiraled outward until it embraced building and people, cattle and apple trees — all the interlace of life of which this was the sweet singing heart. When I came to myself again I was staring at a triple knot carved upon the column before me. My eyes followed the pure curve around and around again, aware that there was an answer here to questions I did not yet know how to ask. Voices murmured around me. Somehow we had got through the confession, gloria, and credo, and were finishing the psalm.

Now evening dimmed the air, and the glory that had entranced me had focused to a circle of candlelight. Golden holders smithed by Cíll Dara's first abbot, Conleth, glimmered bravely against the fair white linen of the altar cloth, but there was darkness in the corners. Queen Mairenn swayed a little, and her women moved to support her. Shadow lay upon her face as well, stamping it suddenly with a terrible likeness to the face of her brother as he had lain on his bier.

"Omnipotens sempiterne Deus, vespere et mane et meridie majestatem tuam suppliciter deprecamur: ut expulsis de cordibus nostris peccatorum tenebris, ad veram lucem, quae Christus est, facias nos pervenire," the priest sang.

Omnipotent eternal God, in the evening and morning and noon we supplicate and entreat Thy majesty — memories of Brother Ambrosius's teaching supplied a halting translation — *that Thou mayest expel from our hearts the sins of darkness, and make us to come to the true light, which is Christ. . . .*

Had we sinned the sin of darkness when we conjured that bitter knowledge from my father's head? And if that were so, what payment would be required? I dared not look at Queen Mairenn's face again, afraid of what I would see.

"Tuus est dies, Domine, et tua est nox. . . ."

Thine is the day, o Lord, and thine is the night. . . .

The moment before, I had seen only glory, and now I was in darkness. And yet there was still a light on Brigid's altar. When the service had ended I followed the others outside, a little comforted.

Esseilte swore softly and set her hand to her lips where she had grazed it against the quern.

"You need not do this — truly we have enough — " The young nun with whom we were grinding the grain looked up quickly. Sister Fedelm was a farm girl, and clearly nervous at having to instruct the High King's daughter. I suppressed a grin and bent back to the labor, for I had fallen easily into the way of it again. But Esseilte shook her head, resuming her work with a kind of penitential fervor I had not seen in her before. We had brought the grain out into the kitchen yard, for the morning was a bright one. Beyond the hedge the rolling grassland of the Curragh shimmered in the morning sunlight like the waves of the sea.

"We have come to you for your prayers," Esseilte answered. "It is only right that we should help with the work that supports them." Suddenly I understood that she had seen the same thing that I had in the face of the queen, and she was afraid.

"They say the querns ground of themselves, in Brigid's day. . . ." Sister Fedelm said wistfully.

"That they did not!" a snort of laughter interrupted her. I had thought the old nun asleep, there in the morning sun, but now she bent toward us, still cackling. "The Blessed Brigid was still our mother when I came here forty years ago. As I grow old I remember my young days ever more clearly — a joy it was to be in this house then, but the cows must still be milked with both hands, nor did the ground till itself!"

The old nun could have been here when Padraig came, I thought as she settled back again. Age had ripened her like an apple at the end of winter, with skin wrinkled and rosy but the meat still sound.

"But Brigid did do miracles — you can't deny it!" The younger nun gestured toward the glittering grassland, as if its reality could prove her words. "Brigid spread her mantle over all this plain to win it for the abbey—was not that a wonder?"

"Indeed, it did take a miracle to get such a gift from the Ui Cellaigh king, but as I heard it in my youth, it was a wonder of wit, and no magic. The old man told her she could have what her mantle encompassed, and she unraveled the good wool, thread by thread, to bound her claim."

"Even all the threads in a queen's cloak could hardly extend so far! It was the power of God that stretched them," exclaimed Sister Fedelm. Esseilte glanced a little self-consciously at the fine blue wool of the cloak that lapped her, for despite the sun, the air was still chill.

"That may be so," the old woman answered her, "but the Lord of Heaven loves those best who spend all to serve Him, and that was always Brigid's way. For her, the cows would let down their milk thrice in a day if she had promised it to the needy, and the grainpits seemed always to hold another measure when all the bread was gone. If the wonders are fewer these days it is because our hearts are smaller than hers."

"But does Brigid still answer those who call on her?" asked Esseilte. "My mother seeks the blessing of her holy fire at noon-tide—will Brigid hear?"

"She will listen," the nun answered with absolute conviction. "But only the poor in spirit have room to receive her generosity. How much is your mother willing to give?"

The sun was high and the pile of grain ground down to meal by the time they summoned us to attend the queen. I had seen the hedged enclosure behind the church and wondered how one entered; when Sister Fedelm led us into the sanctuary I realized that the church itself was the gateway. Coming out into the light again was a shock after that cool dimness. Blinking, I stumbled against Esseilte and felt her take my hand. In a moment the world steadied and my balance returned to me, but my skin was still tingling as it did sometimes on a day of high wind.

The walk through the church seemed to have taken us much farther than the distance we had gone—inside the enclosure one could see nothing of the abbey but the timbered wall of the nave, for the holly hedge was thick and high, and the sounds of the busy community around us came like echoes from another world. Inside the circle the grass was still lush and green. In the center was set an open shelter whose conical thatched roof was supported by thick beams, and within it a low hearth of stone, and upon the hearth a burning fire.

We moved across the silent grass and the nun whose day it was to tend the flame came out from the shelter to meet us.

"Sister, why have you come here?"

The queen's glance moved to the fire, then back again. She bowed her head. "I am come to ask the Lady to ease my soul and relieve my body's pain . . ." she said in a low voice.

I felt Esseilte's hand tighten on my arm, and heard the other women murmur at this confirmation of what we had suspected before. Mairenn was not a woman who admitted weakness easily, nor would she have sought this remedy until all her herb-craft had failed. But there could be no secrets here.

"In return for her favor I am prepared to make a rich offer-ing —" She gestured, and one of her women held out a purse of gold. But the nun shook her head.

"Do you think you can buy the favor of Brigid?" The nun softened the reproof with a gentle smile. "You may offer your gift to Mary's sweet Son when your time here is finished, but as for Brigid, it is the Holy one Herself who must say what She requires."

Mairenn nodded and moved past, and we followed into the shrine.

A few mats had been placed around the hearth in concession to the knees of worshippers who had not taken penitential vows. Esseilte and I settled ourselves on one of them, on the other side of the fire from the queen. Here at the center, the air hummed like a sleeping hive, in which the occasional snap from the fire was the only audible part of a vibration too deep for mortal hear-ing. It was a living silence, like the living light of the holy flame. My ears rang, and I struggled to draw in the weighted air.

Mairenn's lips were moving. And whether in the passion of her entreaty she forgot that she was not alone or whether I was now so tranced that I perceived her soul speaking, I heard. . . .

"Ah, Blessed Brigid! Thou art here, as they told me, the old power allied with the new! Sweet Lady, I have always served Thee! Why hast Thou forsaken me?"

For a few moments there was silence, and then the whispering of the fire began to answer her.

"Was it truly Me you were serving?"

"I sought the land's weal, Lady, as well as I knew how!" Mairenn's face grew stern with pride.

"*Look into your own heart, Queen of Eriu. Have your motives justified your means?*" The fire sank and rose again.

"*Without Diarmait's justice what peace would there be? And without my spells how could he maintain his power? Thou Thyself hast blessed my workings, or how could they have prospered?*"

"*What is done for life's sake I bless, but not what is done for destruction —*" the implacable whisper replied. The queen shook her head, desperate, uncomprehending.

"*I ask only for the health to serve Eriu! What must I give to have Thy favor again?*"

"*Look into the fire and learn. . . .*" The flame shivered as if a wind had touched it, then it began to grow as if some smith were drawing out its living gold in great twisted strands. I blinked at that brilliance, but as sight failed, hearing became sharper. Now the fire's whisper was a crackle. Words came —

> "*I am the fire on the hearth that bakes the grain to bread,*
> *I am the fire on the altar that consumes the offering;*
> *I am the fire in the forge that anneals the soul.*
> *Give me your hatred, and I will refine it into compassion;*
> *Give me your vengeance, and I will forge it into forgiveness;*
> *Give me your pride, and let it fuel the sacrifice.*"

Esseilte cried out, and I knew it was not my inner vision only that saw a great column of light blaze up until it seemed the thatch must surely catch fire.

Mairenn whimpered and turned her face away.

"*I am a princess of the royal house — the blood-price must be paid! Honor is life to me —*"

"*Daughter, it is hatred that is gnawing your life away — the honor of Eriu belongs to Me!*" snapped the fire.

Then the voice roared out of the flame.

> "*I am the fire of Life!*
> *I am the fire of Death!*
> *I am the fire of Love!*"

The other women caught the queen as she fell back, arms upraised to ward away that splendor. Strands of grizzled hair clung to cheeks that glistened with tears.

"Brigid, Brigid, I claim Thy mercy!" Mairenn cried aloud. "I will give — !"

Her hands fell then, and I suppose she fainted. I do not know, for I saw only the light, and within it a form of flame whose face

shone with the terrible beauty I had seen once before in the flare
of sunlight from the water of the holy well.

"Branwen, what happened at the fire today? What do you think
my mother saw?" The blankets fell back as Esseilte raised herself on one elbow to look at me. Lamplight backlit her golden
hair and the smooth curve of her bare shoulder, leaving her face
in shadow. Outside, cold stars glittered above empty fields, and
the wind was harvesting the leaves from the oak trees. There
was no hearth in the guest hut, but the bed made a warm nest
for Esseilte and me.

"I think she saw Brigid," I said carefully. Esseilte had not
asked me what *I* had seen.

"When the fire blazed up? How could anyone see anything?
She was dazzled!" She lay back again, staring up at the inner
curve of the thatching.

Dazzled I had been, I thought then, but not by the fire. Had
Esseilte truly seen nothing more? I was glad I had spoken cau-
tiously. Mairenn was her mother, not mine. It would have been
presumptuous to claim more knowledge. But to myself I could
no longer deny it. Was it because my life had depended on sensing the meanings of others that I could often hear words unspoken by men, and sometimes, as it appeared, the voices of
other powers? Esseilte had never had to listen to anything but
her own will.

I lay motionless, tasting that knowledge, wondering what payment Mairenn had finally offered for her healing, and whether it
would be enough.

"She sounded . . . broken, Branwen. She sounded afraid. My
mother has never been afraid of anything! Oh Branwen, is that
what it means to grow old?" Esseilte rolled over and gripped my
arm. "It makes me afraid, too," she added softly. "I always used
to envy children whose mothers loved them. But at least I knew
that mine would protect me! If something happens to her, what
will I do?"

I turned on my side and hugged her. Was it a comfort to me
to know that Esseilte felt herself orphaned too? But even then I
could not say so.

"You still have a father—" I said instead.

"The children of princes do not have fathers," she answered
bitterly. "They have sovereigns who will use them for the kingdom's good whether they love them or no! Do you think a man

who executed his own son for stealing a nun's cow will hesitate
to marry off his daughter where policy requires?"

"Esseilte, we've known since babyhood that you must marry
someday—" My fingers combed through the silky tangles of her
hair, gentling her as if she had been a nervous mare.

"Someday is now . . ." Esseilte's voice came muffled against
her arm. "You heard what Fergus said. You saw how he looked
at me!"

"Oh Esseilte"—I held her closer—"are you afraid? He stared
at you because he found you beautiful!"

"Beautiful!" She sat up suddenly, shaking off my arm. "Do
you think this body beautiful?" She cupped breasts still high but
with a woman's fullness now, ran her hands down smooth sides
and across the sweet curve of her thighs.

Her breast was as white as the snow of one night. . . . The poet's
praise of Deirdre came to me then. I felt an odd inner pang, as
on some summer morning when the beauty of the waking world
is too beautiful almost to bear.

"Yes . . ." I said softly, sitting up to look at her. "Yes, Esseilte, you are fair."

There was a harsh edge to her laughter as she pushed back
her long hair.

"Then pray that the man I am given to will find me so! Don't
you understand, Branwen? This body is the only weapon I
have!" She burrowed back down into the blankets again, sobbing.

I sat with my arms clasped around my knees, listening to the
wind whisper in the thatch above us as Brigid's fire had whispered to Mairenn. The queen was not beautiful, and yet she had
power. For a moment I glimpsed an answer to Esseilte's fears,
but she was Mairenn's daughter—she knew as well as I did
what the queen could do. If she did not claim that magic, Esseilte must believe she had no gift for that kind of power.

Did I?

I had shared the queen's vision, but my birth denied me initiation into her mysteries. Remembering the anguish in Mairenn's
voice as she faced the fire I thought that perhaps I should be
grateful. A price had been paid for that mastery.

"Branwen—"

Esseilte's whisper distilled from the whistling of the wind.

"Branwen, you won't leave me, will you? Promise you will
stay by me wherever I must go—"

I had made a promise to her mother, and I still trembled when I wondered when I would have to pay. But for me, this question of Esseilte's had been answered long ago. Esseilte was the only one who cared about me in this world. What set my eyes to stinging was the realization that perhaps it was the same for her.

"My oath and my life on it, heart's sister — " I fought to keep my voice steady. "Did you need to ask that of me?"

She shook her head with a shudder and I realized that she was shivering. I swore softly and eased back down beside her, pulling the covers up over us to keep out the cold. Esseilte held on to me like a little child awakened from an evil dream. Murmuring softly, I stroked her hair, and presently her head grew heavy against my shoulder and her sighs became the regular breathing of rest.

But I was wakeful, willing warmth to surround us like Brigid's holy fire. Esseilte and I lay with breasts like nesting doves and thighs entwined, and at that moment I thought that we were one being, born into separate bodies by some mischance and now united again. As I held her, the heat around us became a blaze, and from the bright stillness at its heart there came a voice that whispered, *I am the fire of Love . . .*

I knew then that like Queen Mairenn, if the power were given me I would pay the price required.

We returned to Temair, and if the queen seemed scarcely better, at least her health failed no further. She seemed to be hoarding her strength, though we could not guess what she was waiting for. Meanwhile, the gold of harvest faded to gray. The Festival of Samhain passed quietly, but as winter tightened its grip the tension began to grow.

We avoided Fergus, but the queen herself informed Esseilte that King Gabran had formally asked the king for her, and there were those who made sure we heard the rumors that if the marriage took place, Ainmere of Emain Macha had threatened war.

"I never thought to be grateful to the Ulaid," Esseilte said to me that day, "but so long as he does not seek me for *his* son, I will bless Ainmere's name!" But we both knew that if Diarmait could have gotten peace with the North for his daughter's bride-price he would have taken it, and Esseilte would have gone to Ailech without a word.

Then for a time it began to look as if she would be married to the tanist of South Laigin after all. But before that gossip was cold the rumor came to us that it might be more useful to have young Curnan of Connachta as a son-in-law than a royal hostage. This was ill news indeed, for Curnan was the man who had fouled the Morholt in the Samhain race the year before — a lad of chancy temper for all his good looks, whom Esseilte liked even less than she did Fergus. If Diarmait had ordered it she might have gone to Curnan's bed, but I would not have wagered on their both living through the month after. I suppose the king knew his daughter at least well enough to guess the same, for there was no more talk of that alliance.

Still, it was clear that Esseilte's marriage had become part of the interlace of enmities and alliances in which King Diarmait was entangled. And as the sun's power weakened, thoughts began to turn toward the ritual that must take place on Midwinter's Day at the great white mound in the curve of the Boinne that the bards said belonged to Oengus Og, who was a lord among the Sidhe. Already the teams of dancers had been chosen from among the king's hostages and young warriors. The straw disguises were being woven, and the other gear had been taken from storage for repair. Now the focus of intrigue moved to the ceremony, and the loyalties of the participants and the forces that they would channel became part of the equation of power.

It was the first week of December when Fergus pressed his suit to King Diarmait once more. Old Messach, first as ever with the gossip of Temair, came to tell us. I looked at Esseilte, who had gone white with anger, and then back at our nurse.

"What was the king's answer, then? Do you know?"

For a moment the old woman looked discomfited, then she shrugged. "I heard what Red Fergus said when the messenger went in, but he was silent when the man came out again. Still, he did not look unhappy, and all know that he will be your father's champion in the ritual. Would it be so ill a thing for you to wed him, gosling? You would not have to leave Temair!"

Esseilte put down her embroidery. "I would as soon wed the man who killed the Morholt as the man who has supplanted him! Fergus is a pig — rather than go to his bed I would lie down in the sty!"

Messach limped toward the door. "Mistress high and mighty —" She shook her head mockingly. "You should be grateful a strong warrior wants you — or were you waiting to be courted by one of the Sidhe? But maybe your mother will talk some sense into you!" As the hide curtain flapped behind her I turned and saw that Queen Mairenn had come into the room.

Esseilte got to her feet, embroidery sliding unheeded from her lap onto the floor.

"Is it true?"

"Is what true?" the queen echoed calmly. She eased down on a bench by the window.

"That Father is going to give me to Fergus?"

"Fergus's father has asked, certainly," Mairenn answered in the same smooth tone. "But your father will not give him an answer until after the ritual."

"Then I am to be his prize? In the old tales the maiden always goes to the warrior who kills the dragon!"

"Perhaps. Much will depend on the way the ritual goes." Mairenn sighed. "It is necessary that you understand, Esseilte, for there is no assurance of victory. The royal champion represents the king, and must complete the rite in every detail. You and I have no voice in the ceremony, yet we must be there. Our prayers, if you will, may make the difference between an empty ritual and the full renewal of your father's power."

You will be doing more than saying prayers, I thought, looking at her, *if everything I have heard is true.*

"If all goes well, the High King will make what alliances he likes thereafter," the queen went on.

"I will not marry Fergus —" Esseilte repeated.

"Perhaps you will not have to." She shrugged. "But that does not matter. Now I must teach you what you will need to know for the ritual."

Esseilte looked at her mother and sighed. It was certain that she would get no sympathy now, and it might even be that what the queen had said was true. If Diarmait's champion did not win a clear and complete victory, perhaps no one would marry Esseilte at all.

Eight

THE DRAGON

River mist lay heavy on the mound of Knowth, drawing glimmering haloes around the torches, dropping a glittering veil across Esseilte's bright hair. I coughed and wrapped my woolen brat more tightly around me, mind and body still stiff from the long ride. Around us dim shapes stirred as if the air had congealed into the forms of men. Many men, for the procession was forming here, and beyond them waited the people who had come to witness the ritual.

One of the queen's women offered us ale mulled over the little fire and I grasped the leather tankard gratefully. Steam writhed above it in curls like the patterns pecked into the ancient stones.

"How long do you suppose it will be before we begin?" I leaned against the side of the mound.

Esseilte's eyes were shadowed as she stared down into her tankard. "The filidh will begin the chanting when it is time. . . ." She nodded toward the huddle of figures whose long gowns glowed with embroidery even in this uncertain light, for the wedding robes of the noblewomen of Eriu were the poets' fee.

Beyond them moved other, stranger, forms. Peaked headdresses and tiered capes and skirts of wheatstraw masked the shapes inside them. Already the dancers had ceased to be human in appearance. I heard a gust of laughter from that direction, hastily stifled as they remembered where they were. Inside the costumes they were still men — king's sons, honored to have this

121

part in the ceremony. But once the music began, once the dance took them, what would they be then?

I remembered Fergus's warnings and wondered if any of these princes would deliberately try to distort the rite. Once it was upon them, would they dare? And even if they willed it, could they resist the forces that would be released by the ritual? I shivered again, and this time it was not from cold. Expectation weighted the air more heavily than the moisture, and not only from the people — it seemed to me as if the land itself were holding its breath through the last darkness of the longest night as it waited for midwinter's dawn.

"They know how many verses it will take to get us to get to the Brugh before the sun rises — " Esseilte continued.

"In this murk, will we be able to tell?" I answered sourly.

"My mother says we will. She says that when Amergin the Archpoet sings the spell, even were it snowing the clouds would part to let the first sunlight through. There is a triple spiral carved into the stone of the inner chamber, and the light flares down the passage to touch it only at this moment of this day. . . ."

". . . To wake the magic," I added. Esseilte gave a nod and I knew that she was thinking of her father, who had been all night keeping vigil in the mound — the king of men guesting in the house of the lord of the Sidhe so that the power of his sovereignty might be renewed.

A cow's horn blew, soft and tuneful in that moist air, and the muddle of robes began to flow into a more orderly line. A torch bobbed toward us, and as I started to push myself upright I saw a pattern in the stone beneath my hand.

"Look — "

Esseilte leaned over to see what I had found. Nearing torchlight showed a roughly scratched shape that shadow limned with sudden meaning. It was a triple-humped serpentine shape whose neck had been pierced by a stake or a spear.

A dragon . . .

Esseilte made a little obeisance and then straightened as the escort came to lead us into the line.

A quiver went through my belly as the mellow moaning of the horns echoed up and down the line, and now a heavy drum-beat added its punctuation, a bone flute twittered plaintively, and rattles filled with bits of old iron began a clangor that bound the other discords into its own almost-harmony. No sweet-singing harps were here, or even the bright braying of pipes. The oldest music was wanted now, for the most ancient of ceremonies.

The heavy air stirred as the music set unseen bodies in motion, presaging the first quiver of the changing tide that would swing the world towards summer once again. It was a river of life that was beginning to flow around us, its power all the more perceptible because it was still invisible to fleshly eyes.

> *"Cold heart of winter, darkest season,*
> *Stark is the weather, nights at their longest.*
> *Sun hastens southward, seeking the warm*
> *Waters of lands that know no storm,*
> *Hope unavailing, for winter is strongest."*

The voices of the singers swelled like the river in floodtide, bearing away all before it. The torches swept forward in misty blurs of light. Outlines wavered as if the forms themselves were fluid, waiting for some further spell to complete their manifestation. Esseilte and I fell into place behind the queen and began to move forward with the music.

There was a flurry of activity behind us and the teazers scrambled into position. Painted bladders bobbed as they flourished their wands, and the ribbons that adorned them swirled sluggishly, damp from the air. Ribbons fluttered from their mantles and headpieces, adding to the impression of fluidity. As we continued onward their movements lost their first stiffness, and they began a few tentative capers.

The singing continued, showing us the face of the enemy we must battle soon.

> *"Rain unceasing lashes the landscape,*
> *Each pond a lake, each lake an ocean;*
> *Sand is swept by stinging waves,*
> *Through vale and cleft wild water raves,*
> *Furrows writhe with rivers' motion.*
> *"On the mountain snow grows deeper,*
> *Keeping deer from finding food;*
> *Eagle turns her back to weather,*
> *Ice that fringes with frost each feather;*
> *Winter white has wrapped the wood."*

The procession turned as we began the long curve to the other mound, making the first turn of the spiral that would become the dragon path.

"Numb is the nighttime, now small birds seek
To keep them safe from strife of storm;
In hill and heath no place to rest
No hole or hollow holds soft nest;
Here's no hiding place from harm."

Around us now gray light was growing, dimming the difference
between light and shadow so that vision was more confused than
before. Slowly a swirl of motion behind the teazers resolved itself into the fantastic form of the carved dragon's head bobbing
on its pole, forked tongue flicking as the rope was jerked by
those who followed, for this was the lifeline that bound the parts
of the dragon together. With the straw masks cutting off the
dancers' vision, it must be serving to guide them as well.

"In the veins the blood has frozen,
Knows the land no motion now;
No life is left on heath and hill
To challenge winter's sovereign chill;
Earth's heartbeat falters, faint and slow."

We rounded the mound of Knowth and started back toward the
Brugh. Mist brushed my face; the air was moving, though there
seemed no diminution in the clouds. Perhaps it was our own
movement that had set things to stirring. Indistinct and hushed
by solemnity, the murmur of the throng that followed was like
the wind. Our pace quickened, and a tingle of excitement passed
down the line — or was it a tingle of fear?

"Leaves are lost from naked branches,
Barren they rattle in the gray morn;
Only ivy's leaves are clinging,
And the king of birds still singing,
Prisoned by the green holly thorn!"

At the end of the procession tossed the holly bush where the
tethered wren, not quite dead yet despite the cold, fluttered frantically. Fergus was there, bearing King Diarmait's armor. He
had greeted Esseilte like a conqueror the night before. I wondered if he were feeling so confident now. A thick-skinned man
might be less vulnerable to the tensions that were tightening my
shoulders, but how could such a man sense and direct the
power?

Something loomed ahead, pale through the mists. We were
coming to the Brugh at last — the white-shining mansion, the pal-

ace of the Dagda and his son Oengus Og. Just so must Brendan's islands have lifted above the gray plains of the sea, outposts of earth in an alien world. The Brugh was an island of the Otherworld surrounded by the daily reality of humankind, but its foundations were in the realm of the Sidhe that underlay our world as the sea supported the land.

"And now the year-wheel in its turning
Yearning for its source, spins round;
The spiral winding without end,
The patterned power anew to bend
Until the spirit is unbound —"

Steel gleamed before us. The line of warriors who had guarded the High King's vigil parted to let the procession through. The people spread out behind us as we circled the Brugh. The air was still damp, but the blood sang in my veins. Esseilte's cheeks were glowing, and the hair sprang out from her brow in glinting curls. The mist that had weighted the air seemed now to ripple. But there was no wind, only this tension between the worlds.

I was still afraid of what was going to happen, but at the same time I found the waiting well-nigh unbearable. I could hear the ripple of excitement behind me as the teazers began to do their office, leaping and grimacing, striking the women in the crowd with the inflated bladders on their wands. I wondered if my own tension were only a reflection of theirs, and half-turned to watch the teazers.

One of them was nuzzling up to a young woman who squealed delightedly. The man beside her pulled back with an odd grace that caught my eye. With his ragged brat pulled over his head against the damp he was like many another, but as if he had felt my gaze upon him he looked up, and I caught the glint of blue eyes.

I stumbled, trying to see, and when I looked again the man had melted back into the crowd. I shook my head to clear it, for this was no time to be fanciful, and as we came around before the entrance to the Brugh I forgot that for a moment the peasant had looked like the harper Dughan.

One of the escort took Esseilte's arm to lead her to her place, downslope to the north of the Brugh while the queen and her women went on to the other side. I followed, pulling the end of my brat under me to keep out the damp of the matted grass as I knelt beside her. There was a murmur from the people nearest as the brightening air revealed the intricacy of the embroidery that weighted Esseilte's mantle and the gown beneath it, and the golden ornaments on wrist and neck and hair. Men were hailing her by names the priests of Christ hoped they had forgotten, for she was the bright face of the Lady who would hearten the Champion when the dragon rose out of the dark, and the maiden who would be devoured by it if he failed. . . .

The poets had gone on with the queen, and their song faded to a murmur of melody, but the music makers were stationed all around the sprawling circle, and the deep drum beat was loud enough to keep everyone more or less together. The dancers paused near us, and as they closed up, the straw blurred together and then it was a serpent I was seeing, with spiked back and sides whose fringes rippled like wavelets on a lake in the wind.

A long horn call broke through the drumming and suddenly all was still. In the hushed silence the voice of the archpoet rang out like a great bell. Mist swirled, the air brightened, and I blinked as a patch of pale sky appeared above us, pearled with pink and silver like the inside of a shell. The opening widened, and I glimpsed the opaline shimmer of the river where it coiled around the three mounds. The Boinne, I thought, Lady Boann herself protecting her family's stronghold, for in one of her aspects she was held to be the wife of the Dagda and the mother of Oengus Og.

For a moment I seemed to hear the whisper of many waters — the hiss of the rivulets that snaked downhill to join the greater stream and the softer sound of hidden currents that moved beneath the soil as rainfall drained downward into the secret systems that emerged from holes in the earth at holy wells and sacred springs. And Boann was the source of all this water for the heart of Eriu — now I understood why it was here that the Ard-Righ came to renew his power.

Above us the dawn sky curdled with color. Unprompted, everyone had turned eastward. Then the glowing disc of the sun lifted above the horizon; light caught and shimmered in every drifting droplet, and out of that haze of brightness the pebbles of white quartz scattered over the Brugh blazed as if the mound had been dusted with snow. There was a great sigh as the sun rolled up the skyway; then, of a sudden I could see the dark slash of the passageway, saw it brighten as the first rays of the sun spilled down it and into the heart of the mound.

"Out of night, the day —
Out of darkness, light —
Out of ice, the water of life —
Let the ritual begin!"

The archpoet cried out the words, and the air echoed his cry with a cacophony of braying horns and booming drums and the clangor of rattling iron that deepened as the High King came forth from the mound. For a moment he stood blinking, as if dazed by the light of day, but I think it was more than the sudden brightness that mazed him, for he moved like one tranced as his warriors escorted him to his place atop the Brugh.

With a clash of metal the dragon dancers surged into sinuous motion, coiling leftwards in a wide circle around the mound. I twitched a little, seeing them move counter to the way of the sun, for from birth we were taught to go deasil in ceremonies, around churches, when dealing with any holy thing. But when Boann was the wife of Nechtain, she went three times widdershins around the sacred well, and so the power of the waters was released and flowed out in a great flood to the sea.

As the dancers completed the first circuit, I felt a change in the air. A kind of pressure it was, as happens sometimes within walls when the wind is blowing hard outside. As the dancers passed, the mists swirled after them, hiding the river, though sunlight still set the mound aglow. It was as if the air within the circle had thickened. We could see, but outlines seemed to ripple as if we were watching through a glimmering veil.

Again the dragon dancers passed, their movements smoother as their muscles loosened and they learned the ground. Now there were moments when I saw not a line of straw-masked warriors but a single being pursuing its undulant path around the Brugh. As the Dragon began the third circuit, I began to notice something else; perhaps it was only that the mist had thickened, but where the serpent passed, a shimmering hung in the air. Again and again the Dragon danced the circle, nine times coiling around the sacred mound. Each time it passed, that trail of light grew brighter, so that to me at least the inward spiral that it made showed clear.

The air hummed as the ninth circuit ended. All things seemed to drain inward to that vortex of power. As the serpent stopped before the entrance to the mound, the music ceased. Now there was only a deep, steady throbbing of drums. Once the Dragon roared, and twice, and once again — a sound too harsh and huge to have come from the throats of men. Esseilte stepped back a pace and I reached up to steady her. She twitched beneath my hands like a mare in a haunted wood, frightened by something her rider cannot see.

"Na, na, my love, there's nothing to fear," I whispered, trying to send her some reassurance through the palms of my hands.

"No?" she hissed back. "It is not you who will be blasted if the Champion fails, and not you who will be given to Fergus if he wins!"

"He will win—" I answered with more confidence than I felt, for the air throbbed as it does when a thunderstorm is coming, even though the sky above the mists was clear. "And we can take counsel what to do after. Your mother's arts will surely find a way . . ."

"Perhaps she'll poison him—" Esseilte set her hand to her mouth as she realized what she had said, for the maiden's task in this ritual was to lend strength to the Champion. "Branwen!" The words came on a thread of sound. *"Help* me!"

And as if her appeal had given me permission, I felt myself linked into the pattern of power activated by the Dragon's dance—the spiral vortex that was unbinding the serpent power of all the subterranean water, a power that had been collecting for the past seven years in the mound.

The warcry of Midhe struck that pool of power like a stone thrown into a pond as Fergus leaped past us, and Esseilte and I shuddered as the wave of disturbance reached us. No use now reaching into the earth for the strength to uphold us; we clung together, balanced between earth and heaven, as the battle began.

Fergus carried the High King's shield, but instead of a sword he was armed with a blackthorn cudgel that seemed the size of the club of the Dagda when he swung it high. But the Dragon dancers were armed with supple staves that flicked out as the Champion approached, and there were nine of them to his one. Fergus danced forward, and the Dragon curved around him. The sharp thwack of wood split the air.

Esseilte and I had never cared to watch Fergus at practice, but I saw now that more than family connections had made him Champion. He moved with a heavy grace that put him always in the right place to meet the Dragon's attack. The clatter of parried blows imposed its own rhythm on the drumming as the combat inscribed its pattern on the misty air. The bone flutes twittered fiercely, and the people began to clap out the rhythm.

Now the fight swept toward us, the Dragon uncoiling in an intricate figure that brought its left side to the Champion. Straw sides flared as four staves lifted, the hands that held them invisible. Feet flickering in an intricate figure, Fergus spun down the line, striking one stave up and receiving the blow of the next one on his shield. As he reached the end the Dragon was already turning, and the warrior repeated the combination up the other side.

Fergus leaped past the carven head and stood, cudgel at the ready, as it bobbed and feinted, body lashing behind. Then the Dragon curved away and the Champion sprang after it, this time striking the staves down as he faced them and up with a backhand blow behind him as he whirled. We could hear the sound of the blows diminishing as the battle wound around the Brugh. The moves of that conflict had been practiced for weeks before the ritual, but the reality was something more — this dance of attack and defense was the perfection which every festival mock-combat strove to attain.

As the combatants reappeared, I began to realize just how much more than mummery this battle was. The air around them shimmered as their intricate passage focused the power that had already been raised. Now the dance was faster; they fought with a frenzied energy. When Fergus whirled sweat splattered from his brow like rain. The clatter of cudgel and stave smote the ears. Each blow struck sparks for those with eyes to see.

Drums thundered. The Dragon whipped around, encircling the man. Four staves slashed. The serpent swung away. For a moment Fergus swayed, arms flung wide. Then, with willed grace, he fell.

Silence pulsed palpably in my ears. In all that assembly, no one stirred, as if some stark stroke of winter had frozen the world. But force still throbbed from the Brugh; it was not finished yet. I reminded my lungs to take in air.

And as I exhaled, a thread of sound wound through the stillness. Blended voices came clearly from beyond the mound; the voices of the poets, pitched high and sweet like the voices of women, like the singing of the Sidhe.

"Out of the south I am bearing
Benison for all ill sharing —
Show me the warrior who's fallen —
Blessed be my faring.
Healing to hero bringing,
Renewal to warrior winging,
Well may the spell be spoken,
And sweet be my singing."

Out of the shimmer of mist came a figure — the queen? No, it
was Amergin MacAlam the Archpoet, wearing the queen's royal
garments. But he had come from the queen's quarter, and he
carried her power. The sense of Mairenn's presence was vivid in
my awareness, and as the chief poet approached I felt a response
leap forth from Esseilte, so that Amergin moved along a path of
balanced power.

The archpoet halted before the still figure of the fallen Champion. Fergus was not dead, for I could see his chest heaving, but
downed as much by his own exhaustion as by the requirements
of the ceremony. Amergin stretched out his arms.

"I am the cure for all killing,
I am the word and the willing,
Warrior, arise — I have given
Thee grace, all geas fulfilling!"

He brought his hands down of a sudden and stroked the length
of the body, once, twice, again. My skin prickled, and at the
third sweep I saw the air sparkle where the poet's hands had
gone, and a network of light spreading through Fergus's limbs.
The poet stepped back as Fergus began to twitch. In a moment
the Champion was on his feet again. Now I sensed also a path of
power between the Champion and the High King on top of the
Brugh.

Amergin stepped away softly. A quiver ran through the body
of the Dragon and it flowed forward, not yet threatening, but
gathering momentum like a wheel rolling downhill. Ever more
quickly it circled its opponent. I blinked, for the shape of the
mock-beast was hidden by an angry glow. I had no previous
experience of this ritual with which to compare what was happening, but I seemed to sense a menace in the Dragon that went
beyond the demands of the ceremony. Dragon and Champion
were both limned in light — it was no physical combat but a conflict of pure forces that I was perceiving now.

The Dragon lashed out and light clashed with light. The Champion struck and recoiled, parried the Dragon's flashing attack and strove to get past its guard. The enemy twisted round and then came in again. The energy was building, building — my fists clenched till the nails dug into the palms. Now it pulsed from the Brugh in waves that resonated from each white stone, testing men's fragile boundaries. It must be mastered, channeled, earthed — it must —

Fergus fell back, swaying. His light sparked and dimmed as the Dragon's force flared toward him, and his link with King Diarmait was abruptly gone. The force of a Dragon driven by hatred was too great for him. I felt, rather than heard, the indrawn breath of the folk behind me, but the Dragon seemed to draw strength from their fear. Light sparked without pattern. Mist thickened, swirling chaotically. I could still see a lurid interplay of color, but the murmur behind me deepened as the people ceased to see anything at all.

Esseilte started to crumple as chaos buffeted the circle. I scrambled to my feet, supporting her, striving for the oneness we had known at Cill Dara. I felt the flickering touch of the queen's power and snatched at it, sending all my strength through Esseilte and along that line that was rapidly becoming the only order in a maelstrom of disrupted energies.

Then the Champion's light winked out.

Power exploded past me. Dimly I heard screaming, but all my senses were being overwhelmed by the chaos around me. I thought someone pushed past us, but I was too busy trying to barrier myself and Esseilte to care. Only something must have happened, because of a sudden a new pattern rippled through the riot, and the Dragon focused its forces inward again.

> *"Force of female and male, mated, shall bind*
> *Blessing and bane — matter and mind!"*

The spell sparked through the circle. Did my spirit hear it, or my earthly ears? I could see the sinuous spiral of the Dragon again, pursued by a column of light that had renewed its link with the High King. Again it was a dance, order returning as the Champion forced the Dragon to face him. Light flowed back and forward, holding back nothing, and once more the tension built, but now there was a pleasure in it, a straining that something in me recognized though it was not understood. Then the voice of the Champion rang out once more.

"Come cudgel and grail, serpent and wand,
Wed sovereign and soul, renewing the land!"

The column of light fountained, then drove forward, piercing the Dragon's pattern, focusing it, and projecting both powers into the earth below. My ears rang with changing pressure. The component parts of the Dragon scattered as the cord of light that connected them was jerked away.

Force flooded outward, carried by the hidden rivers beneath the soil throughout the land. Racked by waves of glory, I was barely aware as the crowd around us erupted in rejoicing. People surged past; I thought a shadow slipped through in the other direction, but in the confusion I could not be sure. The mists swirled and thinned, dispersed by the movement of so many bodies, and suddenly I was fully in my flesh again and I could see.

Esseilte turned in my arms and clung to me, sobbing. Fergus was just sitting up, the cudgel lying on the grass beside him. The High King's own warriors were climbing the Brugh to escort him down; others clustered around Fergus, helping him to his feet. Someone had started an exultant song of praise. The dancers who had been the Dragon lay like tumbled haystacks nearby. But as people moved forward to help them, I saw very clearly that the tongue and cord that had held the Dragon together was not there.

"Do you think you can break all the daggers in Eriu, or dry up all the streams?" Esseilte broke from my arms and cast herself upon the bed. "Perhaps you can, then — but if you give me to Fergus I will do like Deirdre and dash out my brains against a stone!"

I let her lie there, catching her breath in harsh hiccoughs, and looked back at the queen. Sound gusted from the meadhall as the celebration there reached some new height of drunken glee, then the Grianan was quiet again. Queen Mairenn leaned against the wall, eyes closed. The slanting rays of the late afternoon sun showed her face worn to the bone with weariness. I might have thought her dozing but for the tight-clenched hands.

"My daughter is behaving like a child . . ."

"Perhaps," I answered softly. "But you let Esseilte believe there would be a way out of this marriage if she played her part in the ritual. And she spent her strength for you. But it nearly

went all wrong this morning, didn't it? Listen to them! Do you
think they will let the Ard-Righ refuse anything the man they
think saved Eriu desires?"

"*The man they think saved Eriu?*" Mairenn's eyes opened, raven-
dark beneath bent brows. "Dare you to doubt what everyone
knows?"

I shrugged and looked away. "You were on the other side of
the circle; the High King atop the Brugh; and Esseilte across
from you — all three of you taking the full force of the power.
Esseilte shielded me from the worst of it, and also . . . I could
see . . ." My voice sank to a whisper as I confessed what I had
already admitted to myself, before.

"I thought so —" said Queen Mairenn.

I shuddered, watching her sidelong. This was the greatest sorceress in Eriu. What had I said?

"So tell me, what did you see?"

I heard Esseilte's sobs cease and the creak of the bed as she
turned over to watch us, but the queen's eyes had captured mine
and I could not look away.

"There were men who hated, dancing the Dragon. I think that
they were willing to risk death for the rite to fail. I think Fergus
could not withstand it, even channeling the Ard-Righ's power.
He fell a second time, and the serpent force began to break the
pattern —"

"It is so. I felt it happen, but I thought that the Champion had
taken up the battle once more," said the queen.

"*Somebody* did," I said slowly. "I thought something slipped
past us into the circle, and then it all began to come right again.
I saw the shape of his spirit, and it was not like that of Fergus.
But he mastered the Dragon, and in the confusion afterward he
disappeared."

"There is no proof for this —" The queen shook her head wearily.

"There might be. I think he took the Dragon's tongue away."

"Why then has he not claimed his reward?"

"Perhaps he cannot!" Esseilte sat up, her eyes blazing with
frantic hope. "See how we are wearied, and we came home on a
wagon! Suppose the man got free of the circle, and then his
strength failed him? He could be lying out there still —" Her
voice faltered. The day had grown colder, and even indoors we
were still cloaked against the chill. If my sight had not been

deluded and there was such a man, a night spent in the open could extinguish what life was left in him.

"And how do you propose that we find him, then, wearied as we are?" The queen had closed her eyes again, but there was a subtle tension in her now.

"*You* can find him, Mother, to honor your promise to me!" Esseilte leaned forward.

"Indeed, I did swear that . . . I think I have sworn too many things. . . ." With an effort Mairenn roused herself. "Are you certain you desire this, my daughter? Fergus is at least an evil that we know! If I do this thing for you, I must have your promise there will be an end to it. I will not spend what strength remains to me in the search for a hero out of legend to be your man!"

"You have it! The man who conquered the Dragon *is* a hero, and I will seek no more!" Esseilte reached out to grasp her mother's hand.

"Be it so then." Mairenn heaved herself upright. "Come with me . . ."

Shivering, we followed her to the still-house. I could not help twitching as I remembered the last time we had come here to perform a divination. But the queen was no longer the terrifying sorceress she had seemed, and Esseilte and I were women now.

The queen had herbs drying that needed steady warmth, so I had only to stir the peats already glowing on the hearth to revive the fire. The still-house was smaller and warmer than the Grianan. Mairenn opened one of the chests and drew out a bronze basin, almost black with age.

"Bring me the flagon that hangs on the wall—it is water from Brigid's holy well," she explained as I handed it to her. "I do not know the man, but I can trace the power of the dragon. May the Lady bless what we do. . . ." She poured the water into the basin and settled it on her knees.

> *"Brigid, Thy blessing abide on the water—*
> *Wise one, a vision of virtue bestow now,*
> *Brigid, give Thy blessing!"*

We echoed her words, and waited while the queen's breathing steadied, grew slower and deeper. She stilled, staring into the dark mirror of the water. Silence spread in the room.

Suddenly Mairenn's eyes rolled up and she began to grunt

and twitch. Esseilte leaned close to hear the hoarse whisper that followed.

"In water and on land . . . by night and by day . . . awake and asleep . . . prince and peasant . . . betrayed and betrayer . . . thus shall you find him . . ." The voice died away to mumbling, and I thought she had done. I moved to take the basin from her hands, but her fingers clenched on it. "Where the white willow grows . . ." she said, very strongly. Then her hands fell away from the bowl and she sagged back.

It took a little time to revive the queen enough to interpret the divination. She herself remembered little of what she had seen, but presently we concluded that a man might lie hidden in the willow-meads where Boann's spreading waters made marshland of the low ground. And that was halfway to the Brugh, a distance of some miles.

Sunset was suffusing the sky with colors as lurid as any of those I had seen in the mists of morning as Esseilte and I rode out, escorted by two of the queen's bondsmen. By the time we reached the marshes the sun had set, but the sky still glowed with the memory of light. It was enough to search by, though we would not have long. I had just ordered the bondsmen to light their torches when a cry from Esseilte brought me running toward a dark pool.

"There — don't you see a gleam of metal?" She pointed where the overhanging branches of a willow shadowed the water. I saw a shape that could have been snagged rubbish left by the floods, or some unhuman creature out of one of Messach's tales, or, just possibly, a man.

"Quickly! Get over there and see —" The bondsmen ran around the pool and Esseilte and I followed, slipping in the mud that edged it. My vision blurred and for a moment I hung back, blinking. I thought I had seen, not the water kelpie I feared, but something fairer — the glimmering arms and liquid eyes of a woman who lifted away as we approached, and disappeared.

Whether she had been guarding something or about to prey on it I could not tell. The thing was man-shaped indeed, but was it living? The bondsmen heaved, and with a sucking plop the mud gave up its prey. Hands clumsy with haste, we turned it over on the grass and pulled the sodden brat that had wrapped it away.

Esseilte slipped her hand beneath the tunic — made of a wool much finer than I would have guessed from the state of his mantle.

"His heart is still beating, but slowly," said Esseilte. "And he is so cold!"

She motioned the bondsmen closer, and gold gleamed in the torchlight, not from the man, but from the thing he still clasped in his arms. It was a curving piece of wood, cunningly carved and gilded, but for a moment I could not imagine what it might be. Then I saw the tattered rope that trailed after it, and recognized the tongue of the Dragon.

But Esseilte was bending over the man, wiping the mud from his face with the corner of her brat.

"Branwen, do you have the flask?"

I unhooked the leather bottle from my belt and handed it to her, kneeling on the stranger's other side. The queen had given it to me — it was an infusion of herbs in uisquebagh, and the liquor alone ought to be enough to raise the dead.

Esseilte slipped her arm beneath the man's head and raised it so that she could set the flask to his lips. As she did so, the torchlight fell full on his face for the first time.

He swallowed and sputtered as the stuff went down him, but after a few moments he opened his eyes.

"The sun . . . and the moon . . . risen together!" he whispered, looking from Esseilte to me.

Esseilte dropped the flask and sat back, staring.

"Oh, Branwen," she said in a voice of wonder. "It is our harper, Dughan!"

Nine

BETRAYER AND BETRAYED

"I have a tale for you, harper, that maybe you have not heard—" Esseilte finished ladling chamomile tea into the silver-bound oaken cup and handed it to Dughan. We had brought him to the guesthouse where we had nursed him before, but this time his coverlet was of embroidered woolen, for he had proved himself something more than a wandering bard.

"Will you be my teacher then, Princess?" he said with a half-smile, drinking and setting the cup back down. He was still stiff, but after a day in bed the first terrible fatigue had passed. There was no wound on him, after all; it was only the expenditure of spirit needed to master the forces raised in the Dragon ritual that had exhausted him, and for that, rest and plenty of good food were the cure.

"In the legends of my own land, I am the more learned—" She shot him a curious glance. Was she wondering, as I was, where his true homeland lay, and why he had returned so opportunely? He certainly had a talent for dramatic arrivals.

"It is the story of Ferdiad and Finnabair that I will tell you, and of the dragon of the black linn. You must know that the mother of Ferdiad was a woman of the Sidhe, the true sister of our own Boann—"

Dughan's eyes narrowed a little; his experience of the reality that we called Boann was too recent for him not to wonder what truth might be hidden in this old tale.

Esseilte seemed not to notice. Her gaze had gone a little inward as she marshaled her words for the tale, but I could tell that she was aware of him. She was wearing one of her best robes, of crimson wool worked around the hems with an inter-lace of fantastic beasts, and her hair, unbraided, hung down her back in roulades of gold.

"And Finnabair, who was the daughter of Medbh, Queen of Connachta, and her husband Aillel, heard of his beauty and loved him, and when he knew it, he went to seek her in marriage from her parents in Cruachan."

"And no doubt her hair was curling yellow," said Dughan, smiling appreciatively, "and her eye like the eye of the wood dove when she makes her nest."

"And his eye was deep gray, and his body of great whiteness, and Finnabair thought that she had not seen any that would come up to him a half or a third for beauty." Esseilte responded swiftly, and if Dughan had not been still so weak I think he would have colored in his turn. The chamber echoed with words unsaid, and my stomach tightened. There was no harm in what they were saying. But what were they thinking?

"But the bride-price asked by Aillel was not to the hero's lik-ing, for the king wanted Ferdiad's help when they went to steal the Brown Bull of Cualigne away, and that were to put Ferdiad in contention with Cuchulain, who had been his brother-in-arms and his dearest friend . . ." Esseilte went on.

"Is this yet another story in which love must conflict with loyalty?" Dughan asked wryly. "I know too many such al-ready!"

I saw the color deepen in Esseilte's cheeks and fade again. *Oh my dear,* I thought then, *what tale are you spinning about this stranger in your heart where we cannot hear?* But she only shrugged and went on.

"When they could not come to agreement, Aillel and Medbh feared the hero would carry the girl away and set war between them. And Medbh craved the berries of the rowan tree that grew on the island in the midst of the black linn, and the king laid it on the hero that he must swim across and pluck them for her."

"And of course he did so," said Dughan as Esseilte drew breath. As she started to speak again, I saw Messach hovering in the doorway and motioned her in.

"There's a man come from Inber Colptha asking after this Dughan," she said with her usual abruptness. "Do I tell him that you're here?"

"If you will, Princess —" Dughan spoke quickly. "He must be a man from the ship that brought me. They'll be thinking me dead — please let him come in!"

Esseilte nodded, and Messach went out again. "Do you want me to finish the story?"

"Of course." His attention was wholly upon her once more.

"Well then, Ferdiad was in the middle of the linn, when the monster came up from the deeps of the water and fastened her teeth in his side. And he cried out for a sword, but for fear of Aillel and Medbh no one of them would give him one. But Finnabair stripped off her garments and took her father's sword and swam out to him, and he cut off the dragon's head and brought it to land."

"She was a valiant lady to take such a risk," said Dughan.

"He was a mighty hero," said Esseilte, "to slay such a monster." She smiled radiantly.

The door opened, and a tall man pushed past Messach into the room.

"Oh, my lord, we feared —"

"Gorwennol, my companion!" Dughan interrupted swiftly. "It is Esseilte daughter of King Diarmait that sits yonder. Before you speak a word to me you should give her your greeting!"

Gorwennol turned to Esseilte with almost comical abruptness, stared a moment, then saluted her as if she had been a queen. He was a lanky, sandy-haired man considerably older than Dughan, dressed in clothing whose quality had survived the wear and tear of life at sea.

"Lady, you are fair indeed, I —" He caught Dughan's eye and coughed. "I thank you for taking care of him. What madness has the boy been up to now?"

"Once more she has honored this poor bard with her concern," said Dughan carefully. "But this time there was little need. I'll be on my feet tomorrow, and tell you the story soon." He was avoiding my eye, as well he might, for it was clear he was desperate to make his companion hold his tongue. Gorwennol seemed a good man, but he was no intriguer, whereas Dughan's tongue was as well-oiled as that of any bard. But I was more and more certain that harping was only one of his trades.

"But — Dughan — there are things you must know —" Gorwennol said awkwardly. "Can we talk?"

"Esseilte, come," I broke in, taking pity on the man. "No doubt he has business of their ship that would bore us. You wanted to show me that length of silk your mother has given you?" As I took her arm she stiffened.

"You should be grateful for the interruption —" I whispered. "What will you do if Dughan asks you for the rest of the story? Remember, Ferdiad never got to marry his princess. Whether you believe the version in which he died of his wounds, or the one in which he was killed by Cuchulain, there is no happy ending to that tale."

Esseilte would not meet my eyes, but she allowed me to draw her outside.

"I suppose it's useless to try and keep anything from you," she said finally, but her laugh wavered. "And maybe it was a girl's trick to try and lead Dughan's thoughts that way. But Branwen, what else can I do? He's said nothing to show why he returned here, or what he is going to do. Surely it was not to save me from Fergus — he could not have known. But why did he risk the ritual unless he wanted to claim the Champion's reward?"

She stood in the pale sunlight, twisting a strand of bright hair around her finger. "Oh, Branwen, do you think Dughan has not spoken because of his birth?"

No, not because of that — I said silently. I remembered how the man Gorwennol had greeted him even if Esseilte had not noticed it. But I hesitated to remind her. Clearly he had lied to us about being no more than a wandering harper. What deception was his silence hiding now? Fear of unworthiness would have been an understandable reason for diffidence. But Dughan was not diffident, he was wary. I frowned, suddenly as anxious as Esseilte, if not from the same cause.

"That doesn't have to be a barrier!" Esseilte said brightly. "If he has no land of his own, he can live here and be my father's champion!"

Like the Morholt . . . I stared at her. But my father had been a true-born son of the King of Mumu. Had all these dragon stories deluded her into thinking she was living in some old tale? I knew only too well what a barrier irregular birth could be. If my father had not claimed me, I would have been a slave, as my mother had been.

"Do you want to wed him?"

Esseilte shrugged. "What use does a princess have for passion? Better him than Fergus, anyway."

Was that the truth? Would I rather believe her calculating, or clandestine? But she would not meet my eyes, and I wondered then whether she herself knew what her feelings were.

"Our Dughan is a man who knows well how to keep his own counsel," I said carefully. "So far he has managed none so badly. Be patient — surely he will tell us his intention soon. He came here with a purpose, and I think we can trust him to get some good out of what has happened now . . ."

Esseilte sighed, then laughed, apparently satisfied. I hoped so, because really we had no choice but to wait and see what came to pass. I thought I had answered her very well, considering that serving his own purposes was the only thing that I trusted Dughan to do at all.

By the next day the queen had recovered enough to come to us. Her eyes were shadowed, but there was a peace about her I had never noticed before, as if she also had won a victory. Dughan was on his feet again, though still a little pale, and even more self-possessed than he had been the day before. Esseilte had brought in her little harp and he was teaching her a new tune from Kernow when Mairenn came in.

"You seem to have recovered," said the queen.

"I feel as if I had fought a real monster." Dughan stretched out his right arm and grimaced as if stiffened muscles still pained him.

"You did. Your struggle was not with men, but with the elemental powers. Never think it was not a real battle, for the flesh reflects what happens to the spirit, even though this was a conflict not of the body but of the soul." She came the rest of the way into the room and sat down on one of the benches.

"I don't understand," said Esseilte. "There are so many tales of monster serpents that live in loch and linn, and they are physical beasts that can tear flesh from bone. Are these only stories, or does our ritual come somehow from those tales?"

"I have learned the legends of many lands," added Dughan, "and dragons are found everywhere."

"I cannot answer you," said the queen. "They knew in the old days — the Druids knew — but though we still have our history, the new priests teach that the great ones of old were men, not gods. The ancient magic behind the stories is being lost. I also have wondered," she went on. "The world is full of places of power. Perhaps when the rituals are not correctly done that magic goes bad, and transforms some innocent water-creature

into a monster. The priests say they have the power to banish
such beings, and maybe after a time the old forces will fade and
it will not matter whether we do the rituals . . ."

"But you do not think so — " I said then. On Mairenn's face I
saw a fleeting, rather bitter smile.

"A man may deny God and his own soul and still live, even
live well. But not forever. The time will come when the body
sickens because of that denial, and in that day, if he does not
learn to listen to his spirit, he will die."

"But this was a thing of the land itself," I objected.

"It was indeed," said the queen.

For a moment the floor seemed to tremble, and I reached out
to the wall, afraid of falling. But when my senses steadied, nothing had changed. And the queen had said that the soul-sick man
might live long. The days of earth were centuries. Whatever evil
was to come of men's neglect would not be in my time.

The others had gone on to new topics, and the queen was
speaking again.

"You have saved us, harper, and we have saved you. Now
what are you going to do?"

Dughan eyed the queen. "With the tongue of the Dragon in
my possession I think I can discredit Fergus, and I have an alliance to propose that will bring your daughter great honor."

Esseilte and I both stared.

Mairenn nodded. "I persuaded the High King to put off his
decision for three days. Fergus will come before him to make his
claim tomorrow, at the Feast of Christ's birth. What is your
plan?"

"My position here is somewhat delicate" — a flick of the finger
indicated the harp — "and I must be assured of safety."

"You have the protection of the hearth of Temair, my oath on
it," answered the queen. "For I think you are more than a
harper. Are you a fugitive?"

"I might be, if certain things were known. I killed a man in
Kernow. But I swear that I fought in honor."

"You are a warrior, then. I thought so."

Dughan's lips twisted wryly. "Among other things. I have
been well-taught. But I would rather make music than war."

He could afford to say that. After the dragon fight, one did
not question his courage.

"And your plan?" Mairenn came back to what concerned us
now.

"Can you trust me just a little longer?"

She looked at him narrowly, perhaps for the first time feeling that tickle of unease that had troubled me for so long.

"You will deliver me from Fergus, I know it!" Esseilte's eyes were shining. "We must find you fresh clothing and clean your gear so that you will do us credit."

"And perhaps I could take a turn in the sweat house? For surely no one will believe me a warrior if I hobble into the hall like an old man crippled by the bog-mists!" said Dughan.

"Tonight we shall dress him as befits a hero!"

Esseilte held up the cloak she had selected from her mother's stores. It was fine wool dyed a rich purple and bordered with gold. Dughan's own cloak pin was good, but plain, so Esseilte had brought a penannular brooch of chased silver that had belonged to the Morholt. The tunic that was to go under it was deep green, with bandings of Greek cloth woven in red and gold, and applications of rich embroidery.

"A hero indeed, but a dirty one, if he doesn't get into the sweat house soon. Are the hot stones ready?"

"The men are tending the fires," she answered, laying the garment down. "Do you show Dughan the way, Branwen, while I finish furbishing his gear."

I nodded and went outside where the harper was waiting, talking to one of the High King's armsmen whom he had gotten to know when he was here before. He turned as I came out and we walked down the hill toward the sweat house.

"You've recovered well from that wound in the thigh." Side vision showed me no trace of a limp in his walking, but I should have guessed that from seeing him fight three days before. He must have been exercising, or perhaps he had hidden the extent of his recovery even before he went away.

He colored a little, as if he had heard my thought, though weather-browned skin did not show it as well as the pallor I remembered. His face had firmed out as well. No longer gaunt, his profile made a clean line against the winter sky.

"You still do not trust me, do you?"

"Trust comes from knowledge, and all I know is that you are not what you have wished to seem."

"Wise Branwen, with the shine of pale wheatstraw in your hair . . . are you always so eager to ferret out what you might be happier not to know?" It seemed to me there was bitterness in his smile. "There have been things I could not tell you, I confess it, but you must believe I have never acted in dishonor or ingratitude."

"I am only concerned lest my lady be harmed. Did you think it mattered to me?" I strode ahead to speak with the attendants as we came to the low, whitewashed structure, round and dark as a womb inside its stone walls.

"You were long in coming, mistress. 'Tis ready and more than ready, with the air in it like the High King's ovens by now." Gap-toothed, the man grinned as Dughan unwrapped the big cloak and stepped out of his clogs. For a moment he stood naked in the thin sunlight, white flesh pebbling at the touch of the wind.

He was as white of skin as Ferdiad, I thought watching him, and fine-tuned with training as he was now, just as beautiful. Indeed, this man was very different from the wasted creature Esseilte and I had pulled out of the sea.

Then the attendant pulled open the door and Dughan dove in. I felt the steamy breath of cold water cast on hot stones on my face and heard a great whoosh of breath as the heat hit Dughan, then a grateful sigh as he eased down on a bench to let the hot air relax strained muscles and ease racked bones. The door closed, and I settled down to wait on the bench outside.

The harper had twice called for more hot stones when Esseilte came running down the slope toward us. As she got closer I saw that she was clutching a sheathed sword. Except for the spots of color burning on each cheekbone, her face was as white as scraped vellum. But what brought me to my feet, heart pounding, was the terrible burning brightness in her eyes.

"Open the door —"

One of the men began to protest that it was not time yet, but Esseilte's glare silenced him. Had somebody died? I wondered, but all was peaceful, and a death would not explain what she was doing here with Dughan's sword.

"Esseilte, what —" My voice failed as I realized she was not seeing me at all.

"Open the door and then go away, all of you." There was something in her tone that compelled obedience. As the door swung open the men were already scuttling off, but I followed Esseilte inside.

An oil lamp flickered madly as the door swung shut again. Steam swirled in the shadows, and for an instant I seemed to be back in the misty chaos where the dragon had been slain. But these vapors weighted the lungs and set the sweat starting from skin. I pulled off my cloak and peered through the shadows.

Steel rasped as Esseilte unsheathed the sword. A pale blur moved on the other side of the firepit and I realized the harper was sitting there.

"Who is it? Is something wrong?"

"Is this your sword?" As Esseilte passed through the mists her outline wavered. For one terrible moment I fancied it was not steam but battle-fury that was distorting her form. Would her body become monstrous while the hero-light burst forth from her brow? Then the steam eddied away and I could see her clearly. And in that moment it was not Cuchulain whom Esseilte resembled, but the Morrigan.

"You know it is mine. Why have you brought it here?"

At that moment I did not understand what was happening any better than he, but it seemed impossible that he should not sense the danger that faced him now.

"A poor sword for a hero, with such a nick in the blade," said Esseilte. She let the sheath drop and turned the blade so that a flicker of lamplight ran down the steel, and now I could see that a bit was missing halfway down the blade. My stomach tightened with the beginnings of an awful certainty. The harper's eyes went from the sword to Esseilte's face, and back again, but he did not move.

"Perhaps you really are a peasant, and have been cutting wood with it," she said spitefully, "or perhaps the blade bit something nobler . . . never mind, I can fix it—do you see?" From her belt she pulled a piece of silk and let it fall open. It had been wrapped around a fragment of steel. My fist went to my mouth, for that was something I did recognize. When I saw it first, Queen Mairenn had just plucked it from my father's skull.

"A pretty weapon for a wandering harper, but that was a lie, wasn't it? You've no need to borrow finery, do you? No need for place or patron—you have one of your own! The King of Kernow's champion was noble. Who are you really, *Drustan*?"

"The King of Kernow's nephew, and heir to the lordship of Léon . . ." he said tiredly. "But Dughan also, for that word means 'sorrow' in my tongue."

"On my tongue also, for a sorrow you have been to me, and a traitor too!"

"Betrayer and betrayed, Esseilte!" he snapped back at her.

"There was poison on your uncle's blade! Where else could I come for healing but here?"

"You knew we would as soon have drunk poison ourselves as have cured that illness!" she cried. "You escaped your fate once, Drustan—was it guilt that drove you back here to find it again?"

I found my voice finally. "Esseilte, come away. We are not the ones to deal with this—Esseilte, in the name of Blessed Brigid, put down the sword!"

"Oh no," she said softly. "I have a use for this blade. Drustan of Léon owes me an honor-price for my uncle, and if he thinks to pay it with an offer of marriage, he will soon learn differently. For the death of the Morholt I will have compensation, and a recompense for the insult and the injury to me. An enemy who remains an enemy may be treated with honor, but what price will wipe out the pain when the enemy has won favor by deception in the guise of a false friend?

"I call the gods I swear by to witness—" Esseilte lifted the sword—"may the earth gape to swallow me, may the sea rise to cover me, may the skies fall and crush me if I accept marriage with this man!"

Slowly she moved toward him with the heavy blade trembling in her hand. Her skin glistened with sweat, and her hair hung lank about her face, with moisture-darkened tendrils clinging to her brow. I felt my own garments growing sodden, and a heaviness in my flesh, as if I were melting into the earth floor.

"You brought death to one of my mother's blood, and my mother's blood shall bring death to you!" The sword swung toward Drustan's naked breast.

"Your mother promised me her protection . . ."

"Perhaps she did, traitor, but *I* am not so bound! Do you know, even now, what a fair man you cut down in his flower? He was the last hero left to Eriu, was my uncle—none higher in courage, none more generous of spirit than he—" Esseilte's voice grew louder as she warmed to her theme, like a bard at a funeral, but I knew that she believed what she was saying now.

And could I say that her wrath was entirely wrong? Perhaps Dughan, or Drustan, had fought honorably, but that had not been the end of it. To come here and win his way into our hearts for his own advantage—*that* was the injury. For the pain he had brought us, perhaps the man should die! But not at Esseilte's hands! The words of the queen's cursing echoed in memory.

Mairenn had set this thing in motion, Mairenn was the one who must deal with it now.

I stumbled to the doorway and drew in a grateful gasp of cool air. One of the attendants had crept back to his post, and I motioned him nearer.

"Go up to the Grianan and fetch the queen here. Say to her that Branwen sends you. It is a matter of her honor, tell her. In the name of the Morholt, tell the queen that she must come!"

His eyes widened, but as I ducked back into the sweat house he was already in motion. The new air and the cooling of the stones had allowed some of the steam to settle. Esseilte was closer to Drustan now, the sword a little nearer his bare breast.

"And so you understand, false one, that your blood belongs to me —" She took another step, and the point lowered, seeking his heart.

I had never seen a man sit so still. Only his eyes moved, watching her as the hunter whose spear has broken watches the wolf pad toward him across the snow.

"Esseilte, you must not," I said softly. "If you kill him, who will save you from Fergus? The time of the warrior queens is over; if you do this, no man will want to wed with you at all!"

"Do you think that I care? This is a hero's deed! At least I will have a name to carry down into the dark!" The sword blade quivered with strain. "You will not stop me, Branwen. The oath we swore must be honored. You will not deny me my due!"

And still Drustan had not moved.

The blood pounded in my ears like a great drum; shadows shifted around us like a fluttering of dark wings, and I knew that death was with us in the room.

"I will not deny you . . ." I whispered.

"Nor will I —"

It was as if the darkness had spoken. Drustan looked up at her, and his eyes were windows into night.

"You see," he said gently, "my breast is offered to your blade. It is no shame to me to die at the hand of one so courageous and so fair. Better that, than to be killed by my own kindred, as my brother died. It was my uncle Marc'h who sheltered me, but his lords have never loved me. Better to be killed by you, than to die by knife or poison in the hand of a man of Kernow.

"I never meant to do evil — only my duty to my lord and his land. For that, I owe you nothing. I came to Eriu for healing because I thought I owed it to my uncle to try to live. I did not know you then, or your mother. I am willing to pay for having caused you pain. My life has been borrowed from fate since I was very small, Esseilte. And it has never been so dear to me that I will much regret its loss. . . ."

Esseilte's eyes were huge and lightless against the pallor of her skin. Shadow met shadow as she stared at Drustan, and for a moment their two faces were stamped with an odd identity. I felt as if an invisible wall had slammed down between us. I could not have reached them now no matter how I tried.

As if of its own weight, the sword came to rest below his left nipple, where the line of the ribs showed beneath the firm muscle of the chest. Where it touched, a dark thread of blood snaked across the sweat-slick skin.

Drustan's nerve broke first. "For Christ's sweet sake, Esseilte," he cried out, arms thrown wide, "make an end!"

"Oh!" Esseilte shrieked suddenly. Light scattered from the blade of the sword. "May the Morholt forgive me! I cannot thrust it in!" She swung up the blade and it flew free and clanged against the stones of the wall. The sound merged with her shriek of frustrated fury as she dove for the door.

It opened as she reached it. Light glowed in the last of the steam, then darkened again as a bulky form blocked it. Esseilte collapsed, gasping, as Queen Mairenn pushed past her into the room.

"Branwen . . . what does this mean?"

The queen's voice released me, and I stepped carefully across the muddy floor to pick up the sword. Mairenn looked from the huddled shape of her daughter to Drustan, who was still sitting on the bench with his face hidden in his hands, and then back again at me. I found the bit of steel that Esseilte had dropped, and brought it to the queen together with the blade.

"It means death. . . ." I held them out to her.

Mairenn's fingers closed on the fragment, and with a hand that trembled she fitted it into the notch in the sword.

"When bit and blade lie together, the slain man's kin shall hold the life of his slayer in her hand . . ." the queen said in a terrible voice. Then she looked down at her daughter.

"I could not do it!" Esseilte whispered. "My blood burned to see his flow before me, but I could not make my hand obey!"

"You are Drustan?" Her voice cut through Esseilte's renewed sobbing and the man lifted his head at last.

"He is the nephew of the High King of Kernow," I said quietly.

"This is not Kernow," Mairenn said sharply. "And he is in my hand now!"

"I am also under the protection of the hearth of Temair." Drustan shrugged wearily. "If that means anything. I thought none in Eriu knew my name, but I am at your mercy, lady. Do what you will with me. . . ."

He lifted his head and I winced, for I had seen just that look in the eyes of a stag hunted until it could run no more. Yet neither as Drustan nor as Dughan did he seem a man to be defeated so easily, unless . . . suddenly I was certain that the hunters that had brought him to this despair drove him from within.

But even with no will behind them, his words had power. The queen's hand went to her breast. "Ah, Sweet Brigid, is this what you are asking of me?" she whispered, eyes closed, face twisting. For a time the only sound was the rasp of breaths drawn in with pain.

"If I spare your life, what comes to my girl? She will never wed with you now," Mairenn said at last.

"I never expected it. This changes nothing that I have said to you." He spoke as if it had taken an effort to turn his thoughts to living once more.

"Drustan of Kernow, why did you return?" Mairenn's words grated painfully.

"To make some recompense for what you lost because of me, Queen of Eriu . . ."

I stared, wondering how that could possibly be true.

Mairenn shook her head. "Queen of Eriu you have named me, and for the sake of that which lies dearer than my soul I will not act against you. But it was my geas that called you here, with or without your will. The curse that I laid against your name still stands. Though the blade turn in my daughter's hand now, one day she will bring death to you. Be warned."

"It changes nothing," Drustan said once more. He stood up, and though his voice was still weary, in his face the lines of strain were easing away. "The Greeks say that a man's fate may not be evaded, whether or not he knows its name. I will serve you both as best I may."

Esseilte choked and pushed past her mother. In a moment I

heard her retching outside the door. The queen sighed and nodded, then went after her. I stood where I was, still holding Drustan's sword.

When my ears told me that the other two had gone I held it out to him.

"The spring is just behind the building. Rinse off the mud and then come back with me. There is still tonight's banquet to get through."

But while I waited for him I wondered if I ought to invoke the High King's justice against him. It was not for Drustan's sake that I had tried to stop Esseilte from running him through, but to spare her that memory, and I was realizing now that the curse bound not only him, but her.

Ten

ALLIANCES

"Branwen, I cannot do it. I will not go in!" Esseilte turned in the doorway to the meadhall and I caught her by the arms.

"You are a daughter of heroes — will you disgrace them?"

She shook her head, shuddering. I sighed and pushed her forward; goading her with words.

"Do you want Drustan to think you are afraid?" That touched her, and she began to move, but the look she cast me was venomous as we went on into the hall.

The entire population of Midhe seemed to have gathered there before us, every profession in its quarter and the subject kings established with their attendants in the compartments closest to the hearth. Even Eithne of Mumu was present with her new husband, a lesser prince of the southern Ui Néill. They had decorated the beams with swags of holly and evergreen in honor of the festival. The light of hanging lamps glowed on rich mantles and glittered on ornaments.

In all that company, only Esseilte wore the somber stuff of mourning, a dark blue gown and mantle, and no ornament except the shining fall of her hair. There was a little murmur of admiration as we settled into our places beside the queen, and I realized that they took Esseilte's pallor and burning eyes for excitement, and the starkness of her dress made her seem by contrast all the more fair.

Fergus got to his feet and bowed as she went past. He was laden with gold like a maid at her wedding, and wearing a crim-

son cloak that clashed with his fox-colored hair, but I do not
think Esseilte even saw him. Her eyes were searching the hall
for the one face she most desired not to see.

Presently then they brought in the roasted carcass of a young
bull, garlanded with savory herbs, and the harpers left off their
sweet music as the warriors of Midhe began to chant Fergus's
name. He rose up, grinning, already flourishing his blade. The
rich scent of well-cooked meat filled the hall.

"A fine beast this is, and a fine company is gathered to eat it —"
Fergus strode forward to where the servers had set the great
roast down.

"Carve the cow, Fergus!" "Let the Champion's portion go to
the dragon-slayer!" "The meat and the maiden, Fergus — claim
your due!" came the answering cries.

"And is there any among you all who would deny me the right
to make the first cut of the beef?" He looked at King Diarmait
for confirmation, and lifted his sword.

"I would deny it!" A woman's voice cut coldly through the
babble. Only the High King himself did not seem surprised as
Queen Mairenn came out to face Fergus across the fire. "The
Champion is he who destroyed the Dragon, and it was not Fergus who did that deed, but another man!" A confused mutter
swelled and sank again. Fergus himself stood slack-jawed and
staring.

"Woman, how say you? It was my son who bore the blackthorn into that circle and none other —" The King of West
Midhe sounded more confused than angry.

"That is true, but no shame to him if the powers he battled
there overcame him. Fergus did indeed begin that battle, but he
did not end it. I saw him fall, and a second man come into the
circle. He it was who mastered the Dragon before its fury destroyed us."

The muttering around us swelled to a roar. "Proof!" they
cried. "Give us the proof of what you say!" "Show us the man!"

"No shame to you, Royal Woman, if in the morning mists you
were mistaken —" After a moment Gabran of West Midhe recovered, but his tone was sharper now. "Hard for any man, or
woman, to say for sure what passes near a mansion of the
Sidhe!"

"I have looked upon greater powers than those and lived!"
Mairenn's eyes flashed, and for a moment it was as if we saw

Queen Medbh herself standing there. "But it is not my witness only that confirms it. My daughter saw also—"

I felt Esseilte stir beside me, and laid a quieting hand on her arm.

"Women's fancies!" Gabran shook his grizzled red head. "And the maid is no impartial witness here."

That was true enough, but Gabran would have been surprised to know the nature of Esseilte's biases.

"Before you deny my witness, tell me who carried the Dragon's tongue away?" asked the queen. This was unexpected, and for a moment silence held them all.

"The crowd rolled up around us." Fergus found his voice finally. "Some one of them must have taken it!"

"It was not there when we raised you up, and that was before the folk came in." Amergin the Archpoet stood up in his place. "We wondered, for we did not believe any of the people would touch such a thing, and the piece has not been found."

Eyes moved to the dragon dancers, and Curnan of Connachta flushed uneasily; but all knew that they had been struck senseless, and could not have carried anything away.

"Judgment!" came the cry. "Let the king's justice decide!"

"If you deny Fergus his claim, you must prove your objection," said the High King. "If any has knowledge of this thing, let him stand forth now. Where is the dragon's tongue, and where is the man who took it from the Brugh?"

The brush of a sleeve against a harpstring thrummed unexpectedly in the sudden silence. It went on—too long, I thought. I could feel Esseilte trembling.

"Both man and proof are here. . . ." Cool, resonant, in that stillness the voice from the doorway carried clearly.

There was a ripple of movement as folk moved aside, and I saw Drustan's dark head. Esseilte's instinct had surely been right in selecting his clothing, though she cared little for that now. He had the bearing of a prince of the Sidhe as he entered the High King's hall. Behind him came the bondsman who had gone with us to search for the dragon-slayer, with a cloth-wrapped bundle in his arms. For those first few moments people were too astonished by this unexpected interruption to speak. Even Fergus could only gape as they marched up to the High King's compartment.

Then Drustan reached out and pulled the cloth away.

"It is the tongue-piece that was lost . . ." said Amergin Mac-Alam. The bondsman bowed, and the archpoet took the thing and carried it away.

"This proves nothing!" shouted Fergus. "It was I who fought the Dragon—you all saw me!"

Drustan turned to look at him. Some of Fergus's bluster faded as his hot gaze met the cool blue of the harper's eyes.

"You fought well, but not to mastery," said Drustan gently. "I do not say you lie, but you were between the worlds, where all things are transformed. You knew that you were fighting, and when you came to your senses again the Dragon was destroyed. No wonder if you believed you had done the thing that all men were praising you for." Drustan faced Diarmait once more, and let his trained bard's voice fill the hall.

"But at the climax of the conflict I saw Fergus fall, and felt the backlash of power. You who were in the circle"— his glance moved from Amergin to the High King and from him to Queen Mairenn, and then to Esseilte, who kept her eyes on her hard-clasped hands—"say if what I tell you is so—"

"It is true," said Diarmait slowly. "But how could you know?"

"There are places of power in my own land, Ard-Righ, and I have played a part in the ceremonies. I knew enough to see that a moment more would bring disaster, and I knew how to enter the circle. I took up the blackthorn cudgel and let the force flow through me to complete the task that Fergus MacGabran had begun."

"Perhaps it is so," said the chief poet softly. "He does seem to understand . . ."

"No!" bellowed Fergus, starting forward. "Don't let his borrowed finery deceive you! I know him now! This is nothing but that wandering bard Dughan, a hedge-poet with no honor-price, and a lying dog of Kernow for whom it is death to enter this hall!"

The High King's law kept Fergus's sword from Drustan's head, but his rage struck like a physical blow. Drustan rocked back and then found his balance, waiting in a fighter's half-crouch to see what the other man would do.

"You have been accused, stranger. What say you now?" The High King's face hardened as it had when he decreed the Mor-holt's exile. I understood then that this was a sovereign whose justice would be swayed by neither need nor fear. Perhaps he did not desire to give his daughter to Fergus, but he would put truth above preference and even over policy.

"I am that man you knew as Dughan," Drustan said quietly, and waited while the babble of surprise rose and fell. "And a bard sometimes, but also a warrior. As for my birth, my father was Meliau, lord of Léon in Armorica. Decide for yourselves what the price for killing me should be!" He had straightened proudly, and in that moment there was no man among them who could deny the truth of his words.

He had convinced them, I thought as I considered the rapt faces around us. But I wondered if even Drustan's agile tongue would have been able to save him if I had told them that he was also the slayer of the Morholt, whom they had loved.

"And do you claim the place of the Champion?" asked the High King. Fergus's fingers tightened on the hilt of his sword.

"Let Fergus MacGabran carve the beef, for he is your Champion, and belongs to this land. I claim only the other prize of that competition, the Lady Esseilte who is called the Maiden of Temair."

"You shall not have her!" Fergus lunged and Drustan sidestepped neatly. "Knave I name you—there is no proof for what you say!" He came after his rival, and Drustan gave way before him until he turned to stand at bay before the royal compartment.

"Ard-Righ, let someone restrain him before I am forced to break your law!"

King Diarmait nodded, and two of his warriors stepped forward to pinion Fergus's flailing arms. The sword clattered to the floor. Drustan's color had risen just a little, but his voice remained calm.

"Fergus MacGabran, you shall not again insult me! I have told you of what blood I come, and even were I only the bard you name me, you would be wrong to attack me. It is not for myself that I seek the maiden, but for my lord and uncle, Marc'h Conomor, who is lord of Ker-haes in Armorica and High King over Dyfneint and Kernow."

I stared, and I suppose all others in that hall were doing the same. But for me it was as if the confusion of furze and bracken on a moor had resolved itself suddenly to reveal the hidden nest, and the meaning of all the contradictions in Drustan's character came suddenly clear. This, then, was the reparation he had promised us. The Morholt's honor-price was an alliance with

Britain that would bring Diarmait advantages that could never have been won by the sword. It was a princely compensation, I told myself, but if I were still struggling to reconcile this truth with all Drustan's deceptions, would Esseilte see it so?

The last vestiges of color faded from her face, and for a moment I thought she would faint in my arms. I realized then that despite all Drustan's protests of disinterest, she had not believed him. She had been braced to do battle if he tried to take her, but there was nothing for her to fight against now.

Over the hubbub around us came the sounds of commotion from the door. Diarmait's warriors were forcibly escorting six strangers into the hall. One of them I recognized as Drustan's friend Gorwennol, and as the group came closer a kind of defiant aristocracy in their bearing gave them a likeness beyond physical kinship, and I began to suspect who they must be.

"Foreigners, Ard-Righ — foreigners from Kernow," said the man in the lead. "I remembered your order and brought them here. What is your will?"

"Maybe you can cheat justice with talk of lordships in Armorica, but what about your friends?" spat Fergus.

Gorwennol looked alarmed. I remembered that he spoke a rough sort of Irish, and the others would be able to make out a few words of what was going on. Finding themselves guarded while Drustan stood at liberty, they must have wondered. The looks they turned on him and on the High King were equally wary.

"For their sake I will have to hope that the High King is able to alter his edicts for the good of his kingdom," Drustan said quietly. "These are the envoys of King Marc'h, come to negotiate an alliance that may be greatly to the advantage of Eriu. If you are as loyal as you are loud, Fergus MacGabran, you will advise your lord to consider what they have to say!"

His gaze turned to King Diarmait again, and the High King allowed himself a faint smile.

"I present to you the chief men of Kernow — Mevennus Maglos, and Wydhyel map Ladek, Karasek of Nans Dreyn, Fragan Tawr, Bretowennus Lord of Penryn, Wyn Dwyel and Beli map Branek and my good companion, Gorwennol —" The British names rang harshly amid the softer speech of Eriu.

"Release the British envoys, lads. I do not think I am in any danger here. And then you may bring more couches so that our guests may join in the feasting." Diarmait gestured the warriors away. Then he held out his hand.

"Domini Dumnonienses, salvete!"

Greeted thus in a language they knew, the British began to smile. I saw that faint, betraying color come again into Drustan's face as he realized that perhaps it was going to be all right after all. Fergus was still standing, the fight draining out of him as he began to suspect the same.

"Fergus MacGabran, there are people perishing all around us because of the savor of that fine beast there," Diarmait said gently. "You are still my Champion, man — do you make the first cut of the beef that we may all get to our feasting."

MacGabran's face worked painfully. But he had lost, and he knew it now. Best to save what honor he could. But he sliced into the carcass before him as if it were Drustan's head.

After that the evening became more civilized. I ate eagerly, for great emotion tended to make me hungry. The beef, though not as hot as it had been, was fat, and so tender one hardly needed a knife. Esseilte sat stony-faced beside me, eating nothing, but drinking cup after cup of mead. At first that worried me, but this was not the heavy stuff the men would be drinking later, but a light, honey-flavored liquor that seemed to have no more effect on her than water from the stream.

Conversation eddied around us, in Irish or Latin, or sometimes in British as Drustan conferred with the men of Kernow.

"What Marc'h seeks from you is the peace that MacErca had with Artor," said Drustan. "In the last century our people took back Demetia from the lords of Mumu and Laigin, and since then your raiding parties have left us alone."

I stared at him, wondering how he could maintain such impassivity. For he, more than any other, had reason to remember the one time in recent years when our warriors had gone raiding into Kernow.

"I have heard that Marcus Cunomorus is a strong ruler. Why does he need an alliance with me?" Diarmait asked politely, using the Latin form of the British name.

"Not for the sake of Britain — the Saxons lie quiet in the eastern territories our treaties have given them. But in Armorica the situation is still unsettled. My uncle hopes to establish a strong British rule in that province that will be able to resist the expansion of the Frankish kings, a rule as secure and strong, if you will, as yours is here." He smiled. "It will take time, and he must be often overseas. He cannot put forth his power on the continent until he knows that his western coasts are secure."

The High King nodded. "And what does your king offer in return?"

"Trade," answered Gorwennol. "Trade, and tin. Our connections in Armorica link us to the continent, and goods flow freely to and from Fawwyth and Lan Wedenek and Porth Mawr."

"I have traveled widely," added Drustan, "and the seas are more peaceful now than they have been for a generation or more. The piracy that devastated the coasts of Armorica is ended, and though internally the empire's old provinces still are troubled, the ocean is an open road for those who know the way. If you and my lord can come to an agreement, Ard-Righ, the Race of Heroes will rule the seas!"

"But trade between Domnonia and Hibernia is the first step," said Gorwennol. "We will work out the details of the exchange when we know better what things you need."

"A trade agreement could be useful," Queen Mairenn agreed, "but why does King Marc'h also seek a bride? He is a man of my lord's age, I believe. Has he no heir?"

One of the Britons cast a quick glance at Drustan, grinned, and then answered in that swift, clipped way of speaking that made it hard to understand them even when one knew the words.

"Lord Maglos says that the king has a son by his first wife who will inherit his lands in Armorica," Drustan answered calmly. "But the lords who stayed in greater Britain wish for a ruler born in their own land. They want Marc'h to marry again and give them an heir for Kernow. There is precedent — in the time of Bishop Padraig, Vitalinus the High King whom men now call Vortigern made an alliance with Eriu by marrying his daughter to the son of your King Loegaire."

There were undercurrents here beyond my understanding, and we would have to understand them if we were to survive. But Esseilte's pallor had become sickly. She rose quickly, making her excuses to her parents without ever looking at Drustan, and I followed her out into the dark.

"Get out of here and take that twanging sound-loom with you!" Esseilte turned on the queen's harper, who had been playing softly in the Grianan, and sent her stumbling from the room with her instrument clutched in her arms. "I never want to hear harping again!"

The queen's women scattered before her like so many clucking hens as she strode to the compartment we shared and threw herself upon the bed.

"I should have killed him! *Why* could not I kill him? I thought my mother would do it for me—but she has failed me! Oh, I should have accused him of the Morholt's murder in front of them all." Her words came muffled against the blanket. I drew the curtain, afraid that others would hear, and trimmed the wick to make the little lamp burn more brightly.

"Esseilte! Let it go, my heart . . . your father needs that treaty—there is nothing to be done about Drustan now." I sat down on the bed beside her and laid my hand on her shoulder. It was shaking—I could not tell whether with anguish or with rage.

"I thought if I were forced to wed Drustan, I would have another chance to kill him when we were alone. But now they mean to marry me off to some old man and exile me to a foreign land. Even if I had been married into the Ulaid, it would still have been Eriu! Branwen, what am I going to do!"

"You will be a queen, Esseilte," I said softly. "You will have power. And Drustan will be only the chief of your warriors, and one who is not well liked, I think, by his uncle's men. Do not lose your courage now, my love."

"Ah, what's the use?" All the fight went out of her with a shuddering sigh. "They've bound me like a heifer for market. At least that poor beast they butchered for the feast tonight did not know that it was going to die."

"Esseilte! Esseilte! Remember that I will be with you. Whatever you are going to, it will not be alone!" I put my arms around her, and after a little she fell into a fitful sleep. But I lay wakeful, listening to the shouts of the men in the meadhall, and knew that I was afraid.

For three weeks the Britons remained with Diarmait, proving that the men of Kernow were every bit as skilled at argument as the folk of Eriu. But in the end they came to a very good understanding, and a treaty was written that detailed the bride-price that was asked for Esseilte, and the support and assurances that King Diarmait was prepared to offer in return.

It was the last day of January when the foreigners set sail for

Britain. A few weeks later a trader brought us news that they
had reached Lan Wedenek safely. Then it was our part to wait,
while storms of winter whipped the sea, and the King of Kernow
weathered who knew what lesser tumults as his advisors drew
up their reply.

In the Grianan we worked on Esseilte's wedding clothes with
a subdued desperation, as if we were getting ready for war.
There were gowns to be made up in the style of Eriu, and
lengths of wool and linen to be woven for future garments in the
fashion of Britain, and bands to be embroidered for ornamenting
them as well. Bed linen and hangings were prepared also, and all
the women's tools that were Esseilte's dower, for the queen was
determined that her daughter should not go a beggar to her new
home. The few Greek traders that had slipped through the gap
between winter and spring storms pulled out their beards in anguish because they had no more to sell.

Esseilte's task was a silk tunic for her new lord, embroidered
in the manner of Eriu. She worked at it sullenly, and there were
times when I unpicked the stitches and redid them while she
slept, lest she should shame us all. But at least she was not being
asked to strain her eyes and prick her fingers for the sake of
Drustan.

And at least we were spared the constant irritation of his presence, for he had gone with the envoys back to Kernow. Gorwennol remained to tutor us in the tongue of Britain. By the time the
cold released its grip and gentler rains began to bless the land
with spring greenery, Esseilte's cheeks were regaining a little
color, and at times she was even heard to wonder what kind of
life she would find in Kernow. The tightness in my chest began
to relax.

It was just after Easter that the British ship returned. Drustan
was with them, but we did not see him. We might not have
noticed even if he had come, for the imminent prospect of departure was like bright sunlight that picked out myriad details that
no one had thought of before. And then, suddenly, all was
packed and ready for loading, and it was the night before we
were to set sail.

"Branwen!"

I turned at the whisper and saw old Messach in the doorway.
"Messach, what—"

She beckoned again, and I set down the folded shifts that I

was carrying and went to her, having learned by long experience that Messach communicated in her own way.

"The queen wants you, sweetling, but quietly. Herself is not to know —" A jerk of the head indicated Esseilte, who was packing jewelry into a leather-bound chest beside the fire.

"But I'm busy here — she must realize —"

"She said I was to fetch you, and you know what she is like, especially now!"

I sighed and slipped through the door after her, for I did know. Since midwinter the queen had grown thinner, and easily tired, and illness had not lengthened her patience. Even if my absence upset Esseilte, surely I owed something to the woman who had raised me with a mother's care if not a mother's love. It was only as I neared the still-house that I remembered the promise she had extracted from me when she answered my call to her a little over a year ago.

Mairenn was waiting for me, wrapped in a heavy cloak beside the hearth. Shadow lay heavy beneath the eaves, and despite the burning peats the place had a damp smell, as if it were some time since it had been used. A shiver made me draw my own shawl more closely around me, and I was not certain if it came from cold or memory.

"Royal Woman?" I came the rest of the way inside and shut the door.

She lifted her head and I felt the gaze of lightless eyes.

"Daughter of my brother, come here."

Slowly I moved to the hearth and sat down on a three-legged stool beside the fire. A round pot of fragrant tea was hanging from the hook. The queen gestured to me to ladle out for her and myself, and drank with a sigh.

"There are things I must tell you. You will be leaving tomorrow, and I will not see you again. . . ."

"Esseilte —" I began, but a curt wave stopped me. Mairenn had never been one to waste words, and now . . . and now . . .

"Esseilte does not know. But you knew, did you not? I will not live long."

I nodded, accepting all at once the weight of evidence I had denied.

"My daughter is willful, and seeks the vision in her heart rather than the wisdom in the world. That is not bad in itself, but there are things she will never be able to understand. I tried to make her learn my secrets. I was wrong — I should have taught them to you . . ."

I stared at her, as shocked by what she had said about Esseilte as by the implications of her words to me.

"It is too late for that now, of course. You are both leaving Eriu, as I desired."

"But why?" The protest burst out without my will.

"I have put what strength remains to me into trying to see what will be. I cannot divine all futures, but I know that evil times are coming for Eriu. Without my understanding for balance the High King's wisdom may be too inflexible. There will be battles, and Temair will become a place where sheep graze on a hill of memories." Her voice had hoarsened. She drank from her wooden cup and set it down again. I shuddered, remembering my vision on Samhain Eve.

"Do you think that things will be so peaceful in Kernow? You heard what Abbot Columba had to say about that British monk's manuscript!"

"I have seen Esseilte dressed in silk and seated in a place of honor in Kernow. Whatever evil touches her there will not come from the contentions of Eriu. If sorrow is fated for my daughter, I think it will be partly her own doing." Her lips twisted wryly. "So much has been given to Esseilte, and yet she will always want more. I have seen it before in those who were ill in childhood. They burn their lives like candle flames!"

I took a quick gulp of my own tea, found it cold, and reached for the ladle. This was plain speaking indeed, and I was not sure I was ready to see Esseilte so clearly. Had the queen also used her arts to look into my future? I was even less certain I would like what she might have seen, but I knew even as I poured more tea that I was going to ask.

"*You* do not know what you want, my child." Mairenn smiled. I nodded. I had never thought there was any point in wanting things for myself at all.

"How it will happen, I know not," she went on, "but I have seen you upon my own path, the hidden way of the Earth and Her power. Your mother was from Kernow. It may be that its soil will speak to you."

"I do not understand. . . ."

Mairenn leaned forward, and the folds of her headdress swung out like dark wings. "Do you not?" she asked softly. "At the holy well and Brigid's shrine did you not hear Her speaking?

Did you not see Her strength uncoiling at the Brugh na Boinne?"

"I saw — oh yes, I saw!" I whispered. "But I was afraid, and still I do not understand. The monks say that to worship the old powers is sin!"

Mairenn snorted and sat back again. "Old — new — what does that mean? If the power is real, do you think it is going to disappear just because men say a different name when they pray?"

"Abbot Ruadan teaches that the Old Ones were evil," I said slowly, "not that they were unreal."

"Is greenery bursting from the earth evil? Or the swelling of the moon in the sky? Or new life emerging from the womb? Those are the powers I serve," said the queen.

"Not only — not always —" I kept my gaze on the glowing peats, thinking of a cauldron I had stirred over just such a fire. It seemed a very long time ago. "You have used what you know to curse as well as to bless, and in this very room."

I waited for the queen to blast me, but she only sighed.

"So I have, and perhaps I am paying for it now. But that is not the fault of the old powers. . . . Do you think the priests of Christ will do better when they rule? I fear what may happen if men are forced to choose between the honor of the Church and the honor of the king!"

"But Eriu is a Christian country," I objected, "and so are those realms in Britain that the Saxons do not rule. Whether the priests do well or ill, they lead our worship now."

"As the king leads the land," agreed Mairenn. "The priests fix their eyes on the glory of heaven, and the king on the honor of earthly rule, but the earth supports both the high-seat and the altar. Without that third power to keep the balance, both king and priest will fall."

I looked up at her, then quickly away, struggling to catch hold of the image, a bright pattern that would have enabled me to understand it all. King . . . queen . . . priest . . . all linked in an endless triple spiral that whirled down into a darkness of times past and future until. . . .

Mairenn's grip on my shoulder brought me back to the dark room and the glowing fire.

"I thought so," she said with some satisfaction. "You have no choice, my child. The old powers have touched your spirit, and you must decide whether to serve them as a priestess or a slave."

I shook my head, hands clenched on my mug and feet pushing

against the stones of the hearth in an attempt to reclaim the reality I had always known.

"There are no priestesses anymore."

Mairenn shrugged. "In the old days all knew what they served, and why. It is more difficult now, but there are those who still keep the old knowledge alive. Do not be surprised by where you find them. The life of the land is strong, and will not be denied."

I could feel that life in the solidity of the stool on which I was sitting, in the pungence of the air I breathed, in the heat of the fire and the cooling savor of the tea. From somewhere outside I heard the mournful call of an owl.

"I wish you could have trained me. . . ." I found myself saying then.

"I *am* training you —" The darkness of her robes surrounded me as she leaned forward. "Thus do I welcome you to the circle of life!"

For a moment thin arms gripped me; the queen's kiss burned my brow. Then she released me and sat back again, but my forehead still throbbed as if she had marked me with an invisible brand. I looked up at her, striving to read the meaning of what had just happened in those dark eyes. But even now their glittering surface gave away no secrets. Would I ever understand?

"On the table is a chest bound in brass," said Mairenn. "Bring it to me here."

The thing was solidly made. I grunted, lifting it, and set it down before the hearth with care. She gestured to me to open it, and I fumbled with the clasp. Even before I got the top up a heady wave of scent told me what must be inside. Pungent and aromatic, sweet and tart all mingled, carefully packed within the casket was a selection of glass vials and flagons full of tinctures and infusions, and healing herbs done up in twists of cloth.

"This you will take with you, and the book as well —"

Neatly fitted into the top of the chest was a book in wooden covers, a book of vellum leaves whose edges were browned and tattered — Queen Mairenn's own book of recipes and spells. . . .

"You cannot mean to give this to me!"

"To whom else should I give it? At least my blood runs in your veins!" she said quickly. "But the hour grows late. Pull out the large flagon that's packed in the corner there."

I drew it free — a lovely thing of pale green Roman glass. A dark, sweet-smelling liquor swirled inside.

"It smells wonderful!" I breathed in appreciatively.

"Don't drink it," Mairenn said with a dry smile. "It is a gift for my daughter's wedding day. It seemed to me that Esseilte may find it hard, being married to an older man. So much will be strange to her, and so different from her dreams. It will be easier if there is love to sweeten living and make her forget past pain. That flagon holds the last, best flower of all my skill, an infusion that will warm the body and inebriate the soul until all that is needed to awaken passion is the touch of a lover's hand. Let Esseilte share it with the king, and they will begin their lives together by sharing joy."

I smiled and thrust the flagon into its place again. Clearly Mairenn knew her daughter better than I had suspected, and the potion might turn out to be very useful indeed.

"When I took you from your father's arms, I did better than I knew. . . . Go now—there will be a great deal to do tomorrow, and much of it will fall on you."

I clasped the cover of the casket and stood up. The fire had faded to a feeble glow and I had to strain to make out gaunt features and the glitter of her eyes. As I began to turn, her thin hand closed on my gown.

"Once, I made you swear to do whatever I asked of you. Now, I have given you your inheritance. What will you do for me?" The queen looked at me, and the skin where she had kissed me tingled once more.

I bowed my head. "I have already sworn faith to your daughter. With the skills your gift may give me I will guard her as well as I may."

"That needed no oath—that is your destiny," Mairenn said harshly.

"But what else—" I swallowed, beginning to understand. "Is it vengeance you want of me?" I whispered then. "Am I to be your instrument to punish Drustan?"

She did not answer. As I picked up the casket and went out of the still-house, Mairenn remained by the hearth, a shadow in the darkness, a shadow on my soul. White wings and black wings flickered dizzily. It was only as I walked up the path to the Grianan with the herb-chest in my arms that I realized that the brightness I had seen in my aunt's eyes was the glitter of tears.

Eleven

THE WATERS OF SORROW

"'Tis cold as a curse, this wind!"

"Wind? Only a bit breeze — t'set us on our way!" the sailor answered in rough Irish. "At sea — that's wind! Skin hair off bull's hide!"

He laughed and swung the end of the chest over the rail. Two more crewmen carried it off to be fitted into the stack of gear they were stowing amidships in the bark that would bear us to Kernow.

"Easy for him to brag, an' me with my feet all frozen in the sea!" muttered the loader, wading back for another box.

Five days to reach Kernow, Drustan had said, if wind and weather held fair. I looked at the British bark. They called her *Flower o' the Broom*, and a big, solid creature she seemed beside the leather-hulled curraghs of the fishermen — like an ox among racing ponies — but we were going to feel cramped enough by the end of the voyage if Esseilte continued to treat Drustan like something nasty found under a stone.

The first flowers of the broom which had given the ship her name sparked defiantly against the dull gray-green of the shore. The whitewashed houses of the fisher-folk of Inber Colptha huddled beneath lowering clouds, and even the bright cloaks of the High King's household could not banish the chill. A cold dismal morning it was to be leaving the land of Eriu. Another bark was drawn up farther down the shore, loading a cargo of hides, several leashes of rough-coated hunting dogs, and a half-dozen shiv-

166

ering slaves to carry back to Gaul. At least Esseilte and I were departing with honor. But we were still going into exile.

The three girls who had been chosen for Esseilte's household came hurrying toward me, cloaks fluttering.

"Oh Branwen, when will we go? It's cold I am, and the wind whipping my hair like oatstraw off the threshing floor!"

I smiled in spite of myself, for Sionach's fly-away fair hair had indeed pulled loose from its braids. Cairenn came to a halt beside her, black hair held firmly by a kerchief, and red-headed Breacc scurried after her. Their glances went past me to the sailors on the bark, and they stifled giggles. They were scarcely two years younger than I was, but I had already begun to feel it might as well have been two decades.

"They have to finish lashing down our boxes, my dears — you'd not wish the boat to founder in the middle of the cold gray sea because the balance was wrong?"

Three pairs of eyes rounded as their attention came back to me. The girls shook their heads.

"Then go back to the hut and wait there with the princess. Even with all we are taking, they must finish soon!"

Drustan was already on board, his crisp orders directing the raising of the leather tent that would shelter us during the voyage. He seemed to know his business; the stories he had told us of his travels had not been all a fabrication. An incoming swell lifted the ship suddenly; the sternline snapped and the roof sagged. Drustan leaped to the rail to catch it and grabbed the rope as it whipped past. A rattle of orders brought seamen running, and Drustan jumped down again. He saw me watching him, and waved.

"Branwen!" The captain touched his arm and spoke and Drustan nodded, then turned to me again. "Bring the others quickly, or we'll lose the ebb of the tide!"

The waiting that had seemed eternal was ending, and for a moment I wanted to pretend I had not heard. But my feet were already bearing me back along the strand to the hut where Esseilte and her father were sheltering.

As she came out into the light I could see that she had been weeping. Even King's Diarmait's stern features were marked by the aftermath of emotion, and I realized that perhaps his justice was not as effortless as it appeared. I followed them toward the ship. Drustan and Gorwennol and the captain were waiting, wet to the thighs from wading ashore.

"Lord Drustan, I give my daughter into your care. Guard her well, for the sake of both our lands," said Diarmait. The cold wind tugged at his beard, and I saw how much silver was mingled with the auburn there. The queen was not the only one who had aged this past year.

Esseilte stood beside him, mute and trembling. The High King set his hands on her shoulders.

"My child, we all do what we must for the sake of the land. Some must die to defend it, and some must leave it behind. . . ."

"When men die for their homeland they have hopes of a better world," murmured Esseilte. "I do not think Kernow is heaven, Father, but I will go."

"It is a hero's sacrifice, daughter. Eriu will remember you." He bent and kissed her upon the brow.

"We must get aboard, Ard-Righ, the tide is going fast —" Captain Gorgi interrupted. "There's no need for the women to get wet though — we can carry them —" Sionach giggled as he held out his arms.

"I will bear the lady Branwen, if she permits," said Gorwennol shyly. "Lord Drustan is the king's kinsman, and should carry the princess."

"I will not." The words were soft, but clear. "All else I have consented to, but that man will not touch me without my will."

Drustan stared at her, and his face darkened beneath the tan, then grew pale. His eyes went to Diarmait's in mute appeal.

Diarmait put his arm around Esseilte's shoulders. "Your mother carried you beneath her heart till you were born into this world. It is only justice that I should carry you now . . ."

Without waiting for a reply he lifted her and strode into the water. Grinning, the captain scooped Sionach into his arms, and two men from the High King's household took Breacc and Cairenn. Gorwennol lifted me like some holy relic. As I looked back over his shoulder I saw Drustan following us, alone.

And then Esseilte and I were clinging to each other beside the mast. We staggered as the anchor was dragged in and the ship was released to the tide. Chanting, men hauled on the lines and the square leather sail rattled up the mast, flapped loudly until the sailors angled it to the proper trim, and then strained taut and full. I sat down suddenly as the *Flower* leaned into the wind, and felt the new purpose in her motion as we headed for the entrance to the bay.

Gulls screamed around us like women keening a departing

soul. At each lift of the ship I saw the white houses clustered above the strand and the mingling of wood and meadow beyond. The cloaks of the royal household still glowed on the shore, and one of them, the tallest, lifted his arm in farewell. Esseilte clung to the mast, staring at those figures as they dwindled and finally disappeared.

From somewhere near I heard a soft singing.

> *"The land of Eriu I'm calling,*
> *Where curraghs course the fertile sea,*
> *Free down the vales sweet waters falling,*
> *Fair the heroes' home to me —"*

It was as if my heart were speaking, and it took me a few moments to realize that the song was coming from Drustan.

> *"The land of Eriu I'm singing,*
> *Stags that on the mountains bell,*
> *Wells of water, blackbirds winging*
> *Wild with beauty, there I'd dwell."*

I listened, hearing in that song a truth beyond all his deceptions. Prince and merchant and warrior — Drustan had as many faces as Lugh Samildanach, and all of them shadowed. But I had forgotten that first of all he was a bard.

> *"The land of Eriu I'm leaving,*
> *Losing the lakes where lifts the crane*
> *Against the dawn. But I go grieving*
> *Gray sea's sighing sings my pain. . . ."*

Like a physician lancing a wound to heal it, he pierced the heart with his singing and released the sorrow festering there. As the last words faded, the will that had held Esseilte upright failed and she collapsed weeping into my arms.

When I could see again, Inber Colptha was only a grey shape upon the horizon, which soon disappeared.

When the wind blew from the east, *Flower*'s rigging thrummed like Drustan's harpstrings. The sound when it backed northward was quieter, and one became aware of the tuneful gurgle of water beneath the bows. For three days we had been coasting southward with the shoreline of Eriu like a shadow upon our right hand. Our first misery was past, and the sweet music of a ship in motion was becoming familiar to us now.

I smiled to realize what I was thinking, and picked up my embroidery again. Esseilte was still gazing toward the shore. The clouds had thinned to let through a little watery sunshine that picked out the green of the headlands and touched unexpected gleams of color from the sea.

"We will have to find something useful for those three girl-children they sent with us to do —" I said cheerfully. Esseilte murmured a reply and I went on.

"This morning I caught them going through my herb-chest — looking for a remedy for seasickness, they said, though since that first night they've been as steady as sailors! Pure mischief, I think it was. I'll get a lock for the casket when we reach Kernow. Some of those potions could poison if taken wrong. As it is, I marked the most dangerous —"

I stopped short, realizing that I had almost told Esseilte about the love potion, which I had also marked "poison" lest someone should take it for wine. But it would not have mattered what I had said. Drustan was making his way toward us from the bow, and Esseilte's bleak gaze was fixed upon him.

Like the rest of the crew he went barefoot on board, but with no need for disguise his clothing was as rich, though as somber, as the garments Esseilte wore. There was a peace in his eyes that had not been there in Temair. Was it because he was going back to Britannia, or because he was between worlds when he was on the sea?

"There are things you should know before you reach Kernow." Drustan waited until the ship slid down the next swell and let the motion carry him to us.

"Nothing that you could teach me, traitor —"

I looked from Drustan's stony face to Esseilte's, and sighed.

"You will be queen of a realm as various as the four fifths of Eriu," he continued as if he had not heard. "Perhaps more so, for the movement of peoples has been more recent there. You need to know something of those whom you will rule."

"You are all British and Roman, are you not?" I asked quickly.

"Yes," he answered. "But that is not as simple as it seems. When the Romans came, Kernow and Dyfneint belonged to the Dumnonii. My people, the Cornovii, came from around Viroconium. They were brought south by Vitalinus to defend Dumnonia from the men of Mumu who had settled on the coast. In Artor's time, the kings of the Belgae and the Durotriges betrayed their race to ally with the Saxons and died at Badon, and Artor added their lands to those Marc'h's grandfather Cato already ruled."

"Then the claim my people have upon that land is older than your own!" Esseilte said spitefully. "The Morholt was a man of Mumu. Is that why you murdered him?"

"And the claim of the Cruithni to rule Eriu is older than yours!" Drustan responded, stung from his composure. "The Fir Domnann were far cousins of the Dumnonii, and the first Tuathal became High King of Eriu four centuries ago with aid from Rome! One tribe replaces another on the land, Esseilte, and each new people calls it home!"

"Is that how you justify your conquest of Armorica?" Esseilte said sweetly. "By that reasoning, the Saxons have a right to keep the districts they hold —"

"Perhaps . . ." Drustan sighed. He rested his elbows on his knees and rubbed his eyes wearily. "But the tribes of Britain have always fought each other. In language and traditions, British and Irish are kin. I even understand why you must hate me, for among my folk it is the same. But the Saxons seem different, like the Franks in Gaul. Since my great-grandsire's time they have been the great enemy. And yet perhaps the land will one day accept them too . . ."

I saw Esseilte's fingers curl white-knuckled against the palms of her hands. If Drustan had attacked her she could have fought him and worked off some of her anger, but it was impossible to strike a man who lowered his guard and presented his breast to his foe.

I felt sorry for her. I felt sorry for them both.

We anchored overnight off the Sacred Cape, and at dawn headed eastward across the Hibernian sea. To go so long without the sight of land was frightening, though the sailors did not seem concerned. Still, I think everyone was relieved when a fair wind brought us in sight of Porth Mawr with the last of the setting sun.

We felt our way into the bay in the dusk, guided by the twinkle of lights on shore. Lanterns showed us where other ships lay already, for the white sands of the little bay were a famous anchorage, and most of the trade of Demetia and Gwynedd passed through Porth Mawr. In the morning we took on food and water and rounded the point southward.

For most of the next two days our course paralleled the coast of Demetia, where fierce dark mountains greater than any hills I had ever seen brooded above the green shore. We were moving into the firth of the Sabrina that separated the west of Britain from the Dumnonian peninsula. Twisting trails of smoke showed us where Carmarthen and other, smaller settlements lay hidden. Fishermen hailed us, and from time to time we passed a larger vessel, for there was a considerable traffic across the Sabrina Sea. And then the fertile fields of Glevissig faded behind us as the *Flower* altered course for the coast of Kernow.

"You told my father you are heir to Léon in Armorica. Why then are you running errands for the King of Kernow?" Esseilte said brightly. Bitterness and anger had both failed to shake Drustan's wary courtesy as he continued his attempts to teach her. What was she going to try today?

He smiled rather wryly. "Inheritance in Armorica has its complexities, perhaps because no British title in that country predates the time of Maximus, and most of its lords still hold territories on this side of the water too. My grandfather Budic was the third generation to claim land there. He had to fight for his rights in Demetia and in Armorica both, before he defeated his brother and became lord of Kemper."

He looked up as the clouds spattered us with a few drops of rain, then the same wind that was bearing us southwestward hurried them away.

"Budic is an old man now, but still vigorous — he, and Macliavus of Venetorium, and my other grandfather, Pompeius Regalcis, whom we call Riwal, are the masters of Armorica." Drustan grimaced at the third name. "My uncle Theodoric is his heir, but Meliau my father was his favorite, they say. Budic married him off to Riwal's daughter Gwenneth, on condition that Léon, whose lordship had fallen vacant, should be her dowry."

"There was no male heir?" I echoed. "Was there a daughter then?"

"Auroc's daughter Pritella married Jonas of Dol, who claims it for their son Iudual. But Riwal holds it still . . . or I should say, once more . . ." Drustan answered bitterly.

"I am beginning to understand what you mean about complexity." I glared at Esseilte, who looked as if she were seeking something cutting to say. "But that does not explain how you ended up in Kernow."

"Perhaps Meliau chafed at Riwal's overlordship, or perhaps Riwal feared that Budic was using his son to extend his own power. It doesn't matter now. Riwal killed him," Drustan said flatly.

"He attacked his own daughter?" asked Esseilte, startled into sympathy.

"No. My mother was dead already," answered Drustan. "She died a few days after I was born. But Riwal did seek to destroy my older brother and me. Marc'h's first wife, my aunt Budicca, was still alive then, and they sheltered us for a time in Kerhaes." The sea shimmered with tarnished silver dapplings as the clouds curdled and thinned above us. Drustan's face shifted from light to shadow and back again as he went on.

"Riwal sent his assassins after us. My brother Melor was taken to Britain for safety, but they killed him finally near the great ring of stones. I was sent south to school in Gaul and elsewhere. I was nearly grown before I learned my true parentage and my name. . . ."

Drustan sat very still, and for a moment I saw the lost and lonely child he must have been. Then one of the sailors sang out the sighting of a seal, and the mask of disinterest hid his true feelings once more.

"I seem to recall that the great Artor himself died by his own son's hand. If this is how your people treat their families, I suppose I should not be surprised when they betray those they call enemy," said Esseilte.

"Esseilte!" I exclaimed. Her search for something hurtful to say had clearly been successful. The clouds were thickening again, and I pulled my brat over my head as they began to weep once more.

"Don't you understand that the greatest treacheries are those between kin?" Drustan exclaimed. Like the clouds, his eyes had darkened. With what inner storms?

"This petty vengeance is unworthy of you, Princess." He got to his feet. "But I have no need to respond in kind. The lords of Kernow are not kind to foreigners — I have reason to know. Pray that your beauty will win them — you will get no more help from me!"

Another day of sailing brought us angling past offshore islands where bright-billed puffins darted among clouds of cormorants and gulls. The shoreline was fortified with tortured cliffs of dark-brown stone that repelled the charging waves in fountains of glittering spray. A brisk wind had driven the clouds away, and bright sunshine struck sparks of teal and tourmaline from the dancing sea.

And then the big sail was hauled round and the *Flower* leaned into the wind toward the curving estuary of Lan Wedenek. As we came around the point it dropped abruptly and the ship's motion steadied. Behind the sand bars and beaches that lined the estuary we glimpsed a countryside of round green hills and sheltered copses beneath the great blue bowl of the sky.

One of the sailors at the bow pointed at the low island we were passing and they all laughed.

"Oh indeed, I saw it —" one man exclaimed. "Drustan took him down like a woodsman tops a tree! The Irish scum will think twice before they try that again!" His companion tried to hush him, glancing sidelong at Esseilte. For a moment all three turned, then, too quickly, they looked away. Esseilte's knuckles whitened as she gripped the rail.

"That is the island then . . ." she said in a low voice. "And there is not even a stone upon it to show where the Morholt died. . . . A sorry, poor place it is to have been the death of such a hero. Oh Branwen, how can I live in a land where the Morholt's blood cries out for vengeance from the soil?" Her cheeks glistened as tears mingled with the spray.

She turned as the bark moved onward, still weeping silently, and watched the island until we eased in toward the harbor and it disappeared. Then she went back into the tent and did not emerge again.

At Lan Wedenek we got fresh food and water, and news that King Marc'h lay now at Lys Hornek in Penwith. We set sail again, therefore, and continued southwest along the coast toward Porth Ia, on the Heyle. But as if Esseilte's renewed grief had upset the weather, the wind that had been so kindly turned foul, and to keep from being smashed against the hungry rocks, the *Flower* must beat her way to the safety of the open sea. When the winds abated at last, we were out of sight of land.

"Captain Gorgi says the worst of it is over." I pushed the doorflap aside and bent to enter the tent. "By morning we'll head back toward the coast, and maybe make the Heyle by nightfall if all goes well."

The sea was still lively, and the movement of the hanging

lamp made it hard to read Esseilte's expression. She was sitting on her pallet, plucking nervously at the embroidered coverlet.

"Tomorrow?"

"He said so—" I began straightening gear that had tumbled about during the storm. "Will you come out? The clean air is like wine, and the sun is dying with a blaze like the Samhain fires!"

Esseilte shook her head in sudden decision. "There is something I must do. Go to Drustan, and ask him to come here to me."

I stared at her, and she forced a smile.

"You were right, Branwen. This sulking of mine is foolish now. The enmity between us must be ended. I promise you— bring him here, and by the time we come to land I will have made my peace with Drustan."

My expression must have shown my astonishment, for she looked at me and laughed.

"Dear Branwen, you have been more patient than I deserve. I do thank you for all your care. I will not trouble you like this again." The brass lamp swung from the brace overhead as the bark rocked in the swell. Light and shadow flickered across her face so that I could not tell whether what I saw there was a smile or a grimace of pain.

"Esseilte. . . ." I looked at her helplessly, trying to reply. But there were no words for the bond between us, and after a moment I went out to try and do her will.

Drustan was still in the stained tunic in which he had fought the storm. Wearied as he was, and suspicious of Esseilte's sincerity, still he gave in with a graceful courtesy that reminded me of the harper we had rescued. This, at least, was not dissimulation. I found myself liking him more than I had at any time since those first days when he was recovering from his wound.

Esseilte had changed her dress while I was gone. Her hair hung loose now, and instead of the wool tunics we had been wearing on shipboard she was dressed in a loose robe of purple silk fastened with bow-brooches in the ancient style and a crimson mantle trimmed with knotwork of gold. Drustan took an involuntary step back when he saw her. I supposed that her magnificence was intended to make him feel inferior. After a moment he seemed to realize that too, for he smiled grimly and came the rest of the way inside.

"Royal Woman—" He bowed as if he too had been arrayed in silk and gold. "I am here."

"I see you." She made a little, helpless gesture in reply. "I have thought long on what you have said to me, and I know that I cannot reign in Kernow if you and I are enemies. This is the last chance we will have to resolve what lies between us, Drustan."

"As you will, lady," he said more gently. "The enmity was by no choice of mine."

Esseilte nodded. "Branwen, leave us alone, and keep those three girl-children away. It will be hard enough to do this without—" She stopped, swallowing. "What I have to say is not for the whole ship to hear!"

There was nothing I could say. She had dismissed me. I backed out of the tent and left them alone.

The sun had sunk beneath the horizon, but in the western sky the memory of its passion still glowed. Its reflections glittered like spilled blood in every ripple of the restless sea. I stood for a few moments, wondering at the terrible beauty the world could sometimes show.

In the stern, someone was singing—

> *"Westward my gaze, but east, o'er the sea,*
> *Fresh blows the wind, toward my own country—"*

The sailors were gathered around the little brazier, cooking the evening meal, and the girls were with them. As I came toward them someone nodded toward the tent and laughed.

> *"My sweet Irish maid, where do you go?*
> *Do your fluttering sighs fill my sails now?"*

I stopped, realizing abruptly what kind of gossip could start if Drustan and Esseilte remained too long together unattended. I moved back to the tent and eased down beside the door.

At least they were not quarreling.

I could hear a murmur of voices from within; Esseilte's light tones, and Drustan's occasional low reply. And then, suddenly, the wind failed a moment and I heard her speak quite clearly— "Now you shall pay for the Morholt's death at last!"

I thrust through the door. Still on my knees, I saw Drustan set down one of the pair of silver-bound drinking horns.

"But you drank too—" he said into the silence.

Esseilte smiled triumphantly. In one hand she held the second horn, and in the other a green glass flagon that I knew only too well. I fell back as if I had taken a gut wound, looking from him to her.

"I did. I told you, the drink was poison, but the war between our peoples must be ended. I myself shall pay the price for killing you!"

Esseilte's face was flushed, her eyes were glittering, but with an inward look, as if her attention were more on the messages her body was sending her than on his words. New color had come into Drustan's face as well, and in the silence his harsh breath seemed very loud.

"You are wrong. . . . The war will never end!" My own voice sounded terribly in my ears. "What you have drunk together is not death, but love!"

Slowly they turned to look down at me.

"I marked that bottle poison to keep anyone from touching it," I said then. "Oh, it is my fault for not guarding it! What you drank was a potion of your mother's making, Esseilte, meant to bind you and your lord in love. . . ."

Esseilte's eyes dilated and the empty flagon slipped from a suddenly strengthless hand. The motion of the ship brought it rolling across the deck to me and I snatched at it futilely.

I should smash it, I thought then, watching their faces change as they began to understand. *I should smash it and cut my own throat with the shards of glass. My carelessness has betrayed us all!*

But I had not the queen's foreknowledge. Even knowing Esseilte's grief, how could I have guessed that she meant to kill herself and him? If I had warned her about the potion she would have found some other way. At least she was still alive. . . .

My hands clenched on the flagon's smooth surface as Esseilte carefully set her drinking horn upon the chest, her lips curving in a strange smile.

"Love? Or death — or are the two the same? Either way, Drustan, your life belongs to me. . . ."

"It changes nothing. You will be my uncle's wife."

She turned her head to one side and then to the other, enjoying the heavy swing of her hair; worked her shoulders back and forth in a luxurious movement that seemed to ripple through the rest of her body.

"But you will not deny that you desire me — " she questioned softly.

"I desire you," he answered, and now there was no music in his voice at all.

Esseilte's eyes were downcast, and still on her lips there played that little smile. Then she looked up, and he started as if she had touched him.

"I could ruin you, Drustan, but I am caught in the self-same snare." Her breathing faltered in a sudden catch of wonder. "Instead I will claim you for my own!"

Drustan closed his eyes, shaking his head.

"Esseilte, what are you doing?" I managed to speak at last. Outside the sailors' song mocked us.

> *"Sigh away, wind, wanton or mild —*
> *Sigh, Irish maid, you wild, lovely child!"*

"I do what I must, Branwen. Twice I have failed to kill him; I will never be able to do it now. But his life must be mine. No other choice is left to me." For a moment she looked at me, then her fierce gaze returned to the man.

"As Grainne claimed Diarmuid, I will claim you; as Deirdre claimed Naoisi, Drustan!" A pulse beat heavily in Esseilte's white throat, but Drustan stood stiff as stone.

"I don't understand."

"A geas of shame upon you if you deny me, Drustan. You will never know peace, you will never know rest, you will never know honor, not anywhere!"

"I have known the first two rarely enough in my life, Esseilte," he said with a ghost of his old self-mockery. "But surely I never will have them if I listen to you. Honor is all that is left to me."

"There is no honor for you if you refuse me! But together we will find glory; we will make a song that will never die!"

"Wait, both of you!" I cried. "Esseilte is not yet married. When we reach shore you must tell your king what has happened. There is no reason why she should not wed you in all honor, and all be well."

Drustan shook his head slowly. He was trembling now. "The alliance," he said at last. "Marc'h might still honor it without the marriage, but his lords would not. They hate me, and Marc'h has already suffered for favoring me above closer kin. He dares leave no weakness behind him when he goes back to Kerhaes. . . ."

"In Eriu it would be the same," Esseilte echoed him. "My

father told me, before we parted, how needful this bond of kinship with Britain is for him."

I stared at her. The queen had made me swear to make Drustan pay for the Morholt's death. Was this indeed how it must happen? Had Mairenn set a geas upon me to leave the casket unattended so that this could come to pass? *My fault! My fault!* Indecision held me mute as Esseilte turned back to Drustan again.

"Oh man of my heart, I am not asking you to carry me away as Diarmuid fled with Grainne. We will keep faith with our lords so far, that we will serve the needs of our nations in the sight of men. But the compulsion is upon you to serve me when we are alone! And you, Branwen—" The brightness of her eyes fixed me and I could not look away. "If the fault was yours, then you must pay for it by guarding us, for I will die surely if I do not have this man now!"

I stared at her. Was this truly what was required of me? The lamplight behind her made a radiance of her bright hair. She seemed to grow taller as I looked at her, blazing with beauty like a woman of the Sidhe.

And then it came to me that this service, also, I had sworn to her mother without qualification or questioning, and to Esseilte herself also, at Cíll Dara. Choices I had not known that I was making were all laying their own geas upon me now. I nodded slowly, and she smiled.

"Drustan . . . come to me . . ."

"Esseilte, I cannot, I must not! My lady, let me go!" His voice cracked in agony. Outside the tent a sailor's pipe struck up a dance tune. My pulse raced to the rhythm of clapping and the beat of bare feet upon the planks.

"Drustan of Léon, look at me!"

As if ensorcelled, he obeyed.

Esseilte loosened the pin from the brooch that held her mantle and let it drop, unhooked the clasps that held her gown and allowed it to fall, untied the drawstring of her smock and pulled it away. The skin of her breasts was like new milk; the nipples budded rose-pink at the touch of the cold air. Drustan stared and the white showed around his eyes like those of an over-driven stallion.

"Drustan, my hero, my beloved, come to me. . . ."

Esseilte's whisper stirred the still air. My final words of pro-test died unborn. It had gone too far. If I called for help now others would see her nakedness and both of them would be lost. It was too late; it had been too late from the moment they drank the potion. Only Drustan could have stopped it now, and he was moving stiffly toward her, staggering as the ship moved beneath him, but continuing on.

His hands closed on her bare shoulders. She lifted her head and his lips sought hers with the inevitable sureness of the incoming tide.

"Until death, Drustan," she murmured when his mouth lifted reluctantly at last.

"Until death." He sighed as he had sighed once in Temair, rendering his life into our hands. His hands caught in the shining masses of her hair.

And then a larger wave angled the deck beneath them, and the two of them, clinging too close for balance, fell together onto the bed. The swinging lamp sent a tangle of writhing shadows around the room.

Drustan had forgotten I was there, and if Esseilte remembered, she did not care. Gut twisting, I pushed through the door, stumbled to the side of the ship and hurled the empty flagon into the sea.

The wind harped in the rigging, and the timbers creaked to the gentle rocking of the sea. From the stern came laughter and a snatch of song. Only I was left alone.

Oh Esseilte, I thought, as I huddled in the doorway, trying not to hear when the first fury of their passion spent itself, and when they began the slow sweet exploration of each other's bodies once again, *Oh Esseilte, you have found your story at last, and what is left for me?*

But even as I raged against them for laying the burden of their safety upon me, for the first time in my life I tasted power, for I knew that their two lives lay within my hands.

Twelve

THE BELTANE QUEEN

The trees along the road from the Heyle were just coming into leaf, translucent red in the spring sunlight as if blood, not sap, flowed through their veins. Where the road dipped downward hyacinths and violets peeped from beneath the white splendor of the hedges of thorn. But when it breasted the ridges the wind blew all softness away, and as the sun sank behind us the air seemed to glow with the brilliance of the yellow broom.

We had landed at Porth Ia just at sunset the day before. That night we guested with a sweet-voiced woman whom men said was the daughter of the great Theodoric, a ship commander from the land of the Goths who had been one of Artor's generals. It had been too dark to see much of the country then, and we had been too tired even to admire the strange Roman fashion of the villa. But the morning sun had risen upon a new world.

Only one thing had not altered, and as Esseilte kicked her mare up beside mine, I knew what she was going to ask of me.

"Let it be, Esseilte." I kept my eyes on the pure line of the hill we were climbing. "To keep silence is sin enough, but at least it is a passive deception. . . ."

"That is all I am asking," she responded in a low voice. "Just be still, and let it happen. It will not matter if the king thinks you are shy, or afraid, just as long as he thinks you are his queen!"

Goaded finally beyond discretion, I turned on her. "Can you tell me that it is only a matter of lying like an image while the

man takes his pleasure? Esseilte, can you say that to me, *now*?"
It was not only what she knew, I realized suddenly. We were too
closely linked for me not to have sensed some of her ecstasy.
Was that another reason for my discomfort?

Color came and went in her cheeks and her gaze flew like a
homing dove to the head of the line, where Drustan sat his gray
stallion like the prince we now knew him to be. And as if she
had touched him, Drustan turned. For a moment the flow of
force between them was almost visible, for any who had eyes to
see. Then Gorwennol spoke to him, and he forced himself to
look away.

"And you had better learn to govern your eyes," I hissed at
her, "or it will not matter what lies we tell!"

"Marcus Cunomorus was bred in the ways of Rome" — she
turned back to me — "and the Romans require virginity in their
brides. If the king finds me no maiden there will be questions,
and then what use our lies? We must go all the way with the
deception, Branwen, or we should not attempt it at all —"

No one would ever care about *my* maidenhead, I thought bitterly. The only value it might have was to convince the King of
Kernow he was getting a virgin bride, so that the King of Eriu
would get his daughter's maiden-fee. Was I denying Esseilte or
myself if I refused to sacrifice it for her?

"Eriu was another lifetime," she went on. "I would flee with
Drustan now, as Grainne fled with Diarmait, as Deirdre went
with Naoisi, if his honor would allow it. But if I could constrain
him to desert his lord, how could I ever trust him to keep faith
with me?" A branch of broom clutched at her cloak and she
struck it angrily away.

I sighed. Had my consent to guard their secret committed me
also to this second, and more dangerous, deception? And could
any of us possibly imagine what it might mean to maintain such
a lie life-long?

"It cannot succeed, Esseilte," I said finally. "How could any
man ever mistake me for you?"

She tipped her head to one side like a bird, and laughed at
me. "Easily! We are the same in height and shape, and darkness
will disguise differences in feature and coloring. Drustan says
that even he sometimes confused us before he knew us well!"

I stared. It was true that we shared a family likeness, but
Esseilte was beautiful! We had come out from under the trees
again and the sunlight crowned her with gold.

"And the king does not know me at all," she went on. "He will see a woman in royal robes, Branwen. He will see what he expects to see!"

The leaders of our escort had disappeared over the top of the hill. A horn blared, and after a moment other horns, mellowed by distance, answered it. My pulse quickened.

"The Rock! Kerrek Los! There it is — we will be there soon!" came the shout from ahead.

"Branwen, I beg you, tell me you will do it! The wedding is set for tomorrow morning — who knows when we can talk privately again!"

My lips tightened, but were they holding back submission, or denial? My horse collected itself for the last push up the hill, and then we were on the crest, and saw below us the gray, tree-girt mass of rock rising from the glittering azure of the bay. Strangely, what I felt most in that moment was recognition.

Was it my mother's blood speaking in me? Abruptly I saw Esseilte's plea from a new perspective. The land lay open before me. What matter if the price was one night with its king?

"Very well," I said then.

Esseilte gripped my arm, and I pulled my gaze from the island to meet her eyes.

"My oath on it. I will take your place with the king. . . ."

Horns sounded again. Horsemen were galloping up the road beside the stream. Bright cloaks blew out behind them, and the westering sun struck sparks from ornaments of gold. In the lead was a man on a white stallion, who seemed somehow to focus all the glory of the day.

We drew rein to await them. I forced myself to breathe again. The leader rode with a supple mastery that denied the silver in his dark hair. Now I could see weathered features, sculpted by power. Drustan spurred down the hill to meet him; they clasped arms, then came toward us together, the younger man like a half-made copy of the elder, holding his gray half a pace behind.

But it had not needed that resemblance to tell me that this was Marc'h of Kernow.

"Benedictio Domini super vos —" The voice of the abbot carried easily above the murmur of the sea and the whispers of the crowd. Today the settlements ashore were raucous with Beltane festivity, but before ever the Christians built their oratory on the seaward side of the island, Kerrek Los had been sacred ground.

The gold thread on the abbot's cope glittered as the clouds that had covered the morning sky began to thin. But the king wore gold tissue from Byzantium, and in that sudden light he blazed like the sun. Esseilte's features were blurred behind her crimson veil. It was just as well. She had been as white and shaking that morning as if we were readying her for execution. Drustan, standing with the king's guard of honor, looked little better. And indeed, there was little joy for any of us three in this day.

"Beati omnes . . ." replied his acolytes. The first of them paced around the wedding party, swinging the great censer with a clashing of brass chains, and clouds of frankincense swirled upward. The sweet smoke caught at my lungs.

"Paulus Aurelianus is in fine form this morning," said the man behind me. I recognized Karasek of Nans Dreyn, who had been one of the envoys. "But it is a surprise to see him. I thought he was fixed in Léon—"

"He is indeed. This is a visit only, to settle some business of his family," said his companion. "No doubt the king will offer him a bishopric again, but I don't give much for his chances of persuading our Paulus. Better to be an independent abbot in Armorica than bishop in a High King's hall. Still, it is an honor . . ."

For whom, I wondered. The censer had been followed by two lads with tall candles, and another who asperged the circle with salted water. That done, the abbot lifted his hands above the couple who stood before him. There was intelligence in his thin face, and even a hint of humor, unexpected in a churchman.

"Deus, qui multimoda subsidiorum remedia fragilitati humanae beneficia confers et tribuis incrementum. . . ." Was marriage a remedy for human frailty? This wedding was more likely to compound a sin. "Sic temporibus priscis Ruth Moabitem benedixisti, sic in novissimis per apostolum tuum secunda matrimonia concessisti. . . ."

"Second marriage!" whispered a woman nearby. I turned my head to see. She was little and dark, and I remembered now that her name was Kew, from Dynas Ban. So the man standing next to her must be Lord Perran.

"But surely this is the third for the king—there was that woman from Kemper, and then poor Tryphyna! And this one is young enough to be his daughter—he ought to be ashamed!"

"He needs the alliance," murmured her husband.

"And to marry in May, too! It is ill-omened! Can winter woo summer and win?"

"My dear, you are mistaken. This is a marriage of British tin and Irish gold!"

I shivered despite the sunlight. It was true, and it was the only reason that Esseilte and Drustan were not halfway to Alba even now. But there was no way we could be faithful to all vows.

And now Esseilte and Marc'h were repeating those false promises — Marc'h in a firm voice, not knowing that even tonight he would be unwittingly forsworn; Esseilte so softly that I had to strain to hear her —

"Volo . . ." *I am willing.* . . .

Gulls circled overhead, mocking her words.

The priest bound their clasped hands with his stole and lifted them for all to see. And thus their joining was blessed and witnessed according to the forms of religion, and only three of us among all that multitude knew it for black perjury.

A wedding in the old way was made by the marriage feast and the formal bedding of the bride. They had set up trestles for feasting on the green slope on the landward side of the island, where trees climbed until the granite core thrust through. Sheltered by the summit, the air was mild, but colored awnings shielded the feasters, for the weather varied between intermittent sunlight and an occasional scattering of rain, as if the day could not decide whether to weep or to smile.

The first entertainment was the reading of the marriage treaty. Only the tierns — the chieftains — listened. I recognized Mevennus and Wydhyel, who had been among the envoys; the big man, Fragan Tawr; and a little gnarled man with a shock of pale hair whom they said was Withgy, the king's horsemaster. While the reading was going on they served us with loaves of white bread and red wine. Esseilte ate little, and I not much more, for the sun marched relentlessly across the sky, and I could not help but wonder what the night would bring.

The servers brought in pies of layered meats — pork and lamb and squab spiced with leeks and onions and smothered in thick cream. Across from me, Drustan and Gorwennol were talking with the churchman who had performed the ceremony.

"You do not seem distressed to be once more in civilized company!" Gorwennol laughed.

"Why should it distress me?" said the abbot mildly. "Any man is happy to revisit his homeland."

"But you left it for Léon . . ." said Drustan.

"Which is *your* homeland—" countered the churchman.

"Only by birth. Pompeius Regalis saw to it that I should have no real home," Drustan answered bitterly. "Does he trouble you?"

Paulus shrugged. "He has little call to. Léon has not yet recovered from the plague six years ago. There were villages where not one inhabitant survived. In my territory there are few folk except for my monks and me. Armorica is a land dedicated to God."

As if in ironic commentary, the servants took away the pies and began to pass dishes of baked suckling pig and slices of smoking venison.

"So you found the desert you were seeking when you refused a British bishopric," said Drustan. "When I was in Eriu, I heard Columba and Brendan arguing whether it was possible to achieve the kingdom of heaven without entirely leaving this world. You have made a hermitage in the wilderness, but still you are here, robed in silk and gold. When you go back to your solitudes, will they satisfy you?"

"Does your life satisfy *you*?" Paulus looked at Drustan narrowly. I thought he must be the only one of them all who had seen through Drustan's forced gaiety. "What prize is there worth pursuing, in this weary world?"

"I think that I have found one . . ." A kind of radiance shone suddenly through Drustan's pain. "It is called love."

The abbot shook his head. "The love of woman can only lead to sorrow."

"So they say." Drustan looked down at his clasped hands. "But perhaps my sorrow, nobly borne, will expiate my sin. For there is a joy when we are together that takes me out of this weary world as surely as any voyage to the Living Lands. . . ."

"Do you think so?" asked the churchman. "The world reaches out hot hands to drag both lover and saint from their ecstasies. But God is always waiting—human lovers are less enduring. I think that you have only begun to taste the pain. My son, I will pray for you. . . ."

I had wondered how Drustan would bear this day. Garbed in gray silk and silver, he looked more princely than I had ever seen him, and in an odd way, priestly. And that was not so fanciful, I realized, for in his words to the abbot there was the beginning of an answer to my question. Drustan had become the

priest of a cult whose goddess was Esseilte, and whose religion
was earthly love. It remained only to find an answer for her, and
for me.

Now the king's bards were making their contribution to the
entertainment with a series of marriage songs remarkable more
for policy than for inspiration. Yet I could sympathize with their
difficulty. If Esseilte had been cursed with bowlegs and a squint
they would still have called her beautiful. But who, hearing only
those platitudes, would guess that they were literally true?

Almost as difficult, I thought then, to do justice to the king. I
drew my veil half over my face to hide my staring and watched
him from across the table, knowing that our lives might depend
on reading him correctly. His movements compelled the eye, for
everything he did seemed for that moment to be the only thing of
importance in the world. It took me somewhat longer to realize
that this was an illusion, for at the same time as he was carefully
choosing the best bits of meat for his bride, Marc'h was also
listening to the conversations among his lords. I had heard they
called him the Horse King, which was the British meaning of his
name. But his occasional comments were like the subtle twitch
of a rein by which the charioteer keeps a difficult team pulling in
harmony.

Tonight, I thought, there would be no distractions. Tonight all
his attention would be directed toward me. . . .

"Drustan! Let Drustan sing for us!" It was a woman's voice,
honeyed with memory. "There is no one who touches an instrument so sweetly as he!"

Esseilte straightened, looking from the lady to Drustan, who
sat on the other side of the king. Abruptly I was as certain as she
was that the woman had been Drustan's mistress in the days
before he came to Eriu.

But Drustan was shaking his head. "I am sadly out of practice—I would do the queen no honor today!"

"Still, I would hear you!" Esseilte's eyes flashed beneath her
veil. "Show them the music you taught me."

He colored, then gathered himself to meet her challenge. A
servant brought his harp and he bent over it, testing the harmony of the strings. I wondered suddenly if Marc'h, who had
been so aware of everything else that was going on, had noticed
Drustan's suppressed tension today?

A ripple of sound from the harp silenced the murmur of conversation. Drustan waited a moment, then began to sing. It was

a praise-poem, remarkable less for its words than for the painful sweetness with which he sang it, but the final verse struck home —

> *"Happier than warrior whose foe lies sore stricken,*
> *Happier than saint who sees heaven's doors open,*
> *Happier than king with companions rejoicing,*
> * Is the man who is matched with the queen in love's striving."*

He finished, and only now did he dare to look at Esseilte, and then only for a moment, but his breathing had quickened. No one seemed to notice, or if they did, perhaps they thought it only a harper's pleasure at the finish of a fine song. And fine it had been, with the beauty that hovers on the sword-edge of pain. Only the woman who had first called for Drustan to play was frowning.

King Marc'h took the wristlet of gold from his arm and held it out to the harper, smiling as a man smiles at the triumph of his favorite son.

Westward the dying sun set the banks of cloud blazing like the Beltane fires that flowered on the hillsides. Seen through the silk of Esseilte's wedding veil they glowed crimson, and the deepening blue overhead shone purple as the cloak of a king. The bridal litter lurched as the bearers started across the causeway. I pulled shut the curtains of the litter and adjusted the hawthorn wreath that held the veil over my face and hair. Drustan's gray curvetted just ahead. He had taken Esseilte up behind him with my mantle wrapped around her. I saw her eyes glittering with excitement as she turned to look back at me.

They said that the king had gone on to Lys Hornek where he was lodging, and Esseilte and I had thought it best to change clothes on the island, for there was no telling whether we would have the privacy to do so once we reached the fortress. The pace of the bearers steadied as they splashed through the shallow water and I leaned back against the cushions, breathing deeply to steady the beating of my heart.

The women who followed were singing, a sweet melody that set the skin prickling on my arms, though I could not say why.

> *"When wood and meadow are clothed in green,*
> *When fires like flowers on the hills are seen,*
> *Then shall we welcome the Beltane Queen!"*

The men added their voices to the chorus, deep voices echoing across the whisper of the waves.

"Here we come bringing the Beltane Bride,
Among the leaves of sweet springtide
Blessed the lord who is laid by her side!"

Now the men sang alone, and the litter jerked as we started up the slope of the shore. Darkness was drawing a purple cloak across the sky, jeweled already by the first stars.

"Hawthorn in hedges is blooming now,
Bright is the blossom that blows on the bough,
White is the light of the radiant brow."

Again all joined in the chorus, and then the women continued,

"She who beareth the hawthorn crown,
Weareth her glory as a bright gown,
Like beams of sunlight streaming down."

I was shaking, but it was not cold that made me tremble. Did the singers know the meaning of their song? I wanted to cry out, *This is sacrilege, I am not the queen!*, but fear held me still.

Excitement pulsed as we swung onto the road. My bearers moved to the music, and the procession became a dance. Every houseplace was garlanded with green.

"He who beareth the rod of might,
Weareth a mantle that's made of light,
Her lord and her lover by day and by night!"

We had gone perhaps halfway around the bay when hoofbeats drummed suddenly. The litter lurched to a stop amid screams and laughter. Torches flowered from shadow; a white stallion reared and whinnied his challenge to the world. My escort scattered as horsemen clattered past, ringing me with fire.

"Fire on the hilltop, fire on the stone,
By these signs the hour of their union is known,
When king shall lay claim to the queen as his own."

The white stallion shouldered up against the litter, huge in the torchlight, and the man who rode him towered like a god. Unwilled, my fingers loosened their grip upon the shafts.

It was not to be a simple wedding night in the fortress, then. Tales half-heard and half-remembered fluttered through my memory. But the British had been Christians longer than the folk of Eriu. How could I have known that the King of Kernow would follow the old ways when it came time to bed his bride?

For a moment the stallion danced sideways. The curtain was ripped away, and the rider reached in. His hands closed on my arms and he hauled me up onto the horse before him. I felt the beast gather himself beneath us as the king pulled me hard against his chest, his arm like a band of iron. I could feel his breathing, and the heat of his body, and gasped, as if I had touched fire. Then we were leaping down the road with the torchbearers streaming in a river of flame behind us.

> *"When midnight blazes like the sun,*
> *When a river from out of the rock has run,*
> *Then lord and his lady and land are all one!"*

Faintly, I heard the ending of the song.

"I am sorry. I hope you have not been too uncomfortable. We are almost there now . . ."

It was the first thing the king had said to me. At the beginning the ride had been too wild, and after that perhaps he feared my answer. I was angry and afraid, but not for the reasons he must suppose. Nor for the reasons I had expected. It was the power in the man himself that frightened me, or perhaps it was my own response to it that made me tremble. My awareness of him was so acute it was almost pain, as if I had lost my skin.

He was waiting for my answer, but I found it hard to breathe. Mute, I shook my head, and his arm tightened around me once more.

Tall stones seemed to leap out of the darkness as the torches neared them — two menhirs stood like sentinels before us. My skin prickled as we passed between them. The king pulled his cloak more closely around me, but it was not cold that sent the tremors through me. Behind lay rolling countryside, still and dark beneath a sky sown with stars like daisies in a field. Ahead the torchbearers were circling. Where they passed, I saw a ring of stones.

"I had you brought to the Heyle because this is the oldest part of my kingdom," said Marc'h, reining in. "This is the far headland that the Greeks called Belerion when they came to the Rock to trade for tin. But Penwith was ancient even then. The Old Ones worked mightily with stone. This is one of their sacred places. . . ."

"Yes," I murmured. "They dwelt also in Eriu. Perhaps Drustan has told you how the dragon-power flowed through him at the Brugh na Boinne." The circle before us might not have been impressive by daylight, for the stones were not even man-high, but on Beltane Eve I could feel its power.

"The High King of Logres is called the Pendragon, did you know?" he asked me then. "The Romans named this isle Britannia, after the Lady whom we call Brigantia and who is known as Brigid in Eriu, but Logres is the true name, the hidden name of the land. . . ."

Nineteen warriors now stood guard with their torches, one with his back to each stone. The king slid off the stallion and pulled me down into his arms. The horsemaster, Withgy, came to lead the stallion away, and Marc'h carried me inside.

Within the circle the bracken had been cut away so that grass could grow. In the center the king paused a moment, then, very carefully, he laid me down with my head toward the direction from which we had come. Above me the stars wrote their ancient wisdom across the sky. The new moon was already high. My pulse was fluttering like that of a frightened bird. The king sat back on his heels, his silhouette dark against the torchlight. His nearness took my breath away though he was only touching my hand.

"Do not be afraid. I will not hurt you. . . . Lie still, and let the peace of the place ease you." His eyes lifted and unfocused, as if he could see across the miles to the Rock and the bay from which we had come.

I could see the steady rise and fall of his chest, and tried to match my own breathing to his. I remembered how I had sensed the power in the Brugh, and sought to extend my awareness outward to the stones. I must have started then, for his gaze came instantly back to me.

"What is it?"

"The stones are shining . . ." I whispered. "It is not the torchlight. The stones themselves have a golden glow!"

The king's grip on my hand tightened. "You can see that? I hoped, but did not dare expect it — but they say that the Queen of Eriu is a sorceress. Did she teach you her skills?"

I nodded, for that much at least was true, and saw his sudden smile.

"Then perhaps I have found my queen at last! They will have told you that May is unlucky for marriages, but not for the Great Marriage. That is why I brought you here, for the wolves are gathering to devour us, and how can we resist them unless the gods themselves empower the land?" His face flushed, and I realized that here was the passion that drove him as Drustan was driven by the love he had spoken of that afternoon.

"But the ceremony this morning—" I began.

"In His own place I honor the Christian God, but I will worship every deity men ever gave a name to if they will help me to save my people. And this is the most ancient of magics by which a king may bind himself to his land. I need a child from you, my queen. . . ." He held his hand above my womb, and as if he had touched me, my body yearned for his.

"The cycle of sovereignty must be fulfilled," Marc'h continued softly. "Artor betrayed his own oaths to the Lady, and his son nearly destroyed Logres. He rules now in the hidden realm, and I in the kingdom of men, but there is no prince to come after me. I am no longer young—when I pass in my turn, who will defend the land?"

Perhaps what he said was true. My mind remembered that he was of an age with Diarmait, but my flesh felt the force in him, and my breath stopped as he touched me again.

"I have reigned in Britain since I was twenty years old, and in Armorica as well. But always there has been something lacking—" he exclaimed. "Surely more than Christian prayer is needful, if we are to hold against the barbarian! The Saxons are quiet now, but in time they will grow hungry once more. Britannia is ruled by half a hundred warring princes, and in Gaul the Franks nibble at the edges of Armorica. When will we have a Wor-Tiern—a High King, again? I cannot build a kingdom unless I am blessed by the Lady of the Land. I will not ask your forgiveness for forcing this upon you, for I think you can match me, my lady."

And what, I wondered then, did this magic do for the queen?

He brought my hand to his lips, turned it, and kissed the palm. The touch raced through my flesh like fire. My nipples began to tingle; I felt an unfamiliar throbbing between my thighs. Then he reached to undo my girdle and the shoulder clasps that held my gown and lifted the heavy silk away. The shift beneath it was of fine linen, and this he ripped so that I lay naked before him.

"You are very beautiful, my queen," his voice softened with another kind of passion. "Already I feel the power in me rising to serve you." He unfastened the great brooch that held his mantle, let fall sword and swordbelt, and then stripped off tunic and undertunic. His torso was lean, all muscle and bone, the white skin mottled here and there with old scars. Arms and shoulders showed the peculiar uneven development of the horseman who fights with sword and shield — sword arm knotted with muscle and pectoral prominent, while the shield arm was braced by a wedge of muscle between shoulder and back. He loosened the lacings that held his braes, stepped out of them, and stood before me as naked as I. Only then did he bend to lift back my veil.

I felt my eyes widen, realizing that there was more than one reason they called Marc'h the Horse King. The meaning behind all the poets' phrases became suddenly clear — the rod which was given to a king at his crowning, the revitalizing Spear of Lugh. He stretched himself out beside me, and I began to tremble.

As Marc'h began to touch me the verses of the marriage song rang once more in memory. Almost immediately I understood that this man handled a woman's body with absolute authority that was utterly unlike the clumsy pawings of the lads at Temair who had thought the Morholt's bastard daughter would be easy game. His fingers traced the outline of my lips and they parted, stroked down my throat to cup first one breast, then the other, shaping them to throbbing awareness. My nipples yearned for him to touch them.

I should not have been surprised. This was a man who had bedded two brides already, in addition to the many other women who were available to a king. Perhaps it would not be so painful, despite his size.

The king's lips tasted mine, then brushed downward where his hands had been. His tongue circled first one nipple, then the other, teasing, tasting until they hardened, throbbing. His mouth closed upon one while his fingers pinched the other, kneading, sucking, until I moaned. Almost instantly he lifted and his mouth claimed mine, hard, tongue thrusting as his fingers slipped suddenly between my thighs.

He slid his fingers gently across the secret softness there, then pressed harder, parting the petals, like a man searching through the moss for a hidden spring. I felt the first welling of those sacred waters as if I were melting, and understood why the Lady of the Land was worshipped at Her holy wells. My mouth opened beneath Marc'h's as my thighs opened to his hands. The power of motion had left my limbs, all awareness draining toward the sweetness he was awakening between my thighs.

Then the king's body covered me. I felt his weight, his hard

rod following the path his hands had blazed; he gripped my hips
and thrust suddenly and I was pierced by Lugh's burning spear.
I cried out, but almost immediately the fire was quenched in the
cauldron and I trembled to the first rush of power. I tried to pull
him against me, wanting more, but he held me still.

"Not yet —" His voice was harsh, and I saw the twitch of rigid
muscles as he raised himself to look down at me. "Don't move,
my lady, or we will achieve no more than any man and maid can
do. I think you are capable of something greater. It has been
generations since this land had such a queen! Will you try?"

I stared up at him. "What must I do?"

"Lie as if you were sinking into the earth beneath you, as if
you were part of it, and tell me what you feel."

My body had become one organ, wanting him. With an effort
I shifted my awareness outward, letting it sink deeper, deep — I
began to feel a pressure, like a current in the sea, flowing in the
same direction I lay.

"Something is moving —" I whispered, searching for words.
"From feet to head, from feet to head and on . . ."

"The power is moving!" he answered exultantly. "Let it flow
through you — let it go!"

The warmth where we were joined had become a fire. I trembled as it moved upward, setting new fires in my belly and beneath my ribs. It throbbed in my breast and I felt my spirit rush
outward to encompass his, and I knew then it was this, not our
bodies' joining, that would bind me to him.

"Brigantia!" He sank down upon me, legs twined, breast
pressing mine, his head coming to rest against the tangle of my
hair. No space now between us — we were a single body. We
breathed one breath, and I felt the power rush upward once
more to flutter in my throat.

"My beloved," I whispered, wondering if one could die of this
delight, "my king. . . ."

He drew a trembling breath, struggling for mastery, and lifted
his head a little. There were tears in his eyes, and I reached up
with one finger to wipe them away.

"Swear to me," he whispered, "swear that you will be queen
. . . in spirit as well as body . . . that you will spend your life for
the land!"

Long experience had given him greater control over his physical responses than I had of mine, but I sensed that his desire
was greater also, and wondered at the overriding passion that

compelled him to delay the pleasure for which I felt his body clamoring.

I hold the truth of you now, Marc'h of Kernow, clasped between my two thighs, I thought then, *and in a moment I will understand. . . .* I found a voice to answer him.

"I swear. . . ."

As if the words had broken some barrier, the glow pulsed to my forehead, throbbing just where I had received the kiss of initiation from the queen. Immediately my awareness sharpened. The air around us glowed like the clouds at sunset, and light rayed out from our joined bodies to each of the shining stones. I understood then that this was the awakening to power that Mairenn had promised me.

Marc'h trembled and clung to me, but I felt the power filling my body until I was like a vessel that must brim over or explode.

He groaned and sought my lips again like a man seeking water in a thirsty land, and at that touch, the power burst free from the crown of my head, and I became part of a river of light that flowed onward through distances beyond my imagining.

"Ah. . . ." Very gently, the king began to move in me, and the river brightened. "Reach out and touch the Kerrek," he whispered, and instantly I was there, tapping into the deep power of that water-washed granite core. "Now, the serpent stone!" For this I had no image, but awareness sped onward past three circles to focus in a delicately balanced tier of stone.

"Farther! Find the shrine on the moor, and then the humped hills—" The distance grew greater, but the king's strokes were becoming more powerful, and each time he thrust, the energy that carried me onward grew. Now I scarcely heard his words. The current rushed strongly toward a tor that reared up from surrounding marshes. Below it I found the balancing purity of a holy well. But still I was moving, like a river flooding toward the sea, pouring into a mighty circle of stones.

Unknowing, I had begun to move in harmony with the man within me. Ever more swiftly our bodies met and parted in the oldest dance, ourselves being also the music. Our hearts drummed out the rhythm of life. Sensation had long ceased to be localized; every nerve tingled, every muscle strained in ecstasy. And all that force funneled through me along the line to the stone circle, where it crossed other currents—

And then the king cried out, the great shout of a spirit transcending mortality. Like lightning striking a standing stone, his life-force drove through me, burst into the nexus of currents in the stone circle and fountained, flowing outward to every end of the land. And as the land received, it responded, sending back through my convulsing body a golden wash of pure power.

If anything had blocked it, both of us would have been consumed, but for that moment my flesh was the soil, my blood the rivers that nourished it, my breath the wind, and the life within me one with the life of everything that moved or grew. . . .

I had touched the Goddess before as water and as fire. Now I knew Her as the land itself. I was Logres; I was Brigantia. She filled and fulfilled me until even the world could no longer contain my spirit, and I knew union, not with the man, but with a white radiance that was more than king or queen or goddess or god.

The glory slowly drained away. I became aware that I was a mortal woman holding a mortal man close-clasped within her arms. My whole body ached with a sweet languor. The stars were writing a new inscription in the heavens, and the moon sank toward the western sea.

"Tiernissa — Lady and Queen . . ." he whispered into the tangle of my hair. "Do you know how great a gift you have given me today?"

I sighed, for he had named me more truly than perhaps he ever would again.

I am the Lady of the Land . . .

I could return Esseilte's wedding garments, but never could I give her the fullness of what had happened here.

No matter how men might honor her, it was my maiden blood that had mingled with this sacred soil. The hawthorn crown was mine. In the only sense that really mattered, the ritual that Marc'h had chosen to consummate his marriage had made me queen of the hidden kingdom that was the soul of Kernow.

Thirteen

THE HIDDEN REALM

In the week that followed Beltane, the king and his household
began a leisurely progress northward, guesting with the prin-
cipal families along the way. Thus we came presently to Dynas
Ban, a ditched and palisaded stronghold set on an eminence near
the headwaters of the river Fal. Before ever the Romans came to
this land the mach-tierns of Dumnonia had lived there, and now
that they were gone, the British princes had fortified it again.
Despite the grimness of the place, Lord Perran and his wife Kew
did their best to make us welcome. Small shame to them if our
stay was soured by undercurrents of emotion they could not understand.

Who among us did understand? Not Esseilte, whose tongue
had grown sharper as the days went by; or Drustan, whose gaze
moved unhappily between her and the king; not Marc'h himself,
whose smile was fading as the woman with whom he thought he
had shared the sacred marriage remained cold in his bed by
night and distantly courteous by day. And certainly not I, who
for one night had dwelt in the Land of the Blessed to which I
might never return.

We rode out onto the moor south of the fortress in the morning. Banked clouds in the west promised rain, but meat was
needed for the table, and perhaps Marc'h thought that exercise
in the open would ease the strain. And indeed I felt my spirit
open to the great arch of sky above me, gray though it might be.
I gazed around me with delight, lowering the barriers with

which I had tried to protect myself from human emotion, allowing my eyes to see the moor with the clarity of vision I had
learned on Beltane Eve.

This was another country from the friendly landscape of field
and pasture that surrounded the fortress. Here, earth's granite
bones poked through the thin soil in rocky tors and outcroppings
of stone. The red-stemmed heather and thorny tangles of the
furze grew sparsely over the scars where miners had streamed
for tin, or formed a mat that caught at the horses' fetlocks as we
passed, setting pale lavender bells nodding. In this expanse of
gray and garnet and brown the yellow flowers of gorse flickered
like guttering candle flames.

The king rode ahead with the hounds playing before him like
porpoises about a ship's prow. I reined in a little, watching his
easy grace in the saddle, feeling the movement of his body as if it
were my own. The eternal wind fluttered the folds of his red
cloak and blew back his dark hair. I remembered the silky feel of
that hair beneath my fingers and shivered, gripping the reins.

Since Beltane I had struggled also with an expanded physical
awareness, not only of the king's body, but of my own. The wind
touched my face like a lover; I was acutely aware of the movement of the horse between my thighs. As if I had been gifted
with a shapeshifter's spell I listened to my body, and could not
tell if its strangeness came from my new womanhood, or the
power I had channeled, or whether there might be some other
cause.

"Do you desire him?" The voice froze the dark currents of my
abstraction into a pattern I had not wanted to see. I turned to
meet Esseilte's eyes, as gray this morning as the stormy sky, and
as cold.

"Yes," I answered steadily. In all my protests against her plan
I had never considered the most telling — that the King of Kernow might be a man I could love. "Does it matter?"

"It might." She was watching me with a warrior's intentness,
and I stared at her, uncomprehending. We had hardly spoken
since Beltane — with people always around us, conversation was
of necessity superficial, but there had been a time when we had
known each other's thoughts without speaking. When had that
changed?

When Esseilte laid the bonds of love upon Drustan . . . came the
silent answer. *When you were carried off by the king.* . . .

Ahead, Perran was arguing with his huntsman while Marc'h

and Drustan added their comments, laughing. But Esseilte and I had fallen behind the others, and the wind swirled around us as if to cut us off from the world.

"I will not betray you," I said then, beginning to understand.

"Will you not? Love makes people do strange things." She shuddered suddenly. "*I* could not kill Drustan!" Her gaze sought him as mine had followed the king. The argument appeared to have been decided, and the main party began to move again. I nudged my mare to follow, but Esseilte blocked my way.

"Did you like the weight of a man's head against your breast? Did you like the touch of his hand between your thighs? Will you forgo such play forever, now that you know how sweet it can be?" She was trembling visibly now. Her hair, curling fiercely in that moist air, escaped from its braids in a wild cloud.

I stared at her. *She* had not been able to give up Drustan.

"If it *was* love! If that old man could teach anyone passion!" she added. I stiffened, but the undammed torrent of her words rushed on.

"Now I begin to wonder about your protests," she hissed. "Perhaps you always planned to reveal the whole deception! Do not expect me to believe that you have not thought of it! Why should you lie alone when you could be queen?"

"Because I swore an oath to you!" I exclaimed, stung into answering passion by awareness of how persistent that very temptation had been. But I had loved Esseilte long before I ever saw Marc'h of Kernow. I had thought that she loved me too. . . .

"And what will that oath be worth if you should prove to be with child?" Esseilte brought her horse up close to mine. The wind howled about us, then sank again. "Are you? Has that man planted his seed in you?"

"It is too soon —" I shook my head, trying to dash the quick tears away. But they would not stop, for in the deep places of my soul I had dreamed of this too. "In Blessed Brigid's name, I do not know!"

"Then pray that you are barren, my cousin," Esseilte said softly. "For I will have no child born to challenge Drustan's right to Kernow!" Her features were like stone, her eyes staring. The woman who faced me was not anyone I knew.

"That is as the Lady wills —" I began, but she laughed.

"Do you take me for a fool? Did you think I would not find

the key to that chest of herbs my mother gave you, or know how
to read her spells? I can brew up a tea as well as you!"

Appalled, I remembered the recipe Queen Mairenn had
showed me, to be used if Esseilte seemed likely to bear her lord
too many babes too soon. I began to shake my head once more.

From ahead of us came shouting. The heather pulsed as the
dogs dashed after some invisible prey. But in a moment they
retreated, yelping. Leaves thrashed as something fled toward us,
then my horse reared. As the thing — a hare — darted from between its feet, I had a vague impression of whiteness, as though
it had not yet lost its winter coloring. For a moment it paused,
and I caught the gleam of burning eyes. Then the hare disappeared. Suddenly there was evil in the wind's shrill song.

"And when we return, you will drink that potion, Branwen."
Esseilte nodded compulsively. "Then we will know!" I had seen
just such a look on the face of Queen Mairenn, when she called
down vengeance upon the Morholt's murderer.

"I will not!" My heart was hammering like the horses' hooves.
I blinked, trying to see through the patches of darkness that
swirled around me.

The riders were turning back toward us. "Did you see the
beast?" they called. "It's an evil omen — we're turning back —
we'll get nothing today!"

Esseilte seized my arm. "Ill-omened for you if you try to betray me!" Her eyes burned like those of the demon-hare.

"Never —" My horse squealed and leaped forward as I jerked
my arm away. Esseilte called out, but I could not hear her. I
leaned forward, slapping the mare's neck with the reins, not caring where she bore me as long as it was away!

Thunder clashed overhead and the sky crashed around me. My
mare came to a halt, sides heaving, and I pulled my cloak over
my head, peering through the swirling veils of rain. I could not
see Esseilte. I could not see any human soul. The world had
contracted to this wilderness of wind and water. I knew neither
how long we had run, nor how far we had come.

Had Esseilte gone mad, or had I?

Rain roared on rock; thought dissolved in anguish. The horse
was moving again. A lightning flash brought a moment's bitter
clarity — a rock-strewn slope and Esseilte's stony eyes. . . .

Madness was better.

Wind tugged my cloak from strengthless fingers — *I am*

wind. . . . Water soaked hair and gown, ran into my open mouth — *I am water.* . . . Wind and water swept downward, following the rivulets that ran off stone into rich grass, vivid green even by stormlight, patched with hummocks. The horse stepped forward. Her hooves sank suddenly into that green ground, she lurched, whinnied anxiously, then heaved convulsively and fell.

I am earth. . . . The rich tang of peat, soft sphagnum, and the delicate foliage of butterwort and gentian. Air sucked in lifted me; exhaled, let me sink further into that welcoming embrace. *I am Logres . . . I am the land.* . . .

Nearby something was struggling — that was wrong. Softness . . . I wanted softness and sleep. . . . Something struck my shoulder — pain focused my gaze on the mare's head, tossing desperately as she fought the bog. Already she was mired to the belly, and every heave only worked her deeper in.

If I do not move, the bog will swallow me too.

The mare dropped her muzzle into the muck and lay for a moment, wheezing as she sucked in air. Then she lifted her head, groaning, and began to fight again. Pity stirred in me at that sound, and with it an awareness that I was very cold. Brown furze edged the green. I turned and rolled toward it. The bog's slick fingers clutched at my garments. The cloak was left behind as I rolled again.

Furze scratched my outthrust arm. My fingers closed on sharpness, pulled, and felt something that did not yield. The stench of the dark water rolled over me — something worse than bog — dank, rotten, slimy even to smell. Clinging to my tenuous support, I looked back.

Only the mare's head still showed. But rising behind it was something else — a horse-shape distorted into madness by poking bone and sagging, scaly skin. Bulging eyes burned with the demon-hare's fire. Fanged jaws gaped and the stench became stupefying. They snapped shut on the mare's neck. There was one scream, then snaky limbs drew the horse down.

I dug my fingers into the thorny stems of the furze and pulled the rest of my body onto solid ground. The fury of the rain had lessened, but the light was fading. Long tremors shook my body. In this moment of respite I knew that I must find shelter or die, and perhaps the poor mare had bequeathed me her valiant spirit, for now my body was as determined to survive as it had been to give up before.

I clambered higher and staggered to my feet, stripping off the hampering remains of garments that no longer offered any protection. For a moment light seemed to glimmer ahead of me. Was it a dwelling, or only a break in the clouds? I stumbled toward it across the uneven ground, and found myself on a rising slope. Now the light was to my left. Again I moved forward, shivering as the wind chilled wet skin. And once more the light shifted and I followed it. Awareness diminished to the bare consciousness of movement. The struggle was without plan or purpose, but it kept the blood flowing in my veins.

And then I fetched up suddenly against a stone. For a moment I had thought it was a man, for it was a little more than my height, and broad in proportion. I put my arms around it as I tried to catch my breath, grateful for the support. As my hands learned its contours I realized it was a menhir; that knowledge triggered deeper senses, and I became aware of a pulse of power within.

As I had learned to tap into the current in the stone circle, I reached inward. The power intensified—

"Is it the time?"

Shocked, I let go, breaking the contact, for the words had come from inside the stone. I looked at it carefully, but it seemed as solidly rooted as before. Gingerly, I touched it again, and was aware of the presence, more alive than it had been before, not evil, but intensely *other*.

It is not time, be at rest. I need shelter. Do you know the way? I projected clearly. Perhaps this was more of my madness, but it seemed to me that an answer came—

"Follow the road. . . ."

In the stone circle, I had seen the land mapped out in lines of light. Now I strained for that kind of vision again, and in the failing daylight, saw the stone I held grow luminous, and a faint pathway beyond it.

It was clearly no human road, for it went straight over all obstacles. But as the hidden sun gave up its last illumination, something loomed out of the mists like a doorway into night.

It was a barrow, and I knew that there was scarcely a man of this land or my own who would not prefer to die on the open moor rather than to enter here. But the capstone seemed solid, and a place that had housed the ancient dead for so many centuries might well prove secure enough to shelter me from the storm.

"O ye people of the earth, in the name of the Mother and the

Bride I claim refuge!" I murmured, and then, with my last strength, crawled inside.

As the numbness left my limbs, I became aware of the throbbing of wrenched muscles and scratched skin, and a deep, regular ache in my belly that curled me into a whimpering ball. I do not know if I slept then, or lay tranced, or in delirium, or if what seemed to happen after that was the same as the truth of waking day.

The agony was gone.

The massive sides and great capstone of the barrow shone with inner light, as the heated rocks in the sweathouse glow. The patterned rings and spirals pecked into the stone blazed in lines of fire. Wondering, I reached out and with the tip of one finger touched the ridged rock. My skin began to tingle. Unthinking, I traced the ridge halfway around the edge of the circle. At the central division it doubled in on itself; I started to pull back, and found that I could not take my hand away. Faster and faster my finger moved inward, around and back and around again until it found the cup mark within, plunged toward the center—

—And passed through.

I stood in a lofty hall of stone.

"She is come! She is come! At last the queen has come!" sweet voices called from the spaces around me. Horns' mellow music echoed from the walls.

With folk fair as dream the great hall was filling. Like the stones of their dwelling, they shone from within. Calling and laughing, they clustered around me. I had never had such a welcome as they gave me in that hall.

My rags they replaced with a gown of green linen, spun softer than silk, clasped with brooches of gold. With a cloak of fine fox furs they weighted my shoulders. Over my wrists, they slipped ridged golden armlets, set on my breast a broad shining crescent, and a wreath of white hawthorn settled on my brow. Then they led me, rejoicing, toward a high seat of honor that was spread with the softness of a red stag's hide. Bone flutes and small bow-harps struck up a wild music.

"Tiernissa hail! The queen of the sun-folk has come here among us—come see, come see, come hither and see her!"

Like the sound of a tree full of birds came their calling. Red-gold the hair of some, their skin swan-white and shining; earth-dark locks on others, with eyes like glowing coals. And some of them shone in bright-chequered garments, and others were wrapped in fine furs and worked leather; they glittered in ornaments of gold and fine silver, they were weighted with necklets of jet and of amber. But each one I saw bore the same stamp of beauty; in each limb the same lightness, in each eye the same pale fire.

"The sun-folk forget us!" cried some. "Why give her honor?"

"She will speak to them for us," the others replied.

"We have been here from before the beginning; through the centuries' cycles still we will remain! Men live on the land, but they never can own it until they are one with earth's spirit again!"

More came, and more — the hall rippled with color, the air throbbed with singing and shimmered with laughter. Some of the songs were like those of my people, others far older. They sang of ancient chieftains, and of wars and of conquests, of the hunting of monsters through forests of darkness. Songs of Belerion, tales of the Greek tin-traders borne hither by biremes with swelling purple sails. And there were chants pounded out by a hammer, spell songs of the wise ones who set up the standing stones. Visioned forth by the music, time's river swirled around me; past and present commingled in a single endless stream.

Then the music deepened. Drums set a steady beat, feet stamped out the time, rock shook to the tread, air pulsed rhythmically. The fair folk drew away; in the wall I saw a door. Moonlight was flooding through, music louder than before vibrated through flesh and bone, my heart pounded painfully. A sharp shape blocked the light, at once like a man, like a stag, like a stallion. He called to me —

"The mother moon rides fair and high — the moor is all abloom with May, come dance the Dance of Life with Me and bless the hours before the Day!"

"The Bucca, the Bucca! Behold the Lord! With harp and drum and flutesong greet Him, and strike up the Dance!" came the answering cry. "The Dance! The Dance! To the moor let us fly!" Suddenly all that throng was swirling like leaves caught by the breeze around the hall, sweeping me up with them as they poured through the open door.

And there on the threshold the Bucca was waiting. His wild-maned head and sleek loins were wreathed with convolvulus and tormentil spiked with purple heather and sprays of golden broom. Ivy twined the sweep of his great horns. Heavily muscled He seemed, with the pungent scent of a healthy animal, and yet His face looked like the face of the King.

"Come dance the Dance of Life with Me, Lady of Kernow—" he repeated. "For I am your Lover." He smiled, and joy fountained through me, nor did I hang back when his strong arm circled my waist and we joined the rush and the tumble as the fair folk streamed onto the moor.

The wasteland through which I had wandered was remade by moonlight. From leaf and stem came the glitter of crystal, pool and rill shone silver where they caught the moon's cool rays. And now that still splendor was glimmering, warming, for the fair folk trailed radiance wherever they passed. Each bunch of heather took life from their touching, until all the white world was a-shimmer with joy. From every living thing a form of light unfolded, spread glistening wings, became part of the dance.

The Bucca bore me into the circle. Around and around we whirled, and in and out again. Power flowed as it had when Marc'h and I lay together. Once more I saw light veining the landscape. Awareness expanded outward to encompass the world.

The moon approached her zenith. The Dance burst outward in a fountain of light, and when all the bright sparks settled, more of the fair folk were coming out of the hill. They bore drinking horns that were bound round with silver, and great golden platters heaped high with fragrant food. The Bucca sat me down upon a stone hollowed out like a high seat and took His place beside me. The tray of cakes came round to us, and I stretched out my hand.

"Wait—" said my companion. He grasped my wrist so that I could not touch the food. "If you eat, you will never return to the world of men. . . ."

"I will become one of you?" I asked. He nodded, still holding my hand. I looked at the beauty around me. Here was neither pain nor labor. Here was no Esseilte, with her hateful, hurtful words.

"Why are you warning me?" I asked then, remembering old Messach's tales. "I thought the folk of the Otherworld tried to tempt mortals into their realm!"

"Because of who you are, because of what you have become—because you can walk in both worlds. Artor and Morgaine rule now in the Blessed Isle over those spirits who wait to come again, but the living lands must have a Sovereign. If you return, you can speak for us in the world of men."

"I do not understand—are not you the King?"

He laughed, horns gleaming in starlight. "I am Lord of this Land and yet no King of Men, though at times the King bears My power. When the Sovereign falls, the child of light must take up the Crown; the Sovereign passes to the lands beyond to become King of Shadows; in each generation the Cauldron of Renewal must be recovered so that the holy child may be reborn. You are the Cauldron who must bear the Crown."

This, then, was the fruit of my initiation in the circle of stones. And the fair folk needed the link between the worlds as much as did the King. I remembered how Marc'h had wept in my arms. I had thought that I must sit at his side to be his Queen. But perhaps it was not so.

"You will not be alone," the Bucca added then. "We are with you in sunlight and moonlight, in falling water and growing grass, if you remember to open your eyes and see . . ."

I thought of Esseilte, forsaking all other goods as she struggled to tryst with her lover, and pitied her.

"I will go back." I let the faerie food go by.

The moon stood still overhead. All the sounds of the night became a single chord. Moonlight poured down and all the glowing lines of light across the landscape flowed into the circle and fountained upward to join in one column of radiance.

"Earth and Heaven are united." Did the Horned One speak to my ears or to my heart? *"The Lady comes. . . ."*

The Light shimmered into rainbow rays of pale fire that shaped a woman's form. The Bucca had risen, arms lifting to salute Her, whose Lover He was in this world, as His power had filled my lover in the world of men. But it was I who received the full force of Her gaze. I recognized the Power I had touched at the final moment in the circle of stones.

"My daughter, you will bear My blessing into the world!" Her light flowed around me, and then I saw no more.

"Daughter, daughter, how have you come here?"

It was a man's voice—an old man's voice. I opened my eyes and flinched from the harsh light of dawn. When I tried to speak, a croak was all that would come.

"My child, be easy—there is no need for talking—you are in safety now. . . ."

I had been safe where I was before. Now awareness of my body was coming back to me, and pain was everywhere. After a moment, I tried sight again and found it easier, but it answered neither the old man's question, nor my own.

A weathered crag of rock loomed above me, like an island in the purple sea of the moor. A round cell of stone had been tucked into it like a nest in the crotch of a tree, from which a thin trail of smoke curled against the pale sky. I lifted myself upon one elbow and saw that I was lying upon the rocky path that wound up to it, clad in the tatters of my shift and gown.

Dried blood smeared my thighs. I lay back with a groan. Esseilte would be spared a temptation, I thought dimly. If there was to have been a child, it was certain there would be none now. The seed of the spirit was all I would bear in this mortal world.

I felt the softness of a blanket being wrapped around me. I opened my eyes again and saw a skinny man in a worn white robe, almost bald and so weathered that there was no guessing his age. But there was surprising strength in those thin arms. He carried me up the path and into the darkness of the hermitage, and laid me down upon a pallet before the fire.

He already had water heating, and he bathed me as tenderly as a mother, and with as little awareness of gender. When he was finished, and had clothed me in a gown that was only a little less worn than the one he had on, I tried to whisper my thanks.

"It is our blessed Lord you should be thanking," he smiled, "for giving me this refuge in the wilderness where I can care for you. My name is Ogrin. Now rest, while I make up some good broth for you. . . ."

For the next few days I woke only to eat a little and then sleep again. My world was bounded by the flickering light of Ogrin's turf fire. But after a time I began to be aware of some things. It was the hermit's own bed I was sleeping in, while he lay on bare earth by the fire. When he was not tending me, he prayed, sometimes weeping, but mostly with great outpourings of praise. At first it made me uncomfortable, as if I had surprised someone in the act of love, but after a time I began to understand that to Ogrin, prayer was as natural as the singing of the swallows that nested in the crags.

Then came a morning when I could no longer bear to lie still. The weakness in my legs astonished me, but I managed to make my way outside and sat down on an outcrop of stone, sucking in great drafts of the sweet spring air.

Had my eyes grown so unaccustomed to the light? I blinked, rubbed my eyes with the heels of my palms, and opened them again. But it was the same. I saw a radiance around each leaf and blade of grass. The hermit was hurrying up the path, and the light that surrounded him was more brilliant still. *I am seeing haloes*, I thought, *like the illuminations in the holy books, but it is only the fire of life that glows in everything. . . .*

"So you have come seeking the blessing of the sun? I am so glad!" Ogrin stopped before me, clasping his basket of herbs in his arms. "Surely on such a day as this no one could doubt the reality of Paradise!" He turned to gaze out over the rolling land behind him, glowing amber and amethyst under a sky which poured out light like a shower of gold.

My lips twitched, for I had been thinking of the radiance of the moor under moonlight. "Paradise, or Tír na nÓg . . ." I said. "I have seen the Otherworld, and it is very beautiful. I was with the fair folk, before you found me," I answered, wondering if he would think me damned, or simply maddened by my wanderings, "and I know . . ."

"Were you?" Astonishingly, he simply looked interested. "I have seen them too, sometimes. They are fair indeed, dancing beneath the moon."

"I danced with the Horned One—" I added. I think that I was hoping to shock him. My vision of the Lady was too holy a thing to share.

"Him I have not seen," said the hermit, "but that he is a great lord among them I have heard."

"But who are they?" I asked him. When I had been with the Bucca, all had been clear, but a mist dimmed memory as I tried to reconcile what I had experienced with what I thought I knew. "Some of them were like the men of the past, but I was taught that the soul goes to hell or to heaven, so how could they still be here?"

He shook his head. "Flesh and bone belong to the earth that bore them, and the immortal soul to God, but I have wondered sometimes where the spirit of life goes when we leave it—perhaps there is some third part of a man that clings to the land he loved, at least until all memory of his time is gone. I think also that there are some souls that choose to stay, to watch over us, and sometimes to aid."

I remembered what the Bucca had said about Artor. Did he wait in the Land of the Blessed until he should be needed again?

"And of course there are other beings that never were human — spirits of tree and pool that I also have seen," Ogrin went on.

"You do not call them demons?" I challenged.

"If they are in this world it is because the good God made them, and who am I to question His handiwork? They have never done any harm to me. . . ."

I stared at him, beginning to understand why the fair folk had left me at Ogrin's door.

"I have listened to the words of many mitered abbots" — I thought of the fulminations of Ruadan — "and never heard such mildness toward the Old Ones before."

Ogrin shrugged uncomfortably. "Well, I daresay all those great men of the Church are right, and I am wrong. But I am too aware of my own unworthiness to judge other creatures, whether or not they have immortal souls. If the Creator is all-powerful as scripture tells us, how can their existence threaten His sovereignty?"

Tears welled from beneath my shut eyelids. Only then did I realize how I had feared that when Ogrin knew where I had been, he would shun me. Perhaps there were some things I would not tell him — not all my secrets were my own — but the last barrier to healing had disappeared. I felt his hand brush my head in blessing, laid my head upon my knees and simply cried.

"Weep, daughter," said the priest. "If it eases your spirit, let the tears flow. For it is written that after sorrow, cometh great joy. . . ."

The next day I walked easily, and in another, I was helping Ogrin gather herbs and tend his bees. He handled them fearlessly, and I made shift to follow his example, though I could not follow the words he crooned to them.

"You speak to them as if they could understand —"

"Who is to say they do not? I think sometimes human words hide more than they reveal!"

"At Cíll Dara they say that the Blessed Brigid could speak the language of the bees," I said when we were done.

"You are from Eriu, then, daughter? From your speech I thought so. I am told that there are men of great holiness there . . ."

"Perhaps," I answered, thinking that none of the great

churchmen I had seen seemed as blessed to me as this old man. Then I looked at him sharply. I had not meant to tell him who I was or where I was from.

He met my gaze steadily. "You must go back to your people sometime, my child, for your time of healing is almost done. Had you the calling, I would build you an oratory beside my own. But I think your path lies among men. . . ."

He must have taken my silence for assent, for he went on.

"Sometimes I know when people are coming to me . . . all the way into this wilderness they come for counsel, as if I could tell them anything they could not learn at their own firesides! But they do come—" he added in wonder. "And one will be here tomorrow who can take you back with him, if you will."

"I suppose I must go then, but it may be I will be among those who return to you for counsel." I looked around me, drinking in the serenity of the moor, and then back at him. "And I will ask for your blessing before we part."

"I will give you the blessing that Mary asked for her Son," said Ogrin. He lifted his hands above me, and I saw the power come out of his palms in a golden glow.

> *"God over thee, God under thee,*
> *God before thee, God behind thee,*
> *Thou on His path, my child, and He in thy steps.*
> *The augury made by Mary for her own offspring*
> *When He was for a space amissing,*
> *Knowledge of truth, not knowledge of falsehood,*
> *That thou shalt truly see all thy quest.*
> *Son of beauteous Mary, King of Life,*
> *Give thee eyes to see all thy quest,*
> *With grace that shall never fail before thee,*
> *That shall never quench nor dim."*

Fourteen

BANNHEDOS

"Branwen, will you not talk to me?"

I added another handful of fluffy, cream-colored wool to the end of the thread I was forming, and began twisting as it took the weight of the spindle. Esseilte was still waiting when I looked up again, trying to think what to say. Too much had happened. The Branwen who had been brought to the king's fortress above the Fawwyth the day before was not the same woman Esseilte had driven away from Dynas Ban.

The murmur of conversation from the women in the sheltered porch where we were spinning rose around us like the humming of Ogrin's bees. After the first babble at my appearance, Crida, who managed the household, had drawn them away, recognizing our need to talk alone. The three girls we had brought from Eriu were with them, discussing Sionach's approaching marriage to one of the seamen from the *Flower o' the Broom*. No need to worry about how *they* were settling in.

"I am here . . ." I answered finally. Looking at Esseilte fully for the first time, I noted a new definition in the fine bones of her face and thought that perhaps she, too, had changed. Her bright hair was covered now by a matron's veil, her skin even paler than before, while mine had been browned and my hair bleached by the spring sun. It would have been easier to tell the difference between us now.

"I came back to you. What else is there to say?"

"Branwen, Branwen —" She shook her head. "Could you say

211

that you forgive me? That day I was a madwoman surely, torn between fears till I no longer knew what I said. On the boat, my course seemed so simple, but I could not know what it would be like to have to plan every glance, every word. And you had been so strange—"

I looked at her, and the swift color rose in her cheeks, then drained away.

"And that is my fault too, I know it well," she added. "I saw it only too clearly when the storm broke and I thought you were lost. Drustan and the others were out on the moors three days, searching, and I was grief-mad indeed when they returned with no sign. The king's men said that the bog must have taken you for sure!"

Beyond the palisaded walls and the ditches and the gorse-clad earthworks of Bannhedos, the land fell away in a long slope of wood and meadow toward the river where brown water gleamed in the morning sun. I closed my eyes, remembering the sucking stench that had devoured my horse, and felt Esseilte's hand on my arm.

"By God and the Lady Mary, Branwen—where have you been?"

Not in any place a Christian would recognize, I thought with a shiver of memory. *Except, perhaps, for one.*

"I wandered, I suppose, and the hermit found and tended me . . ." I set the spindle twirling once more, and let the silky fibers of the carded wool wind downward toward the shaft.

Esseilte's face told me that she knew there must be more—so the old link between us had not entirely disappeared—but I had no words to tell her about the kingdom under the hill. And yet she was part of my reason for leaving it. I wondered if I had chosen well.

"Yes, I suppose we will always have some secrets from each other now—" she sighed. "But there are secrets between us as well. Why did you come back, Branwen, my sister? What do you mean to do?"

I felt my own color change at the question, but little Sionach was coming toward us with wooden goblets and a jug of cider. By the time she had poured for us and gone away, I had recovered my self-command.

"I came back for the sake of this land, and for your sake, and for the king . . ." I answered steadily.

"Will you betray me after all?" Esseilte's thread snapped, and she fumbled, trying to rejoin the two ends. "How can you serve both me and him?"

"That is the thing I must learn." I wound the spun thread tightly around my spindle and dropped it into my lap. "What do you mean to do about Drustan?"

Esseilte stopped struggling with her thread and looked up at me with a smile like the sun breaking through the clouds at dawn. "He is my life, Branwen. He is the bright heart of the world. Even when I cannot touch him, only to see him is the shining of the sun."

"Then you will not give him up?"

"I would die," she answered simply. "For the sake of the alliance, I will live upon the crumbs of time we can snatch together, but rather than give him up entirely I would make him carry me away."

I frowned, trying to think my way through the tangle. Even in my preoccupation, I had heard enough to know how needful the support of Eriu was to the king. Once more I could see Marc'h's ardent face in the torchlight as he told me his dreams.

I thought I had chosen, on the boat, and when I thrust the faerie food away, and yet here was the choice to be made again. *Ah, Marc'h, my beloved,* I thought then, *to serve you, must I betray you once more?*

"And you need my help to see him, do you?" I challenged. "To tell lies for you, and to guard your chamber door?"

Miserably, Esseilte's blue eyes lifted to meet mine. "I need you, my sister. My life is in your power. . . ."

"You asked me a question, out there on the moor." My whisper was harsh, and I strove to control it. "Now I will answer you. You say that Drustan is the sun in your heaven — I tell you that Marc'h of Kernow shines as brightly for me. Drustan would give up all for love, but more than any woman, Marc'h loves his land. I do not break my vows, Esseilte. Because of my love for you, I will never betray what has been. And because I love the man who is your husband, I will shield you as best I may — "

"I don't understand — "

As she leaned forward, wool and spindle fell from her lap. Unthinking, I snatched them up and automatically began to mend the broken thread.

"Do you want Marc'h yourself, then?" she asked.

"Sweet Lady," I muttered, blinking at the tears that blurred my focus on the wool. "What does that matter now? My price is a higher one—" I looked up at Esseilte. "Both for myself, and for you! I will help you to Drustan's bed in secret if you will go to the king's bed openly. He is a good man, Esseilte, with much to bear. Be kind to him. . . ."

"That is the bargain?" She bit her lip.

"That is the penance I set you—" I wondered what Ogrin would think of my theology. I handed the spindle back to her with the spun thread wound around the shank and the raw end caught neatly in the notch at the top. "See, I have made it whole for you. Do not break it again!"

I was speaking of more than the thread, and Esseilte knew it, but before she could say anything there was a stirring at the door into the hall and the women began to rise.

It was the king, his eyes lighting with pleasure as he came toward us. How could I have forgotten the proud grace of his walking, the aura of power that glimmered around him even in his own hall?

If I had seen him before I spoke with Esseilte, would I have been able to give him up again?

Drustan followed. A radiance came into Esseilte's face then, and Marc'h, thinking that it was for him, quickened his step. My eyes flinched away from them and I caught Drustan's gaze and held it desperately as the two people we loved most in the world went into each other's arms.

They called Bannhedos a villa, but it was in fact a hall and out-buildings within a fortress, rebuilt like Dynas Ban on the foundations of an older stronghold. The circle of the fort itself was over two hundred feet across, with a half-circle added on where the stock could be penned at need. But the Saxons had never come so far west—these Domnonian hill-forts had been refortified by British princes against their fellow chieftains and peasant marauders like the bacaudae who used to ravage Armorica. Still, for some years now Kernow had been peaceful, and the great timbered gates stood open to the road.

As the weeks passed I came to know the countryside around it well, for there were times when the constraints of the lie we were living galled past bearing. Then I would exchange the strapped slippers I wore indoors for stout brogues and strike out across the meadows, or pick my way down the path beside the stream to the broad river where the white swans breasted the incoming tide.

It was more than the exercise I was seeking, though there were times when only exhaustion could ease me. At the uncertain hour between day and evening, I might see a swan's shape shift to that of a maiden, and sometimes in the green silences of the forest I felt eyes watching me. The king's servants called the fair folk piskies, and set out milk and bannock for those that helped them. I knew that they were more, and an occasional shimmer of music or a spray of fresh flowers upon my pillow told me that they had not forgotten me.

I began to make a place for myself in the royal household, and if there were sometimes whispers when I came in from one of my tramps with a wreath of eglantine twined in my hair, there were none when folk came to me to poultice a wound or to make a tisane to bring a fever down. I had the time, and the need, to master the contents of Queen Mairenn's spell-book now, and soon I had an additional purpose for my rambles, for I needed herbs to replenish my store.

I was returning from one such walk with my basket full of eye-bright and cinquefoil when I heard hoofbeats behind me.

"A warm afternoon for so fair a maiden to be climbing hills —"

I knew the voice even before I turned. Marc'h was smiling down at me from the back of the white horse. *White horse, white horse, give me good luck.* . . . One of Crida's sayings echoed in memory. My heart began to hammer, remembering the horse, and the smile, only too well.

"But worth the labor if you've need of a tonic, Mach-tiern," I managed to answer him.

"Well, there's no need for two legs to bear the burden when four are at hand — let me take you up behind me, Branwen —"

I stared at the king. I had stayed far from him all this time, afraid that if I touched him, some knowledge of the flesh would give me away, but they were all looking at me now. How could so reasonable an offer be refused?

I was still struggling for an answer when one of the escort called out and pointed down the road. A small procession was jogging up the road from Welnans toward the dun. I could see the king's attention visibly slipping away. The white horse snorted and struck at the ground, sensing his master's distraction.

"Visitors? I had better be there to receive them —" Marc'h saw me still standing in the road and gestured behind him. "Lady, you will forgive me? Yvan, there, will carry you home —"

Before he had finished speaking, the white stallion was springing down the road with most of the escort thundering after him.
Yvan, a fair-faced young man whose proximity disturbed me not
at all, nudged his own mount forward. I set my foot on his and
swung myself up behind him, and at a pace he judged suitable
for a lady, we followed the king back to Bannhedos.

Would Marc'h have guessed? Would his touch have destroyed
the peace I had so hardly won? I did not know if I were glad or
sorry that we had not been tested, but I knew that I must take
care to avoid any intimacy.

"Theodoric has come!" "Budic is dead and his son has fled
Kemper!" The fortress was buzzing with rumors as we arrived. I
hurried toward the queen's quarters, trying to remember what I
had heard about those names.

Dinner in the hall that night was spiced by the anticipation
with which men await the tale of other people's disasters. And
yet this Theodoric, a big blond man who showed the Gothic
blood of his grandfather, was Drustan's uncle, and Marc'h listened to him with the air of one who was very much involved.

"There is no suspicion regarding the death of my father," said
Theodoric, setting down his drinking horn. We had dined on
roast mutton and pies of conger dressed with onions and leeks in
cream, reclining in the Roman manner that was so like that of
my home, and now the serious discussion had begun. "He was
an old man, God rest him, and he died in his own bed, which is
a fate not many can aspire to in these times!"

The young man beside him crossed himself piously. They had
introduced him as one Winwalo, a half-fledged priest who had
been studying in Kemper. But his family had some feud with
Macliavus, and so he too had been forced to flee.

"And Macliavus, you say, attacked you?" Marc'h leaned forward, eyes glittering. He had been matching his guest horn for
horn all evening, but while Theodoric grew expansive and a little
sentimental, the only sign that the king had been drinking was a
slight flush across the cheekbones, and that might have been
excitement.

Drustan leaned against the hearth with his harp on his knees,
fingering the strings as if this had nothing to do with him at all.
Esseilte, who was sharing a couch with the king without quite
touching him, looked from the harper to the Armorican lord and
back again. I could see her thinking —*Drustan is the only surviving*

child of Budic's elder son. If this Theodoric fails, then Drustan is heir to Kemper. . . .

"Macliavus had a pact with my father!" Theodoric shook his head sorrowfully. "They both pledged to support each other's heirs . . . but Budic was hardly in his grave when they came down on us, in the dawning . . . I was abed. . . ." He flushed, and I was suddenly certain that despite the fact that his wife had died some time before, he had not been in bed alone. "But I got out in time — no thanks to the men who should have guarded me! I was lucky to escape alive!"

There was a sympathetic murmur from the warriors who had dined with us or come in afterward to hear the news. Mevennus Maglos and Beli map Branek were nodding soberly, and Meriadek, who captained the king's guard, fingered his dagger.

"Damn him!" muttered Marc'h. "Does he think that because I was married to his bitch of a sister I will forget that Budic's daughter bore me a son? I will have to act now, and I am not ready. Macliavus knows that, surely — and I thought he was my friend!" His voice had not risen, but there was an edge to it that set the fine hairs stirring on my neck. The moment pulsed with the potential for violence.

"Are you seeking my lord's help to retake your land?" Esseilte's soft question to Theodoric broke the tension, but I realized now that Marcus Cunomorus might be a dangerous man to cross.

Theodoric eyed her appreciatively, and Drustan became suddenly attentive.

"Your husband has his knife in that pie already, domina — I know better than to interfere in his plans. But I have other prospects —" He grinned, and Marc'h looked at him narrowly. "I've had letters from Rheged, brother-in-law! King Urien has a sister in need of a husband, and a high-seat in Glevissig in need of a trustworthy man to keep it warm."

"You?" Marc'h sat up, frowning.

"Why not?" The blond man's throat worked as he swallowed more cider. "There's folk in Demetia that will remember my grandfather's name — didn't he win their land back from the Irish in Artor's time? I think they will welcome me. And when the resources of Glevissig are mine, I can take back my inheritance in Armorica without asking help of any man!"

Marc'h sat up, thinking, and the others, released from his

gaze, began to discuss the implications of what Theodoric had just told them. Gorwennol leaned close to Drustan, whispering impassionedly, but Drustan's eyes were on Esseilte, who had turned on her side, and was plucking early grapes from their stem and eating them, one by one. Her arms, bared by the loose sleeves of the Roman gown, were like white marble. As if Drustan had touched her, she looked up at him, her eyes in that half-light as deep a purple as the fruit in her hand.

Very slightly, she smiled and held another grape to her lips, circling its smoothness with the tip of her tongue before sucking it in. I felt myself go hot, watching her, and Drustan's fair skin had a color that owed nothing to the rushlamps they were lighting now. I looked quickly around, hoping that no one else had seen, and flinched as my gaze crossed that of Meriadek the captain, who was watching Esseilte like a beggar at a feast.

I rose from my own couch and moved between them, bent over Esseilte and took her arm, digging my fingers in where no one could see. She gasped and looked up at me.

"Haven't you had enough grapes, my lady? They can be dangerous if you eat them the wrong way . . ." I said sweetly, taking the bowl away. Her beautiful eyes began to glisten, but I could not afford to pity her. "If you are bored, perhaps Lord Drustan will give us a song—" *And then, if you must look at him, at least everyone else will be looking too!* She began to rub her arm, eyes fixed on the floor, as I crossed the room to Drustan, bending so that I could speak without being overheard.

"The king needs time to think, and the rest of us need something to occupy our minds—" I hissed. Drustan's gaze fixed on mine like that of a drugged man. "When you were Dughan, you had a song or a story for every occasion—what can you give us now to keep idle tongues from telling what they think that idle eyes have seen?"

"Give us a tale from Armorica, Drustan," said Gorwennol, and from the relief in his pale eyes I realized that he must be in Drustan's confidence, and had understood me. Drustan blinked like a man waking from sleep and his hands moved to the harpstrings.

"She's gone out of tune, with the lamps, and the body-heat of all these people warming the room," he said thickly. I could see him regaining his balance as his clever fingers went through the familiar motions of turning the pegs and testing the strings. After a few moments Drustan took a deep breath and looked up at me.

"In tune again, kind Branwen, and at your command. . . ."
His blue eyes held the old shadow of self-mockery.

"Then sing —" I gestured around us, where the people who
had heard him tuning were already beginning to still in readiness
for the entertainment, and eased backward into the shadows.
Harpstrings released a shimmer of sound that reminded me
oddly of the music I had heard beneath the hill.

"Listen, oh my noble companions, to the story of Gradlon, a
hero of Armorica in our grandfathers' day, and how he won a
woman out of faerie for his bride — not the Gradlon Mor who
was Lord of Ys, for of his ending we know a different tale, but
perhaps a man of that city named after his lord, who sought
service in other lands after Ys was drowned. . . ."

The harp struck out a chord of command, and while its overtones still were humming, Drustan began to chant the tale. In
Diarmait's hall he had sung of the heroes of Eriu. I should have
known that here he would sing the legends of his home.

> *"Gradlon has valiantly served a king,*
> *Who gives him neither cloak nor ring,*
> *For fear that having his reward*
> *The lad would bear away his sword —*
> *Have pity for the young Gradlon —*
> *Who has no kin to help him on . . ."*

I looked at Drustan sharply, wondering whether he had con-
sciously chosen a story of a man whose situation was in some
ways similar to his own. Drustan had wealth enough for his
needs, to be sure; the gleam of gold at his wrists as he played
was proof of that, but for all the affection Marc'h bore him, he
seemed almost as much a stranger here as Esseilte and I.

> *"An ancient gelding he bestrides,*
> *"As out into the woods he rides,*
> *And where the crystal water flows,*
> *Behold, the world a wonder shows —*
> *A Lady clothed in rainbow light,*
> *Whose radiance overwhelms his sight. . . ."*

Drustan looked at Esseilte then, and the brightness in his face
told me, at least, whose beauty he was thinking of.

"'Oh I have waited long for thee,
And now my lover thou shalt be,
Abundance blessing thy fair head,
And my white body in thy bed.'
She says, and takes him by the hand,
'Yet, my beloved, understand,
That never shalt thou speak of me,
Nor say how love hath come to thee.
Remember this, my sweet Gradlon,
Or all our happiness is gone . . .'"

The chant continued, recounting how the lady spread for the warrior a feast of meat and drink beyond mortal sweetness, and gave herself to him most sweetly of all, and when he came home again there was new clothing in his chest, a new horse in his stable, and servants all about him, richly clad.

Does he see Esseilte as a faerie mistress who has seduced him? I wondered. At least Drustan understood that secrecy was the inevitable price of such joy. Verse by verse, the story went on, telling how Gradlon was goaded into boasting that his own lady outshone all women, and even as the words left his lips, knew that by saying them he had lost her.

"'Thou hast a year, thou hast a day
To prove the words that thou dost say —'
The King commands, but Gradlon sighs,
She's gone — what matter if he dies?"

And the year went by, and the day, and the warrior was brought to his trial. But my natural pity for the hero's plight was tempered by the knowledge that at least here there were no dangerous parallels.

"The warrior stands alone and bound,
And none to plead his case is found.
Bright through the air the death sword swings,
And suddenly a bridle rings —
Like lightning stabbing through the sky,
Like sunrise when the day is nigh,
The Queen of Beauty doth appear,
The Lady of his heart is here . . ."

The faerie woman came to the king and his warriors, and threw back her mantle so that they could gaze upon her beauty. But Drustan's version of the story made it very clear that acquittal from the king meant nothing to the lover without the forgiveness of his lady.

> *"The white horse carries her away,*
> *He mounts his own, begs her to stay!*
> *She fords the stream whose other shore*
> *Is not this world, but just before*
> *Its waters drown him, her fair hand*
> *Grips his, and to the lovely land*
> *Go the two lovers, there to dwell*
> *In bliss where all is ended well. . . ."*

A shimmer of harpsong sang the lovers to Avalon and the story to an ending, and I felt my eyes prickling with quick tears. Did Drustan understand what he had sung?

Theodoric had fallen asleep where he lay, and Marc'h, laughing, gave orders for him to be covered warmly.

"Let him sleep, and hope he does not have a sore head come the morn!" said the king. "The cider of Kernow may seem mild, but there is a kick to it, as many a foreigner has found to his cost!" Fragan Tawr laughed wolfishly, and the other warriors echoed him.

Esseilte was gazing into the air before her as if she saw the doorway opening to the Otherworld. But the road to that place is not traveled by dreaming, but by opening oneself to a greater reality. Marc'h's hand brushed her shining hair in a brief caress, then closed on her shoulder and gave her a gentle shake, as one might waken a sleepy child.

"Get to your bed, domina, there is no need for *you* to sleep in the hall! I have accounts to go over before I can join you —" He gestured toward the loft where he and his clerks tallied rents and taxes. I suspected that it was not corn and cattle he would be counting this night, but the strength that the gatherings of each hundred could supply in arms, and men. "Do not wait up for me. . . ."

I put my arm around Esseilte to help her to her feet, and felt her suddenly wide awake beneath my hands. A quick glance showed me Drustan's hands whitening as he gripped the curve of his harp. But as I escorted Esseilte toward the royal chamber that had been built onto the end of the hall it was not Drustan's hot gaze that I felt following us, but that of Meriadek, captain of the guard.

When I had brushed out Esseilte's hair and extinguished the candles, I slipped through the door into the little walled garden that Marc'h had made for his queen. The full moon was rolling up the sky like a silver chariot, but I had no time to let her radiance bless me. I stood still, letting senses for which I had no names identify the life in plant and flower, the small night-creatures going about their work, more distant presences of men in the warriors' quarters and the hall, and clear as a lamp to me, the vivid spirit of the king. Here, I could sense the silence of the sleeping countryside, and one other, standing as still in the garden as I. . . .

I moved through the silver shadows and took his hand. It was cold, shaking with the intensity of his desire.

"Drustan . . . Drustan . . . how can you bear to love in the shadows when you yourself have sung the bright beauty of the Otherworld?"

"While Esseilte is in this world," he said hoarsely, "there are no shadows. I am dazzled by her light. If moonlight were to take the shape of a woman, it would be she."

I stared at him, remembering the Lady who had blessed the feast of faerie. Had Drustan somehow glimpsed the same vision? His submission to Esseilte on the ship had been a compulsion of the senses. But somehow it had been transmuted into this pure fervor that reminded me oddly of the hermit Ogrin as he said mass. But Ogrin's deity was eternal. Could any mortal spirits sustain such a passion life-long? I knew what pressures had forced Esseilte to bind her being to this love; I still did not understand what drove Drustan, but now I perceived its power.

"My poor friend." I squeezed his arm. "My poor friend. . . ."

"Branwen, are you weeping for me?" Drustan seemed to remember my existence finally, and put his arm around my shoulders. "Don't you yet understand? I never had a family or a home. I have been like a storm-tossed mariner, and now at last I have a guiding star!"

"But where is it leading you, Drustan?"

"Does that matter? All I need to know is that Esseilte will be there. . . ."

"Do you think she is your faerie-mistress? Do you think that she will carry you off to the Otherworld one day?" I asked sharply.

He laughed a little, remembering how we had once talked of the Blessed Isles. Then he sobered. "The bed in which we lie together is the heart of all worlds. . . ."

I sighed, shaken by memory. When Marc'h and I were united,

we had been the center and the crown. Could I say that Drustan's vision was any less true than my own?

The night grew more silent. The dim swells of land beyond the dun lay in dreaming peace. Wordless, I led Drustan to the bed of the queen, and then, as I had done before, lay down myself in front of the doorway to the hall, waiting to warn them when the king should come.

Theodoric set out for Glevissig the next morning, garlanded with good wishes, and provisioned with Crida's honeycakes and enough cider to make him sleep as well tonight as he had the night before. It was a fine summer morning, and the cloaks of his men looked very gay against the green of the fields. Marc'h watched those bright specks out of sight, then took Esseilte's arm and led us back into the hall.

"I had hoped not to leave you until we had started a child, but there are matters moving in Armorica that demand my attention," he said painfully. "The council will take care of Kernow, and Meriadek can command this fortress, but I should leave a man to watch over you, my lady. Whom would you prefer?"

Esseilte stared at him, and I hoped that he could not interpret the play of emotion on her face. At least she had the self-control to keep from looking at Drustan.

"Give me a man of your own family," she said finally, eyes downcast. "Leave Drustan. He can talk to me in the speech of my own country — it will be something to comfort me when you are away."

Her eyes had not betrayed her, but there was a lovely color in her cheeks. I saw Meriadek watching her, and had a sudden conviction that she should have named any name but Drustan's. But it was too late now.

"Well enough." The king nodded. "Drustan has guarded my back so long I will hardly know how to fight without him, but perhaps it will not come to battle, at least not now. I will not grudge my best warrior for the sake of my queen!"

Did you hear that — I thought at Drustan, whose burning gaze should have ignited the bracken he was looking at on the floor. *Is your heart wrenched by this man's trust in you?*

"Will you go soon?" Esseilte faced Marc'h again. "I should see to your gear." Mairenn had trained her well, and she knew what was expected of her.

"By the end of this week, I fear," he sighed. "When I have gotten the replies to the messages I sent at dawn."

She nodded, and turned toward their chamber. I started to follow her, but the king put his hand on my arm. I started at his touch and looked up at him, trying to keep from trembling.

"Branwen." There was a kindness in his smile that in its own way hurt more than a look of love. "I must leave a man here for the sake of my honor, but I know who will really be caring for my queen."

I felt the quick color flame into my cheeks, and hoped he would think it was embarrassment.

"If I could, I would watch over more than your queen. . . ." I shut my lips, wondering what had possessed me to say that to him.

"Perhaps you can —" It was the king, not the husband, who was eyeing me now. "I have seen how my people come to you. They trust you, who have been but a few months among them, more than they do my poor Drustan, though he has lived half his life in this land. . . . You will hear what folk are saying, and still more, the things they do not quite say.

"It is a thing that most men do not notice, but kings — kings are required to know. Drustan can hear when a harpstring is barely off the true" — Marc'h shook his head in wonder — "but he does not hear the voices in the land. My chieftains sense that, I suppose, and so they dislike him. They constrained me to marry, did you know? But for that lack in him, I would have resisted, and made Drustan my heir for Kernow."

I looked at the king in wonder, remembering what he had said to me about the cycle of sovereignty. Drustan should have been his heir indeed — should have been the prince who could take up the mantle of kingship when Marc'h passed to the inner realms. But Drustan was flawed.

And this king who could hear, if he willed it, the same voices I heard in the rippling of the waters and the whispering of the trees, had not noticed that his wife was betraying him with the man he loved best in the world! I understood then that if Marc'h did not know it, it was because he did not choose to see.

"Be his ears, Branwen —" He focused on me again. "Be his eyes and ears and guard him as you guard the queen."

"I am pledged to that already," I said truthfully, swallowed, and went on, "and I will serve you as best I may, my lord — you, and this land —"

"Yes." Marc'h smiled. "I do not understand that, but I believe that is so —"

Oh my king, you are hitting too near the heart!

I eased back just as he reached out to kiss me on the brow, and felt his lips brush my hair. My vision darkened, and the blood roared in my ears, but I could hear the rustle of dry bracken as he strode away.

Oh my love, my dear love, guard yourself as well. . . .

Fifteen

THE CIDER PRESS

That summer the apples hung heavy on the bough, sun-ripe skins stretched over hard sweetness, turning blood-red and gold among the green leaves. In the orchard at Nans Yann they weighted the branches. We came there often, those last days of August, when the whole land ripened toward harvest in dreaming peace.

I sat with my back against a sturdy trunk, listening to Drustan's harping and fending kittens away from the newly spun yarn which Esseilte was trying to wind into a ball. The kittens were part of the farm in the valley below Bannhedos which had been Esseilte's parting gift from the king. It was green there, hill-hallowed, cooled by the breeze off the river in the heat of the day. While Marc'h was in Armorica, there was no need to keep court in the dun, and so Esseilte had left its management to Meriadek and moved to the farmhouse at Nans Yann with me and our Irish maidens . . . and Drustan. Old Wyn Vedras, who farmed it with the help of his three sons, lived in a second dwelling nearby, which formed, with the barn and outbuildings, a rough square. His wife Senara cooked for us, and the tenants from the king's other holdings nearby helped with the harvesting.

The ripple of harpsong was interrupted by an oath, and a startled gray kitten shot past my feet, knocked over his sister, and tangled them both in the yarn. Drustan was sucking on his finger, glaring. A third kitten leaped sideways, arched in alarm,

226

and then, when the harper did nothing more alarming, sat down and began to lick her paw. Esseilte looked from him to the kittens and began to laugh.

Drustan lifted one eyebrow. "The queen is amused?" He flexed his fingers and carefully plucked one string. The kittens stilled for a moment at the sound; I grabbed a furry body, and began to disentangle it from the wool.

"If you had seen your face!" Esseilte bit her lip, trying to keep from laughing again. Her own face glowed, sun-ripened like the apples by the long lazy days.

"Shall I be your jester, then?" He ran his fingers through his dark hair until it stood up like stubble in a scythed field. Agile fingers skipped over the bronze harpstrings, plucking a dissonant scale.

> *"Seven silver apples on a tree,*
> *See them fall —*
> *All the proud priests prance,*
> *Lest worse befall!"*

He sang in a high quaver, dropping his jaw at each phrase so that his face lengthened in an absurd parody of one of the chief-poet's more sententious followers.

"Did that mean something?" I asked. I was almost certain it was nonsense, but the poets often cloaked their secrets in terminology no less obscure, and Drustan had never been known for humor.

"Woman, who are you to question the ancient mysteries?" he intoned, rolling his eyes as if he were about to have a fit. "By being knocked on the head, the wise gain inspiration. The location of all treasures above the earth, and under the earth, and in the depths of the sea is known to me, but I prefer to wear rags. I have lived as a worm in an apple, as a maggot in a horse-dropping, as a louse on the back of a Saxon. . . ."

Esseilte was in no doubt about his meaning. She covered her face with her hands, shoulders shaking. The ball of yarn unrolled across the grass and all three kittens shot after it.

"I am the master of the magic milkpail, the which no matter how much milk is put into it, will turn it all sour —" he continued mercilessly. "I am the singer of the sacred incantation which is so secret that no one knows its tune; I am the warrior of the ghastly grimace which causes all my foes to collapse with giggles. . . ."

"Oh, Drustan, no more!" cried Esseilte weakly. The kittens had begun a furious battle for possession of the ball of yarn, chewing on each others' limbs and growling ferociously.

"I am the lover of the faerie woman who lives in the fortress of delectable feasting, the hair of her head streams down like butter, her body is formed of thick cream, her lips are two sweet red berries. Every night I devour her entirely, and in the morning she is restored." Drustan's tone remained light, but his voice had deepened, and Esseilte's breast rose and fell rather quickly.

I looked away, and saw Cairenn and Breacc coming across the grass with a pitcher of cider. Sionach had married her sailor at the beginning of the summer, and now Cairenn was courting with the son of the chief at Welnans.

"Very witty —" I cut in suddenly, abandoning my attempts to untangle the yarn. "I have never heard such a performance from you before!"

Drustan blinked and then reddened, realizing that we were no longer alone.

"Neither have I. My life has not given me much reason for laughter. . . ." His gaze moved instinctively back to Esseilte. His eyes, wide and unguarded, in that moment seemed as intensely blue as the wings of the butterfly that fluttered past.

"We thought you would like some of the cider," said Cairenn brightly. "The men in the fields liked it, but they had to go back to work again . . ."

"Thank you." Esseilte took the wooden cup with a grave courtesy. "I am sure the harvesters appreciated your kindness."

It had been a year of bounty, the heads of corn and barley bending their slender stalks by the end of July, and the sheep and cattle growing fat in the moorland pastures. When I saw the laden wagons bringing the grain in for threshing my heart eased, for I knew that the ritual I had performed with the king had blessed the land.

"It's the last of the old year's cider," said Cairenn. "They will press the new after the barley harvest is done."

"Indeed," answered Drustan. "Only the cider of Armorica can compare with that of Kernow. They make it from the little apples, as small and hard as a maiden's breast." His glance flicked from one girl to the other, and they giggled, but I knew for whom his words were intended.

"Then they crush the fruit to sweet pulp in the mortar. The pestle crushes it — in and out, in and out of the mortar it grinds, and the flesh of the fruit grows soft, the juices begin to flow. . . ."

Drustan's words hung heavy in the air. Breacc and Cairenn had gotten very pink as they understood his meaning, and even I felt a sweet warmth between my thighs. Esseilte sat with her eyes closed, the fine linen of her gown quivered with the rise and fall of her breathing.

In public, he never touched her. . . .

Sitting together as we did now, or walking, or dining in the stone farmhouse, there was never a motion that could have been interpreted to his dishonor, or to hers. But they spoke. Words teased the imagination, stretching out the sweet torment until by nightfall she swayed, weak with desire.

In the darkness it was different. When the moon rose, Esseilte's lover would kneel before her like a worshipper at a shrine. I did not need to see what happened between them then. I, who had seen the stones of the circle shining, and who had danced with the Horned One in the hollow hills, could see the power that throbbed in this little valley when they lay together. This passion, however hidden and unlawful, was still a sacred thing.

"The spirit of the apple tree is pressed out in pain. Only thus can it preserve its fire . . ." Drustan added dreamily. The stillness that followed was weighted, and after a few moments of it Cairenn and Breacc, still blushing, took the pitcher and cups away.

The sun had gone below the rim of the hill, but the diffuse golden light of evening filled the valley like cider poured into a bowl. The little stream that wound past the farm buildings and through the orchard toward the river chuckled softly to itself; a dog barked farther up the hillside, turning the sheep toward their fold, and Drustan's gentle touch on the harpstrings distilled those homely country sounds into a nobler melody.

"Bard, tell me a tale —" Esseilte sat quiet in the twilight, the skirts of her gown spread around her like the petals of a flower. Drustan responded with a ripple of music, then struck a single sweet chord as if the sight of her had given him his theme.

"In Artor's time there was a prince whose wife died, leaving him with a boy they called Culhwch, because he had been delivered in a pig-run. When the prince married again, his new lady wished to secure her place by marrying the boy to her own daughter, but Culhwch would have none of her. And in retaliation, the step-mother laid upon him that he should marry none but Olwen, the daughter of the giant, Yspaddaden Pencawr—" he began. He looked up again at Esseilte, and smiled.

"And though Culhwch had not seen Olwen, at the speaking of her name he knew and loved her, for she was the Lady of the White Track, and where she passed, the earth grew radiant with flowers. But though his heart knew her, no man in all Britain could say where she was to be found.

"Culhwch's father sent him to Artor his kinsman to receive manhood and claim the king's aid. And Artor received him gladly, for of all men in this island Culhwch was the fairest, and the king pledged to him the service of his most famous warriors until the quest should be done . . ." The harp struck up a swift striding music; a cavalcade of heroes rode the realms of the air—

And a distant pattering of hoofbeats beat out the rhythm.

I turned to listen. A horse was being ridden fast down the lane from the dun. That sudden irregular drumming transformed the stillness. Drustan's harping faltered, and Esseilte reached for her veil, for farmers do not ride at such a pace coming home from the fields.

Movement blurred the shadows beyond the trees. Then the horse became visible, and as it came down the hill, we recognized the rider. It was Meriadek.

Drustan set down the harp and got to his feet. The steward pulled up. As Meriadek saluted the queen, the horse stood, blowing gustily. His rider brushed back a lock of hair that had been blown across his forehead by the haste of his ride, and assumed the smoothly contained appearance I remembered.

"Is there news?" Esseilte spoke steadily.

"The best of news—" Meriadek said pleasantly, but his dark gaze flicked nervously from her to Drustan and back again. I remembered how he had watched them at Bannhedos. "Your lord is coming home!"

"When will he be here?"

"By the week's end, if the wind holds fair. He sent a ship ahead to bring word. Will you come with me back to the dun?"

"Soon—it will take me some time to pack." Esseilte's voice was cool. "Will you dine with us?"

"I must return. There is a great deal to do!" Clearly he wanted her to come with him immediately, but he must know as well as we did that Crida had the domestic management of the fortress well in hand. There would be time for a leisurely return . . .

I could see Meriadek hesitate. His narrow face creased as if that thought had occurred to him too. The horse jerked up its head as if Meriadek had given an involuntary twitch to the rein. But Esseilte was already turning away, and he did not dare dispute that dismissal. He released the rein, and the horse sprang back up the lane.

We looked at each other as the hoofbeats died away to silence once more. The peace that had filled the valley seemed suddenly fragile. More than a summer's day was coming to an end.

"And the tale?" Esseilte's voice trembled a little.

"What?" Drustan turned to her, still frowning.

"You were telling us a story. How does it finish?"

"Yspaddaden's death lay in the marriage of his daughter," said Drustan harshly, abandoning the poet's cadencing. "The heroes spent their lives to fulfill the geas he set upon them to win her, the quest for the Treasures of Britain. The cauldron of rebirth was one of them —" He glanced at me and I remembered the tale he had told me of Branwen. "Artor and all his host went into the Otherworld to seek those Treasures, and with him only seven men returned."

"A high price. . . ." I said then.

"Is not the price always high, for love?" Esseilte was standing very still, facing Drustan.

"Have I begrudged it?" he asked.

She did not smile. "We have barely begun. When the king returns, will you still keep faith with me?" Her veil had fallen back and a little vagrant wind lifted the fine hair at her brow, but she did not move.

"You are the breath in my body, the blood in my veins!" he said in a still voice. "Why do you play with me!"

"Because the price is a great one, and I think that you and I may pass through Annwyfn also, before we are done." She faced west, as if she could see all their future painted in the colors of the dying day.

"If I *could* deny you, I would have done so, Esseilte!" he said gravely. "As I have heard men in agony deny their God. But your presence in the world is an answer to all doubting. You are *she who must be gazed upon* . . ."

He stood, hands open and empty at his side, as if even the power of motion waited on her will.

"Does the fall of the tree make a sound if there is no one to hear it?" Esseilte asked, smiling a little. "If I am beautiful, it is because you are here to see . . ." She turned to him again, and as their eyes met, the exaltation in his seemed to flow through that link until their two faces were the same.

Perhaps they might have stood there until darkness fell, and I with them, rapt in the same contemplation. But an early owl called, and suddenly I was cold.

"Night is coming," I broke the silence. "We ought to go in —"

As we gathered up the yarn, the air shimmered around us. A silvery flutter caught the last light like an unseasonal snowfall. Esseilte covered her face with her veil. I felt something touch my cheek and gasped, brushing it away.

"They are only moths," came Drustan's quiet voice. "We know that summer is almost done when the silver moths come home from Gaul."

From Gaul, I thought, *like the king. . . .* I straightened then, letting the moths spiral around me. *Did you see him, my sisters, did the wind that bore you here also fill his sails?* My heart began a slow, heavy beating in my breast.

More than the summer had come to an end.

The tang of crushed apples weighted the air, acid, sweet, with an odd mustiness that caught at the throat as fermentation began. There were rumors that the king's ship had been delayed, and so we stayed at Nans Yann, waiting for word, while Esseilte pretended to pack and everyone else prepared for the cider-making as the harvest went on.

I stood in the barnyard watching, shivering a little as the great presses groaned. Slowly, agonizingly, they squeezed the spirit of the apples out into the trough. The men added barley straw to the crushed pulp before they pressed it, turning the reeking mass and pressing and turning it again until the last trickle ceased.

So much pressure, I thought, so much pain, but the result was a fiery golden liquor that would warm body and soul through the gray winter days.

From the slope above us came a long horn call. Esseilte came running out of the house and stood beside me, looking up the road as the first of the riders came into view. Bright cloaks flowered against the green. And in the lead was a white horse, moving ever faster as the rider spurred him down the hill.

"He is here then — so soon! We thought we would have more time. . . ." whispered Esseilte. Her eyes were wide, and a little frightened.

"Drustan is down in the river pasture, helping to move the cattle, and by the time he returns Marc'h's household will be all around us. You must tell him to meet me tonight in the orchard —"

"What?" I struggled for breath, feeling as if I were being pressed like the apples as Marc'h drew near.

"I must speak with him! Tell him to mark the apple twigs and send them downstream to us when he is there." Her hand closed on my arm. "Sweet heaven, Branwen, it was your own idea! There is no time to find another way of communication now!" By this time everyone on the farmstead had seen the royal party, and the yard was filling fast.

I forced the fragment of my mind that was not focused on the king to remember. The stream that watered the orchard curved past the farmhouse, and it had occurred to me that anything put into the water upstream would pass the pool where Esseilte and I washed. Surely no one would suspect if she went out for a drink of fresh water in the night. And then, if all was clear, upstream to the shadow of the oldest apple tree. . . .

"I will tell him . . ."

Esseilte let go of my arm and began to adjust the golden circlet that held her veil. "Very well. Now I can pretend to be a queen . . ."

Startled, I looked at her, wondering if somewhere deep within she understood that her sovereignty was a pretense indeed. And then the king's escort was clattering into the farmyard. Geese scrambled from beneath the horses' hooves, squawking in outrage. Marc'h drew rein in the midst of them, swaying easily as the white horse reared. The summer's campaigning had fined him down, I saw. He held his shoulder a little stiffly — had he been wounded? If so, it could not be serious, for he mastered the horse with a precise economy of motion, as if war, like the ciderpress, had strained out all but the essential spirit of the man.

Esseilte took the eared cup that Cairenn had brought her and moved forward to meet him, her draperies swaying gracefully.

"Blessed be your homecoming, my king — here is the first of the cider to refresh you. . . ."

He took the cup from her hands and drank, his gaze swiftly scanning the crowd as he lowered it again. For a moment his eyes met mine, and I thought he smiled, but perhaps it was my imagination, for immediately he was bending to thank Esseilte, handing her the chalice and sliding down from the horse to embrace her. Someone took his stallion's bridle and led it away as the people thronged around them.

The blood sang in my veins. Esseilte had said she could not endure without Drustan near. But could I endure the presence of the king? To see him every day, to speak with him? Even, if I were not careful, to touch him at times? Could I bear all that and still give no sign of what he was to me? I had not realized that the summer had been a respite not only for Drustan and Esseilte, but for me.

Blessed Lady — I prayed to the power I had seen by fire and moonlight, the presence that I had touched in the sacred spring and the ring of stones. *I am being crushed as surely as any of those apples . . . how can I bear it? Lady, I beg you — wring some bounty from my pain!*

"A fair land and a fair harvest . . . It is good to be home . . ."

I opened my eyes and found Marc'h at my elbow. The smell of the white horse was on him, and his own scent, that I would never mistake for that of any other man. A great fist clutched in my belly, and for a moment the air darkened so that I could not see.

My lips moved, but it was not I who answered him.

"The Land rejoices in the coming of the King. . . ."

Harvest passed, and Samhain, and for a time everyone was busy with the winter slaughtering. Salted and smoked and pickled, the joints of pork and beef and mutton joined the binned grain and barrels of cider in the barns, and earth wrapped a mantle of mist around us as we settled in to wait for spring.

Though there were times when we must keep court in the dun, Esseilte still dwelt for the most part at Nans Yann, and as often as he could, the king joined her. Sheltered in the folds of the hills, the farm was warmer than the fortress on the ridge, and I think Marc'h enjoyed the informality of living there. With time I grew accustomed to being in his presence, and if it had not been for Meriadek, we could have been happy.

On an evening when the clouds had for the moment cleared and a full moon was blessing the crisp air, we sat around the great hearth that was the center of the farmhouse, enjoying the sweet warmth of an applewood fire.

"Will Jonas be able to muster any real resistance if you move against him in the spring?" Meriadek leaned forward, cocking his head to keep an eye on the rest of the company while he looked at the king. He and Mevennus Maglos had come down to us that afternoon from the dun with letters from Armorica. Marc'h was still studying them, and the rest of us had drawn close to the fire.

"Jonas is an oyster, and the walls of Dol are his shell!" The king gave a short bark of laughter and laid the roll of vellum down. "By himself he would not worry me. But Samson is another animal entirely. Rumor has it that he is intriguing with Chlotar. I think he has backed the wrong cock in that family — there's a deal of life in Childebert yet, and a flock of hungry princes waiting for the Frankish throne. And Jonas is not the man to win a kingdom, or I misread him."

"But it was men of Dol who gave you that stiff shoulder," pointed out Gorwennol.

The king swung his arm back and forth a little as if to disprove it, and Drustan looked up from his harp, flushing.

"My lord — does it still trouble you?"

"Only a little," Marc'h protested. "I don't heal as quickly as I did when I was your age! But I will be well enough by the time we fight again."

"I should have been with you!" Drustan's eyes caught the light of the fire as he straightened, and I thought that perhaps for the first time since we arrived in Britain, he had forgotten Esseilte.

"Na, na, my lad — do you think you can be my champion every time? I have taken wounds even on campaigns when you were with me, if you will recall!" He drank from the cider jug and passed it across to Drustan. "'Tis not swords but crosiers that are pricking me just now! I used to think that if I could only get Father Samson out of Welnans my difficulties would be over. But when he was haranguing me from his chapel there at least I knew what he was up to!" Firelight danced across Marc'h's lean features, making it impossible to read his true expression.

There was a little laughter from some of the others.

"He will never forgive you for not offering him what you tried to force on Paul Aurelian—" said Gorwennol. "Samson wanted to be Bishop of Kernow."

"I suppose the blood of Maxen Wledig speaks as strongly in him as it does in any man of our house, though it comes to Samson through his dam," the king replied. "He was still with Iltud when I came to study there, and he was a tyrant to the younger boys. It is an ill thing when a man confuses the miter with the crown!"

"Columba of Derry plays that game in Eriu," I said then. "He was born a prince of the northern Ui Néill, and he is a lordly man, and proud." I looked to Esseilte for confirmation, then remembered that she had complained of a headache earlier and gone to bed. Drustan gave a twisted smile.

"I remember him. He had just finished reading that book that Gildas wrote, and I nearly betrayed myself by insisting that you did not share the sins of your ancestors!"

"Did you so?" The king smiled in return. For a moment their faces were very much alike. "Ah, why cannot these churchmen understand? Nowadays the priests call Artor Christ's defender, and exhort us all to adopt his virtues, but they were quick enough with their curses when he took their gold to buy arms or their grain to feed his men. I remember how he struck the table and swore because the Bishop of Isca Dumnoniorum refused to pay a tax upon his corn."

"You knew Artor?" I asked involuntarily.

"Does that make me seem so old?" He laughed at me. "I was a child in my grandfather's house. Cato had been one of Artor's captains—he was one of the few to survive Camlann—and the High King stayed with us when he visited Dumnonia."

"What was he like?" I asked. "I have heard so many tales—"

Marc'h laughed. "I suppose—it always amazes me how quickly such stories grow. Is it better, I wonder, to be remembered as a legend—even an evil one—or not remembered at all?"

Esseilte had wanted to become a legend, I remembered. Did she still, or had her love for Drustan become itself the goal? But for their story to be remembered, it would have to become known. . . . I thrust the thought away.

"Artor was a big, fair man, or had been so in his youth, and of course he seemed beyond mortal stature to a child. The Roman blood of our line did not show in him, nor the ancient blood of the hills, but one saw the kingship—even when he was old. He had no need to raise his voice to show his power. You did not look at anyone else when Artor was in the room."

And in that, my lord, you are surely his heir — thought I.

"There were stories about him even then," Marc'h went on. "I worshipped him. When my grandfather did not chase me away I played at their feet and learned what I could from their talk. Artor's trouble with the bishop was just the beginning; I fear our descendants will find these priests harder to control than we . . ."

"But if the Church is so troublesome, why need we support it at all?" I shivered as I spoke, imagining I felt Abbot Ruadan's harsh glare from all the way across the Irish Sea. But I drew for strength on the memory of Ogrin the hermit, who had needed no authority of king or bishop to support his faith.

"Did you think that it is only Christian priests who behave in this way?" The king's attention was wholly upon me, and I trembled for a different reason now. "Wherever there is prestige and property, men will fight for earthly, instead of heavenly power," he went on. "I suppose that there were chieftains among my ancestors whose complaints about the Druid hierarchy sounded much the same! But the people need shepherds, and also, the Church is our last link with the empire. . . . A scholar like Iltud, who was my own teacher, compensates for more than one Samson!

"Let the Church care for its faithful — the king must care for all. My father was no saint, and yet I think he was not so bad as Gildas paints him. As for me, when I stand before the high seat of the King of Heaven, I hope He will agree that my own sins were committed for the sake of my land. Most of them, any road — " He smiled reminiscently, and his glance moved toward Drustan once more.

Drustan was sliding his harp into its worn sealskin case. His eyes flicked up to meet the king's, then shifted away. A branch popped in the hearth and fell in a shower of sparks like faerie gold.

"Are you leaving us then?" Marc'h asked.

"I think I must if I'm to wake in time . . ." came the soft reply. "I've promised to go with Withgy to look at some horses, and we'll be leaving early."

"When it's a question of a horse, how can I deny you? Go in peace — "

Drustan came forward and the king brushed his bent head

almost in blessing. Then he was swallowed by the shadows. The moon was shining through the high window, and abruptly I knew why he had gone.

"Will you have to fight Dol when you go back to Gaul?" I asked quickly.

Marc'h's gaze came from the darkness into which Drustan had disappeared, back to me.

"I may fight Jonas, or Riwal, or even Macliavus my old ally," he answered, smiling. "In Armorica there is no lack of enemies. They are strong men all, except perhaps for Jonas, and every one of them trumpeting like a stallion around a mare at the scent of power! When I go back again, I shall be able to pick and choose my foes."

I nodded, as if I did not realize he was not taking me seriously. In truth, I scarcely cared who ruled in Armorica as long as Marc'h was safe. It was Kernow that concerned me, and the inner realm of Logres to which it belonged.

"And when you go back to Ker-haes," said Meriadek in a thin voice, "who will go with you? Are you going to let your nephew hide behind a woman's skirts a second time?"

I felt my skin go cold. Everyone was looking at the steward, disturbed by his tone before there was any evil in his words.

"Come now, it was not by Drustan's will that he was left behind," the king answered, reaching for the cider jug as if he, alone of us all, thought this was only idle chattering. The fire flickered madly, as if somewhere someone had opened a door to let in a draft of chill air.

"No indeed, it was the will of the queen . . ." said Meriadek silkily.

Marc'h's hand paused above the jug, then very deliberately, he turned.

"What do you mean?"

All the color left the steward's face, but his inner demon drove him on. *Jealousy*, I thought. *It has eaten him from within like the rot in a pillar and now it will spread to bring the house down upon us all. . . .*

"Do you not know? *She* chose him to be her keeper. She chooses to stay here with him still, rather than ruling with you in the dun. She sought her bed early, and now he too is gone. To sleep, he said, but I do not think so. If you do not believe me, my lord, go see if your queen and the man to whom you entrusted her are where they ought to be!"

The silence rang in my ears. Even the fire seemed to make no sound, or perhaps it was the shock that had deadened my senses. Why did no one speak?

I forced myself to stand. "You dare accuse your queen?" I spat at Meriadek. "Will none of you who have so often praised her beauty deny this? And you" — I glared at Gorwennol — "will not the warriors who have fought at Drustan's side speak in defense of him?" I stared around the circle, challenging them, but they were silent, as if some intuition had told them that what Meriadek had said was true.

"Then I see that it is left to me! I will bring the queen here to give you all the lie!" I started to turn. Drustan had not been gone so very long. If I went quickly I might be able to call Esseilte back before more harm was done.

"Ah no!" A hard hand jerked me around. I stared into Meriadek's burning eyes. "The dishonor could only be with this woman's connivance! Do we hunt the fox with the vixen?" Still holding my arm, he gestured in appeal to the king.

"If there *is* dishonor . . ." Marc'h spoke at last, and I winced at the undertone of pain. "Yet there is reason in your objection, if there is reason in this at all! Maglos — " He nodded to the older man. "Go you to the queen's chamber and see that she is there."

But of course she was not, and so we wrapped ourselves in our cloaks and went, all of us, out into the silver night to search for her.

From the front entrance to the farmstead the way to the orchard led through the hazel-copse. The knobbly ends of the coppiced trunks stabbed the moonlit sky like the tormented limbs of demons, and I shivered from something more than cold. Marc'h hung back, but I tried to hurry them, hoping that Esseilte and Drustan had not yet achieved their meeting. To find them in the orchard would be damaging enough, but to find them in each other's arms would be damning.

The moon was approaching its zenith, full and brilliant in the frosty air — so cold, and so serene — it seemed impossible that anyone could contemplate violence here. And yet I could hear Meriadek's hoarse breathing above the chuckling of the stream. In that clear light the apple trees seemed made of silver, and the water glimmered like the fountains of faerie. If I shifted focus, would I see the spirits or the trees, or were they sleeping through the cold?

If I had known how, in that moment I would have called the Bucca to my aid and disappeared, but Meriadek was pulling me along. I stepped on every branch I could, hoping the noise would alert someone. The point of the steward's dagger had already shown me the unwisdom of trying to call.

Then we reached the stream.

"Here, lord king," Meriadek whispered harshly. "They meet here, beneath the largest tree. . . ." He pulled back into the shadows, but Marc'h remained on the bank of the stream, staring into its ripples as if the truth were written there.

And perhaps it was. I stared past my captor's shoulder, straining to see if any twigs were floating down the stream. But even if he should see one of Drustan's messages, would he recognize the scratches in the wood as the ogham writing the harper had learned in Eriu? Or be able to read in them the lovers' linked names?

Esseilte . . . Drustan . . . Esseilte . . . Drustan. . . .

The moonlight struck silver from the king's hair — I had not realized how many new strands of white this last year's campaigning had set there. It bleached all color from his cloak, and sent his shadow dark across the stream. Then I saw him stiffen and pull back, for now there was another sound in the stillness. Footsteps were coming from upstream, soft, but steady, as if the walker recognized the need for caution, but felt no fear.

Drustan . . . my heart cried. *Be careful! You are betrayed!* But there was no link between our spirits. He came steadily onward, and stopped short only when he was almost in front of us by the stream. Then it was silent again. Drustan was very still, unnaturally still, I thought suddenly, like a man rapt in contemplation of the moon. But he was looking downstream.

Surely a man waiting for his lover would shift a little with impatience, even sit down with his back against a tree to wait for her. But Drustan never moved. Had he somehow sensed our presence? If that was so, then why did he not run away?

A moment's thought brought me understanding. Marc'h and Gorwennol might hang back, but not Meriadek and Mevennus, and Drustan must know that any such ambush would include his enemies. Even if he could have escaped them, flight would be an admission of guilt, and he would not leave Esseilte to face their accusations alone.

And so he stood like a sentinel, and presently a light step upon the frosty grass told me that Esseilte was answering his call. In a moment she came into view, the white hem of her bedgown fluttering beneath the heavy folds of the mantle she wore.

I had never dared to hope that she would fail him. She was hurrying, and again I sent forth my silent cry. And she stopped. She halted a few paces downstream, as suddenly as if she had heard me, or as if her eager gaze had somehow pierced the shadows that hid her enemies. Cloak and gown settled into carven folds.

My heart beat so heavily I was sure that she must hear it, and abruptly she shrugged and sighed.

"Well, Master Bard — I have come as you requested. Your reason had better be compelling to justify risking my health and my reputation in this cold!" Esseilte sounded odd, but no one who did not know her well would have realized how unlike her usual voice it was. *She knew!*

The strain had gone from Drustan's shoulders. He took a step forward and bowed. "Domina, it is indeed a question of your honor, and perhaps your health as well, and the weal of Eriu. I have to tell you that we are accused of being lovers, and if that story gets to Marc'h he will send you away, and where will your father's alliance be then?"

"Lovers!" Esseilte laughed shrilly and her mantle fell back so that the moonlight shone full on her fair hair. "With the man who murdered my uncle and betrayed my mother's hospitality? Is that how a man wins a woman's love? You deceived me; you deceived us all. Because of you I will never again see the green hills of Eriu." She was shaking with emotion, and I shivered, for no one who heard her could doubt the truth in her words.

"Remember, Drustan . . . don't you remember the sweathouse where I tried to kill you when I learned your name? My mother's curse on the Morholt's murderer is yet unfulfilled. Those who gossip about us would say that you should fear, not love me, if everything were known, for surely I will be the death of you one day." I saw Marc'h twitch at her unexpected venom, and wondered how much Drustan had told him about his adventures in Eriu.

"For the sake of my marriage, I have tried to seem friendly when we are together," she went on. "Where I have hated I have had to seem to love, and to hide the truth of my heart from all. But God knows it was only because of that alliance that I ever consented to cross the sea with you!" I repressed a desire to cheer, for what she had just said was most certainly true.

"Lady, you know and I know the truth of our dealings together, but the world can hardly be expected to understand—" he said sarcastically. I remembered the playfulness of the summer. Had those flights of fancy somehow prepared them to improvise this comedy?

Esseilte stared at him for a moment, then lifted one white arm toward the sky.

"The Lady of the Sacred Flame knows the nature of the passion that fills my heart, and if ever I sin against that love, may that day end my life as well. Do they think that the royal daughter of Eriu would care so little for her honor? Do they think I go after men like a mare in season for my body's ease? The vows that I have made are dearer to me than life, stronger than death; in love lies my hope of immortality! Do they think that I would jeopardize that for a momentary satisfaction?" She wrapped her mantle around her again and faced him defiantly. I did not feel like cheering this time, though I was sure her words would convince the king, for I remembered only too well what vows his bride had made.

"I know the truth that is in you better than anyone!" said Drustan very softly. "You are my queen, and I have sworn to protect and honor you. But the gossip will continue as long as I am here. You have already cost me one year's campaigning. I had hoped to go back to Armorica with the king in the spring. Will you speak to him on my behalf?"

"Drustan, you are truly mad!" came her answer. "If they think I am your mistress, I am the last person under heaven you should ask to plead your cause. If I say anything in your favor they will be at me like so many wolves, calling it proof of my interest in you. I am sorry this has happened, for despite my real feelings it is more pleasant for Marc'h if we can pretend to be friends, and I would like to spare him pain." She pulled her mantle more closely around her so that only her face was visible, pale in the light of the moon.

"I have already spent too much time away from my bed, and I am freezing here. It would be just my fortune for this meeting to provide fuel for the flame you have warned me of. You must make your own peace with the king, Drustan.

"I will certainly not make the mistake of asking for you as my guardian again! Marc'h would give you that duty only if he wished to show the world his trust in us both, and if he listens to liars, all hope for that is gone. . . . Drustan, farewell." She began to pick her way back through the trees.

"Lady, may your steps be blessed," Drustan called after her. "I have always wished the best for you and the king. . . ."

"I believe it," she answered softly, half-turning, "and I wish that fate had allowed me to love you. I thank you for your warning, but I beg you, do not put me in such jeopardy again!" Then the trees hid her. Drustan's shoulders slumped, he sighed, and after a few moments he started upstream the way he had come.

Meriadek's hand fell from my arm as the king turned, and his shadow withdrew from the stream.

"Did you hear?" Marc'h asked harshly, facing us. "Did all of you hear?" The other men nodded. "Was that a meeting of lovers?" he went on. "Then let no one speak of this again! And as for you" — as he came to Meriadek his voice shook with violence barely contained — "I do not want to look upon your false face or hear your lying words. Get out, before I kill you and dishonor my blade!"

Sixteen

THE NIGHT SONG

The golden ball spun skyward, blazing in the spring sunlight, challenging heaven as if propelled by the breath expelled by several hundred throats. Poised precariously on the great stone, the king stretched to follow its flight. Men surged around him as the bright sphere reached its zenith. For a moment the ball seemed to hover. Then a great shout shook the earth as it fell.

"Lan Wedenek! Lan Wedenek!"

Sound pulsed through my bones as the ball disappeared into a tangle of villagers. A heaving knot of warriors slammed against the pillar and Marc'h danced to keep his balance, laughing.

"Hai, hai — go get it! Good lads — after it, there it goes!" He urged them on like hunting dogs. "Run with it, Iestyn! Yvan, watch out —" Gold flickered as the ball spurted through clutching fingers. One of the king's men caught it and darted away. "Ah, there's none like the men of Kernow!"

"He should save that ferocity for the enemy," Esseilte said sourly.

"Oh, no — it will fire up their spirits —" Drustan leaned over the rail of the platform where we were standing as if he wanted to plunge into the fray.

"With cracked heads and broken arms? What if the king's men lose?"

Hurling was not native to Eriu, but we had ball games that were similar enough for me to guess what the outcome would be. The two goals — the holy well on the cliffs, and a sacred pool —

were both within a mile of the town. Each side would strive to goal the ball while the other prevented, and short of deliberate fouling, there were no prohibitions on what the players could do.

The struggle rolled back across the market square, children and dogs fleeing like birds before the wave. Even the sound of it was like the surf on the beaches a few miles away. Marc'h straightened, the shape of his head clear against the bright sky. The crying of gulls came clearly from the little harbor, but when the wind changed it brought the intoxicating scents of new grass and spring flowers.

Hawthorn in the hedges, I thought, swallowing. *It has been just a year since we came.*

"It would be no dishonor to lose to men of Britain," Drustan continued. "If even the fisherfolk of Kernow are so formidable, the men of Armorica will have no chance against us at all! But the warriors Marc'h has gathered for this campaign are in hard training. I do not think we will fail!"

On the other side of the square, Gorwennol emerged from the scrimmage, the golden orb cradled tightly beneath his arm, and began to wriggle toward the east road. Drustan waved to him.

"Do you not?" She turned on him suddenly. "And no grief to you, is it, either way? I wonder that you have held yourself back from the fray, eager as you are to be off to this war!"

I sighed. Since that night last autumn when the king's shadow on moonlit water had revealed his suspicion, we had been moving toward this day. To prove his good faith Drustan must go to war — in the moment of crisis that had been obvious to both of them. They had sworn, also, to refrain from physical love, but now it was Beltane, and the spring hosting was completed. Marc'h had summoned the Triggs of the North Coast — the gatherings of men from each Hundred who were fit for war. Tomorrow they would sail for Gaul.

Ball and game forgotten, Drustan stared at her. "My lady knows better than any why I have not played the warrior this past year, and why I am standing with you here." His voice shook with words he could not say.

"Oh, aye," she said bitterly. "Did you think I had forgotten your prowess? Look yonder where the green gleam of the river shows between the walls. There is a sandspit in that river — don't you remember? Does the blood you shed there still stain the ground?"

Lan Wedenek . . . I thought. *Of course, this is where the Morholt died.* I had forgotten that until now.

Drustan straightened. "My blood flowed that day too . . . do you still blame me for defending my people? Now, when this is your country too?"

Esseilte shook her head. Did he think she was forgiving him? I understood better. Kernow was not Esseilte's, despite the gold that banded her brow. It was I who felt power throb from the ground as the hurlers fought for the golden seed of life that was rolling past. I wondered suddenly if it was Drustan's country either?

"And I would never have come to trouble you in Eriu if your mother had not poisoned the Morholt's blade—" he went on grimly.

"A pretty tangle, is it not?" Her eyes were on the heaving mass of men who wrestled for possession of the golden ball, but not her thoughts, no, and he knew that very well. "Who will cut through it for you?"

"In Jesu's name, Esseilte, do you think I wanted it to be this way?"

Two burly fishermen had Gorwennol in a wrestler's grip, struggling for the ball. For a moment his eyes sought Drustan's in a silent plea.

Esseilte laughed.

Drustan jerked like a horse that feels the spur. A vein jumped at his temple.

"Esseilte," I whispered, "you must let him go!"

Her swift glance went from me to the man before her. He was shaking as I have seen a stallion do, curbed beyond enduring. Esseilte was trembling too, in fine, invisible tremors that I felt as I held her.

She lifted her hand.

Drustan vaulted the railing. His war-cry pierced the din as he dove into the knot that surrounded Gorwennol. Someone yelped and the scrimmage heaved. In moments we saw Drustan's dark head rising from the fray like a seal from the wild waves. Gold gleamed between his hands. He snarled, and men fell away before the force that was in him. His lips drew back in a grimace of laughter as he darted toward the open end of the square.

"Drustan! Drustan! For the honor of Kernow!" shouted Marc'h, triumphant on his stone, and the other warriors took up the cry.

"Eh lads, get after him then—" cried one of the local men. "Will 'ee let the foreigner carry our gold away?"

The tangle of friends and foes resolved itself into a flowing mass that streamed behind Drustan as he headed out of the square and raced cross-country toward the holy well.

"They will kill him . . ." whispered Esseilte, eyes fixed on the gap through which Drustan had disappeared.

"Not if he wins for them—he will be a hero then!" A straggling mass of spectators followed the hurlers. Someone brought out the king's horse, and Marc'h mounted without touching the ground. Hooves clattered on cobbles as he reined the horse around. Gaily he waved at us, then he too was off to see the end of the game.

"For a little while," she answered softly. "Oh Branwen, what have I done?"

"Hush, love, hush." I held her. "An hour or two and it will be over. We'll go back to the dun to wait for them."

"A good run! The best I've seen in many a year!" exclaimed Koren Medek, pounding his knee. "You have some good players, my lord! They outran us fairly!" Flushed by wine and the firelight of his hall, his face wore the look of a vanished youth when he too had carried the golden ball to victory.

"Your men made us work for it!" exclaimed Gorwennol. "They run fast for folk who tread the bottom of a boat more often than the top of a hill!" He had a cloth tied around his brow where he had grazed his head on a stone, but for the moment it did not seem to bother him. He would have a headache tomorrow, I guessed, between the blow and the wine. I hoped that he was not subject to seasickness as well.

Marc'h grinned and passed the wineskin back to the lord of Lan Wedenek. The remains of roast lamb and an assortment of pies still weighted the table. Koren had not stinted in feasting the victors, even though his villagers had lost, and the king had distributed enough Gaulish wine to gladden the hearts of both sides.

"They do indeed!" Marc'h agreed. "There's one man of yours, Koren, who had mine running like hares—a little ferrety fellow who stuck to the ball like a thistle, and clever with it, too. He had my team convinced that the big wrestler was carrying it, did he not, until he was halfway to the goal!"

"He fooled me," agreed Gorwennol. "But he didn't deceive Drustan!"

"Nay, how should he," came a low whisper from behind me. "Our Drustan is the master of that trade . . . how can you trust a man with no kindred?"

"True, but this time it won for us! Don't complain!"

I turned quickly, but could not tell which of the men behind us had spoken. Not Mevennus Maglos, who was dour and trusty, but perhaps it had been Karasek of Nans Dreyn who was Meriadek's friend. The whisperers were still with us, despite a winter during which Esseilte and Drustan had disciplined themselves like Egyptian monks to suppress every look, every word, every touch that might betray their love.

Had it all been for nothing, then? Drustan had never been loved by the men of Kernow. Perhaps the rumors would have started even had there been nothing between him and the queen at all.

"I saw him." Mevennus wiped his moustache. "He tripped the little fisherman with as pretty a wrestler's throw as I have ever seen, and then he was off with the ball again, running like that black horse you had, my lord, that always came from behind to win."

"Hai, Drustan — are your ears burning? Hear how he is praising you!" Marc'h grinned as Drustan came in. His hair clung damply to the fine curve of his skull as if he had been given a rough cleansing, and the red of abrasions and rapidly purpling bruises stood out against his fair skin. But his eyes were very bright, as if he were still pulsing with the energy that had brought him the victory.

"Drustan! Drustan! Hero of the day!" shouted Gorwennol, who seemed to have gotten a head start on the wine.

Esseilte's eyes widened as she saw what had been hidden by the mud before.

"His ears may not be burning, but I should think the rest of him must be in considerable pain!" she said through stiff lips.

The color that had not come into Drustan's face at Gorwennol's praise rose swiftly at Esseilte's words.

"It is not as bad as it looks," he said swiftly. "I will be checkered like a chief-poet's mantle for a little while, and these fingers must rest before I can harp again —" He held them out, and I winced. "I think someone stepped on them," Drustan added. "But there's nothing that won't heal!"

"It is not your sword-hand, may the Lord of Battles be praised!" said the king. "Wrap it well, and it won't interfere with your use of your shield."

Esseilte made a small, quickly stifled sound beside me, and I realized that for one confused moment she must have really hoped that the injury would keep Drustan out of the war.

"The Morholt would not have held back for so small a thing," I whispered. "Will you deny the same fortitude to his conqueror? Your uncle fought for glory. Drustan fights for you!"

"Does he?" she asked softly. "Look at him — he belongs to the men's world now!"

The king's men had closed around Drustan, offering him their drinking horns, congratulating him on this or that piece of clever action in the hurling, according him this moment of public praise whatever their private opinions might be. His face bore a faint flush of pleasure. Even so soaring a passion as theirs had been did not meet all needs. Perhaps both he and Esseilte were realizing that, now.

Esseilte let her hands settle into her lap with a sigh. "He will have glory, and I will wait at home. He has left me," she said softly. "He is in the same room, but he might as well already be upon the sea . . ."

Through a momentary gap in the shouting I heard music, and presently Lord Koren was shouting for silence.

"Unite, and unite, and let us all unite,
For summer is a-come in today,
And whither we are going, we will all unite,
In the merry morning of May."

"What is it?" asked the King.

"'The Night Song,'" came the answer. "Do you not have this custom on your coast? It is near midnight, and our young men and maidens are off to the woods to bring in the May. But they'll sing first to every household in the village to bring them good fortune. That is their story, at least — by the time everyone has rewarded them with saffron cakes and mugs of ale it is a wonder that they can see to cut the branches and pick the flowers!" The old man laughed.

"I warn you young men every one,
For summer is a-come in today,
To go to the greenwood and fetch your May home
In the merry morning of May."

The singing was louder now, and men threw open the great doors to the hall to let the singers troop in. From their flushed faces and giggles, it appeared that they had already made the circuit of the rest of the village, building up their courage to serenade the king.

> *"Arise up Lord Koren, and gold be your ring,*
> *   For summer is a-come in today,*
> *With a cup of ale the merrier we shall sing,*
> *   In the merry morning of May."*

Koren's people were already going round with the ale-jug. The singers held out their mugs and continued to sing with them in their hands.

> *"Arise Lady Branwen, all in your gown of green,*
> *   For summer is a-come in today,*
> *You are a fine lady to wait upon the queen,*
> *   In the merry morning of May."*

Startled, I tried to hid behind Esseilte, but Gorwennol pulled me out into the open, laughing. I felt my face flaming. I had always stood in Esseilte's shadow — always! I blushed again to find myself so shaken by a single moment at the focus of a village festival.

> *"Arise up our Queen all in your gown of silk,*
> *   For summer is a-come in today,*
> *And all your body under as white as any milk,*
> *   In the merry morning of May.*
> *Arise up Lord King, and joy you betide.*
> *   For summer is a-come in today,*
> *And bright is your bride that sits by your side.*
> *   In the merry morning of May."*

The village rarely had such visitors, and they were making the most of the occasion, with verses adapted or invented to suit us all. They hustled Marc'h and Esseilte out to stand beside me and old Lord Koren. Marc'h had his arm around her. She stiffened as he pulled her against him and he laughed. He was not drunk, but he had not been behind in enjoying the wine, and a lifetime of rule had inured him to attention. Still laughing, he swung her high.

"Marc'h, what are you doing? Put me down —" Esseilte hissed at him.

He grinned and set her upon the trestle table. Drustan stood up where he had been drinking with the others, his eyes darkening as he watched them.

"Here is your high seat, my queen! Will you not bless your people?"

Esseilte's lips clamped together in a tight line. It was a danger signal, but Marc'h was too mellow to see it. He pressed his drinking horn into her hand.

"Drink to them as they have toasted you!"

"I've drunk enough this night, and so have you!" she said in a hard voice. Her gaze sought Drustan, but he did not move. What could he do? Surrounded by such a company, what did she suppose he could say?

"No such thing! Not on the Eve of Beltane!" The king put his arm around her, and gestured toward the singers, who were forming up again before the door. "They're going to the woods now — to the new leaves and young grass, sweet in the moonlight," he added more softly. "Too dark yet to gather greenery, but I've no doubt the young men will find their flowers . . ." He turned his head and bent to kiss the sweet hollow where the smooth skin of her neck curved into her shoulder.

Esseilte had gone utterly still. *Stop, Marc'h,* I cried silently, *can't you feel how she's hating this? You can't court her this way, not here!*

"The sweetest of flowers . . . I know where they grow." He lifted the veil and stroked down her bright hair, down neck and arm until he cupped her breast within his hand. "Come with me, Esseilte, come into the greenwood and we'll welcome in the May. The power will flow through us, as it did last year — do you remember?"

"The only thing I remember is that I have been up since dawn, stood for several hours watching grown men chasing a silly ball, and sat for several more while they drank themselves silly." Her tone congealed the warm murmur of his words. A swift twist took her out of his arms to the floor.

"Esseilte," he began, still not understanding. "You are my queen. . . ."

"Am I?" she said icily. "Then I suggest you stop treating me as if I were your slave!"

The words of the departing singers mocked the silence.

> *"Now fare you well, and we bid you all good cheer.*
> *For summer is a-come in today,*
> *We'll call once more unto your house before another year,*
> *In the merry morning of May."*

The blood left Marc'h's face as he straightened, blinking, then returned in a rush. His eyes burned. Suddenly I understood how he appeared to his enemies.

"Indeed, domina, and would you like to find out how I treat my slaves?"

Esseilte whitened, but she did not flinch. Drustan took a half-step, then jerked to a halt. The king started to reach for her.

"My lord — Marc'h —" I said in a low voice. "You must not! It is *Beltane*!"

Though Esseilte would not help him honor the festival, still he must not profane it. My body trembled with the need to touch him, to offer myself to him, to tell him that *I* remembered what had happened a year ago. But I could not. I *must* not. This was all I could do for him, or for her.

"Yes, it is Beltane," he echoed harshly. "And I have a camp full of warriors to see settled, or they will have to be poured on board ship come the morn."

I looked quickly around me. Before the others had quite understood there was danger, the moment had passed. Only Drustan swayed where he stood, and Gorwennol clapped him on the shoulder and made him sit down, joking about mixing wine with ale. I could not help wondering — if Marc'h had laid hands on Esseilte, what would Drustan have done? Would his love for her have been stronger than the love and loyalty that bound him to his king? I sat down myself, then, with a hollow sense of disaster averted — but for how long?

"Branwen, see me to bed. I am not well —" said Esseilte hurriedly. The shadows around her eyes were like Drustan's bruises.

"Not well . . ." the king echoed, so softly that only we could hear. "Nor am I, nor is the land, nor will it be if you do not turn to me . . . Esseilte . . . Esseilte . . . are you just a cold Irish bitch, or is there something more? We began with such promise!" He stared grimly after us as Esseilte and I moved toward the door. As I closed it I heard him calling Drustan and Maglos and the other men.

"Come with me to the camp then, and we'll see if they have drunk all of the wine!"

> *"Unite and unite, and let us all unite . . ."*

The strains of the May song came raggedly through the trees, striking my ears in what seemed a deliberate mockery, for there

was only disunion here! Aided by my herb tea, Esseilte had sunk
into a troubled sleep at last, but tension jumped through every
nerve in my body; for my own ills I had no medicine.

For Esseilte, tonight was only one more denial. But I understood precisely why Marc'h had gone down to the camp to
drown his sorrows. Was it the hawthorn, or the singing, or some
invisible conjunction of forces that sanctified the festival, that
stirred me so? I knew only that the memory of what I had
shared with the king the year before was alive in every inch of
me. The cool night air caressed me, and I shivered as if all my
senses had focused in my skin. Was it I who wanted, or the
world around me that ached with need?

Unable to be still any longer, I pulled my green mantle around
me and moved slowly down the slope behind the dun. Bushes
quivered, dim in the starlight, and I heard a low laugh. One of
the men from the dun, I thought, with his lass. More quickly, I
walked past, unwilling to disturb them, though I was unable to
bear awareness of their joy. But it seemed to me that every
clump of greenery hid its pair of lovers as I went on. Now I was
running, desperate to escape the passion that beat against my
senses from everywhere. What man and maid did beneath the
hedgerows was part of the night's celebration, but it only
touched the surface — the land wanted more.

When I came to myself once more I was standing in an open
field. On every side the land rolled away in hills and hollows,
guarding its secrets. This was a gentler land than the moors on
which I had wandered, where woods filled the folds between
high cropland and pasture. In the distance, torches glimmered,
and the music of the night-birds mingled with snatches of song.
But there was no one near.

At Beltane, as at Samhain, the doors opened between the
worlds. I took a deep breath and let my awareness sink inward.
The Bucca had said that I might call upon Faerie, and in the
year since I had met him, I had never felt the need as I did now.

"Bucca — are you listening? Horned One, I need your help —
where are you? Can you even hear?"

Doubt wrenched the words from me. When I wandered the
moors I had been ill. I had told none but Ogrin what I had seen
there, fearing that those who did not call my visions demonic
would think them delirium. But until this moment, I had never
doubted that what I had seen was true.

I sank down upon the grass, weeping, rubbing my eyes with

the heels of my hands. What was real? Surely the grass I was sitting on, the cowslips, tight-closed against the night, the sweet pungence of wild thyme. . . . I clung to my knowledge of those simple things. Blindly I reached out to the coolness of the dew that wet the grass and let it soothe my aching eyes.

When I opened them, the world was transformed. At Ogrin's rock, I had seen the life in every blade of grass as a haze of golden light. It was silver in the starlight, a cool radiance that outlined each leaf, and within each leaf every vein.

This much, at least, had not been a dream. And if that were so. . . .

Ah, my sisters, little sisters . . . I sighed, looking at the flowers through half-focused eyes. *Will you not show yourselves to me?*

The radiance grew. I caught my breath, seeing forms grow luminous around me, not quite human, but more than flower — the nodding harebell, slender sedges and meadowgrass, worts and daisies — suddenly they were weaving around me as if the stars had come down to the meadow to hold festival.

It was true! It was all true! The forest shimmered as oak and elm and hazel, alder and willow released their dryads to join the dance. I willed the beating of my heart to steady and drew breath to renew my invocation.

"My Lord and my Lover, hear how I am calling! My Stallion, my Stag, my Shining One, hear me now!" The night grew quiet, listening. Instinct drew me to my feet, and my arms opened wide.

> *"I am the womb of every holt.*
> *I am the blaze on every hill.*
> *I am the queen of every hive,*
> *All living things obey my will. . . ."*

My throat pulsed with words that were not my own.

"I am Queen of the Logres that lies within, I am the White Raven, the Brigantia of Kernow! Come to me — *come to me!*" The throbbing life around me stilled, waiting, as I waited, for the answer to my call.

Then, with a heart-pounding pulse of drums, all the forest's night creatures came rioting from beneath the trees. The darting vole and the mole with velvet fur slipped through the grasses, fox and vixen tumbled like puppies among the flowers, lumbering badger and swift squirrel pushed toward me, and bounding above them, the red and fallow deer. But they were only the war-band, heralding their High King's coming. With a burst of sweet piping, he was suddenly among them, bluebells twined around his sleek flanks and his gleaming branched horns.

I felt as if I had been asleep since last I had seen him. This— *this* was reality, and the strivings of men as meaningless as a dream that dies with the day. The world whirled as his strong arms closed around me. Then it steadied, as if my feet had rooted in the soil. I breathed deeply, drawing that strength into my soul.

"It has been long since you called on us—"

"A long time, and a bitter time, for me," I agreed.

"What do you need?" The Bucca's deep voice vibrated through my bones.

"I need my husband, I need my lover, I need my king!" I cried, daring for the first time to put into words the desire that the land was forcing through me, and all that I as a woman had been denied. . . .

"Listen to the singing, and I will bring him to you—"

It seemed to me at first that they were singing the Maying song. But they did not sing with human voices, and their words were in no human tongue. There was birdsong in that music, and flowers opening to the sun, cool sap rising, and hot blood running, life pulsing around me as it beat within me until I could no longer tell which senses were the world's and which my own.

> *"Blessed the Lord who is laid by her side . . ."*

I recognized the song they were singing now.

A great stillness seemed to fall about me as I saw him coming, tall and kingly with the great stags attending him, and the glamor of Faerie lighting his wondering eyes. I blinked, for it was hard to focus on his glory. But I did not need to see him now. Nonhuman hands helped me to slip from my garments, as they helped him. Naked he came to me, skin slid against skin and I felt his hardness thrust against my belly.

I gasped and clutched at his strong shoulders, for all my awareness was dissolving, pooling in urgent sweetness between my thighs, and there was no strength in my legs anymore. But he was as eager as I was. Strong arms lifted and laid me down upon the sweet grass. His soft lips were everywhere upon my body, brushing my skin until it tingled, tasting me like a man long hungered until I whimpered with desire.

My own hands slid down the smoothly muscled body that

crouched above me. He sank down beside me with a groan, growing bolder as my thighs opened and his gentle fingers could probe deeper and all my life melted beneath his hands.

"Now, oh my king, my love — I cannot wait for you — fill me now!"

His arms wound around me as my legs gripped him, arching to meet the first aching thrust. There was no holding back this time, but the whole of the land was already in me. Again and again he thrust into me, as the stallion takes the mare in strength and glory, and the glory filled me until my spirit could hardly contain it. I gasped, nails scoring smooth skin, and he cried out as all the power that was in him sped to its goal like the golden ball with all the energy of the hurler behind it.

Awareness spun outward on a tide of pure power, pouring across the land. I felt it open, as I had opened, and relax again, content. And then, released, I sank into a cauldron of darkness in which all needs were satisfied.

When I came to myself again, a pale light was fading the stars. I stirred, feeling the chill as my flesh parted from that other body that had been joined to it so sweetly. With a sigh I looked down at him —

— And grew still. For even in the light of the false dawn I could see that this was not the king. How could I have mistaken Marc'h's lean and battle-scarred body for this one, whose smooth skin stretched tightly over muscles built by long hours with hay fork and hoe? But I had not been thinking at all. I had been a body driven by needs that were greater than its own.

He had a sweet face, I thought as I pulled myself the rest of the way free and looked down at him. The shock of sun-bleached hair fell across closed eyes as thickly lashed as those of a child, above lips that were tender, tempting kisses even now. The Bucca had done the best he could for me.

I wept as I put on my clothes again, but I did not feel betrayed. The boy, whoever he was, had served me like a king.

I came back to the dun as the first risers were stirring, my mantle heavy with flowers. They thought I had gone out early to bring in the May for the king's household, and so, in a way, I had. A garland of sycamore and cowslips bound with ribbons already hung over the doorway, a little askew, as if it had been put up before there was light enough to really see. We could hear singing from the village, but in the dun everyone was busy with the last of the packing for the men who were going away.

Esseilte would not wear the wreath that I had made her, but despite her jibes I kept my own.

It was mid-morning before the king came up from the camp with his sword-band behind him, all of them looking rather frayed and fragile — for those who had not been defeated by yesterday's hurling had succumbed to the gift of royal wine. A good many of them were swearing to stay faithful in the future to good British ale, which seemed a pity, when they were going into Gaul.

Marc'h himself appeared to be the least affected of them all, which rather surprised me, considering the mood in which he had left the dun.

"Have you some secret remedy for the wine-sickness then?" I asked him. "I should add it to my collection!"

He looked at the hawthorn in my crown of flowers and smiled. "No secret. By rights I should be as low as any man in my company, for surely I out-drank them all! But I had fair dreams. . . ."

I looked quickly away lest he should see those dreams reflected in my eyes. Perhaps it was beyond the Bucca's powers to extract a drunken ruler from among his warriors, but he had done the next best thing. No matter whose body had embraced me in the darkness, the spirit that had joined with mine had been that of the king. Perhaps the ritual we performed had done some good for the land as well as for me.

But as I turned, my gaze met that of Drustan. If Marc'h's dreams had shown him Paradise, Drustan's appeared to have taken him through hell.

"I have some tea that may help the headache —" Gently I steered him toward the hearth. "Sit down."

"How is *she*?" he asked in a low voice.

"In better temper than most of your companions, surely, though that is scant praise," I answered him. "I gave her a sleeping draft — I wish I had been able to do the same for you!"

"At the time . . . the wine seemed an excellent medicine," he said with a ghost of his usual irony.

I handed him a mug of tea which I had made with marjoram and betony and some other herbs. He winced, but drank bravely, and soon I was busy dealing out the concoction to the rest of them, who would have drunk poison if they thought it would get them on board the ships at the appointed hour. I suspected that seasickness would clean out their systems faster than anything I could give them, but I did not tell them so.

It was noon before we were ready to go down to the harbor, and the village festival was in full sway. We could hear the deep, steady boom of the drums all the way from the dun, like the earth's deep heart beat throbbing through the rocky soil. As we came down to the water the procession swung down the road from the chapel to meet us, dressed in garments of bleached linen with colored sashes, gay with ribbons and flowers.

"Where are the Irish dogs that make such boast O?
  They shall eat the gray goose feather,
And we will eat the roast O.
And in every land O, wherever we may go."

I supposed they had a right to gloat a little, with the marks where the Morholt had tried to burn it still black on the palisade that surrounded the dun, though I winced at the fervor with which they sang.

"Thou might'st have shown thy knavish face,
  Thou might'st have tarried at home O,
But thou shalt be an old cuckold.
  And thou shalt wear the horns.
Hal-an-tow and jolly rumble O,
For summer is a-come O, and winter is a-go.
And in every land O, wherever we may go!"

And that struck near the bone, if anyone had known it, but the singers were laughing, and Marc'h watched them and smiled. Flute and drums beat and twittered, and the leader, who wore a red tunic, much embroidered, that surely had once belonged to the lord of the dun, danced aside, waving his ribboned wand with the pig's bladder bobbing at its end.

I gasped, uncertain for a moment whether what I felt was amusement or alarm, for the Horse of Lan Wedenek was a gross apparition like a parody of the Bucca, with a horse's snapping skull at one end and at the other its tail, swathed in a black horsehide draped over a framework that swung at each step. Bobbing back and forth it came, threatening the bystanders who retreated, laughing, while its attendants cavorted around it. After a few moments I realized that it snapped at the men, but the women, especially the young women, were dragged under those flapping skirts and not released until they had been smeared liberally with the soot that gave the horse its color. Then, I began to understand.

Esseilte stood with her cloak wrapped closely around her, for dark clouds were scudding in from the west and the wind was cold. But it was not the wind against which she sought that protection, it was the day itself — the procession, the people, and above all, the ships that were beginning to pull at their anchors as the tide came in.

Some of the men had embarked already, but Marc'h waited, his lips beginning to curve in that smile which I was learning to distrust. The Horse danced toward us and the rest of the king's household began to give way. But Marc'h held Esseilte's arm. He could not know to what use Esseilte put her mother's herb-lore, but he must have realized that her failure to bear him a child had caused her no pain. Yet an heir was one of the things for which he had married her.

She glared at him as she realized he was not going to let her go, but she had been bred up in a king's house, and knew better than to fight him before the people. Drustan stiffened beside me.

"He is not hurting her!" I hissed, gripping Drustan's arm. "I think he has realized that he cannot win her love, but he does have the right to her fertility. Would it not be better if she had a child?"

"Ah, how can I say?" He covered his eyes as if his head were hurting him. "We have talked of it, but she will not torture me by bearing a child to him, and she will not shame him, by foisting upon him her child by me. . . ."

"Perhaps it is as well, then, that you and the king will both be in Armorica," I said reflectively. "Whether she is blessed by the Horse or no, without lord or lover no one will expect her to get with child!"

The grotesque head swung past her; the reeking skirts brushed across breast and belly, leaving a smear of black upon the pale blue wool. The king released her then. She fell back with a stifled sound of disgust, trying to brush the soot away.

I caught her as she stumbled. "Do not touch it — you will offend them, and you'll only make it worse, trying to get it off that way."

Esseilte's hand fell, and she sighed. From the ships came a whistle. The king gave his wife a formal embrace, and then turned to me.

"Guard what has been entrusted to you," he said gravely. It

was not quite the same charge he had given me before, but I nodded. It was Drustan who gripped my hand with the anguished appeal. "Take care of her!"

The tears ran unchecked and unheeded down Esseilte's cheeks as the king's flotilla moved out of the harbor and into the estuary, gathering speed with the ebb of the tide. The Horse and his procession had moved on, but their singing drifted back through the cooling air.

> *"Awake, Mabon, thou art our champion O,*
>   *For summer is a-come O and winter is a-go,*
> *And every day God gives us his grace,*
> *By day and night O.*
> *Where is our defender, where is he O,*
>   *He is out in his long-boat all on the salt sea O,*
> *And in every land O, wherever we may go.*
> *And for to fetch the summer home, the summer and the May O,*
> *For summer is a-come O, and winter is a-go."*

Seventeen

WINE OF THE GAULS

Throughout that summer we waited for news, patient as the dogs that hang about the gates of Bannhedos, waiting for the scraps that are thrown outside. But without Drustan to steady her, Esseilte could not be still. From Lan Wedenek we moved up the coast to stay with the monks of Lan Juliot, then inland to Dynas Ban, down to Lys Hornek and the fortress of Chun, then back to Bannhedos again. The king's letters followed us, terse reports dictated from Ker-haes or various camps in the countryside, and with them an occasional fervent epistle from Drustan, when he could trust the messenger.

Marc'h had re-established his alliance with Macliavus of Venetorum. With his southern flank protected, he was free to pursue his plans for the northern coast that the British settlers had called Domnonia after their homeland. We read how the forest of Broceliande, whose fastnesses hid so many mysteries, had cloaked the eastward advance of the Cornovian army. From the plebes and the pagi of Ker-haes and Cornovia they came to join the hosts he had brought from Kernow, princes and chieftains leading their kin and the men who had sworn to them. Across the Black Mountains they had made their way, following the old Roman road to Subis and then to Redon in the country of the Gauls.

Other reports told how they had pushed northward through the line of hills to strike at Dol. From the letters we learned little but the bare facts of the campaign, but the messengers were sometimes more informative. It had been hard fought and bloody, and there were grim gaps in the telling whose meaning I did not want to explore. But it was clear enough that the king's own household spearheaded the battle, captained by Drustan. News of the conquest of Dol came in August, when the fighting was mostly over and Jonas of Dol was dead. The story current among the men of Ker-haes was that he had died from sheer fright at the approach of his enemy.

That summer we heard also that Queen Mairenn had died. We had returned to the guesthouse at Juliot's monastery by the fort of Durocornovium to wait out the warm days at the end of August. I found myself wondering if Mairenn had made her peace with the powers she served before the end.

"It seems hard, somehow, to picture her in heaven," said Esseilte, pausing beside me on the path. A low wall of zigzag slates held up the bank behind it, starred with orange lichens and crowned with white rockrose. Below us, the white-washed buildings of the monastery lay in dreaming peace on the rock-bridged island. Esseilte plucked a spray and we continued down the path.

"I shouldn't think the perfection of the celestial city would offer sufficient scope for her energy!" Neither of us wanted to admit that some of Mairenn's deeds might have earned her another fate entirely. Images of the queen as I had last seen her fluttered dark wings in my memory.

"I think she has gone to the Sidhe," I answered her. "The queen would not have wanted to abandon Eriu. . . ."

The slanting light of afternoon hazed the grass with gold, and the yellow flowers of the gorse glowed like tiny suns. I could feel the life in the land, storing up warmth against winter's storms. This was my land now, and if it were allowed, I would stay to guard it when my own time came. Like Morgaine, who had also been a hidden queen. . . . My forehead burned where Mairenn had once kissed me.

May the Lady welcome you, mother of my spirit — I thought then. *I understand you better now.*

Esseilte sighed and gave up the attempt to keep on her veil. She had grown thin after Drustan had gone, but today her face was glowing with sun and sea-air. Would anyone confuse the two of us now? Esseilte's vibrant beauty had become more delicate, the fine bone structure of her face bared by strain. Her skin was paler, and her hair, covered by the veil, a darker gold, while my expeditions into the countryside in search of herbs had made me sun-colored all over, tightened my waist, and built up the long muscles of leg and thigh.

"Why do I feel sorrow, Branwen? My mother might as well have died the moment we sailed out of Inber Colptha, for we knew that we would not see her again. Why should knowing she is gone bring such a sense of loss?"

I stared across the emerald waves as if I could see through the haze that veiled the horizon to Eriu. "Because," I answered slowly, "it means that we can never go home. Even if we could take wing and fly across the sea it would not be the same. We would be like Oisin when he returned from the Land of Youth. Now we are alone."

"Alone indeed, when we have neither the comfort of the old life, nor of the new." She stared southward toward Gaul. "And yet, do you know, Branwen — sometimes I feel that Drustan is near. At night his spirit seeks mine, and my longing is like a beacon to show him the way. I knew when he was wounded — before the letter that told us, my arm ached, and I knew that an arrow had struck him there."

I looked at her, remembering vividly standing in a moonlit garden a year ago, listening to Drustan. What these two had was not a relationship, but a religion, with two deities, and two worshippers. And yet even this mortal adoration had some power to ennoble the spirit, and who was I, still tormented by my hopeless love for the king, to condemn it entirely?

"Where is he now, Esseilte?" I said softly.

She took a deep breath and closed her eyes. As I watched, all the life in her seemed to flow inward. She swayed and I reached out to support her.

"He is near . . . he is coming nearer — oh Branwen!" Esseilte's eyes flew open and she gripped my arm. "He is coming here!"

Faintly through the thin soil I could feel the vibration of hoof-beats. I shaded my eyes with my hand. Something was moving on the southern road. A single horseman, whipping his mount ahead of the rest of his company: *Drustan* . . . All at once I was as sure of it as she. And my own inner vision told me that he had come to take us to Armorica.

"It is a pity that Jonas's cub escaped us — " Drustan swayed easily as the boat leaned into the wind. "Men say that the king's old nemesis, Samson, hid the boy and then got him away."

We had taken ship at Lan Wedenek the day before with Drustan and a picked escort of his own men. Some of them I remembered — his old friend Gorwennol, Hadron Hardhand and Wynek ap Vab and little red-headed Dinan.

Esseilte looked up and Drustan smiled as he went on. There was a glow in her face that owed nothing to sea-air, as if a lantern were burning within.

"Is that so terrible?" she asked. "It was not he, but his father, who was Marc'h's enemy."

Drustan sighed. "His survival will make it harder for the people of Dol to accept Marc'h's rule, and I would rather not have to compel them to recognize the advantages of unity again. . . ." A summer's campaigning had browned and toughened him. But his eyes were gray as the sky, shadowed by grim memories. Only when he looked at Esseilte did they grow clear as the sea.

I broke the silence. "Where is Iudual now?"

"In Lutetia, crying on Childebert's shoulder and asking him for aid," answered Drustan.

"Will the Frankish king help him?" I asked. "What interest can he have in Armorica?" I pulled the folds of my brat tightly around me to keep out the cold wind that was filling the sails. The sky was gray and featureless above a heaving pewter sea.

"What interest do any of these barbarians have in our lands?" said Gorwennol bitterly, hunkering down beside his friend. Lanky and grizzled as ever, he looked as if the fighting had worn even more hardly on him than on his lord. His cheek was marred by a new scar. "The rest of Gaul is Frankland now; why should they stop there?"

"The king thinks they might settle for an alliance if they see that we are united against them, and strong —" Drustan grinned mirthlessly. "He has been writing to Childebert too . . ."

I remembered how Marc'h had spoken in the circle of stones. The Franks and the Saxons were the wolves. Would a show of strength impress them, or would it be taken as a challenge? And would transplanted British tribesmen whose forefathers had only briefly recognized Artor's rule accept an imposed unity?

Esseilte and Drustan had drawn closer together. She laughed softly. I moved to stand between them and the crew and found Gorwennol by my side.

"Has it been bad?" I asked.

He shrugged, looking down at me. "When is war good, Branwen? But this fighting has been more bitter than most, for the

Wor-Tiern cannot afford to show mercy. There have been deeds that the worst of us do not like to remember. . . . I am a dull fellow, you know — if I were as poor a hand with a sword as I am with a harp I would have died long ago. But Drustan is a man who feels others' pain — how does he bear sights that have sickened my soul? I tell you, Branwen, every time my lord fights I fear."

"What do you mean?" I glanced at Drustan, who was laughing, pointing to something dark that bobbed among the waves, perhaps a seal.

"You have not seen him in battle, have you?" said Gorwennol. I shook my head. It was Drustan the tormented harper, Drustan the impassioned lover, that I knew.

"Drustan may be the most dangerous warrior we have. You wouldn't think it to look at him, would you — " He gestured toward the prow, where Drustan had taken Esseilte's hand as gently as if he held a butterfly. "It is not his strength, really, as much as his skill and speed — not even those — " he corrected himself. "I think he stops caring what happens to him when he takes the sword in his hand, as if he feels his death would be an expiation . . . for many things. . . . Perhaps he will defend himself better when the queen is by."

I remembered how Drustan had faced Esseilte in the sweathouse. There had been a moment then when I thought he would have welcomed the sword. Had separation from Esseilte renewed his despair? It might be so, but I wondered if divided loyalties might impose an even greater strain. What fate waited for us in Armorica?

I shook my head, trying to sort out my confusions. "I do not understand how the king can manage this war. Last summer, he was Theodoric's ally against Macliavus — how does he justify supporting his enemy?"

"Ah, well, Theodoric is becoming a great man among the Cymri. He has been busy fighting for his brother-in-law, and Unhintic has borne him a son. Perhaps when Urien has conquered the rest of the North, Theodoric will have time to worry about Kemper. Oh, he has been busy, that lad, and then there was the Irish business — " He stopped suddenly with a quick glance at Esseilte.

"What is it?" I asked.

"Oh, just a story we heard . . . a man of Connachta called Aed Guaire killed a steward who was on business of the High

King and fled to Britain for refuge — to Glevissig, actually. But I
suppose Theodoric considers himself bound by Marc'h's alliance
with Eriu, for he has sent him back again, and I daresay King
Diarmait will know how to deal with him. He seemed a formidable old bird . . ."

I nodded, but I wondered, for it was well-nigh unthinkable
that anyone would even defy the Ard-Righ's law. The boat lifted
beneath me, then swooped down the slope of the wave, and I
shivered, for it seemed to me that the kingdoms of earth were
becoming as uncertain as the shifting surface of the sea.

The wind stayed cold, but fair, and two days more brought us
through the black islets that guarded the passage to the western
coast of Armorica, and toward the rocky point of Vanis which
once had sheltered the city of Ys that now lay drowned beneath
the waves. Then we turned landward at last, making for a deep,
protected bay.

The boat slid toward the shoreline under shortened sail. I
could see rolling country covered with thick forest, with the
ragged black silhouettes of mountains rising in the distance beyond them. This was a shadowed land, stony and secretive,
and though the men who settled it might have given it the names
of their homeland, it seemed harsh after the open moors of
Kernow.

An order from Drustan brought the bow around and we eased
past a low-lying island into the narrow harbor. On the island,
men were laboring with wood and stone to build a tower; they
waved as we passed by.

"Fortifications," Drustan explained. "Marc'h has given me the
island to defend, and a fort there will command the bay. But we
are going to his villa at Plebs Marci just beyond the ruins of the
old Roman town."

I lifted my eyes, searching the tumble of overgrown masonry
where an occasional column still stood witness to vanished glory.
They said that when the men of Britain first came into this land
hardly a town was peopled, and where the men of Rome had
banqueted, the wild sow rooted and the bull and the bear
roamed free.

Beyond the ruins I could see woodsmoke twisting into the air.
Plebs Marci — Marc'h's town — the heritage of Armorica was British now. . . .

* * *

Cold weather swept down upon us hard and early. At Samhain Marc'h moved his household to winter quarters in his fortress at the headwaters of the Aon. Ker-haes was a stronghold within a natural fortress whose encircling walls were the Black Mountains and the hills of Arré. But it was also the crossroads of central Armorica, and muddy messengers straggled in from Aleth or Redon, Geso or Venetorum as the season drew on. The eastern coasts lay uneasy in the Horse King's grasp, and Riwal was said to be raising the rest of Domnonia to resist any attempt to extend Marc'h's rule.

It was a hard winter, and all passions seemed frozen by the bitter winds that swept down from the hills. There were times when I thought that no fires could warm the massive stones of Ker-haes's walls. Marc'h had brought his queen to Armorica in hopes of getting her with child at last, but her resolve to bear no heir to dispute Drustan's claim remained firm, despite increasing evidence that his valor in the campaign had done nothing to increase his popularity. Yet it seemed to me that if the king got little joy of his lady, no more did Drustan, for close-quartered as we were, there were few chances for them to be alone. By the time the Black Months were drawing to an end, we were all longing for spring.

The cold was reluctantly loosening its grip at last when we had visitors of another kind. Beneath the delicate green haze of budding oak-trees that lined the Redon road I saw them riding, big, fair men on heavy horses, mud-splashed to the shoulder, for the rains had been hard the week before. Beneath the mud, though, their mantles were lined with fur, and the watery sunshine picked out the gleam of gold. The one in the lead was young, his eyes pale as the spring sky and his hair blowing wildly. As he came out from under the trees three crows flapped up from the branches and flew away, cawing.

Horns blew from the gate in welcome. As I hurried down to the hall I heard the rolling cadences of Frankish Latin and British voices answering, warm with welcome. I stopped, dizzied by intuitions to which I could put no name. Suddenly the winter's constriction seemed a safety which we would look back upon with longing all too soon.

King Childebert's response to Marc'h's offer of alliance had come.

"Wine and blood they run, blent in one,
Wine and blood they run!
'Tis the Gauls' bright blood, runs in flood,
'Tis the Gauls' bright blood!
   Fire, fire, steel oh steel!
   Fire, fire, steel and fire!
   Oak, oak, earth and waves!
   Waves, oak, earth, and oak!"

Drustan struck the harp fiercely as he chanted the verses and the chorus, bawled out by half a hundred voices, echoed back from the rough-cut granite of the walls. Trophies from last summer's warring hung from the heavy beams; standards and captured weapons quivered as stamping feet shook the hall. The raiding song had accompanied the men of Britain through their conquest of Armorica, altering to fit conditions, and the chorus was older still. It was a war song, and a drinking song. Marc'h seemed to have an endless supply of Gaulish wine to wash it down, and the Franks an endless capacity for consumption.

"I've drunk wine and gore in the war,
I've drunk wine and gore!
Wine and blood they feed fat indeed,
Wine and blood they feed!"

Chramn dashed his silver-banded cup against the table with a thunk that sent wine upward in a crimson fountain as the song swung to its rousing conclusion. The enamel and gold in his ornaments glinted in the candlelight.

"Ah, we'll drink deep o' that wine, come the spring! Father'll see then if the old blood runs true . . . he'll see then that he was wrong!" He set his elbows on the table and rested his fair head on his hands, gazing sadly into the dark wine. I still blinked when I looked at him, for even the Irish were rarely quite so colorful — he had put on a loose coat of purple, with cuffs embroidered in gold, over a green silk tunic pinned with a chip-carved eagle brooch set with garnets, and red-leather strapping cross-gartered his linen braes.

"Indeed," said Marc'h calmly, "Chlotar was mad to banish such a son. But your uncle loves you, and your uncle, not your father, is the over-king. . . ."

"Tha's true!" Chramn lifted his head with a grin that reminded me of a puppy that has just been patted. "Father thinks that when old Childebert dies he'll have it all. 'N he can leave it to Arnegund's brat. My brothers don't understand. . . . But it's my uncle's crown, isn't it? An' he's going to leave it to me!" He giggled happily. "I'm goin' to be king of the Franks, and you're goin' to be my frien'. . . ." Chramn draped one brawny arm across Marc'h's shoulders. I could see Drustan repressing a smile, and Karasek of Nans Dreyn snickered behind his hand.

Marc'h sighed indulgently, and after a moment removed the arm.

"But King Childebert, may God preserve him, is going to live a long time. Don't you think he also needs friends?"

"*Got* friends . . ." muttered Chramn. Marc'h gestured to Esseilte to fill the Frankish prince's cup with more wine. Chramn looked up at the movement and covered her hand with his paw.

"Pretty lady — pretty queen!" He seemed to notice the sudden chill in the eyes of the men around him and released her, laughing again. "*My* wife's pretty too. Miss her, y'know . . . and the babies. Got a little daughter and two sons — you got sons?" He grinned up at Marc'h and Esseilte, who flushed painfully and eased away.

"My son Budic is my heir for Ker-haes . . ." the king said evenly, not looking at his queen. "He holds Dol for me now."

Heir to Ker-haes, and how much more? I wondered. Bretowennus of Penryn and the others were nodding approvingly. I had heard that there was another son, Tremor, by Marc'h's second wife Tryphyna. But the marriage had been a failure, and the boy a damaged, poor-spirited thing who had taken vows with the monks in the town.

"We could be strong friends to a ruler, my son and I —" Marc'h went on. "Think you that your uncle understands that, Chramn?" He watched with a steely patience. This was the question he had waited through almost a week of lavish hospitality to ask.

The Frankish prince shrugged and took another swallow of wine. "An alliance? He might accept you as a subject king. . . ."

"Subject to a barbarian?" came a harsh whisper from Mevennus Maglos. "Artor made the Saxons *his* subjects, and this Frank-king's fathers were scratching their fleas beyond the Rhenus when ours ruled Rome!"

Silence grew heavy in the room.

"Our chieftains will never support that —" said Rigan of Tregor, a lord of Domnonia who had quarreled with Riwal and become Marc'h's ally. "Hard enough to make them bow to a

Wor-Tiern of their own race. We will have a hard summer's fighting before Pompeius Regalis gives in. The British of Armorica will never accept subjection to a foreigner!"

"Proud British — proud Franks — somebody'll have to give in. . . ." Chramn nodded wisely. Marc'h frowned.

"My warriors may have something to say about that —" He gestured around him. "Don't make the mistake of thinking that because Drustan, here, does not match your stature, he cannot match you in arms. The men of Dol know better, and I have a dozen who are almost his peer!"

"*Almost!* Will you make that cuckolding pig your champion?"

I looked around quickly, for the whisper had been almost too faint to hear. It was Meriadek, whose service during the summer had won him back a place among the companions, though the king still looked through him as if he were not there. What disturbed me was that Karasek was listening.

"Aye, he does think a lot of himself, does lord Drustan . . ." the older man agreed.

I thought that Drustan's flush had another cause. He avoided talking about his triumphs. What I saw in his eyes now was not pride, but shame, whether for the deeds themselves, or because no valor could compensate for the trust he betrayed in his heart every time he looked at the queen.

"Brave men . . . never doubted it . . ." mumbled Chramn. *"Valiant Briton, thine the white wine, valiant Briton —"* His pale head nodded, lowered until it rested upon his crossed arms. After a moment we heard a grunting snore.

Marc'h sighed and motioned to the other Franks to come put their prince to bed.

The eagle screams, plummeting, talon-stretching, sharp beak tearing the air. Shrieking defiance, the stallion rears. Knife-hooves slash, mane tosses . . . rage pulses between them . . . thunder rolls across the sky and rattles the shutters . . . the stallion trumpets defiance . . .

Horns blared again and again. I felt the bed beneath me shiver as I struggled toward consciousness. I heard the hollow thud of struck timbers; I thrust a tangle of sleeping furs to the floor as a second splintering crash told me that the gate had given way. A babble of women's voices rose above the din.

Esseilte! I threw a fur over my shoulders and ran for the door. I could hear the queen's crisp orders shocking the women into a semblance of calm. She looked up as I pushed through.

"An attack—I don't know who. Marc'h is already down there—" She gestured toward the yard below. *And Drustan . . .* She did not need to tell me. He slept in the room on the other side of the royal bedchamber. He would be a step behind, or perhaps in front of, his king.

"Go to the cellars then, if you are frightened!" Esseilte snapped at the other women. "You'll be safe, but of course by the time our attackers find you they will already also have found the wine. . . ." Visions of rape replaced the fear of dying. The outburst that followed was more subdued.

"From the roof we can see—" I began. She nodded, and I snatched up her heavy mantle and bundled it around her. Together we scrambled up the narrow spiral and into the chill pre-dawn air.

Torches danced like piskies in the space below, but I could hear yells, and the clangor of steel. This was no faerie flitting, but the human face of war. It was a measure of the uncommon peace in which Esseilte and I had lived that we had never looked upon battle before. Memory supplied details of the outlines the gray light dimly revealed, the tower below us with its cluster of outbuildings, the long shape of the feasting hall, and the circle of stone around us that had failed to keep out the enemy. There was movement there; the uncertain light caught the red gleam of swinging swords. It was a daring attempt, made all the more effective by its sheer unexpectedness. Lights showed in the village beyond our walls, but all our warriors were in the dun. If the villagers were sensible they would stay within doors until the fighting was done.

The torches that had ringed the base of the tower drew away again. Dark lumps lay here and there on the ground. All those who had broken out of the buildings had been killed, then. For a few moments there was silence. Then I heard the sounds of something being dragged. Esseilte gripped my arm.

"Come out, Marc'h of Kernow! A guest is knocking at your door. Where is your welcome?" For a moment, grouped torches revealed the face of the speaker clearly—a tall man, gaunted by age, with a beak of a nose and a shock of once-red hair. A wolf-skin pinned with a great ring-brooch broadened his shoulders; red light glinted on the rivets in his bull-hide shield. "Come out to me, old horse, or we will roast you in your stall!" His men roared approval.

The sky was paling, and I became aware that what I had

heard was the sound of wood and brush being dragged against the walls. The upper levels of the tower were timbered. With enough encouragement, they would burn.

Esseilte let go of my arm with a sigh. "Is the tale truly to end this way? Fire is a clean death, but I would rather have burned in Drustan's arms!" I looked at her in wonder, for her voice was quite calm. Then an inner darkness buffeted my awareness like dark wings, covering her next words.

"In his arms you will burn. In my arms you will die . . ." I said in a voice that was not my own.

Esseilte was still talking when my senses returned. Had I spoken aloud? The moment was forgotten as a door opened below us and a shadow emerged.

"Pompeius Regalis—" The figure paused. "I am sure you will understand why I do not invite you in. . . ." Marc'h's voice held a note like the echo of thunder.

Beware . . . I thought then. *You think you have trapped him, Riwal, but I have heard that note before . . . beware!* I shivered, not entirely from the chill in the air.

"Why not, since you keep such hospitality? A Frankish prince, no less, I am told—now I wonder what you and he have found to say?" There was a creaking noise that I supposed was Riwal's laughter.

"What business is that of yours, old man?" came Chramn's voice from inside. "If I am harmed do you know what Childebert will do to you?"

"Have I threatened you?" asked Riwal. "You and your men are free to go whenever you will. In fact I insist upon it. I have no quarrel with your uncle, none at all, as long as he keeps to his domains. . . ."

"What if I refuse?" Chramn's voice was perceptibly less slurred than it had been, and my respect for him rose.

"You will not refuse—" Marc'h interrupted Riwal's answer. "He is right, my prince—this quarrel is an old one, and it must be settled between him and me."

"Ah, you do understand. I am glad. Come out then, Horse King—I have a thirsty blade." Riwal lifted it, redder than torchlight should have made it. Somewhere a cock challenged the dawning day.

Shield up, Marc'h moved out into the yard to face his foe. There was a blur of movement as warriors who had been hidden in the shadow of the walls rushed in behind him. But another blade flared from the darkness. One assailant fell, blood spurting from his neck as the sword sliced through; another reeled back screaming as he clutched at the stump of his sword hand. The falling weapon clanged against stone. Steel clashed as Marc'h and the third man traded blows, then the king's weapon slid soundlessly into his opponent's breast. There was a shaken silence.

"It is unseemly for a High King to receive guests unescorted," said a new voice. "My lord, I am here . . ."

It was Drustan — of course, who else could it be? He sounded a little breathless, but I thought his eyes would be laughing, as I had seen them once on shipboard, when he battled a storm.

"Is it Gwenneth's whelp?" growled Riwal, looking him up and down. "At least he doesn't favor me —"

"Be silent!" Marc'h's voice cracked across that of his enemy. "She was your own daughter — will you dishonor her name?"

Riwal let out a harsh bark of laughter. "'Twas not I who dishonored it! But I see the boy looks puzzled. Can it be that —" His words were lost as Marc'h's sword swept up and around. Almost too late, his own, longer weapon came up to guard.

The two blades kissed and parted in a slither of steel. Riwal's warriors started forward, but Drustan was before them, and they hesitated, unwilling to share the fate of their companions, even though Drustan wore only the tunic he had slept in, and had come out without any shield.

The light was strengthening. I could see all too clearly how swiftly Riwal moved — like an eagle striking, despite his age. But Marc'h was warming now, unleashing the power that I remembered. A feint to the right wrenched Riwal around to meet it, and he barely got up his shield. His return blow echoed on the king's. Then the two shields crashed together. For a moment the two men strained, flailing with blades that turned as they struck so that only the flat could land, breath puffing out in clouds of mist in the damp air.

My lord, my love, may the Morrigan speed your arm! went my soundless cry.

As if he had heard me, Marc'h leaped back, striking over and around his enemy's shield. The blow should have struck Riwal's shoulder, but the other man was already retreating. His sword whirled by Marc'h and onward, swinging straight toward Drustan's unprotected side.

Esseilte's voice and mine joined in a single anguished cry.

Drustan started to turn, his blade snapped outward and his grandfather's sword rasped past it, slicing down the ribs toward the groin. Drustan staggered and clapped his hand to his side. Marc'h's shout shook the timbers as Riwal's men started forward, but one leap brought the king within range again; his sword came up in a long sweep that knocked the shield aside and sliced up through the soft belly, caught in the rib cage, and thrust on through into the old man's heart.

Bright blood welled between Drustan's fingers, but his own lifting blade held off the rest of the Domnonians as Riwal collapsed, sword and shield flung wide. Then Chramn and the other warriors who had been caught in the hall spilled out the door, blades glittering in the bloody dawn, and the Domnonians ran. Their lord lay where he had fallen, staring into the rising sun with dulling eyes.

"Why did he hate my mother?" asked Drustan faintly, leaning on his sword. "Why did he want to kill me?" Birds were beginning to sing in the trees outside, oblivious to the deaths and doubts of men.

Marc'h only shook his head. Drustan swayed then, and the king moved swiftly to get an arm around him and help him inside.

"I can't complain about getting rid of old Pompeius so easily, but 'tis a pity we didn't lose Drustan as well! Eagle and chick in the same snare — it would have been so poetic." The dry tones stopped me short. I stood still on the stairs, gripping the tray.

"I hate him," came a second voice. "He dirties the queen by his very existence!" I recognized Meriadek's bitterness, and realized that the first speaker must have been Karasek. Clearly they had not realized that this stairway led up to the royal chamber in the tower.

"Never mind. His wound is healing, but the man's not immortal. We'll have other chances."

"No . . ." said Meriadek hoarsely. "Haven't you seen how she looks at him since the raid? And with spring so soft in the air and the flowers blooming, the flesh grows hot with desire. They will be at their dirtiness again, the Devil damn them!"

It was not only Esseilte and her lover who were tormented, but I had no sympathy to spare for Meriadek's pain. For two years I had borne a greater sorrow than he.

"Do you have a plan?" Karasek spoke idly.

"We must watch them! If Drustan goes to her this evening, I will ride out to bring Marc'h back more quickly. They do not know he is so near!"

I took a deep breath of the scented air. What Meriadek had said was true — it took an effort to resist the beauty of the day. Taking care not to rattle the dishes on the platter I held, I crept back up the stairs.

"Yes — Drustan is coming to me tonight," Esseilte answered when I had repeated what I had heard. "Are you surprised?" Her needle jabbed viciously into the silk she was embroidering.

"I will warn him not to come," I began, but she shook her head.

"Meriadek spoke true. This is the last chance we will have before they march on Domnonia. Drustan must go with them — Marc'h means to make him Lord of Léon. But I have seen how men battle now — when I close my eyes, warriors march between me and sleep. Drustan must go to war, but I will not release him until I have felt his heart beat against mine once more — until I have felt his life throbbing between my thighs."

Shivering, she stabbed her finger instead of the cloth. A single drop of bright blood bloomed crimson on the silk.

Staring at it, she whispered, "I have seen Drustan's blood like this upon the ground. . . ."

I swallowed. "I understand. But you will be watched. You must both take care!"

Drustan came to his lady in the evening when the pink dusk lay lightly upon the shadowed hills and the first stars were pricking bright holes in the luminous sky. Meriadek and Karasek were playing fidchel at the foot of the stairs, but Drustan only laughed when I told him.

"Did you see nothing but the fighting, when you stood on top of the tower? The logs of the upper story slant inward. With the bark still on, they present no obstacle to an active man. For the sake of a wager, I have scaled that wall drunk, and taken no harm! Go up and tell those two vultures that your lady has a headache and has retired. Tell them to keep good watch, and let no one come in!"

He was still laughing as he slipped through the narrow window, but Esseilte wept as she clasped him.

"Are you real?" She gripped his shoulders. "Are you truly well? Twice I have fought for your life, my beloved — I cannot bear to think what the third time will be!" I saw him wince a little as her arms tightened around him, but she was weeping again and did not see.

"Esseilte, Tiernissa, why are you so afraid? It will take a better man than Riwal to bring me down!" Drustan murmured into her hair.

He tipped up her chin, and her eyes closed as his lips brushed her brow, her eyelids, along the curve of her cheek and then, very gently, found her mouth at last. Her trembling eased. Then he laid her upon the great bed, and I took my lamp up to the roof to keep watch for the king.

There was time and enough to warn them, when I saw the torches of his escort bobbing along the road. By the time he reached the dun, Drustan was descending the wall. I could not help but laugh at Meriadek's crazed insistence that the queen and her lover were still there.

The king's brows bent in that look of danger I had seen before. I had not thought he would believe the man, but perhaps he, too, wanted an excuse to banish him finally.

But I ceased to laugh when Esseilte threw aside the bedclothes to confound them, and we saw the linen all stained and smeared with red. Drustan's blood . . . his wound must have opened during the climb, or perhaps during their lovemaking, and in the darkness of their passion neither had known.

"My lady, are you ill?" For the first time since I had known him, Marc'h seemed old. I had feared his anger, but far worse was this unvoiced agony. Esseilte looked at the ruined cloth, and the color drained from her face as if she had had an open wound indeed. There was a moment of silence, then she turned to me.

"My moon must have come upon me early. Branwen, will you help me to change?" Her voice was strained, but surprisingly steady. Both of us met the king's shadowed gaze. He had been married three times, and must have known a woman's cycle well enough to realize that the pattern of those stains was wrong, but our eyes beseeched him — *believe it, please say that you believe!*

But Karasek, quicker-witted than his fellow conspirator, had already scrambled back down the stairs to the hall where Drustan's sickbed had been made up near the fire. In a moment, shouting rang hollowly from below.

"Wor-Tiern, come down! Here is the wound that has stained your honor! Come here, my lord, and see!"

Even a king had no choice but to go down to them. Drustan had stopped struggling when he saw us, but they had mishandled him. He stood tense in the grip of his captors, blue eyes blazing. There was blood on his bedding too, and the clumsy bandaging with which he had rebound his side was blooming in a spreading stain.

"It is not proof . . ." Marc'h said heavily. "No—" He held up one hand as the uproar began anew. "Not unless I had found them together. But who will doubt their guilt when they hear of this day? Ah, Drustan, the peace was a battle, too, and you have failed me. Who will follow me if they think I allow you to dishonor my bed at will?"

"My lord—" Drustan began, but a sharp gesture from the king cut short his words. Marc'h eased stiffly down on the wolfskin that covered his carven chair.

"No, do not betray me further with protestations. After this, there is no way either of you can remain with me!" His heavy gaze moved from Drustan to the queen. "Will you go back to your father? No—" he answered his own question, "for that would break the alliance. . . . From what I have heard, the Ard-Righ has worries of his own, but a formal repudiation would be something he could not ignore.

"Let him think you have followed Grainne—oh yes." He smiled painfully. "I am familiar with that tale, though perhaps I should have studied it more. It is a fine story for the fireside, but will you like living it as well?"

Esseilte's eyes widened. She made a quick, helpless gesture, as if she had suddenly realized what was happening, and I put my arms around her, unsure whether I was trying to protect her or seeking support as a tide of warring emotions buffeted my awareness. I flinched from Esseilte's shock and confusion . . . Drustan's anguish, and more terrible than either, the sickening dark tide of Marc'h's uncomprehending pain.

"Drustan of Léon." The king's voice rang suddenly like a brazen gong. "I declare you landless and stripped of all command. If you have indeed put Esseilte's love above all other loyalties you shall eat the bitter fruit of your devotion. Let the wilderness shelter you—neither you nor she shall find refuge in my domains."

"But they have sinned!" squeaked Meriadek. "They must die!"

"Be silent, or it is *you* who will die!" roared the king. "I should have killed you before. Esseilte is my queen! Drustan got that wound fighting for me! I have no proof that they have betrayed me—I banish them because if I do not I can never hope to lead the men of Armorica to unity!"

Eighteen

BROCELIANDE

"Where is my daughter? White Raven, keep faith with me!"
The words of the dream echoed in my ears. But Mairenn had
come to me as a black raven, wings of darkness overshadowing
my dreams. Even in the depths of the forest, my eyes were darkened. *"Remember your promise to watch over my child!"*

The hoofbeats of our mounts sounded softly in the listening
silence beneath the great trees. The summer had been very dry,
and heat weighted the still air. Oaks mightier than any in Kernow pillared the path; the forest floor was deep in rustling
bracken, but a few flowers still bloomed beneath the trees.

Soon — I told the darkness within me. *I will see her soon.* . . .

Had that dream truly been a visitation from the Otherworld,
or was Mairenn's image only a shape for my own fears? Since
Esseilte had fled into the wilderness with Drustan, three months
had passed. For a time messages reached me — they had passed
through Subis, and headed eastward into the land of the Gauls
on the Redon road. And then they had disappeared.

I governed Marc'h's household in Ker-haes as if I had been
queen indeed, while he marched out with fire and sword to take
possession of Riwal's territories. Most of Drustan's men went
with him, but I claimed Gorwennol to be my steward, and as
soon as the king's forces were well away, I sent him in search of
the fugitives.

And now he had found them.

I looked behind me, where Gorwennol was following, the

bags tied behind his saddle bulging as heavily as mine. The rest of my escort had been left in the village at the edge of the Roman road. They could at least pretend they did not know where we had gone. Gorwennol smiled, and pointed ahead through the trees. I saw a sudden gleam of light on water. Wavelets kissed to life by the breeze glittered in the afternoon sun. Pungent woodsmoke drifted from a lean-to cobbled together out of logs and leaves.

Is this a fitting shelter for the daughter of the High King of Eriu? I thought angrily. Then I smiled. If the stories were true, Grainne had slept in harder beds than this, and Cormac, her father, had been a greater king even than Diarmait MacCearbhaill, for all the poets called him Cormac's heir. Then I heard someone coughing. I kicked my mare into motion, calling Esseilte's name.

"I am all right, truly, Branwen —" Esseilte let go of my arm and sat back smiling. "I didn't wish you to worry about me!" The flickering firelight gilded the sharp planes of her face, as brown as mine was, and shone on hair bleached to silver-gilt by the sun. But I had never been so thin. "Would you like some more venison? Drustan is a fine hunter; we have never lacked for game!"

I was willing enough, for the day's riding had given me an appetite, and the second-year buck that Drustan had brought down was well-flavored and tender. It roasted now over a good fire of coals, and we cut off slices as the heat cooked them. We had mushrooms and roots from the forest as well — somehow I had not expected such woodcraft from Drustan. Yet he had told us long ago that he had spent his childhood as a wanderer, and picked up a deal of useful lore. But neither that good, lean meat nor the mushrooms would put fat on Esseilte's bones.

"We've brought you flour and oil and a store of dried apples and honey; a new woolen brat of Irish weave and gowns of good linen —" I began, but Esseilte laughed.

"And a palace in a hazelnut shell? Oh Branwen, I know well that if you could, you would do that for me. I have missed you, my more than sister, but won't you believe that I have been happy here?"

"Oh yes . . . I believe you. . . ." I looked at her and sighed. Happiness radiated from her like the heat from the fire. She and Drustan hardly needed to talk to each other, for the one always seemed to know without speaking what the other desired. I would have felt only joy for her, if it had not been for that persistent coughing, which even now she could not quite hide.

"Show me the lake, Drustan," I said when we had eaten. He stood, too quickly, as if he already knew what I wanted to say. Esseilte was dealing with the leftover food with an ostentatious efficiency. I followed Drustan down to the shore. We walked beside the quiet waters as the rising moon dimmed the stars and hunting owls slipped by on silent wings. We walked, and from the camp behind us, I heard Esseilte's dry cough.

It was Drustan who broke the silence.

"Well, kind Branwen, you have come to give me a scolding, have you not? Do not make me wait too long . . ." There was a smile in his voice, and a kind of weary resignation that made me wince even as I replied.

"Not you, Drustan. If she would let me, it is Esseilte I would scold. . . . I don't like the sound of that cough! I have nursed her through such things before, and I know how tenacious they can be. If she does not recover before the rains come, what will you do?"

"I don't know." He turned away, running his fingers through his hair. "I have bivouacked in places that would make this forest look like the Land of Promise. It never occurred to me that it would be so hard for her. Esseilte doesn't want to leave, but when the weather breaks we will have to go. Maybe I can take service with some southern lord . . ."

"But you don't want to—" I said for him. "You've stayed here for the king's sake, isn't that true? Do you fear he will need you when his enemies try to drag him down?"

"Ah, Branwen, Branwen, what can I do?" He ground the heels of his hands into his eyes. "I love them both too well!"

We stood still on the shore. I heard the whisper as the wavelets kissed the land, and above it, the painful sweet music of a nightingale.

"If she is not well by the Feast of St. Michael, you must send me word," I said finally. "And sleep with your sword unsheathed between your two bodies from that time on. I will bring Marc'h here. . . ."

Two days later, I started home. There was no need for Gorwennol to accompany me, for a half-day's ride would bring me back to the hamlet where my escort waited, and I needed the time alone. Away from the lake, the air seemed even heavier than it had been, and the blue of the sky was veiled by smoke or high cloud. I wondered if it was the smoke of burning villages, if somewhere men and women were cursing the Horse King's name.

I had not spoken to Esseilte and Drustan about the war, and they had not asked me. But Marc'h had grown grim after he banished them. To do it had gone against his nature, I knew, and wondered what other cruelties he might give way to when there was only ambition where love should have reigned. I shivered suddenly, though the air was still warm.

This land is not good for him, I realized suddenly. Artor had sprung from Britain's ancient royalty as well as the Roman line, and been consecrated High King in the old way. So had Marc'h. But this was not Britain. . . . *Marc'h is not bound to Armorica . . . he does not hear its inner music, nor do I!*

The horse shied, and I forced my focus back to the outer world, patting her sweating shoulder. Something moved on the path before me. I blinked and saw a small brown viper, with a band of yellow about its neck like the torque of a chieftain, unraveling through the dry grass.

But we were not upon the path! A deer trail twisted down the slope before me, but there was no print of hoof or heel upon it to tell me that men had ever come this way. The sky above was like burnished silver, diffusing the light so that I could not tell in which direction the Roman road lay. Yet it seemed to me that if I could reach the stream at the bottom of this hill I might find a clearer way.

And so I let the mare pick her way downward, pushing through clumps of gorse and thorn that closed behind us until I was no longer even sure which way we had come. There was water here, but it did not seem to be flowing in any particular direction. It twisted slowly through shallow runnels and turned the earth to mud that looked as if it had been soaked in blood.

The land through which I wandered now was a waste of folded gullies and hillocks choked in a scrub of sallow and stunted pine. The trees were tall enough to obscure vision, but too slender to climb for a better view. Here and there the bones of the earth protruded in jagged outcroppings of bronze-colored stone. There were paths — many paths — and all of them were constantly branching. How could I know which way to go?

The sky settled lower, or was it ground mist closing in? Why did no birds sing? The mare's hoof rang on metal and she half-reared, snorting alarm. Grasping for her mane, I glimpsed brown bronze below me, and the dull white of weathered bone, and knew I was not the first traveler to be lost this way. I reined in. I could feel the mare trembling beneath me, her sweat pungent in the close air.

The traveler's usual expedients would not help me here. This land was not mine, but I had to hope that its spirits were akin to those I knew. I took a deep breath of the heavy air, willing the pounding of my heart to slow.

"Brigid . . . Brigantia . . ." I whispered. "Hear me! I have felt Thy spirit in Kernow and in Eriu, and found Thy image in the ruined temples of this land . . . Lady of the well and flame, why hast Thou brought me here? What is Thy will for me?"

The silence grew heavier, as if something were listening. I was listening too. Trying to still the murmur of panic within me, I let my awareness reach outward. The mare had quieted, breathing gustily. I let my gaze move slowly over the tangle of brush and vine, the haggard stone, the slowly moving stream. My skin prickled and I began to understand that somehow I had passed into a place that was not entirely the world men knew. But I had wandered in these realms before.

Lady, speak to me . . . I will try to do Thy will!

My eye focused on a mark in the mud by the mare's forefoot. It was the cloven print of a deer, just beginning to fill with water as if it had been made barely a moment ago.

But I had seen nothing.

There is no good grazing in this wasteland, I told myself. *If I follow these tracks, I will come out into the forest again.* I loosened the rein. The mare moved forward, and the hoofprints continued to appear before me. I took a deep breath, willing my eyes to unfocus, trying to see what my ordinary senses denied.

The deertracks *shone.* . . . They starred the muddy valley floor, bright as flowers on exposed rock faces, glowing in the patches of heather. The hoofprints glimmered, and away sped a shimmer of light as the thing that I was tracking went on before me. The mare's action grew easier as she moved out, and now, above the sound of her hoofbeats I could hear a faint piping.

We made a turn and the path branched sharply. The white deershape flowed up the bank and I gave the mare her head, holding tight as muscles bunched and released beneath me and she grunted up the slope after it. Hooves rang on rock. Suddenly I could see across a broad expanse of broom and heather. The piping had grown louder, a sweet melody that wandered on and on. The land fell away before me in folds of rolling forest, and against its darkness I saw, very clearly, the white stag. Around its neck gleamed a torque of gold.

It was dark when my guide stopped at last. This was no human habitation, but dim shapes against the stars told me that it once had been. I could hear the sweet gurgle of a spring nearby. My mare found the stream it fed and drank noisily. Almost too stiff to move, I slid from her back, and did the same. The cold of the water made my teeth ache, but it assuaged the worst of my hunger. When the horse was finished, I tethered her to a young oak where she could graze, and with my cloak and the horse-cloth made as good a bed as I could in the shelter of an old wall.

I had expected to fall asleep instantly, but though my muscles trembled with exhaustion, I could manage no more than a doze. It must have been midnight, for the full moon was high, when I came awake once more with the sensation that someone was watching me. I sat up, brushing leaves from my hair.

Pale light pooled around the fountain. Now I could see clearly the ruins in whose shadow I lay, the glittering leaves of the great oak from between whose roots the fountain bubbled, and facing it, the proud height of a mighty pine. But in a moment I realized that the clearing held more than trees. Next to the spring something white lifted — at first I thought it the wing of a great bird, a goose or a swan. Then it resolved itself into the heavy sweep of a linen robe. The figure turned a little. Moonlight glistened on a fall of shining hair. Two brilliant eyes met mine.

"Who are you?" I reminded myself that in Faerie, I was a queen.

"The Lady of the Fountain. . . ." Her voice had the same sweet music as the running water; easy to listen to that voice, easier still to obey.

"Why have you come to me?" My voice sounded like a raven's cawing in my own ears.

"You have questions. I can answer them, if you will do what I ask of you — "

"What do you want?" I answered suspiciously. Frightened as I was, I knew better than to make open promises to the people of the Otherworld.

"Nothing that will harm you, my daughter," she said softly, "and it will serve the land. . . ."

I stared at her. How had she known what plea would move

me? True it was that neither my king nor I had done any good to Armorica!

"So be it," I sighed. "What can you tell me?"

She laughed, sweet waters splashing crystal through the air. "I know the future and the past. I know where the tomb of Merlinus lies. I know where Artor went for healing, and when he will return. . . ."

"Artor's time is over." I said harshly. "Tell me what the fate of his heirs will be!"

In the silence I heard a faint humming; the figure before me shimmered, and I realized that it was the source of the sound.

> *"Where death has walked the wild beasts war;*
> *The eagle falls, heart fails the hare;*
> *The fleeing stallion's felled in gore."*

Her voice deepened, as if the earth itself were speaking, or the waters, or the wind.

> *"The wild bull tramples foemen down;*
> *His offspring win a golden crown;*
> *Blood of heroes brings renown."*

As she spoke I seemed to see her meaning, not in figures as men perceive the waking world, but in a maelstrom of bright images, turning and twining and breaking free. Patterns formed and were broken in an intricate interlace of alliances and treacheries.

> *"Lion and leopard leap the land;*
> *A white swan rises from the strand.*
> *The eagle of the east is damned;*
> *He clutches the ermine in his claw,*
> *The land lies under an alien law,*
> *Cursed those who live the deeds I saw. . . ."*

Her voice faded. Somehow the moon had rolled down the sky and fled behind the trees. The Lady's robes were only a gray glimmer in the false dawn.

"The stallion—" I fixed on the one thing whose meaning I thought I knew. "What will come to the Horse King?"

"Let the Horse King trumpet in his own pastures. His place is not in Armorica!" Her voice was fading too.

"But he will not listen to me!"

"When the mare bears her foal, the stallion will run free . . ."

I strained to hear what seemed a whisper on the wind. But

there was only silence now, and beyond it, the first tentative chirruppings as birds prepared to greet the dawn.

"Wait, wait!" I cried. "How shall I fulfill my oath to you?"

"When the river from out of the rock has run . . ."

Faintly, I heard a whisper of melody. Had that been only a fragment of memory from a spirit stretched beyond its strength? But now I saw a silver basin waiting upon the great rock beside the spring, and suddenly I knew what I must do. Very gently I lowered it into the icy stream, feeling my hands numb as water welled into the bowl. Then I stood, offering it to the rising sun.

"Then Lord and Lady and land are all one . . ."

I lifted the basin and dashed the water upon the stone.

Thunder cracked across the sky. The vessel slipped from my hands and rolled across the grass. Clouds were forming already in what had been a clear dawn. As I ran to saddle my mare I felt the first drops of rain. Lightning flared, and I saw through the trees a white ribbon of road. Then the rain roared down; rain for the thirsty earth, splashing on forest and pasture as I had cast the water upon the dry stone. . . .

But though the rain might ease the land, I shuddered when I thought of Esseilte shivering in that storm.

The war-band was back.

At night, the hills around Ker-haes bloomed with fires like faerie flowers. Nor was this even the whole of the High King's army, for Marc'h had left garrisons to hold Dol and Aleth, Vorganium and Geso and various strategic points throughout the countryside, while they finished getting in the harvest. Trecor and Barsa and some few other places where the local chieftains had joined Marc'h willingly were guarded by their own lords, but elsewhere the North lay bruised and bleeding where the Horse King had trod.

But there was no light in Marc'h's eyes. It was not wholly for Esseilte's sake that I must manage a reconciliation, I thought as I watched him finish another flagon of wine. Marc'h himself was suffering, and it did not matter—it must not matter—whether he grieved for Drustan's loss, or that of his queen. He was not drunk. If I had seen any sign that the wine was affecting him, I might have been relieved. But he watched the warriors who shouted and the churchmen who muttered with the same cold gaze. I remembered the glory that had been in his eyes as he came to me in the stone circle, and something within me clenched in pain.

"We need to talk, Marcus," said Paul Aurelian, who had been given the seat of honor at the king's right. Young Winwalo, who had left Theodoric and come back to Armorica as Paul's clerk and attendant, looked anxiously from one man to the other. His home was in Domnonia, I remembered now, near the stronghold Riwal had built above Brioc's monastery. I wondered if he were mourning friends or kindred.

"Yes, certainly, but not here — remember, my men too have shed blood and lost companions in this war, and feelings are strong. If you have come to scold me, let us wait until we are more private. I would not have you suffer any discourtesy," Marc'h said dryly.

"Would you rather we spoke of the tribulations of other kings?" said Paul Aurelian. He gestured to the trader who sat next to Winwalo. Marc'h's eyes narrowed.

"'Tis a sorry story, indeed, and who knows where it will end?" said the trader, an Irishman who had turned up at our gates that morning. Sharp blue eyes swept from the abbot to the king, rested for a moment upon me, and then passed on. "For the Abbot Ruadan and his priests have fasted against the king!"

"But why?" I exclaimed. The fast was a powerful protest against black injustice, a weapon against those who could be reached no other way, for the shame laid upon a man by another's willingness thus to bear witness could make him an outcast. But Diarmait MacCearbhaill was the manifestation of justice — what crime could have brought down the wrath of the clerics upon his royal head?

"The murderer Aed Guaire sought sanctuary with Ruadan, but the king plucked him out of it and condemned him, and so the monks sat down at the gates of Temair to fast against the sentence . . ." He waited expectantly.

"What did King Diarmait do?" Winwalo's curiosity overcame him.

"What should he do, and he a virtuous and royal lord?" the trader replied. "The Ard-Righ himself fasted, and for every prayer of the priests he had another. A few days of hunger drove Ruadan to desperation, I can tell you, for even his enemies agree that Diarmait MacCearbhaill is a godly king." He paused and held out his goblet. I refilled it silently, feeling his eyes price the crimson wool cloth in my gown, and the depth of its embroidery.

For the feast I had put on the glass bangles Esseilte had given me. They clashed sweetly as I poured the wine.

"But Diarmait lost, all the same—" the trader said then.

"He never gave in!" I cried.

"Nay, but Ruadan made him believe that the monks had done so, and so the Ard-Righ broke his fast and the Church had the victory."

"But was there nothing that King Diarmait could do?" Winwalo asked. Paul eyed him in annoyance, and I realized that the boy had forgotten whose side he was supposed to be on.

"Oh, aye—" The trader gave a snort of bitter laughter. "He cursed them. I was there when it ended, and I remember well his final words: 'You, Fathers, are protecting evil. But I am defending the truth in Christ's name. You may kill me, and you may ruin my kingdom; God may love you for your merits more than me, but I place my hope in the loving-kindness of my God. So go. Take the man away free. But you will render a price to the kingdom for this man.'"

There was a silence after he had spoken. Even Paul Aurelian's mouth was pursed as if the tale had left a bitter aftertaste. But the thought that came to me was that Diarmait would not have been deceived if Queen Mairenn had been there.

"You see what comes when the land is infested by churchmen!" Marc'h said wryly at last. "You chose a bad advocate, old friend, if that was intended as a cautionary tale! But I know you will not rest until you are delivered of the burden your colleagues have laid upon you," he went on. "At least they sent you, and not that viper Samson—"

"Oh no," said Winwalo. "Samson is—"

The abbot's warning glance and Marc'h's grim smile crossed. Winwalo blushed to the edge of his tonsure and shut his mouth again.

"Samson is in Lutetia," the king said gently. "Yes, I know." He looked at Paul Aurelian wryly. The abbot took a deep breath.

"Marcus Cunomorus, in my voice all the clerics of Domnonia join to plead with you. To destroy rulers and seize their lands as you have done is against the laws of God and man. Will you not give up this warring, Marcus, and let us have peace?"

"Pompeius Regalis ran upon his fate—though my sword killed him, his death was no fault of mine. . . ."

"That may be," answered Paul patiently, "but that does not

give you a right to take his territories. Deroc is his heir, as the heir to Dol is Iudual."

Marc'h looked at him for a moment, turning his goblet carefully back and forth between his hands. "I will confirm them gladly," he said, "if they will acknowledge that they are my subkings. . . ."

"*Wor-Tiern* . . . I have heard your men give you that name, but why should the people of Domnonia do so? Their fathers carved out those territories, and it is not the way of our people to have a single overlord. By what authority do you call yourself High King?"

"By what authority did Artor rule Britain?" Marc'h set down the goblet and forced the priest to meet his eyes.

"The Saxons were at their throats, man — it is not the same!"

"Is it not?" Marc'h answered harshly. "The Saxons had a sea to cross, and yet they engulfed half of Britain. What sea will keep the Franks from *our* throats when they decide the time has come to swallow the rest of Gaul? Already they hold the South, as well as levying tribute on their cousins across the Rhenus. When Justinian finishes fighting Persians he will turn his eyes back to Gaul. How if we could re-enter the empire as a partner?"

"It is a noble dream —" Paul bowed his head. "But do you think the tribes of Britain will be so eager to go back under the yoke of Rome? You cannot fight your own people, Marcus —"

"Can I not? Think back to the story of Artor's wars — his hardest fights were against his own people, and it was British treachery that destroyed him finally. And yet he made a peace that has lasted two generations, and today men bless his memory!"

"Marcus, Marcus, there is truth in what you say, and yet I tell you that you are wrong! If the men of the northern coasts could see the danger as you do, perhaps they would rally to your cause. But they do not, and you cannot force them to it, my friend. If you try, even to protect them, against their will, you are only substituting a different tyranny! For the love of Christ, let there be peace!"

"For Christ?" asked the king. "It seems to me that this affair is Caesar's. . . ."

"I have heard," I said into the silence, "I have heard that there are priests who would kill the body in order to save the soul . . ."

"That is not the tradition of the Church in Britain, whatever they may do in Rome," said Paul impatiently. He was still watching the king.

"And what will the Church in Armorica do, if I resist you as Diarmait resisted the clerics of Eriu?" Marc'h said gently.

"Albinus of Angers and I will join Samson in Lutetia," answered Paul, avoiding the king's gaze. "And we will ask Childebert to restore Iudual . . ."

"Will you indeed!" Marc'h bared his teeth in a wolf's sardonic grin. "Now I wonder what the king of the Franks is going to say . . ."

The king refused to elaborate, and the feast ended in chilly silence. But I saw Paul Aurelian's face as he left the table, and it seemed to me that he was afraid.

"Your pardon, Mistress of the House, but I must ask — are you the queen?"

The trader stepped from the shadows at the end of the hall. I turned from the men who were clearing up and stared at him, tempted for one wild moment to tell the truth. But there was already enough trouble in those blue Irish eyes. My own narrowed, for it seemed to me that I had seen this man in Diarmait's hall.

"I am Branwen, her cousin. May I serve you?"

"Ye can tell me where the Maiden of Temair might be — " he challenged me.

"No, I cannot," I answered him. "For Esseilte herself has bound me to keep that secret. But I can tell you that she is safe, and happy."

"I'd heard there was trouble between her and the king — " The trader gave me a quick glance. "One hears stories, you know. In Domnonia they even whisper that he has killed her so that he can marry Riwal's widow."

"Trouble . . . yes, there has been. But I hope it is not beyond mending. Tell King Diarmait that, Domnall MacLeite, when you go back to Temair."

The trader smiled ruefully. "I had not thought you would know me. But it's glad I am to hear it — I tell you truly, Branwen, Diarmait has troubles enough without worrying about his child. I would not say it before them all, but Ruadan cursed the Ard-Righ too, before they were done.

"'Your kingdom shall fail, and none of your seed shall ever

reign. . . .' That is what he said to him." He paused, remembering. "'This your royal town of Temair, whence the kingdom of
Eriu has been ruled these many years, shall be left empty.' I fear
for him, sometimes; there has been a change in him since he lost
the queen. And I fear for the land."

I closed my eyes, remembering a Samhain Eve when the
standing stone had shifted beneath my hand, and my own vision
of Temair inhabited only by sheep and crows. But now I had the
prophecy of the Lady of the Fountain to lay beside Ruadan's,
and I feared for more lands than one. I put my hand out blindly
in farewell, and the trader touched it and melted into the dark.

A king without a queen . . . I thought of Diarmait, floundering
without Mairenn, and Marc'h, whose lust for conquest had
grown as Esseilte had drawn farther away. For a moment I
trembled on the edge of some great understanding. Then fear for
the loss of all that was fair in my world swept over me, and I ran
toward the stairs to the tower.

A single lamp flickered on the table in the royal chamber. For a
moment I thought it was empty; then I saw the shadow, like
some monstrous beast poised to spring across the room. I
stepped backward, and at the sound the still shape by the window began to turn. The shadow fluttered wildly, then resolved
itself into the shape of a man. Plain in the lamplight I saw the
ravaged face of the king.

"Branwen—" He had moved into a fighter's crouch, but my
own posture must have showed that there was no danger, for
after a moment he straightened, and his shoulders sagged once
more. "Do you also come to me with tales of doom?"

I swallowed the words that were on my lips, my general fears
for the kingdom precipitating into an uprush of very personal
anguish for the king.

"I wish I could bring you a tale of joy—a tale of apple or-
chards white with blossom, foals playing in the pasture, fields of
golden corn. . . ."

"You have given me a peaceful household, and that is no little
thing when I compare it with the chaos of other years," Marc'h
answered with a faint smile. "Kind Branwen"—we both winced
a little, remembering from whom he had learned that phrase—
"you must not think I have not noticed what you do for me.
Come in"—he gestured—"or are you afraid of me too?"

I shook my head, remembering. In the circle of stones, the

king had put forth all his power, and I had matched it. But I think that even had it not been so, what I saw in his face then would have inspired pity, not fear, as if he were a hurt child who needed me to wipe the tears away.

Marc'h must have sensed that in my movement, for he came to meet me, holding out his hand. Only somehow the movement continued — I do not know if he pulled me to him or I went willingly into his arms. But at his touch, fires that I had banked for so long I thought them dead blazed into triumphant life within me. Blinded, I trembled to the pulse of the heart's red drum.

"Branwen, oh, sweet Branwen," he whispered against my hair. His strong hand moved from my shoulder down my spine, molding my body against his. "I have seen your work, and I have seen *you* . . . a golden shadow . . . a fragrance on the air. . . . Who are you, Branwen, that it should seem so right for me to hold you so?"

Words clamored against the barrier of my lips: *I am your queen . . . how can you not know me?*

Very gently, he turned my face to his. My own lips quivered, awaiting the touch of his. But as he bent, there was one moment of cold clarity when I knew that if I kissed Marc'h now I would never let him go.

"I cannot . . ." I forced my head to turn.

"Why?" he whispered. "I have never taken a woman unwilling, no matter what men say. I feel the need in you — I think that it may be as great as my own. . . ."

Sweet Lady have mercy! my heart cried then, for never in my life had I desired anything so much as this. In the darkness, I heard a raven's hoarse call.

"You want me, Branwen. Why not give pleasure to yourself in giving it to me?"

Pleasure? I wondered wildly. *After what we have shared?* Would the furtive exchange he was proposing betray the glory we had found in the stone circle? And what other commitments, older, if not deeper, might it also betray?

"I cannot take what belongs to Esseilte . . ." *Again* — but that was unspoken. I waited for his reply.

Marc'h drew a little away, his lips twisting in pain. "Not even what Esseilte has thrown away?"

He loves her — I thought then. *Despite everything, he loves her still.*

"Oh my lord, she has not done so," I murmured, knowing

that for the sake of my own truth and Esseilte's life, I had to lie. "Both of them still love you, if only you could see!" It came out on a sob, and I swallowed painfully. Marc'h still held me, but my heart ached with awareness of the gap that was widening between us with every moment that passed.

"You know where they are," he said in a still voice. I nodded, and he released me. "You are a strange woman, Branwen of Eriu. . . . I think that to say that cost you as much as letting you go cost me!"

More, my beloved, much more, I said silently. But I nodded again.

Almost to himself, he added. "Can I do less than you? What is it that you want of me?"

"Go to Broceliande," I whispered. "I will not ask you to forgive them. Only go to Broceliande and see. . . ."

The king nodded, and I fled from the room before grief mastered me. But another part of my mind was already composing my message to Gorwennol.

Summer was ripening into an early autumn when we entered the forest of Broceliande once more. Trees defied the coming cold in bursts of bronze and gold, but in the shadows the air had a crispness that had not been there before. Deep into the wood we traveled, and then made camp, so close to the lake that we could almost smell Drustan's fire.

And in the dawning we moved silently to the hut in the clearing, and Marc'h took a torch to the entrance and looked inside.

I did not go with him. I knew what he would see, for it was I who had told Drustan what they had to do. But I heard Esseilte's voice, high and shaking a little with cold, or perhaps fear, as she came out to face the king.

"I have given my heart's true love to no man but he who had my maidenhead!" She set her hand upon the gleaming blade. "And may this sword that lay between us divide flesh from spirit if I do not speak true!"

Nineteen

THE HUNTING TOWER

It was one of those crisp, clear days that can give autumn a beauty to rival spring, doubly welcome after the almost constant storms that had drenched us since my return from Broceliande. Water still dripped from eaves and splashed beneath the horses' hooves as we rode out of Ker-haes, and our breath left damp clouds of mist in the cold air. But the sky had been washed to a translucent blue, with only a hint of cloud on the western horizon. One might almost count the bare branches of a distant oak on the hill, and the feathers on the falcon that slid across the sky.

"Look at him, Branwen, he is *still* watching me!" exclaimed Esseilte, reining her dappled mare nearer to mine. I glanced back and stiffened as Meriadek favored me with a nasty grin. Karasek was farther down the line. After the close confinement of the past weeks, going through the gates of the fortress had been like escaping from prison, but unfortunately the jailors were coming along.

"Is this forgiveness, to set men to dog my steps and spy upon my every move?" Her mare leaped forward as sharp heels were dug into her side. With her hair bound up and the leather cavalry breeches showing beneath her cloak, she looked like a beautiful boy.

"Esseilte, it was not Marc'h who—"

"Was it not?" She interrupted me. The king rode ahead of us with Drustan by his side, while the huntsmen trotted on foot beside them, holding back the whining whirlpool of hounds.

"They are his men! Do you think that they keep watch upon his queen against his will? Branwen, I cannot live this way! Such constant suspicion only makes me think more on the thing they are set on preventing! At night I lie wakeful by Marc'h's side, planning ways to see Drustan. . . ."

I had lain wakeful too, the first few nights after Drustan and Esseilte returned to Ker-haes. Marc'h would want to make sure of her, I knew. I had imagined his lips on her smooth skin, his hands probing her secrecies, until I thought that I would go mad. Work was the only cure for it, and I worked until exhaustion claimed me and the servants walked in terror of my frown. It had not occurred to me that this would leave nothing for Esseilte to do.

When we came to Armorica, much of the domestic administration of Ker-haes had fallen to me, and since Esseilte had been away, the servants had ceased even the pretense of going to her for commands. She needed occupation, but I could see that it would be difficult for her to find it, for wherever she went in the fortress either Meriadek or Karasek seemed to be waiting — dicing, gossiping, or simply leaning against some wall watching her. Only in her bedchamber could she be alone, and then they waited on the stairs. The windows of the tower had been barred.

"When they look at me they see a bitch in heat. Shall I drink the bitter dregs without having tasted the sweetness? I will have Drustan . . ." Esseilte said grimly.

I sighed. We were all well away from the village now, winding along the road toward the mountains of Arré, where the king meant to do his hunting. Drifts of mist still clung to the folds of the hills, but hawks were scribing slow circles on the pale sky. The war-band had made heavy inroads into our supplies at the fortress, and the country nearby was almost bare of game. Fresh venison would be a welcome change, but I think Marc'h also sensed the need to give everyone a few days of freedom from its walls. I think the king recognized that Esseilte needed the fresh air and the action as much as any of his men. He himself had received a letter from Lutetia, and I supposed he wanted fresh air and action while he decided how to answer it.

Only for Esseilte, even in the open air there was no liberty.

Still, the horses moved more swiftly as we got out into open country, heads bobbing and bits jingling cheerfully. I took a deep breath of clean wind, and urged my mare on as if we could outrun the shadow upon my soul.

We passed the night at a farmstead along the way, the men camping around their fires in the meadow while the king and Esseilte dispossessed the family from the smoky confines of a hut that seemed to spring like a mushroom from the damp ground.

"What was in the letter?" I asked Marc'h when we had eaten. Esseilte already lay curled in her blankets on the other side of the fire. "Are the clerics up to their tricks again in Lutetia?"

"They try—" Marc'h grinned back at me. "But Childebert is corresponding with *me*. He offers me the title of Prefect of Neustria, with authority over all Armorica!"

"Under him?" I added. "Prefect seems a shabby title to exchange for that of Wor-Tiern—" From the meadow I could hear the deep rumble of male laughter as the wineskins went round.

The king shrugged, then smiled again. "For a time it may be necessary. How I would love to see Samson's face when he hears this news!"

"Have you answered?" I laid my hand upon his arm, striving to see his face through the shadows. Marc'h shook his head.

"You must not agree to it! The north coast will never forgive you—"

"But they themselves are asking Childebert's help against me," he objected.

"This is different!" I shook my head in exasperation, seeking words for something that I myself did not clearly understand. Only in my memory the words of the Lady of the Fountain echoed once more.

"Well, I have until spring to give him my reply," Marc'h said, placating me. "Let us rest now, while we can . . ."

We did not speak again, but my dreams were haunted by visions of bloody swords and hate-filled faces, and the war-cry they sounded was "Death to Conomor!"

In the morning the singing of the hounds awoke us, and we were early on horseback, picking our way up tree-clad slopes where great stones stood out like nuts in a cake. The hounds quested eagerly, ears flapping and pink tongues hanging out as they trotted along, and the trackers ranged ahead, seeking for spoor. But though the forest of Uhelgoat was famous for its game—noble stags and the terrible black boar—so far we had found none.

"Drustan, give us a song to shorten the way," said the king. Sunlight sifted through the net of branches, striking golden sparks from his circlet and Esseilte's shining hair. The day was

bright, but it had lost the clarity of yesterday. Contours softened; the dull colors of autumn grew luminous as the light was
filtered through the gathering moisture in the air.

"The ground is too broken for singing, lord, but I can maybe
find a tale that will do!" Drustan replied. He turned a little in
the saddle, waiting until we had closed the gap in the line, and it
seemed to me that his eyes rested on Esseilte and he smiled. We
had come deep into the forest, and as we stilled to listen, I could
hear the hooves of the horses rustling through the ghosts of last
summer's leaves.

"Since we are in the forest, I will give you a story of hunting,
the story of Winomarc'h ap Hoel, whose father ruled Léon in
Artor's time. Now Winomarc'h was a notable warrior, they say,
with one flaw only — he was quite indifferent to women, and
would neither marry, nor seek to lie with any woman in love."

"But that's yourself, Drustan!" Wynek and Dinan laughed. I
saw Meriadek trade sour glances with his partner, but neither of
them interrupted; Drustan laughed also, if a little thinly, avoiding Esseilte's eyes.

"There came a day when Winomarc'h would go hunting. They
started up a great stag, but as they chased it, Winomarc'h lost
his companions. He rode on through the forest, calling, until he
saw a glimmer of white through the trees, and realized it was a
white doe with her fawn, grazing beside a spring."

White deer seemed to haunt Armorica's forests, but perhaps
Winomarc'h had been a newcomer to the land, and did not know
that this was no creature of the waking world. I gazed through
the interlace of bare branches around us and wondered what
strangeness Uhelgoat might hold. The air was thickening above
us as if we were passing through some barrier between the
worlds.

"What hunter would hesitate?" asked Drustan. "Winomarc'h
nocked arrow to his bow and let fly." He patted the flat-bow
slung over his shoulder, short enough to draw in close country,
and powerful enough to spit a man, or a deer. Though we were
seeking venison, the hunters had come prepared for any game,
with short hunting swords banging at their sides, and lances
bound to their saddlebows.

"He struck the deer, but the arrow rebounded and pierced
him through the thigh. And the dying doe cursed him."

Gorwennol had begun to look rather grim, as if he thought
Drustan was unwise to tell this particular tale. But the pro-

cession had slowed to an amble, even the dogs pattering contentedly ahead of us as the men drew closer to hear what he would say.

"'I am suffering for your hate.' said the doe, 'but you shall suffer for love. And never shall your wound be cured save by she who will endure more for you than any other before or since, and you for her. . . .'"

Meriadek looked quickly from Esseilte to Drustan, but the storyteller's eyes were firmly on the forest ahead. Only in both faces a betraying color rose and fell again, and Esseilte's fingers were like claws on the reins. Surely she was thinking that the lady in the story had a rival now.

"And so it came to pass," said Drustan softly, "for nowhere under heaven could he find a cure. And there came a time when his servants had left him by a lake in the forest while they searched for other aid. And as he lay there alone, he saw a wonder. For over the water a boat came gliding with no hand guiding it; a boat of ebony with a silken sail, and in it a bed spread with rich stuffs so inviting that Winomarc'h could not resist the lure, and so got into the boat and laid him down. The boat sped away, and weak as he was, Winomarc'h could do nothing to stop it." Drustan paused, choosing his words.

"And where did it take him?" asked Fragan Tawr indulgently. Drustan, continuing, seemed hardly to remember that his audience was there.

"It bore him across the water to a fair stronghold, where an old lord kept his lovely wife imprisoned in a tower. . . ."

I saw Marc'h stiffen. Esseilte had gone very pale. The brightness was fading from the day and the sky had become a solid wall. A chill wind flowed down the slope above us, lifting my hair. *Beware, Drustan,* my heart clamored, *oh Drustan, be careful now!*

"But he did allow her to go to her orchard sometimes, to take the air. And this orchard bordered on the lake, and when the boat grounded on its shore, the lady saw Winomarc'h, and he her, and they looked, the one upon the other, and for Winomarc'h, it was as if he had never used his eyes before. . . ."

"My lord!" exclaimed Karasek. "How can you let him —" But the king motioned him to silence.

"And she took him into the tower, and with her maid she tended him, but by then the warrior knew that he had been wounded by a greater power than any arrow, and that was love.

But the lady smiled on him, and the greatest of all gifts she gave to him, and healed him of his wound."

"And you have the hardihood to say it? To admit—" Meriadek was nearly incoherent with rage. The others were looking at him in astonishment. I urged my mare up beside Esseilte's, as if I could protect her, and at that moment, the lead hound gave tongue.

The tangle of trees before us exploded into motion, shaken branches transforming somehow into a great spread of branching horns. The tawny body beneath them soared out of the brake, while the hinds he had been guarding scattered in every direction. Over the hysterical clamoring of the dogs I could hear the crashing as the stag plunged away through the trees.

Marc'h's horse half-reared and the king wrestled him down. The music of the hounds was focused suddenly by the long sweet summons of a horn, and the air rang with a musical belling as the huntsmen slipped the dogs from their leashes and the pack poured up the slope after the stag in a swirl of flapping ears and lashing tails. No words could have been heard at that moment, but I saw Gorwennol slash the rump of Meriadek's horse with his whip and send it bucketing after the huntsmen. I clutched at coarse strands of mane as my own mare joined the stampede.

I thrust up one arm to protect my face against whipping branches while I held on with the other, grateful for the stout leather hunting sark that covered my tunic. I sensed a confusion of treeshape and slope as we went by. The men were hallooing the hounds onward. The music changed as different animals found their pace and the chase spread out. The hunters, too, were stringing out along the trail as differences between the strengths of horses and boldness of riders began to tell.

I had no ambition to be in the forefront. When I could control my horse again I reined her down to a careful jog that let me see the obstacles. The trees here were noble—stands of ancient oak and ash splashed with the beech-trees' scattered gold, or pillared aisles of pine. The thick canopy of summer had kept undergrowth from forming so that there was room to ride, but the ground was studded with enormous boulders whose grim bulk was only slightly softened by mats of emerald moss and a scattering of brown leaves.

The stag was fresh and canny, doubling back and forth through the wood and flying across the clearings, but the hounds hung on implacably while their masters labored along behind.

We had come into a broken country where the forest slopes plunged steeply. In summer, it must have been impenetrable, but now the stream plunged through boulders greater than any I had yet seen.

"He'll seek to lose us at the water," someone cried, and the pace quickened. Drifted leaves fluttered like sea-spray as we slid down through the pines. A pool of water brown as ale glimmered through the trees. Something was crashing through the dead vines on the other side. The hunters hurtled after it; I heard splashing and reined in frantically as I burst through the trees into a yammering tangle of horses and hounds.

I blinked, trying to see what had stopped them. Was it my pulse that was hammering so furiously in my ears, or the pressure of the Otherworld? We had been chasing a royal hart — no pale beast of faerie but the golden lord of the forest. Yet what faced us at the edge of the pool was the sovereign of shadow — a black boar. Reason told us that we had surprised him, that the stag had splashed through the water just as the great pig came down to drink. But some deeper perception whispered that the stag and the boar were two manifestations of a single power.

"Ho, my lord, here is a noble foe! See how he challenges you!" cried Fragan. "Will you give battle here?"

I did not see that we had much choice, for the hounds had been driven to hysterical fury by the scent of their ancient enemy. They held him now, the bolder ones darting into the shallows to either side while the rest formed a half-circle on the bank. The water just behind him shelved steeply. The boar would not want to fight in the pool where the dogs could drag him down. But on land he could meet them; already several of the less disciplined hounds had run in on him and been tossed aside.

The king laughed. One of the huntsmen grasped the stallion's reins by the bit as Marc'h untied his javelins. Then the king slid from the saddle, swaying for a moment as use returned to stiffened limbs, and struck the spears into the earth, ready to hand. Drustan was at his side, his own weapons ready, but it seemed to me he faced the beast unwillingly. One by one the other lords joined them, until the boar was surrounded by dogs and men. Some had even scrambled across the rocks at the outlet of the pool and taken up position on the other side. I saw Esseilte farther down the slope, still mounted, and moved my mare forward.

The black beast was not frightened, he was furious — glaring and tearing at the ground. The hounds surged in again, and I winced as the powerful head snapped around, a tusk ripped along a dog's belly, and hurled the body aside. Blood splattered across the dry leaves.

Marc'h snatched up a lance and flung it. The point bit, then sliced across the shoulder and rattled past. The air grew dark with flying spearshafts as the other men made their casts. Now gouts of the boar's blood were mingling with that of the dogs. I wondered if it would be enough to weaken as well as enrage him.

But Drustan, though his spear was ready in his hand, made no move against the boar. Karasek saw it and began to jeer.

"The black boar has protected me for too long for me to attack him now," said Drustan.

"That is true," whispered Esseilte. "I have never known Drustan to hunt boar!"

Abruptly I remembered the black beast that snarled from his shield and shivered. Had a geas been given to him with that shield?

The men were beginning to murmur.

"Let him be!" Marc'h glared at them. "Do you think I cannot make my own kill? Prick him now, stoutly, and let the dogs get in —" Slowly they moved in, jabbing at the boar's head and dancing away while the hounds snapped at his haunches.

But the boar was swift as shadow. Weaving and whirling, he dashed aside spearpoints and ripped at the hounds. Far from being daunted, each attack only fueled his rage, until the black fury that came off him struck like a physical blow. I put up my hands to ward away that blasting hatred. Shouting, snarling like beasts themselves, the hunters did not seem to feel it. Perhaps the red rage of battle was its own protection.

"Pin him now — hold him fast! cried the king. Men rushed in; the boar whirled, caught in a thicket of shining spears.

Marc'h stabbed at the heavy neck, slipped, and Drustan grabbed for his arm and wrenched him out of the way. The boar came after him, and in that moment of distraction one of the dogs leaped in. Strong jaws snapped shut on the tendon; the boar heaved, but the hound hung on.

Then the sharp teeth bit through. The hound was flung howling, but the boar's hind leg gave way beneath him. He reared upward. Roaring, the men threw themselves upon him. Boar spears pierced tough hide.

Only in front was there no foe to hold him. Spears ripped free and men went sprawling as the boar charged. He lurched to one side as his injured leg failed him, squealing triumph as the turn shifted his line of sight to the fallen king. Marc'h tried to wrench himself aside as the huge head lowered to gore.

My ears roared, and all awareness narrowed to a tunnel of vision that showed me the smooth sweep of Drustan's arm as he brought the spear around and flung his own weight behind it just as the boar plunged down.

Esseilte screamed. There was nothing in the world but that tangle of thrashing bodies, and blood that seemed to spread until red darkness was all I could see.

"Pull it off them — for Christ's sweet sake, men — heave!" Fragan's hoarse plea brought back my vision. The boar had stopped moving. As they lifted the huge body, I saw that the butt of the spear had caught in a crevice of rock by Marc'h's side. The boar, attacking him, had rammed the blade down his own throat with a force beyond that of any man.

There was blood everywhere.

"I am not hurt — he did not touch me —" I heard Marc'h speak and began to breathe again. "Look to Drustan!"

I looked to Esseilte, who was swaying in the saddle beside me, holding her as Marc'h got himself upright. He leaned over Drustan.

"Where are you hurt, lad?" he asked gently, gripping the younger man's hand.

"Just the breath . . . knocked out of me . . . I think. . . ."

Esseilte began to tremble as Drustan let the king help him sit up.

"Hush, love, it is all over now," I whispered. "They are both alive."

"I must touch him, Branwen. There is so much blood! I have to know —"

"Don't betray yourself —" I grasped at her rein. "They do not need us now."

"Ah Drustan — Drustan —" said Marc'h hoarsely. "Yet again you have nearly died for me!" Their hands were still clasped. Bloodstained and disheveled, their faces were momentarily stamped with a single identity. But it seemed to me that there was something piteous in Drustan's gaze, like a child who cannot quite trust its parent's love. And in Marc'h's eyes the frustrated emotion with which I had sometimes seen him watch Drustan had never been so clear.

"Well, boy, you are blooded now!" Fragan's laughter broke the spell. Still laughing, the warrior dipped his finger in the boar's dark blood and smeared it upon Drustan's brow.

Drustan jerked as if he had been burned. For the first time he looked at the boar.

"Ah, my brother, forgive me," he murmured then. "But it was thy life, or that of my king. . . ." He reached out to touch the bloody tusk, then, as if all the strength had gone out of him, his hand fell away.

Without our noticing, the high mist had descended, dimming the day.

"Get the beast butchered and give the dogs their share," Marc'h said, looking around him. "The light is going fast, and we've a bit of a march if we're to reach shelter before night falls."

The way back seemed much longer, though we were heading more directly for the road. Perhaps it was because the mists were closing in upon us. I tried to keep close to Esseilte, but everyone was strung out along the path. Damp air caught in my lungs; the trees ahead dimmed as the mist dropped white veils between them. I could hear the others, but saw only a few shapes moving before me through the trees. I urged the mare forward.

"Branwen!" That was Drustan's voice. I yanked the horse's head around. In a moment I saw him, holding his jittering mount with some difficulty as he faced Esseilte, who had brought her mare to a halt beneath the leaning trunk of an old oak tree. Gorwennol waited farther down the slope, but both men were looking at the queen.

"Are we lost?" I asked as I joined them. Drustan shrugged.

"I think we are found!" said Esseilte sharply. "This mist will be excuse enough for getting separated from the others, and who will be able to say that Branwen and I did not spend the night huddled in the woods alone?"

"Esseilte —" Drustan's bay half-reared. "In this cold? You will be ill if you stay out here!"

"I will be ill if I cannot have this time with you, Drustan. The heart stopped in my body when I saw you covered with blood. I must touch the life in you now. I do not care if we have to lie upon a bed of leaves! You were pleased to lie with me upon a mattress of heather in Broceliande!" Her eyes burned as she stared at him. "I have seen how you love the king. But do you still love me?"

"I love you both! Christ help me! What monster shall I fight for your sake, Esseilte? Is there no way that I can prove my love to you without betraying him?" The bay horse tossed its head, sensing his pain.

"Are your oaths to Marc'h more sacred than those you swore to me?" she answered implacably. "Surely I have suffered more for you than ever woman suffered for a man, and not for the sake of some poet's tale! You, at least, have had the release and the glory of making war. What is there for me?" She was breaking him, without pity for his pain, or her own. "My every step is spied on, I must drag out my useless days in a foreign land. If I do not have your love, what is there in this world for me?"

"Esseilte . . . Esseilte. . . ." It was a groan, and a capitulation. Neither Drustan nor I could oppose Esseilte's will, any more than we had been able to that night when the *Flower o' the Broom* rocked off the shore of Kernow. Naked need pulsed in the air between them. But it seemed a long time before Drustan's head bowed.

"Where? . . ." His whisper scarred the silence.

"My lord, there is the old Roman tower —" said Gorwennol at last. "I discovered it when hunting here years ago. I don't believe it is known to the king."

"Very well." Released at last, the bay horse sprang across the clearing. Drustan took the hand Esseilte held out to him and pressed his lips against her open palm, turning his face against it as if only the touch of her could ease the pain that she herself had given him.

"Oh, dear one, oh my dear, it has been so long!" Her other hand went to his hair. "And you are hurt — bruised, anyway, even if the black beast gave you no wound."

"Wait just a little longer, then!" I exclaimed. "Anyone could come upon us here."

Even Esseilte understood that. Reluctantly she freed her hand.

Gorwennol led us back the way we had come. Ravens were already busy at the offal that remained on the hide beside the pool, and we passed that place quickly and picked our way across the rocks below.

Quickly we set our horses up the steep slope beyond it. Even in the fading light the hand of man was still visible, in new trees growing up around old stumps and hollows where the earth had been dug away. Soon the remains of a road led us around the summit, where the bracken-covered mounds of ancient earthworks surrounded the shell of an octagonal tower.

Stiff from the long ride, we dismounted inside the enclosure. Mist drew closely around the hill, as if the land itself was conspiring to conceal us here. I began to relax at last. Even if one of Marc'h's men knew of this place, they would never be able to find it once darkness fell.

"We'll need bracken for bedding," said Gorwennol. "And water for us and the horses — there used to be a well below the tower. I'll gather wood for a fire."

Laughing, Esseilte helped me to cut dry fern from the embankments. There had been two of them, in an inner and outer circle surrounding the tower, and they were still twice man-high.

Drustan had unsaddled the horses and watered them. Hobbles let them graze on the sparse grass. Esseilte emptied a load of bracken from her cloak into the space beneath the most protected part of the tower, then laid the garment over them.

"That will make a bed for us," she said softly. "And softer than many that Grainne and Diarmuid shared. I was never so happy as this last summer, in the wilderness. I should never have agreed to go back to the king."

I could not help but wonder if she were right, for the reconciliation had not worked as I had hoped. Even if we were not discovered, this night would breed suspicion. It seemed to me that she and Drustan would have no choice but to flee together now.

The scent of woodsmoke made me turn. Gorwennol had gotten a fire going, and was carving slices from the piece of the boar that he had been carrying and threading them on sticks which he propped over the flames. There was also the journeybread we had all been carrying, and the spirits in our wineskins. It was not a feast, but to bodies stressed by exertion and emotion, it was welcome indeed. We sat by the fire and ate as night fell.

And then, while Drustan made a last check on the horses, Esseilte went back to the tower.

"Drustan . . ." she called. Her bright hair had escaped from her braids, and she shone against the darkness of the stones like a flame. He took a deep breath and let it out again as if he were letting all the tension of the past months drain away. Then he moved slowly forward and gripped her arms. She set her hands on his shoulders, looking up at him as if now that her desire was in her grasp she did not know what to say.

"My beloved, you never finished the story. . . ." She found words at last. Drustan laughed a little shakily.

"For the lady's own safety, Winomarc'h knew he must leave her, and so, to keep him faithful, she tied a knot in his shirt which no other woman could untie," he said. Esseilte laughed, and her hands went to the lacings at the neck of his tunic.

"Like this, my love?" Her hands moved inside the garment, across his bare skin.

For a moment he stood, barely breathing, with his hands open at his sides, then he reached for her cincture and began to fumble with its knot.

"And he tied a knot in her girdle, that only he could undo . . . like this. . . ." He flung the cord free and pulled her against him. They strained together as if they could touch through all the layers of clothing they wore. Then he knelt as if his legs had lost the strength to uphold him, pressing his face against the hidden joining of her thighs. For a breath's space she allowed it, her fingers tightening in his hair. And then she moaned a little, sank to her own knees to meet him, and pulled him out of view. I heard soft laughter, the rustle of cloth and bracken, and then the sound of their altered breathing as they joined.

"Perhaps you can tell me the rest of the story," I said rather loudly to Gorwennol.

"Yes—" He was suddenly very busy, snapping sticks and thrusting them into the fire. "As you might expect, the old lord discovered Winomarc'h and sent him home again. The lady wanted to drown herself, but she found the magic ship instead, and it took her away." His telling had not the cadencing of Drustan's, but he did know the tale.

"It carried her to her lover?"

"Not exactly. Another chieftain, called Meriadek, found her first, and held her, trying to win her love." He met my eyes then, and rather bitterly, we both laughed, remembering the other man who bore that name.

"And what happened to Meriadek in the story?" I asked then. Gorwennol bent over to blow the new wood into flame.

"Winomarc'h attacked the dun and killed him," he answered me.

*   *   *

A black beast hunted me through my dreams.

Throughout that night I struggled in and out of consciousness, cold waking me to the sorrowful hooting of hunting owls, exhaustion dragging me back to a deeper darkness through which I fled a formless figure that called my name. There were other creatures in that Otherworld through which I wandered. Tusked and taloned, they reached out to rend and slay. If its minions were so fearful, how terrible must be the thing that hunted me?

As the nightmares continued my resolve began to weaken. How easy it would be to stop, to turn, to let myself sink down into the darkness and be consumed. But I was not the only prey in this wasteland. Other beings ran with me, and we were linked so that I ached with their exhaustion and trembled with their fear. And their survival was more precious than my own. This tied me to them, whether for good or ill I did not know. I knew only that the bond was there, and that I had no choice but to run on.

But my pursuers were gaining. I turned with some wild notion of defiance, and saw rearing above me the writhing, weed-dripping shape of the water-horse, fangs bared. I screamed as it seized me and bore me away, but no sound came. . . .

"Branwen! At least you are safe—" Strong hands closed on my shoulders. Still moaning, I struggled in that remorseless grip. Flame flickered through my closed eyelids and I tried to burrow back into my blanket. "Branwen, wake!" A slap stung my cheek and my eyes flew open. "We have searched half the night for you. Branwen, where is the queen?"

Marc'h was bending over me, his face all craggy planes and shadows in the torchlight. I reached out to him, then cold awareness shocked me fully awake. I tried to cry out, but it was as it had been in my dream—my tongue would not answer my will. More men were climbing through the gap in the earthworks, quietly, as if they were exhausted, or perhaps feared the ghosts of the men who had built the tower.

"There's four horses down here," someone called softly.

"And Gorwennol—" another voice said, much closer, with a sneer in it that I recognized. "Old Gorwennol and Branwen, now I wonder . . . Ah, no!" Turning in Marc'h's arms I saw Gorwennol start up, mouth opening and then closing again as the tip of Karasek's dagger pricked his throat. "You just be silent until we have a little look around. . . ." Meriadek stood over them, staring at the ruined tower whose jagged walls snarled against the stars.

"What are you doing?" Now Marc'h had seen the dagger too.

"Guarding your honor, my king!" said Karasek coldly. "Perhaps you will find what you are looking for over in that tower . . ."

I took a deep breath. "Esseilte!" It came out as a croak. I drew breath again, but before I could scream her name, Marc'h's eyes returned to me, narrowing and then widening in pain.

"Branwen . . . oh Branwen, has everyone I loved lied to me?"

His anger I might have borne, but not that naked agony. *Sweet Lady, let this end!* my spirit cried. Mute, I stared back at him.

Marc'h released me suddenly. Stiffly, he rose, took the torch that one of the men held out to him, and started toward the tower. Everyone had grown silent now. Weeping soundlessly, I clambered to my feet and went after him, and even Meriadek did not try to hinder me.

I was at Marc'h's shoulder as he stopped in the crumbling doorway. Drustan and Esseilte lay cocooned in a cloak, so deeply asleep that even when the pine torch began to hiss they did not stir. His head lay upon her breast, veiled by her golden hair. The crackle of the torch and the harsh rasp of the king's breath were the only sounds.

Then Marc'h bent suddenly and tore the cloak away.

For one moment the sight of smooth curves of arms and legs that flowed together as if they belonged to a single being was imprinted on my vision. I clasped my arms across my breasts, not from cold, but from longing for that perfect unity. Then Meriadek pushed past me, shouting.

"There is no sword between them now! Strike the adulterers asunder, Lord King!"

The tableau fragmented as Drustan rolled away, snatching up the naked sword which had lain by his other side and leaping to his feet in what seemed a single motion. Esseilte pulled the cloak over herself in an instinctive gesture of self-protection and stared up at us with sleep-drugged eyes.

"Oh Drustan . . . I trusted you. . . ." Marc'h turned abruptly, flinging the torch away.

But the rest of the men had followed Meriadek. Torchlight glittered red on spearhead and blade of sword. Drustan's eyes followed the king's retreating figure, pleading, but when Marc'h did not turn, they returned to the men. Drustan's own friends had been shocked into immobility by what was happening. It was Meriadek and the others of the king's household who ringed the door.

"Will you come at me like a beast, then?" Drustan's lips curled in a feral grin. "Or will you fight with me like men?" Naked as he was, every line of him quivered with menace. At that moment, he looked as dangerous as the boar he had killed, and I think they allowed him to put on his clothes to hide the force in him beneath the trappings of humanity.

Esseilte was pulling on her own garments as well. In a moment she stood, white and silent, with her hunting knife gleaming in her hand.

"Swear that the queen will be safe and I will come out to you—" Drustan said. "Else I will slay her and myself now and be done!"

"Do not shame me, beloved . . ." Esseilte said softly. "I am a daughter of heroes and a queen, and I can find a sheath for this blade myself if the time has come to make an end!"

"Esseilte, I want you to live, if you can—" he answered in a hoarse whisper.

"Then slay *them*, if you can!" Her mood changed suddenly. "Drustan, kill them and win free! I can survive if I know that you are living, only swear that you will never give to another woman what you have shared with me!"

With his eyes still on his enemies, Drustan kissed her hand. Then he lifted his head again.

"Well—which is it to be?"

"Esseilte will not be harmed. . . ." The king's voice grated, stone on stone.

With a single leap, Drustan was out among them, blade hooking round with a swift, deadly sweep like the boar's, slicing across one man's breast and sending another's sword slithering across the dead grass. Then Meriadek charged him, mouthing incoherent obscenities that only seemed to fuel his fury.

Swords rang as Meriadek struck fast and hard. Drustan feinted and wove like a shadow, but his enemy came in with a swift barrage of hammer blows, and the air around the tower echoed like a forge. Meriadek had ceased his cursing. His breath came in hoarse gasps now, but Drustan fought silently. Meriadek had touched him once or twice already. Drustan danced away, but the wall of the tower was behind him.

"Now I have you, bastard!" screamed Meriadek, launching himself into a run with sword extended to spit his foe. "Oh, I have — "

Until the final moment, Drustan waited. And then, as Meriadek's point arrowed toward him, he took one step to the right and forward, turning, his own blade following up and across and through with the swing of his body behind it.

His enemy's blade shattered against stone, his body crashing after it and then spinning backward, arms still reaching for Drustan. But Meriadek's head flew upward in a smooth arc, bounced twice on the grass, and rolled onward to rest at the feet of the king.

Gorwennol wrenched free from Karasek and ran for the horses. "My lord, my lord, here — I'll have him bridled in a moment — " Harness rang as he fumbled with the gear.

The others seemed too stunned to try to stop him. Neither Drustan nor Marc'h appeared to have heard. They only looked at each other, and were still staring as Gorwennol brought the bay horse to his master. Mechanically, Drustan mounted, let the animal dance forward, hooves drumming dully on the grass.

"I loved you — " the king spoke as Drustan began to pass, and then, as he had said once to Meriadek, "I do not want to see your face again."

Twenty

MODRON'S WELL

On the night before the Midwinter Festival a high wind rattled sleet against the leather coverings of the windows and slammed against the door. The red flames that leaped above the coping of the great central hearth contorted as drafts crept through crevices in the walls. Now and again the storm's force would diminish, but then the wind moaned and whispered outside like the ghosts of those who had been killed in Conomor's wars. I thought I preferred the direct assault of the storm to that dismal whimpering.

The days since the boar hunt had not been happy. When we returned to Ker-haes, Marc'h had called for writing tools and sent his reply to Childebert. His agents in Lutetia waxed eloquent in their reports of Samson's rage when he learned he had been out-maneuvered. That made for an evening's amusement, and it was welcome, for though Marc'h did not mistreat Esseilte, neither had he forgiven her. I slept in her chamber now, and the king slept with his men in the hall. Esseilte herself endured it only because she knew that Drustan was safe in Léon, where Keihirdyn of Barsa had given him sanctuary.

The bad weather resumed with redoubled fury, as if the elements were expressing the emotions of the king. Storm fronts rolled in like invading armies, weighting the mountains with snow and battering at the walls of the dun. Men huddled in the hall, dicing and drinking, and often enough quarreling too. I wondered if they would be killing each other by spring. In other years, we had livened the long evenings with music and tales. In other years, we had had Drustan.

As the feast day drew nearer, the elements roused to new fury; the powers of winter seemed determined to finally extinguish the weakening sun. I did what I could to make the hall festive with greenery, and a great log of oak was brought in to kindle the sacred fire, but even the prospect of a feast did little enough to raise spirits.

I sat by the hearth cracking nuts and tossing the shells into the fire. The king sat nearby, rereading a worn scroll of Marcus Aurelius. I wondered if the musings of a dead emperor could give him a philosophy that fitted his own tribulations. When we heard the first distant hammering over the crackling of the fire, I assumed it was some new sound of the storm.

Then I heard shouting. Were the men already fighting over their wine? Marc'h had put down his book and sat listening like a wolf that puts up its muzzle to catch the first scent of prey.

The door banged open. "Marc'h! Lord King!" Mevennus Maglos gave a swift look behind him. "My lord, there's a messenger from Lutetia who says he must speak —" Another figure shouldered past him and stood panting, with a death-grip on the posts that held the door. Marc'h started forward.

Drenched, muddy to the chin, and hollow-eyed as if he had not slept for a year, still I recognized the height and the deep voice of the Frankish prince Chramn.

"For the love of God, man, get you here to the fire!" exclaimed the king. He held out his hands and the prince gripped his forearms.

"Rode straight here — no stopping. Roads terrible . . . two horses died . . ."

Marc'h thrust him into the great chair. "What is it?" He shook him as the fair man's eyes began to close. "What's happened, Chramn?"

"Childebert . . . died a week ago. They've crowned my father . . . Chlotar!"

Marc'h let him go.

"Could have beaten him . . . if my brothers had supported me," Chramn added without opening his eyes. "— Hate the old man as much as I do, but they never had the balls to stand up to him. They're sniffing around him now like dogs in a shambles, waiting for him to throw them a bone. Bones is all he'll give 'em,

too. Arnegund wants the meat for Chilperic, and she'll leave my
mother's sons to starve."

I poured mead into a horn and carried it to him. Right now he
needed something stronger than wine. Vaguely I remembered
the story — Chlotar had married another princess, Radegund,
when Chramn's mother died, shoved her into a convent when
she proved barren, and married Arnegund, as if five sons by his
first wife had not been enough to prove his virility. Chramn took
the horn and drank, the strong muscles of his throat rippling as
the stuff went down.

When he had drained it he looked up at Marc'h with a sigh,
wiping his mouth with the back of his hand.

"Had to get away — his companions were coming after me.
Knew I could trust you. . . ."

Marc'h's expression was unreadable. But clearly at this moment a fugitive Frankish prince was a distinct liability.

"Certainly you can stay here for a time —" he began.

"You don't understand." Chramn handed me the horn to re-
fill. "You and me, we have to be allies now. When that little rat
Samson could get nowhere with Childebert he took his pet
prince with him to Soissons. He and m'father got along like a
louse and a flea — Chlotar's going to give him an army to restore
Iudual!" He had begun to shake, I did not know whether with
fear or with cold. Marc'h had gone to the hearth and was staring
into the flames. From the look on his face, I did not want to
know what visions he saw there.

"Whatever is going to happen in the future, you are chilled
and exhausted right now," I said bracingly. "Let us get you into
a hot bath and some dry clothes, my prince, lest the weather
accomplish what your father's swords could not do!"

The men who had overheard Chramn's news were whispering
to their fellows. As the word spread, expressions began to alter — but not to apprehension. They looked like the hound pack
when the huntsman comes to take them to the chase. This Midwinter Feast might be a cheerful occasion after all, I thought
then, but it would feel less like a celebration for the birth of the
Prince of Peace than a feast for Mithras, the soldiers' god.

When the prince came back into the hall, warm and clean and
clad in clothes that were only a little too small for him, he was
appreciably calmer. And Marc'h was once more the bland and
polished aristocrat — the heir of Roman Britain hosting the scion
of a jumped-up foederati tribe.

"So we are to be allies?" With his own hands he served Chramn with boiled mutton and cabbage, with barley bread and salted butter and cheese, and a bowl of steaming broth.

Chramn grinned at him. "Once my brothers have had a taste of my father as over-king they may come round to thinking they should have followed me!"

"Yes," said Marc'h, reflecting. "And this war on Iudual's behalf will be a test for Chlotar — a new king cannot afford to spend his strength on fruitless adventures. If we destroy his strength in Domnonia, he will be weakened everywhere. . . ."

"My brothers will declare for me then!" exclaimed Chramn. "And even now, there are those who may be willing to fight for me, once they see I have allies!"

"And when we have conquered —" Marc'h said indulgently. "What then?"

"I shall rule Austrasia and all of Gaul," said Chramn. "But all of Neustria shall be yours, including Namnet and Redon. Yours as brother-king, not vassal, secured by oath to you and your heirs. . . ." Chramn held out his hand and Marc'h took it, forearm to forearm in a warrior's clasp.

"It is a bargain then," said Marc'h. "Now as I see it, here is what we will have to do . . ."

They talked for a time longer, until fatigue overcame the younger man in the middle of a sentence and he slumped down in the chair. When the prince had been put to bed Marc'h turned to me.

"You must start packing for travel, you and the queen. You will leave as soon as the weather clears. There may be danger here, and I want you safe in Kernow!"

Kernow . . . I was suddenly weak with longing for the sight of rocky tors and sheltered woods, for a wide golden sky and the dancing blue of the sea. I had not allowed myself to know how much I missed it. By the time the seas were safe, winter would be ending. Red buds would swell on the branches, and the primroses would scatter their pale gold beneath the trees. *Kernow!* Abruptly I longed for my land as Esseilte longed for Drustan. I wanted to go home.

I saw that Marc'h was smiling, a thing he had not done since Drustan had gone. But when I came closer my answering smile faded, for I had seen that look on the face of Drustan when he was fighting. It was the smile of a man who can afford to take risks because he does not really care if he survives.

❖   ❖   ❖

"Branwen!"

I was already out of bed and running toward Esseilte's chamber before I realized that it was the middle of the night, and we were safe at Lys Hornek, whose lord had married out little Breacc, in Kernow. I stopped for a moment, listening. There were only the sounds of the villa at night: the faintest creaking of timbers, the wind singing in the tiles, and the whisper of mousefeet as the creature ran out to snatch some forgotten crumb.

"Branwen — he has killed him! Branwen, please come!"

I hurried through her door. Esseilte was sitting up with the bedclothes clutched to her breast, her eyes like pools of darkness, staring into darkness, for the lampflame had sunk to a blue spark. I trimmed the wick, and when the flame was burning strongly again, carried it over to the chest beside the bed.

We had returned just after the Feast of Brigid in February, and now it was June, but the nightmares had grown more frequent as summer drew on. In Armorica, the armies were gathering. My own visions of terror came during the day, when I wondered if Marc'h's force would be sufficient, if even now they might be striking him down.

"Esseilte, love! It's all right — I'm here!" I put my arms around her and she clung to me, sobbing. "We are safe in Kernow, and Drustan is safe in Léon. Hush now. It was only a dream. . . ."

"It was the Morholt —" she whispered when the sobs had ceased. "I saw him and Drustan fighting up and down the island, with blood everywhere, and the sun flickering like red lightning from their swords."

"Yes, dear." I stroked her hair. "But that was long ago. It is all over now."

"But this time I was there too! And when the Morholt fell his head rolled to my feet and he looked up at me and spoke. . . ." She swallowed. "*'Child of my heart, why have you betrayed me?'*" Her voice had deepened as if it were indeed my father saying those words, and I felt a little shiver run down the backs of my arms.

"Why are these dreams haunting me now, Branwen? The Morholt has been dead for near five years. And it is eight months since I have seen Drustan. . . ."

"Perhaps that is why —" I took up a corner of the sheet and began to dry her tears. "I think that you are blaming yourself for having lost him, and trying to find some reason for what you feel. But though the king will not see him, he no longer seeks his life, and Drustan can fight for him in Léon, which you know is what he would want to do. . . ."

"Yes," she said sadly. "When I am awake I know it, but when I sleep the terrors spring out at me like armed men." She eased back upon her pillows, but when I rose to go she held my hand.

"Stay with me here, Branwen. There is room enough for two. Perhaps if you are here I will not be so afraid."

And so I came into the bed beside her, finding it as natural for my body to curve around hers as it had been long ago. We had been girls then, frightened of what the future might hold. Now we were women, and we knew.

Oh my sister, I thought then, *would that we had set sail for the Isle of the Blessed then, and avoided all these sorrows!* But then I remembered the moments of glory when I had been part of the life of all things. And I suppose that Esseilte also had memories that she would not trade. . . . I could only hold her, and hope that the Lady would bring some meaning out of our pain.

Great clouds were boiling up on the western horizon as if the folk of the air were building fortresses in the sky. Presently they would begin to attack each other with lances of lightning, and the rumble of their great war-drums would echo across the sky. But I had a little time yet before the battle began.

I turned back to the grassy bank where I had seen the bright yellow flowerets of celandine. Mixed with vinegar, the juice was good for diseases of the skin, and one of the lads who served us in Lys Hornek had been in misery for days from an itchy patch on his neck. I would take the root, too, for the toothache. Murmuring a prayer to the spirit of the herb that I had learned from Mairenn, I dug into earth still moist from rain the night before, and pulled.

The celandine came up easily, always a good sign, and that was just as well, for already I heard thunder. I straightened, and realized that it was not the skies but the earth that had rumbled. A rider was pushing his horse up the road to Lys Hornek. I looked at my basket. I had hoped to find some chamomile or yarrow for tea, but they could wait for another expedition. I shivered — a reaction that had become habitual at the sound of hoofbeats, for too often they meant messages from Armorica.

I pulled my skirts up through my belt and hurried up the back way to the villa, reaching it just as the rider was entering the court through the main gate. Esseilte had come out on the inner porch to greet him, with Brecc behind her, holding her baby in her arms. I set down my basket and straightened my skirts and went out to join her. At Lys Hornek the queen dressed in the Roman manner, as I did, with her hair coiled and pinned and a stola of fine wool draped over her gown, and she was playing the Roman matron, asking Brecc to bring cakes and wine to the atrium before we would hear the news.

"'Tis sure now that Domnonia will fight the king." The messenger set the goblet back on the tray. He was still young — the beard a golden fuzz along his chin — too young to have such anxious eyes.

He had told us that his name was Ladek, from a farm near Din Chun. He had taken a slash in the sword-arm that was proving slow to heal, and so Marc'h had sent him home. I saw how stiff the arm was when he moved it, and wondered whether any of my salves would help him. But I did not say so. Here was one safe from the storm of battle. Why should I heal him only to send him back into it again?

"The Franks are gathering armies like a squirrel gets nuts in the fall, so they say, but we've only seen skirmishing so far. They attack our camps at dawn, try to burn supplies and the like."

I offered him the tray of saffron cakes, and he took one eagerly. I did not suppose that fine baking was among the supplies available to the army, even when food got through.

"But so far there has not been much fighting?" asked Esseilte.

"Not so's to notice. Your lord is well, though the worry sits on him like cloud on a hilltop. He wanted you to know."

"And the lord Drustan, his nephew?" I took pity on Esseilte then.

"Surely — he's still in Léon, jollying up the good lads there to rise for the king. The West remembers how Riwal killed Drustan's da, and they never did give that old bird their loyalty. Happen Lord Drustan may even hold the land against Iudual. They like him well, with his good sword and his songs, especially since he married their lady — Keihirdyn of Barsa's sister, you know? Her name's Essylt too. Essylt Dornwenn — of the White Hands — they call her . . ." Ladek took another cake and sat munching happily.

Esseilte had not moved, but the color was draining from her

skin until she might have been a statue indeed. I rose quickly and shoved the tray into Ladek's hands.

"Take this back to the kitchens, if you will, and ask them to pack up something for the rest of your journey." I dropped the little bag with the messenger's fee on the tray. "We thank you for bringing us word—" He looked confused, but I pushed him out the door. He might think us inhospitable, but that was better than having him spread the word that the queen had fainted when she heard Drustan was wed.

When the boy was gone I turned quickly, hoping to catch Esseilte before she slid to the floor. But the blood that had left her face was flooding back again. From white to red she had gone, eyes bulging, hair untwining from its coils. She looked like the Morrigan. She looked like Queen Mairenn.

"Esseilte . . ." I began.

"You heard!"

I nodded. "But there must be reasons—"

"I should have killed myself that night in the forest," she went on, unheeding. "I should have killed *him*!" She began to walk up and down, the hem of her gown hissing angrily across the cracked mosaic of Orpheus on the floor. "He swore faith with me! How else could I have let him go?"

I sat down heavily. Oh yes, there must be reasons—I could even imagine some of them. The marriage might have been the price for the support Drustan needed to hold Léon. It might have been a ploy to convince Marc'h that he had no further interest in the queen. It might even have been Drustan's desperate attempt to distract himself from his own pain. But I did not say these things aloud, nor did I remind Esseilte that I had seen the man I loved live in marriage with another, and survived.

At that moment I doubted there was anything I could say that she would have heard.

"Fire! Branwen, go tell them to make up a fire in my chamber! I will cauterize this agony!"

I had not known Esseilte had kept so many things of Drustan's. I would have counseled her against it, but even when he began to distrust her, the king had never searched her belongings. Now it was all going into the flames—the letters, the songs, a veil of silk gauze that he had given her, and other trinkets. But when she started to lay the lap-harp he had taught her to play in Eriu on the fire I stopped her.

"If you will no longer keep it, let me give it to that lad Dewi who wants to be a bard." I took it from her hands and thrust it outside the door.

She pulled at the neck of her gown. "If I could burn these breasts that he has caressed I would do so! Or this hair he used to praise —" Before I could snatch it away she had taken her dagger and slashed off a long lock of her hair. I grasped her wrist as she cast it on the fire, squeezing until the knife clanged on the floor. We stood watching as the golden strands frizzled and disappeared and the stink of burning filled the air.

"Burn then," Esseilte said harshly, "and may my passion burn to ashes as you do! I bought Drustan's life with my love, but there is still a geas unfulfilled. . . . *Neither time nor distance may break it . . . neither hate nor love. . . . Death alone shall break this bond!*"

I shuddered as I recognized her mother's words.

"That curse was never broken, only suspended. . . . Now once more do I invoke it upon the man who has wronged me!" Esseilte's voice was terrible. "Across the waters may my words go winging — dark wings for darker words — raven-black, doom-bearing; circling, striking, piercing his faithless heart!"

A damp gust of wind blew through the open window, blowing back the folds of her garments and sending ashes from the brazier swirling across the room. Esseilte laughed then, and her arms swept up in invocation.

"Drustan, Drustan, hear how I destroy you!" she cried. "Until you lie dead at my feet may my curse pursue you. In your going forth and your coming in may you find ill-fortune; in war and in peace, at table and in the bed-chamber — oh, especially there! Let love turn to hatred in the eyes of the woman who calls you husband! May your sword shatter! May your rod soften! In battle and in the marriage bed alike may your weapons fail you, and may the hand you love be the one to strike you down!"

I had thought myself the heir to Mairenn's power, but I saw now that I had only part of it. To Esseilte had gone the dark passions — I could feel the force of her curse spreading outward, like waves from a stone thrown into a pool. I knew only how to bless, and I had no spell of healing for what Esseilte was doing now.

"By the flesh that is now parted, by the breath that bore your lying vows, by the heart that beats in your faithless breast, and by the fire that has consumed our love I swear this: by Morrigu and Crom Dubh, by my uncle's head and my mother's soul, as I will may it be done!"

Fire flared, blinding, a sheet of light that showed Esseilte's face like a carven Fury, her hair tossing in serpent's coils as she screamed. Then thunder shook the world in a mighty hand. I told myself that it was only the storm I had seen building earlier, but I knew better.

The powers Esseilte had called upon had heard.

I put her to bed then, but by evening she was tossing with fever. The storm that raged above us raged also within. In that old building it was impossible to keep drafts out entirely, especially when Esseilte threw off her covers as fast as we put them on. By the next day she was struggling to keep from drowning in the liquid that gathered in her lungs.

For a week I fought the illness with willow-bark and cold compresses and with hot blankets and mustard, striving to get the fever down and then sweat out the demons that had caused it. I wondered sometimes what Drustan would have done if he had learned Esseilte had taken another lover. Lain down and died? Esseilte's reaction was more active, but as I battled her fever I knew well that she could die of it too. By the time the crisis passed and she slept peacefully, I was ready to slide down into darkness beside her.

Strength came back slowly. As summer ripened around us, I recovered my spirits as well. But Esseilte's healing was of the body only, and she remained listless and pale. She ate what I fed her, and drank my potions down, but she did not seem to care whether they had any power.

"Lady, is the queen better today?"

I looked up from the pot where I was brewing up a tea of chamomile and valerian, saw the lad Dewi, and smiled.

"A little — perhaps this tea will help her."

"I am sure it will!"

Ever since I had cured him of ringworm, Dewi had thought I could heal anything. I shrugged.

"I wanted to thank her for giving the harp to me," he said then. "I can play it a little already. Would it cheer her if I came and sang?"

"Do not!" I tried to soften my first response with a laugh. "Right now what she needs is quiet. Perhaps if she recovers you can play for her —"

"Not likely —" His mood shifted suddenly. "They say she

learned to play from the Lord Drustan. I heard him once, when
the king lodged here. She would not want to listen to me. . . ."
His dark gaze went inward. He was a strange child, the son of
one of the women who cooked for us. He had never been
trained, but he could repeat any tune he had once heard.

"You must not say that, Dewi! I like to hear you sing, and I
have heard the great bards of Eriu. It is only that nothing
pleases my lady just now. . . ."

"You should take her to the holy well—"

I stared at him.

"Modron's Well, don't you know it? It is out in the country
beyond the market town. My mother went there when my little
sister was so ill, and the Lady cured her."

"Bless you, Dewi. We will try that!" It could do no harm,
certainly, and my heart leaped suddenly with the first real hope I
had felt since the messenger had come.

The weather had turned warm again by the time we set out for
Modron's Well, I on my mare and Esseilte in a horse-litter. We
saw corn still flattened by the violence of the storm in some of
the fields, but elsewhere it was beginning to ripen. The harvest
would be less abundant than hoped for, but there would be
wheat and barley for the reapers at Lughnasa.

It was nearly noon when we reached the path that led to the
spring. Woodland surrounded it, smaller trees, mostly—hazel
and sessile oak and ash; willow as the ground grew wetter, and
sallow around the spring. It was marshy where the water bubbled up from the roots of the sapling. Bits of rag fluttered from
its branches, some of them new, others fragile with age. The men
had carried in the litter on foot. They set it down beside the
spring and looked at me.

"Lady, the well is a little farther down the path," said one.

"Yes." I glanced at Esseilte, who was sitting up in the litter,
looking around her. In the restless green-gold light that filtered
through the fluttering leaves her face seemed brighter. "Leave
us," I told the men. "We will go on alone."

"Well, Branwen," Esseilte smiled at me when they had disappeared. "Is this where we pray for a miracle? It is very pretty, I
admit, but what do you expect to happen here?"

I smiled. "I have gotten you out of doors for a day of sun and
air. Isn't that enough? But now that we are here, let us see—"

I turned my face to the sunlight, breathing deeply. Lark song soared in the blue distances above us, but here beneath the golden leaves there was only the gentle gurgling of the waters and the hum of insects in the still air.

"This is the sacred tree, the spirit that guards the spring." I remembered the great oak from whose roots came the fountain in Broceliande. "First we must make our offerings. . . ." From my belt I drew the lengths of silk that I had tucked there. The other rags that I could see fluttering from the branches were wool and linen, but I thought the Lady would expect more from a queen. This silk had come from Constantinople, and a pattern of birds was woven into the cloth.

"Do you want me to do yours?"

Esseilte shook her head. "Let us by all means do the thing properly. If you will help me out of this litter I think I can manage it."

"Dip the cloth into the spring, then tie it to the branch, and picture very strongly the thing you want to happen — as the material frays, the power of your wish will be released into the world." I reached for a branch, looked back, and saw the happiness leave her eyes.

"I will make the offering, Branwen, but I have cursed my love. My heart is dead already — what remains in the world for me to desire?"

Swiftly I tied my dripping strip to the branch of the sallow tree. Still holding it, I closed my eyes, fingering smooth silk and rough bark, feeling the life of the tree tingling underneath my hand.

Bright spirit, I invoke your blessing. Please accept my offering and grant my prayer! Now I must think of what I wanted — abruptly I realized that all my own happiness was bound up with that of others. Esseilte content, and Marc'h home and at peace — those were my desires, and without them I did not know what to ask.

Is there nothing? came the question — from the spirit of the tree or from somewhere deep within? *Not even love?* For an instant I glimpsed a child's face that looked up at me with Marc'h's deep eyes.

I love Marc'h and Esseilte! I banished the image. *Now receive my prayer for the one who will not ask. . . .* I tried to picture happiness for Esseilte, but all I could remember was her face distorted by rage. I forced myself to see her at peace, and for a moment the vision came clear: She lay nestled in Drustan's arms. Memory filled in the rest of the picture — stone walls, and Marc'h stand-

ing over them with a torch in his hand — Quickly I opened my
eyes.

"Let's go on to the chapel," I said harshly.

We followed the path through a tunnel of interlaced thorn. I
saw that Esseilte was walking more easily now, and wondered if
perhaps her weakness had come from simple inaction. Then the
greenery opened out suddenly and we saw the chapel.

It was round, in the old style that reminded me of Eriu, with
walls of woven withies from which the plaster was mostly gone.
Here there was no pattern of stones to follow, but my feet carried me instinctively sunwise around the chapel, where saxifrage
and forget-me-not and sorrel jeweled the grass. A sweet perfume
drifted from the curled trumpets of chevrefoil that nodded from
the vines twining up one wall. Abundant water and sunlight had
kept flowers growing past their season. Here, one might indeed
think oneself come to the Land of Promise. I let the warm air fill
my lungs and released it again, dizzied by sweetness.

Then I followed Esseilte into the chapel. Some of the thatch
was also missing, so that sunlight filtered through the framework
and dappled the floor. Only the altar was of stone, and the coping of the pool, with a trough where water came in and another
through which it overflowed. Esseilte sank down on the wooden
bench and looked around her.

"Yes, it is very peaceful here . . . it is good to be alone."

I shook my head. Peaceful it was, but could she not feel the
presence that was growing more palpable with every moment we
remained? I dipped up water in the wooden cup that stood on
the coping and offered it to Esseilte, and in that motion, a
knowledge deeper than memory told me that I had filled a sacred vessel and offered it to worshippers many times before.

I took the cup back from her when she was finished, and knelt
before the pool. The tiny hairs on my forearms lifted from something other than the cool breath off the water. I blinked, for the
forms around me were wavering, and the blood pounded in my
ears like a ritual drum.

*"Water of life in the well; well of life in the Lady; Lady of life within
me —"* Words trembled on my lips that were not my own.

Then I set the cup to my lips and drank, and the world
changed.

The walls that had been flaking were newly plastered. No sun
pierced the thatch, but the temple was full of light, for around

me stood a circle of dark-robed women holding lamps in their hands.

"*White Raven, White Raven, I summon you!*"

"*Matir,*" I murmured, "*I am here. . . .*"

"*Why have you forsaken the trust that was laid upon you, Lady of Kernow?*" It was a voice trained to the full use of language, and I felt it in my bones.

"*What can I do when the king does not know me?*" I replied. "*He seeks his doom in a foreign country. There is nothing I can do!*"

"*It is for you to command him! Tell him who you are!*"

"*My oath to Esseilte forbids it!*"

"*Your duty to the land supersedes all other loyalties —*"

"*And what of my duty to my sister? Is not a human spirit worth as much as soil and stone?*"

"*Without the land —*" the priestess began, but words poured from my lips.

"*Brigantia, hear me! Modron, holy Mother, I dare to call Thy name! Judge me, Thou who art the source of all, for I will accept no word of humankind!*" I bent to look into the well. And all around me came the sound of waters falling, and a fountain of brightness that swept even the vision of temple and priestesses away.

The surface of the waters dazzled, but I held to the coping, staring within. Perhaps it was my own eyes' defense against the glare, but after a moment it seemed to me that the water swirled, and in its curves and shadows I saw the face of a woman with shadowed eyes.

"*Who are you?*"

"*I am the Lady of the Well and Flame. I am the Mother of the Son,*" said that Light. Radiance forever rose in splendor around me and cascaded ever down.

"*Lady, I am torn between loyalties. What shall I do?*"

"*I am Modron. Though they deny Me, every one of My children is dear to Me. The sword shall pierce your heart also, but love . . . and believe . . . and all shall yet be well.*"

The Light swirled around me in a coruscation of splendor, out of which I saw gazing two eyes, infinitely sad, infinitely joyful, infinitely wise. Then I slid down the wave into peace.

When I opened my eyes, Esseilte was bending over me.

"Branwen! Blessed Brigid be thanked for waking you! Are you hurt? What happened, can you say?"

I could not meet her eyes. "What did you see?"

"There was a glimmer of light on the water, and you spoke in a strange language as if you were answering. But I could see no other with us, and I heard no voice but your own," she answered me.

"I think . . . I saw the Lady of the Holy Well . . ." *and the sun in his glory is like a candle!* I shook my head in self-mockery, but any words of mine would have been equally inadequate to explain to her what I had seen.

I struggled to sit up, and this time it was Esseilte who was aiding me. I shivered and hugged myself with my arms, looking around me with eyes not yet entirely focused on this world. I had come to Modron's Well seeking a gift for Esseilte, but it was I who had received the blessing, though I did not yet know what it might mean.

Twenty-one

KEIHIRDYN

"Columba of Derry is a hard man to cross, and this latest dispute has not made him love the Ard-Righ more!" said Domnall MacLeite, squinting out across the dazzle of the sea. After our visit to Modron's Well, Esseilte had taken a dislike to Lys Hornek. By the end of August we had moved her household to Lan Juliot, where the trader Domnall had found us.

"What has happened?" asked Esseilte. We sat in the shelter of the monastery garden, listening to the bees that hummed around the stonecrop in the zigzag slate walls. The topmost leaves of the bean plants fluttered a little in the sea breeze; the cabbages, protected, unfurled their folded leaves to the sun. Farther off I could see the glossy curled leaves of kale and the feathery tops of turnips in their rows. Here, at least, the land was prospering, though elsewhere the crops had been set back by unseasonal storms.

"Well, it was about a book, see you—a gospel that Brother Finnian brought back to his monks at Moville. Columba heard of it and wanted to see it, for they say this book is more complete than the other scriptures we have in Eriu, a very treasury of God's true Word."

"And did Finnian let him read it?" I asked.

"Aye, indeed—but Columba did more than read. He burnt a cow's worth of candles copying it, and when he claimed the copy as his own, Finnian sought judgment from the Ard-Righ. Myself, I tend to hold with Columba," Domnall continued, "for surely the book was none the worse for being copied, but Diarmait said otherwise —"

He squinted for a moment, remembering. *" 'As a calf is to the cow, so is the copy to the book.'* The High King's ruling was that Columba should give his copy to Finnian." He shook his head and took another swallow of beer. "But there will be trouble. . . . Columba has gone back to his monastery, muttering like a summer storm. He will not soon forgive the slight to him."

There was a short silence, while the trader applied himself to his bread and cheese. I shivered, remembering the eagle gaze that had hardened Columba's face before his smile transformed him to a dove again. It had begun with a book, but where would it end?

"Happy the land where the lordship of a book is the only cause of contention," I said finally. Domnall raised one eyebrow and looked from me to the queen.

"And what of Armorica? One piece of news deserves another. I heard last that Chlotar was leading his host into Domnonia to give battle to your lord —"

"There has been a battle." Esseilte coughed, took a moment to recover herself, and then went on. "The king is drawing back in good order, reorganizing his forces to face them again. The Franks are very strong, and the men of Dol have joined them, but in his last letter Marc'h sounded sure that they could be beaten. The tale is not by any means all told!"

She smiled at the trader calmly, and he nodded, honoring her loyalty whatever he thought of her conclusions. I sighed. Samson in Armorica and Columba in Eriu — truly in this year the priests who should have been partners had become the scourge of kings.

"Well then —" Domnall took a last swallow of beer. "I must be on my way, with thanks for your hospitality. Will you see me to the gate, Branwen?"

I could hear Esseilte coughing behind me as we moved down the path.

"Your lady does not look well —" he said as we reached the gate.

"She was ill at the beginning of the summer, and she's been slow to get her strength back again. . . ." I did not explain why.

"It shook me to see her so pale," said Domnall. "Like a wraith of the girl I remembered, she is now."

I looked back, trying to see Esseilte with a stranger's eyes.

Living with her day by day, I had not noticed how thin she had become. *We will go back to Bannheðos where they keep a ðairy herð,* I thought then. *Perhaps the butter and cream that our little black cattle give at Nans Yann will fill her out again. And I will search through Mairenn's book for a better medicine for that cough!*

I had no doubt that I could find a way to cure her. Had I not received the blessing of the Mother of All?

On the gentler south coast Esseilte seemed better. At least the storms of winter made her no weaker than she had been. She was a little short of breath and easily tired, but as spring began to bless the land it seemed to me that the cough was easing, and I began to hope she would regain full health in time.

I wish I could have been as hopeful about the Horse King's wars.

When the roads dried in the spring the armies began to move once more. And once more there came to us a tale of disaster as the Frankish armies smashed Marc'h's forces a second time. Word came to us that he was retreating to the protection of the hills that ringed Ker-haes. Secure in that natural fortress he waited, hoping that events elsewhere in the Frankish empire would draw off Chlotar's strength before the Frank king could break through and crush him.

I waited also, wondering how the Lady's promises would be fulfilled. Surely, I thought, Marc'h's defeats would bring him back to me and to Kernow. Then we would once more celebrate the rituals and renew the land. As Esseilte took refuge in a settled despair, I ruled her household and contemplated my destiny.

"I would shelter you gladly, master, but my lady hates music — every bard or harper who has come to us has been driven away!" Dewi's light voice drifted up from the gate to the farmyard, and I paused to listen, setting down the basket of scraps I was taking down to the pigs in their run.

It was a bright, clear morning, I remember, the early freshness just beginning to retreat before the heat of the summer sun. July was ending, and we had moved down to Nans Yann to be near the river, with no household but the people of the farm. It was a measure of Esseilte's apathy, I thought, that she would consent to live once more in a place where she had been happy with Drustan.

But who was Dewi talking to? I could hear the murmur of a

deeper voice answering, and then the clink of a horse's hoof on stone. Leaving the basket, I moved toward the gate.

"But you like music, don't you, lad? I've seen your eyes on my harpcase — they lit up like a Lombardy merchant's at the sight of gold!" I could hear the man clearly now, and Dewi's giggle. "Have pity, child, on a man all weary from the road. If they'll not give us a bed in the house, we'll lie on straw in the barn and be grateful. Can you help us to that, lad, for the sake of a look at my harp and a touch of her strings?"

"I don't know —" Dewi began. Then I came around the corner of the shed and they all looked up at me.

There were two of them. The bard looked a beggarly sort, his harpcase of better make than his clothing, as if he had fallen on hard times. His servant held the horses — local ponies, both of them — but neither stranger looked like a local man. The servant was a black-haired, black-eyed fellow whose tunic seemed to be of better quality than the ragged mantle he wore. My eyes narrowed and shifted back to the harper. I waited to hear him speak again.

"Lady." Dewi was still sitting on the gate. "Here's a bard come seeking shelter. Can't we help him?" He kicked the gate with his heels for emphasis.

"Mistress —" The man saluted me as the filidh of Eriu salute the woman of a house. "The peace of the Good God to you and to all within —"

I looked him up and down. "There will be no peace anywhere you are, Drustan!"

The harper straightened, and as if I saw the unraveling of some enchantment, all the hints of something other that I had sensed beneath the dirt and the rags came together, and I wondered how even for a moment I could have failed to know him.

"I told you, Keihirdyn, that she would not be fooled." He turned to his companion with a faint grin. The other man stared at me, eyes widening.

"Is this not the queen?"

"This is the Lady Branwen. Now will you believe I did not lie to you?" Drustan turned back to me and gestured toward the other man. "And this — is Keihirdyn lord of Barsa, my" — he grimaced — "brother-in-law."

I shook my head. "Drustan, you are mad to come here! If Marc'h finds out. . . ."

"The king believes that we are skulking about Léon, trying to raise the countryside against the Franks," he sighed. "No one will know —"

"Esseilte will know!" I answered furiously. "How dare you return to upset her just when she has begun to heal —"

"To heal?" His eyes held mine, and there was no laughter in them now. "I heard that she had been ill. . . ."

"Oh yes," I answered bitterly. "What did you expect? When you men are betrayed you can go kill something. But what could Esseilte do?"

"Forget me . . ." he said softly. "I hoped she would. God knows I tried not to think of her. But I am still bound. You must let me see her, Branwen, or none of us will ever be free!"

I fell back a step. Dewi was still on the gate, looking from Drustan to me and back again with wide eyes. His body was still, but his heels drummed against the crossbar.

"Shall I let them in, Branwen?" He slid down. "There's room for their ponies in the barn. . . ."

"Let me see her, and then she may do what she wills with me . . . I cannot live this way!" Drustan's face contorted for only a moment, but the agony still lived in his eyes.

The separation had been death-in-life for him as well, I thought then. Perhaps if Esseilte could punish him she would find release. Perhaps he was right, and any pain was better than despair.

I nodded, and Dewi began to pull open the gate. But as I led Drustan and Keihirdyn toward the house there seemed to be a shadow on the sun.

All those months of war had not hurt Drustan's harping. While we waited for Esseilte to return from the orchard, I began to slice apples for a pie, and he unstrapped the harpcase and sat down by the cold hearth to keep his promise to the boy. To Dewi, there was fascination even in the act of tuning. But when all the strings were adjusted and Drustan began to play, he sank down at his feet, eyes opening in awe.

Like a shower of raindrops the first notes came falling, like sunlight on sea-spray or the rainbow shimmer of a fountain. It was an invocation of pure music, and it was only gradually that Drustan began to add the deep chords that vibrate in the bone. And then, at last, came a whisper of melody — a love-song; no, it was all love-songs, for he shifted deftly from one to another and back again, with triplets and variations, with changes in rhythm and harmony and ornamentation, building a music that was greater than any single song as his love for Esseilte encompassed all that they had shared.

Drustan played with eyes closed, fingers flickering and hands moving with fluid ease as if the music flowed through, not from them, as if he too were only an instrument for some greater power to play. Knife and apples lay forgotten on the table before me. Even in the king's hall I had not heard him make such music. He played better now than ever in Eriu or Armorica, as if his music had needed only the final focusing of pain.

Listening, no one could have been aware of time's passing. Even place seemed uncertain. It was only gradually that I realized that the door had opened and Esseilte was standing there.

A breath of wind came with her, heady with the scent of ripening hay. Drustan's eyes opened, and as the fact of her presence penetrated his rapture, his fingers faltered, the rhythm of the music was broken, single notes fell into silence and whispered away.

"You!" She drew breath with an effort. Drustan set down the harp, watching her with eyes gone huge and shadowed as if she had drawn to her all the light in the room—and all power of movement also. I could not stir as she came forward and took up the knife with which I had been slicing the apples. "What enchantment has betrayed you into my hands?"

She spoke in a whisper. Drustan lifted his head and wrenched open the neck of his tunic so that his chest was bared.

He wants her to kill him . . . I understood suddenly. He waited as he had waited in the sweat-house, his whole being focused on the release that gleamed in her hand.

"You know its name . . . Esseilte . . . you know. . . ."

She licked dry lips, and then she was on him, knife flashing down and then away, red now, dropping with an icy tinkle to the stone floor.

"Ah dear God, dear God, your blood. . . ." Her golden head dropped to the red mouth that had opened in the pale skin of his chest as though her kiss could heal the wound that she had given him.

Then Drustan's arms closed around her, his own lips pressed against her hair as he murmured her name.

I grasped Dewi by the shoulder and shoved him outside, then took a clean cloth from the press and folded it into a pad to stanch the wound.

"Why cannot I kill you? You betrayed me!" Esseilte sobbed, looking up at him.

"I did not—" Drustan shook his head. "I could not complete the marriage, Esseilte. Whether I would or no, I must be faithful to you."

She gave him a brief, bitter smile. "I cursed your manhood, when I heard!"

"Even before that, Esseilte," Drustan said gently. "When I looked at her, your face was all I could see. . . ."

She reached up to touch his face, tracing the lines that anguish had inscribed around his eyes, the new scar that had been placed there by war, fingering the silver that threaded his dark hair.

"My poor love—I see that you have suffered too." She drew his head to hers and kissed him, then let him go. "What brought you back to me?"

"Oh—" Drustan tried to laugh. "Keihirdyn here blamed me for his sister's continuing virginity. He would not spare me unless I could prove to him that my lady was the fairest of mortal women, and even her companion outshone his sister as the moon pales the stars." He glanced up at me, but I would not meet his smile. This was not the story he had told me before. But Keihirdyn was eyeing me with an appreciation that suggested there was some truth in it. Had Drustan truly thought that this youth, with his wiry body and avid eyes, would appeal to me?

I frowned at them both and busied myself getting out cold meat and bread and curds. The best cure I knew for the exhaustion that came after the storms of emotion was food.

"That is what I told myself—" Drustan added harshly. "But it was only a turning of the key in a door that before long I would have battered down."

"Drustan, we cannot go on as we were before." Esseilte sat up, still within the circle of his arms. "We will have to go away together this time. To Alba, maybe, like Deirdre and the sons of Usnach. You could hunt the heron and the red stag and feed us as you did in Broceliande."

And you could die of fever. . . . I thought, but I kept silent.

"I cannot. Not yet—not now." Drustan's face grew grim. "Marc'h puts on a bold face—that man's face never did show how he feels—but he is in great danger unless he can find allies somewhere. The future of Armorica must be decided before the year is over, and the king will need every sword. Have I not

done enough to harm him, loving you? Do not ask me to fail him
when he needs me, Esseilte. You have to understand that I cannot desert him now!"

"Is it so? But you came to me, was that not a choice?" She
leaned back, looking at him, and smiled. I shivered a little,
watching her, for it was like the smile her mother had shown me
that last night in Temair when she gave her chest of herbs into
my hands.

"Nay, I suppose there is no escape for us that way. . . ." She
reached out to lift away a strand of hair that was falling into his
eyes, a motion that was infinitely tender, focused on his physical
reality as if she were hardly paying attention to the conversation
at all.

"Then you forgive me?" Drustan had been prepared for her to
try to kill him, but not for this smile.

"I cursed you . . . do you understand? How can you still love
me when I have betrayed you?"

"You cannot betray me," he said strongly. "You are Esseilte —"

Didn't he understand what she was trying to tell him? There
was no way to call back a curse such as that had been.

"For a year I have tried to wall away the pain," she went on,
"and I know now that it would be better to die than to live
without loving . . ."

The curse could not be undone. Did Drustan understand that
by linking her fate to his once more Esseilte believed that she
was dooming herself, too? I glared at her, remembering the
nights I had stayed wakeful, nursing her. Was any man worth
this? Had I spent all those weary hours so that she could forgive
him and begin the cycle of deception all over again?

"It was no curse, but a blessing, that brought me back to
you," said Drustan.

I felt a slow anger begin to tighten the muscles of my belly,
sliced into the bread viciously and flung it onto the platter.

"Let me help you —" Keihirdyn slid his hand along my arm
and reached for it, smiling at me like a man who has always been
treated well by women and is sure of his welcome.

"I can carry it!" I brushed past him and set the platter down
beside Drustan.

For several days the weather had been warm and still. With no
breeze off the river, the thick walls of the farmhouse made it an

oven by nightfall. Esseilte and Drustan had more pleasant things to do than sleeping in their bed in the loft, and I found it hard to lower my defenses enough to let sleep in. Our people at the farm were loyal, but I wondered how long it would take for one of Marc'h's chieftains to hear about the strange harper who was staying with the queen.

During the day we had music to occupy us, and the tasks of the farm. Keihirdyn followed me from barn to byre, whether because he was attracted to me, or because Drustan had clearly forgotten his existence, I neither knew nor cared. After several years in the king's household, I had grown used to evading men's advances, and he did not trouble me.

But at night I listened to the deep silence of the countryside that intensifies every sound. My nerves jumped at each creaking timber; it seemed to me I could hear the deer slip from the woods to feed in the orchard and the noiseless glide of the hunting owl. I would wake from dreams of faceless warriors with bloody swords and be afraid to sleep again.

It must have been a little after midnight when I was startled awake by hoofbeats. I lay in my narrow bed, heart pounding, wondering if it were indeed the thunder of my own pulse I had heard, or the cat leaping after a mouse, or whether there really had been something there. With my pulse drumming in my ears I could be sure of nothing. I got up, wrapped the sheet around me, and climbed down the ladder from the loft.

Keihirdyn got up from his pallet by the hearth when he saw me. He had been sleeping naked too, and I looked quickly away.

"What is it?"

"I thought I heard hoofbeats . . ." I answered softly. He reached for his sword and followed me to the door. The moon was just off the full, sinking behind the trees of the orchard now, but the meadow was still washed by its pale light, and silver edged each leaf and blade of grass. If I shifted focus, I could see a shimmer of movement above the grass, and I knew that the spirits of the trees were dancing there. The air was fresh and sweet with a damp breath of dew, very welcome after the dry day. I breathed deeply and felt my tension begin to ease.

"I couldn't sleep either," he said in a low voice, still standing behind me. "But I have heard nothing but the normal night sounds, and of course the music my lord Drustan makes as he lies with the queen!" He laughed softly. I felt myself flushing, and was glad the darkness did not let him see.

"I did not believe him, do you know, when he told me that you were more beautiful than my sister. But then I saw you at the gate, so wrathful—like the sun, not the moon—for to me your lady is too thin and pale. Drustan sees her with the eyes of love. I think you are the fairer now . . ."

Though he did not touch me, I could feel the pressure of his presence behind me. Suddenly uncomfortable, I started to move past him, but he touched my shoulder and turned me to face him.

"Oh Branwen, why must you hurry away? During the day you are always so busy. I have wanted to talk to you."

I paused with a sigh, suspecting what would come next, and deciding that I should let him say it and give him my refusal now.

"You are very beautiful in the moonlight, Branwen. . . ." His finger traced the line of my cheek. For a moment astonishment held me still, then I jerked away. "Is your body as lovely beneath that covering as your face is, I wonder?" He continued as if I had not moved.

"Keihirdyn, be still! What made you think I would want to hear this from you!"

"When you are so lovely, and your lady so great a lover?" he laughed softly. "Do you ask me to believe that all these years you have lain alone?"

I thought of the two occasions on which I had known a man—only twice since we came here from Eriu, and each time it had been a sacred thing. The sordid implications of his remark made my face flame.

"Don't speak of what you do not understand, Keihirdyn!" I said sharply.

"I understand you better than you know!"

He laughed again, and before I could move, pulled me against him. I had been holding the sheet around me, and hampered by the cloth, my arms were pinioned against my chest. With one arm he held me, and I had not anticipated the strength of a man trained to the lance and the oar. He grasped my hair with the other hand and kissed me, taking his time, thrusting with his tongue until I gagged though I tried to pull my head away. As I struggled I could feel his manhood hardening against me; I stilled, and he held me closer and ground his body against mine.

"You will not scream—" he whispered when he released my mouth at last. "My lord and lady are too busy at their own games to notice, but the lads in the men's house would hear you and come running, and what would they find here, mmn?" His other hand slipped down to squeeze my buttocks.

I tried to knee him, but the movement only threw me off balance. He lifted me despite all my twisting and snapping and carried me to his pallet. I tensed to roll free when he put me down, but he threw himself on top of me, using the moment when I tried to get my breath again to push the sheet out of the way and work his knees between my legs. I felt my thighs wrenched apart and his rod shoved between them; he lifted my buttocks and then he was ramming himself into me. His teeth closed on my lip as I tried to scream, and then there was only the pounding and the pain.

It was over very quickly.

I lay still as Keihirdyn rolled off me, conscious only of the sick throbbing between my thighs and the sick anger that was boiling in my belly. Moonlight still flooded through the doorway, bringing a whisper of sweet air. How could the land remain at peace after what had happened to me? I was the queen! If this could happen, then all I had believed must be a lie. I waited, expecting the earth to open or the sky to fall, but heard only the distant hooting of an owl. Through the doorway, the meadow was empty and still. Had there ever been anything there, or had I imagined it all?

"You will die for this . . ." I said hoarsely when the galloping of my heart had slowed.

"Will I?" He raised himself on one elbow, looking down at me. "Then I might as well look at what I am dying for!" Now it no longer mattered if he saw me. I did not move as he pulled the rest of the sheet away. My lip was throbbing. I tried to find some secret place within my skull to hide in where I would not have to think or feel the pain.

"So beautiful . . ." His hand slid along the hard muscles of my calf and up the smooth thigh.

"Don't touch me!"

I could see the flash of his teeth as he smiled. He shifted to show me the flaccid dangle of his manhood, and flicked it with one finger, grinning.

"Do you think I can do you any harm with this? But I will swear to you by my sister's honor — I will not enter you again until you ask for it, Branwen, not until you beg for me to put it in!"

"You will wait until Artor returns, then," I answered, turning my face away.

I felt cold and dizzy, but to try and warm myself would be to recognize I had a body, and I did not want to remember that now. I was vaguely aware that he was still touching me — a soft stroking that crept up each leg in turn, moved in soft swirls across my belly, up between my breasts to the hollow at the base of my throat, and then first to one breast, then the other, cupping, squeezing, then fastening firmly on the nipple with a force that nearly brought me back to consciousness and sent a jolt of pure sensation to where the pain had been.

I gasped and started to curl away, but now it was only a faint tickle, not unpleasant, and the stroking began once more. I do not know how long it went on. Perhaps shock had mercifully detached me from my body, or perhaps that constant touching soothed me. When awareness came to me again, the pain between my thighs had been transformed into a sweet pulsation.

I tensed, and the pressure shifted, melting resistance. Slowly, I opened my eyes. Keihirdyn lay close beside me. It was his fingers I felt within me, tracing a fiery spiral upon flesh that ached to feel that touch again.

"Tight as a virgin, you were," he said pleasantly. "But you are opening now . . ."

I shook my head, and caught my breath as he probed deeper. Spirit fluttered frantically, seeking escape from this, but my body would not obey me. Keihirdyn's dark head bent, and I felt his lips upon my breasts, first tickling, then sucking more strongly until the nipples had grown hard and so sensitive that every touch tingled all over my skin.

Then he abandoned them, easing my thighs farther apart and kissing his way downward until I moaned. I tried to push him away, but my hands only tangled in his thick hair. He lifted his head.

"Do you want me?"

I shook my head. That much will was left to me. I would never ask him for what he had taken from me.

He bent again, and I felt the slow sweet fire lick up my body in waves of sensation. He lifted himself above me, and I saw without surprise that he was ready again. He touched me, then slid away. I waited in aching emptiness as he teased my nipples, waited until my body was twisting without my will, seeking his.

He covered me then, skin just touching skin. I could feel the warmth of his body beating against my own.

"This is what you are, Branwen," he whispered, "a beautiful body, a vessel waiting to be filled. This is what you were made for . . . this is what you want, isn't it?"

My hips lifted, I felt the delicious pressure. He started to pull away and my arms closed around him.

"I want . . ."

His whole weight came down upon me, in me, and I began the slow, searing slide down into the dark.

I woke at dawn with Keihirdyn's arm still flung across me. The taste of ashes was in my mouth, and my body ached all over from what he had done to me. I eased carefully out from under, frantic not to wake him, and crept up to my own sleeping place for a gown. In the stream that ran down to the river there was a shallow pool where Esseilte and I bathed. Maybe its chill waters could make me clean.

I felt, indeed, as if I had had a fever. I still shook when I tried to remember what had happened. But if memory shied at acknowledging what had been done to me, it was certain that the world had changed. I went out into a morning whose colors seemed leached of all vitality. Even the sensation of water pouring over my skin was not what I thought I remembered. It was only when I turned to leave the pool that it was different, for Keihirdyn was on the bank behind me, pulling his tunic over his head and casting it aside.

I tried to back away, but he came down into the water and held me, his hands moving over my wet body like soldiers over a conquered land. I felt that touch as I had felt nothing else since I awakened.

"Do you like this?" His hand on my breast sent fire through my chilled skin, but I shook my head. "Truly?" Keihirdyn smiled, and his supple fingers moved lower, stroking until the strength left my legs. I clung to him.

"You must say it, Branwen —" His breath tickled my ear. "You must say how much you want me to fill that throbbing emptiness between your thighs. . . ." He touched me again, and I gasped. I could feel his hardness, but he only grinned as I tried to press myself against him. I tried to draw away then, but he held me, tormenting me with his lips and his hands.

"Ask for it, you bitch! Admit it—you want me as much as any female animal in season wants the male!"

I glared in mingled hatred and appeal, understanding that once more he was robbing me of even the illusion of integrity. It was not enough that my body had betrayed me—he also required the surrender of my will. . . .

I tried to summon up some strength to resist him, but the fire in my flesh was all I knew. Keihirdyn laughed and thrust me to my knees in the water before him, so that his manhood was all I could see.

"Kiss him, Branwen—kiss him until he is ready for you, and tell him what you want him to do!"

And I did it, all of it, until he pushed me down on my back in the shallows and took me, half in and half out of the water, in the pallid light of that dreadful dawn.

In the days that followed I began to understand that my consent was the final proof of Keihirdyn's conquest.

Esseilte and Drustan had always been discreet in their loving, denying their appetites until darkness. And at night Keihirdyn had me in his bed, again and again, so that I came to my tasks heavy-eyed in the morning and Esseilte looked at me with a knowing smile. But she did not know how it truly was with me, nor did I try to tell her. It seemed to me that a part of the madness that possessed me now was the fruit of all those nights when I had lain outside her chamber door, trying not to hear. If I had been a virgin, I might have been able to listen without understanding, but I had had to suppress my own awakening, and now every moan and cry I had ever heard was issuing from my own lips despite my will.

I hated Keihirdyn for uncovering my weakness. But I hated myself even more.

Keihirdyn pursued me in the daytime also. Despite his youth, he had had many adventures with women. Whenever he took me in a new way he would tell me which of them had taught it to him, and how and at what time—upon the straw of the barn with the horses munching contentedly above us; standing against the wall; from the back, I kneeling; or sitting in his lap upon a bench before the fire. He was a master at humiliation. He would torment my spirit until I turned on him, and then tease my body until I begged for his touch.

No matter how I tried to avoid it, if he could lay hands on me, my flesh would betray me, and I learned to give my consent quickly so that we might finish before someone came to see.

Lughnasa came, and the air echoed with the singing of the reapers and the swish as the sharp blades bit into the corn. I went out with cider for the harvesters, and stood half-tranced by the flicker of the sickles as the line of women moved down the field. One would not need to think, doing that. There would be only the stretch to grasp and sever the tough stems, a quick twist so that they would fall evenly for the binders who followed, and then on to the next step, the next handful, again and again.

In the shadow of the trees Keihirdyn was waiting. I knew that on the way back through the wood he would seize me and press me down beneath the trees. A vision bloomed in my imagination; I saw my hand gripping his member, the flash of a sickle, and red blood spurting as I flung it aside. And even at the thought I felt my flesh quicken, and did not know if it were because I wanted to destroy him or because I was already anticipating what he would do to me.

Sometimes I tried to remember how it had been with Marc'h, when I had been the Hawthorn Queen. But that was someone else, another lifetime, a dream. In that life I had scorned Esseilte for her passion, but now I knew that she also was trapped by this aching female body that was so vulnerable to a man's attention.

If there was a Lady, then she had betrayed me, for all my struggles to protect Esseilte and remain faithful to Marc'h and his land had come to this — that I was only a thing of flesh made to serve the flesh of a man.

Twenty-two

THE LAST SHEAF

The tide was going out. From the shore, one saw a sudden ruffle across the brown water as the current of the Fawwyth began to press against the faltering will of the sea. Where wavelets had lapped gently against the sedges now a thin ribbon of gray mud gleamed, textured with broken shell and bits of stone, and the rowing boat that had been bobbing at the end of its tether was settling onto its keel. There was a high overcast, as if the weather soon would be changing, but the day was yet warm and still.

Like the ripples of the river, the music of the harp flowed on behind me, now sounding strongly, now ebbing away. We had come down to take our noon meal beside the water, and the remains of a meat pie lay now on the blanket. Dewi was still working on the honey cakes. Esseilte was leaning against Drustan with her head on his shoulder, and Keihirdyn lay with his head pillowed on his cloak, watching me. But I had turned my back on all of them, and gazed out across the river with my legs drawn up and my arms around my knees.

"Wyn's son Cuby was up to Welnans yesterday, an' he says that the chieftains have come back to the dun," Dewi mumbled through a mouthful of cake. Suddenly there was no sound but the river. I turned, and saw the other three fixing the boy with the same stare. "Not the king, though —" Dewi swallowed. "He's still off east in Dyfneint, they say."

"What is he doing *there*?" Drustan burst out, then laughed as

340

Dewi gazed at him in astonishment. "No, lad, I don't expect Cuby to have told you that! But though the men of the east may accept Cornovi rule, they have not forgotten that Artor dispossessed their own lords after they sided with the Saxons at Portcaster and again at Badon." He shook his head. "The lament they made for Prince Gerontius after that battle was one of the first pieces I learned to sing for the king. I have thought of it often, these past days."

As if involuntarily, his hands went to the harpstrings and he plucked a long, deep-sounding chord.

> *"Before Gerontius, the enemy's dread,*
> *White horses rearing, and the red,*
> *After war cries, bitter the home of the dead.*
>
> *"In Portcaster, I saw sharp spurs*
> *And men who did not flinch from spears,*
> *Who drank from glass as bright as tears.*
>
> *"In Portcaster, I saw them striking sore —*
> *The heroes of the great Artor —*
> *Our labor's lord, Imperator.*
>
> *"In Portcaster, Gerontius was laid low,*
> *And heroes of Dumnonia also,*
> *But before they all were slain, they slew.*
>
> *"Swift the steeds 'neath Gerontius' thigh,*
> *Long-legged, fed on wheat and rye,*
> *Swooping like eagles from the sky . . ."*

The music soured suddenly and he dashed his hand across the strings.

"I think about it," he groaned, "and I wonder how long before they will require a lament for Conomor from me!"

I hid my face against my folded arms. Somewhere deep within me was a woman who wept at those words, but she could not break through the wall I had built around my heart since meeting Keihirdyn.

"You love him . . ." said Esseilte gently. "It has taken me so long to understand. The Morholt loved only glory, not his king. You must go back, Drustan — leave me and go back to Léon!"

He set the harp aside then, and took her into his arms, but I am not sure which of them was doing the comforting.

Ducks were coming up onto the mudflats, and I began to throw them the remains of the pie. A drake hopped over Esseilte's foot to snatch a morsel, and she looked up and laughed.

"The river was fine to look on," said Keihirdyn, "but the mudflats are less appealing. Don't you think it time we were going back to the farm?"

Dewi ran ahead of us, the empty basket bouncing at every step, as we made our way up the path beside the stream. Keihirdyn and I came next, his hand already tracing promises against my back, and Drustan and Esseilte last of all, for she grew short of breath if she did not go slowly.

And then a horse whinnied ahead of us.

"You, boy — where is the queen?"

I stiffened, for I recognized that voice. What was Mevennus Maglos doing here?

"Get back, tell Drustan to hide —" I whispered to Keihirdyn. He sped back down the path and I started forward, from old habit seeking ways to conceal the truth as I had concealed it so many times before.

"Behind me, my lord with . . . Branwen . . ." came Dewi's reply.

Good lad! I thought. We had told him only enough to make clear the need for secrecy, and he was doing splendidly.

"With Branwen, no doubt!" a second voice cut in. "And who else, eh? Is she at her old tricks again here?"

I looked behind me, willing Esseilte to catch up quickly, for I knew this voice as well. I could see her coming, and Drustan at the edge of the path behind her with his sword drawn and ready. Keihirdyn had disappeared.

"Karasek!" growled Mevennus. "Keep your dirty tongue off the queen. Anyhow, Drustan is in Léon!"

"Is he? If I were to see that man laid in the earth I would not be sure he was underground! Let us see what this lad is hiding —" Hooves drummed on the hard earth of the path as he reined his mount around.

"My lady, here are guests come to see you!" Dewi called.

"Are there, then? Well, I am almost there . . ."

Drustan faded into the greenery just as Esseilte reached me. She slipped her hand through my arm, breathing rather quickly.

"There's nought to fear, Tiernissa —" Mevennus bowed over his horse's mane. "Your lord is safe in Britain."

"Is he coming home?"

I hoped they took her heightened color for eagerness.

"Now, that I do not know. He landed in Ker-Esk a week since, and sent us off with messages for the West."

"But I can tell you why —" Karasek answered the question in Esseilte's eyes. "Chlotar is gathering his armies once more, and Marc'h cannot withstand him without allies. He has been negotiating with the sons of Eormenric of Kent to bring a force to fight for him in Armorica!"

"Saxons!" exclaimed Esseilte.

"Jutes from Herulia, actually, but it is much the same. He has been recruiting Danes and other Northmen as well."

"Even if he wins they will never forgive him, with such allies!" I whispered.

"You may tell him so, if he comes here —" said Maglos heavily. "Perhaps he will listen to you. But the situation is desperate, and he is determined to risk all on this last throw —"

Esseilte sighed and shook her head.

"He is the king, and he will have his way, but let us not mourn just yet —" the chieftain added with forced jocularity. "I can take you up behind me to return to the house, if you will, and Karasek can take the lady Branwen."

"Thank you." Esseilte gave him her best smile. Dewi knelt to let her use his back as a mounting block.

"I thank you also," I said, "but I think I have left my shawl down beside the water, and I must go back for it!" Karasek did not look disappointed. He kicked his mount after his companion's. I waited until the sound of their hoofbeats faded, then went back down the path.

"Where is Keihirdyn?" I asked as Drustan stepped out to meet me.

"He was here —" Drustan looked around.

"Go on then, but carefully," I told him. "I will find your friend . . ."

Drustan gave me a complicit smile, but it was not lust I was feeling. A cold certainty had settled in my belly and was spreading toward my heart. I slipped among the trees, seeking a certain thicket, and as I expected, there I found Keihirdyn.

"Ah, my love, shall we have our time together after all?" He patted the grass beside him.

I stepped back. "What are you doing here?"

"Hiding — was that not what you had in mind?"

"Drustan was just off the path with his sword ready in case

the queen should need him. You are here with your weapon still in its sheath. Why?" My voice shook a little and I strove for control.

"It was not my fight—"

"Drustan is your brother-in-law, your companion!"

"Why should I risk my life to defend him? His marriage to my sister is a sham." Keihirdyn gave a short laugh. "I did not come here for him, I came for you!"

"You were afraid!" I was speaking as much to myself as to him, all that had happened between us altering in this new and terrible light. Why it should make such a difference I did not know—at some deep level had I accepted his right to master me?

"The only weapon you know how to use is the one that hangs between your legs, and you only use it on those who are weaker than you. You conquered me, but I thought you were at least a man!"

Keihirdyn was on his feet by now, laughing. Still laughing, he reached for me.

"Why should you care what I do with my sword so long as I have something that will fit your sheath so well!" He made an obscene gesture. I wrenched free of his grip and put a tree between us.

"I thought that Drustan's comrade had conquered me, but now I see that a coward has dishonored me. You will not touch me again!"

I spoke as a corpse might speak, accusing its murderer.

"Dishonor!" Keihirdyn shook his head disgustedly. "There is no such thing. There is only this—" he patted his crotch, "and that—" he pointed at mine. "Why are you so self-righteous? You liked what I did to you, Branwen! You moaned in my arms and begged for more!"

I felt the blood leave my face, but I did not fall. Dimly I was aware that what Keihirdyn was saying was true, and that my reaction was as much against that part of myself that had yielded to him as against *him*. But that made its violence all the more necessary. What I tasted now was the opposite of the chaotic fury I had felt as he was raping me. I knew what had moved Mairenn when she cursed the Morholt's murderer.

Rage is far deadlier when it is cold.

❀　　❀　　❀

"Eh, mistress, we'll be starting to reap the home field this morning," said Wyn Vedras. He gave me a short nod and stood for a moment, considering the dawn sky. I waited with the pail of water dripping in my hand, for it was no use trying to hurry him. "An' we must work fast, for I don't like the look of the clouds."

I looked up at the clouds that hung above the rim of the hill, pink-tinged like wool that has been used to wash a wound. The reapers had been moving from one field to the next as each ripened, and it was always a race between the sun and the autumn storms to get the grain in.

"Happen they'll be rain ere nightfall, and the corn'll rot if it's not in mow . . . neighbors be coming to help in the reaping, but any from the house that would join us would be welcome."

"I will ask," I said, remembering the customs from past years. "The harper is weakened by an old wound, but maybe I can bring his servant along."

When Keihirdyn and I got there, the women had already cut one row. He had come, as I expected him to, in hopes of some opportunity to get me off alone. Since the day by the river I had managed to avoid him, but he was not yet convinced that I would never let him touch me again. I smiled sweetly.

"You see how the women are cutting the stalks and the men are binding them — get some straw ropes and young Cuby will show you what to do." He grimaced, and I slid the back of the sickle teasingly down the side of his face. "I will be right ahead of you. . . ."

I waited until the other women had finished their row and come down to begin again, took a deep breath, and stepped into place behind and a little to the right of the last. I bent to grasp the first handful of rough stems, hooked the sickle through them, and let them fall, then another, and another, falling into the rhythm of it as I went along. It was punishing work, and in minutes the sweat began to pour off me, for despite the clouds the day was muggy and warm. Long before I reached the end of the row my back muscles were screaming, but I welcomed the pain.

The binders came along behind us, gathering up the loose stalks into sheaves, and behind them the little children gleaning the short pieces, while Dewi and the bigger boys carried the sheaves to the setters — old men who knew the art of building the sheaves into shocks, or larger mows with the bearded ends inward and the butt ends exposed. It was hand mows they were making today, to keep the wheat against the coming bad weather, setting the sheaves into man-high cones finished off by fanning out one or two inverted sheaves and tying the bearded ends to the side of the mow.

"They say as how the king's coming back to the dun," said one of the binders. I missed a stroke and slowed, trying to hear.

"Will'ee be staying long then?" asked the man beside him. They finished their bundles and moved forward, and I bent and cut more slowly, staying level with them.

"Dunno. My woman's brother did say a messenger came telling them to have food ready by nightfall."

"Ill luck to them if they've come seeking more men for the king's wars —"

The first man grunted agreement and they went on in silence, but my heart was thudding so erratically I found it hard to breathe.

Drustan had delayed his departure from day to day, as if he were courting discovery. Would Marc'h come here and find him? And when we met, would the king know what had happened to me? I had prayed for Marc'h to come home again, but now I was afraid.

The other women called to me to keep up, and I bent to my work once more, ripping through the wheatstalks and casting them aside, letting my anger and confusion add strength to my arm.

At midmorning we paused for cider and fuggan, the sweet buns they made at harvest time. Wyn's wife Senara brought us a noon meal of pasties, and in the afternoon we stopped once for cider again. I lay on my back, for the moment too lost in the blessed relief of stillness for any other awareness.

A hand squeezed my breast. I had brought the sickle around and the edge was at Keihirdyn's wrist before I thought. He sat very still until I lifted it.

"Not here!" I whispered, forcing a smile. "Not now. There's no feeling anywhere in my body but my back, and that's all pain!" This was the pure truth, and he knew it. He rubbed his hands and looked at me hopefully.

"Hard work on my side too. Haven't we done our share?"

"I have promised to stay, and see, there's only a corner left to do. You don't want to miss the festivities at the end . . ."

The break was cut short, for the clouds in the west were building into great piles, dark with rain. The air had the close stillness that comes before a storm. But folk were laughing as we moved onto the field again. Only I, looking back down the path toward the farmhouse, saw that two figures had emerged from among the trees. I recognized Esseilte's bright head immediately, and knew that the ragged figure beside her must be Drustan, disguised as a wandering bard once more. From a distance it would do. If he were foolish enough to come closer and one of the men recognized him there was nothing I could do. And at the moment I did not really care.

The final rows went swiftly. And then there was only one wisp of corn still standing, like the last survivor of some terrible battlefield. Senara stood over it, brandishing her sickle. The rest of the women spread into a circle around her while the men separated into three bands. I saw Wyn's son Cuby in the group where Keihirdyn had ended and grasped his arm.

"Let the foreigner bind for your band . . ."

Cuby gave me a long, slow smile of understanding, and I slipped away.

Senara bent, and in a single swift motion severed the last stalks and held them high.

"We have it, we have it!" cried the men in her husband's band.

"What have ye? What have ye?" replied those across from them.

"A neck! A neck! A neck!" answered the others.

Senara's little daughter ran to her with a handful of ribbons and flowers, and she began to plait and decorate the neck of grain.

Immediately one man from each band started binding up the rest of the fallen stalks in the row while their fellows cheered them on. Keihirdyn caught the frenzy, and I saw him gathering and tying with a will. But being the least experienced, he was naturally slower than the others. As they finished, a silence fell. Keihirdyn flushed a little, fumbling as he realized all eyes were on him. He met my smile and glared, but I was waiting; we were all waiting, and as he finished, the women flung themselves upon him and despite his shouts and struggles, began to bind him to his sheaf with ropes of straw.

"Let me go! You're hurting me!"

I smiled as I heard his muffled cries.

"Be easy on the poor lad" came a new voice. "He does not understand!"

One of the older women looked up and saw Drustan in his beggar's rags.

"A stranger!" she cried. "That's a far better omen, that a stranger should come into the field!" She pulled her rope away and pointed. The other women set up a shrill cry, and Keihirdyn was left sprawling as they rushed Drustan and knocked him to the earth, pummeling him as he laughed and tried to protect his face with his hands.

Damn you, Drustan! I thought as I watched it. *That pummeling was meant for Keihirdyn! I did not want him to understand!* Keihirdyn was struggling to sit up, looking around him with dazed eyes.

Swiftly, the sheaf was bound around the new victim. Senara tied the "neck" against his breast.

"To the river with him!" they cried. "To the river, and let us see if he will sink or swim!"

"Old Man of the Harvest, we have you now, and what will you pay to be free?" She brought down her sickle until its curve embraced his neck. I could see only his face above the quivering golden heads of grain, as if he had been decapitated already, but his eyes were dancing.

"Gold have I none, but there is music in my fingertips. Let me go, good folk, and I will harp so sweetly for your festival you will forget every blister and pain!"

"Music, oh aye, that's a fit ransom —" they cried. "Senara, let him go!"

Laughing, she lifted the sickle from his neck and drew it the length of his body, severing the ropes of straw. Dewi snatched the flower-decked neck of corn from his breast and dashed off with it, but before he had gotten five steps, one of the girls doused him with water from a pail.

As if that had been a signal, the heavens rumbled. With Dewi leading, the shouting, prancing procession started toward the farmhouse. And as the pace settled, women's voices lifted in song.

> *"When earth grows green in springtime the blessed seed is sown —*
> *Praise to the babe who's born to be a king when he is grown."*

Now the men joined in for the chorus, deep notes underscored by distant thunder.

"With one accord, we praise the Lord who lies among the corn,
For he is mown and stricken down that he may rise reborn!"

Now everyone was singing the verses together. Doors opened in
the farm buildings at the foot of the hill, and the women who
had been preparing the feast came out into the yard to welcome
us.

"When summer sun grows mighty, and rules the world on high,
The boy he grows a golden beard and reaches for the sky."

Dewi raced ahead toward the farmhouse, holding the corn-neck
high.

"But now the birds wing southward, the wind is growing cold,
The weighted head begins to bow; the man is growing old."

A cold wind rolled the clouds across the sky. It was not yet
evening, but already the eastern sky had darkened. Only in the
west did the undersides of the clouds glow bloody in the light of
the setting sun.

"Go down into the dark, old man, and sleep away your pain —
And in the lusty springtime, your staff shall rise again!"

Thunder clapped above us, and we crowded into the farmhouse,
pelted by the first stinging drops of rain.

"With one accord we praise the Lord who lies among the corn,
For he is mown and stricken down that we may be reborn!"

Outside, rain drummed on the thatch and pattered against the
walls. Inside the house the air pulsed with the sounds and smells
of exuberant, overheated humanity, for the rain had forced us to
cram into the building the four trestle tables and benches that we
would otherwise have set out in the yard.

The "neck" hung in a place of honor on the wall, but its flowers were already wilting. The fire had been blazing all day and
despite the damp gusts that came through the open door, the
room was as much of an oven as the covered cauldrons in which
they had cooked the food for the feasting.

Esseilte had retreated to Drustan's side, leaving me to assist
Senara with the serving. Gol Deis they called it — the Feast of
Ricks, and the farmstead was not stinting its bounty. Platters of
pork boiled with turnips and onion were passed; bowls of steam-

ing barley went round, baskets of parched peas and apples stayed on the trestle tables, with a variety of breads and cheese. The round casks of last year's cider were brought in and emptied and replaced again. I drank as thirstily as any, dried out by the heat of the room and the exertions of the day.

Drustan had shed his melancholy, and was working off his forfeit with a will. Tonight his harp held only dance tunes that had folk clapping even though there was no room to turn. Not much remained of the beggarly disguise, but by this time most of the men were too full of cider to notice or to care.

Keihirdyn had remained with the party too, and in the press I could not always avoid him. He grabbed me around the waist just as I was setting a jug of cider down and kissed me heartily—a thing so in the context of the general horseplay that no one else noticed until I gave him a box in the ear that sent him reeling into Wyn Vedras's arms.

"Eh, now lass," said the farmer, setting Keihirdyn upright again with a genial grin, "thee hast no call to be mistreating the young man so, for he labored with the rest of us, so he did!" Keihirdyn's glare promised worse than kisses when he should get me alone, but in my present mood I wanted only enough room to get my claws into his eyes. He had escaped the humiliation I had planned for him, but I would find a way to drag his pride in the dust before I was done. Not even now did he understand what he had done to me! I shoved a pasty at Wyn and headed for the door.

"I thought you liked Keihirdyn . . ." said a worried voice at my elbow. It was Drustan. I blinked at him, trying to find words in the cider-haze. "The din is too great for anyone to hear my harping, and I needed air," he went on. "But I saw what happened over at the table. Will you tell me what is wrong?"

"Does Keihirdyn think a bard's sweet tongue will be more successful than a coward's groping hands? He should not have sent you, Drustan, for you are almost as much to blame as he!"

"He did not send—" Drustan broke off, frowning. "Branwen, what do you mean!"

I had not meant to discuss this with Drustan, but his solicitude had opened the floodgates, and I poured out all the poison that had been collecting within me these past days.

"What do I mean? Are you so blinded by your own passion that you really cannot see what is going on around you, or have you great lovers all allied to make fools of womankind? Keihirdyn has told me how you lured him here, Drustan—did you laugh together on the ship coming over, planning how to trap me? Perhaps I could even have borne it, if he had been a warrior, but now that I know him I would rather lie down with the beggar at the gates of Bannhedos than with Keihirdyn!"

"Branwen!" Drustan interrupted me when I drew breath at last. "I did tell him that you were beautiful. I thought that if he could win you—"

"Do not say it—" Someone handed me a horn of cider and I let a long draft ease my dry throat and handed it back again. "I have heard too many of your lies. I know what Keihirdyn has said to me, and what he has done. If you cannot see why I hate him, then you are as bad as he is, or you are an idiot! Either way, you have betrayed me, Drustan of Léon." I stared at him, seeing suddenly Keihirdyn's face in his, hating both of them—hating all men. "Have I served you and my lady so long only to be treated like a slave?" I cried suddenly.

"I didn't—perhaps Esseilte—" He shook his head helplessly. I looked over to where she sat and saw her smile at us indulgently.

"Esseilte is your accomplice, and a fool!" How was it that I had never realized that before? Was it Esseilte's influence that had sapped my will? Was that why I had allowed myself to be used this way? "Though you have never brought her anything but sorrow, still she loves you! Maybe she is ensorcelled by your sweet singer's tongue and your clever harper's hands, but I will not be so subjected, not anymore!"

My words were a self-feeding fire. Perhaps this was how men worked themselves up to go into battle, for I could feel the power building in me, pulsing against the barriers of my will. Keihirdyn met my glance from across the room and flinched. I laughed.

"Branwen, I swear—"

"Don't, Drustan, for I will not believe you. I have known you for too long!"

He was growing angry now as well, but not foolhardy enough to cross me. Tight-lipped, he moved through the press back to Esseilte's side.

Esseilte had cursed him, and what had that accomplished? I saw her smile as he clasped her hand, and suddenly I hated her, as well.

Feelings for which I had no name tore at my control. I had sacrificed life and honor for the man and woman who cuddled by the fire, and my reward — my eyes blurred — Esseilte's laughter mocked me! Her face and Drustan's flickered bright and dark in a distortion of vision, and Keihirdyn's somehow with them, twisted in lust and a sly glee as they all remembered how they had used me! Laughter like the screaming of ravens rasped my soul. . . .

My consent allowed all this to happen. I have the power to make it end. The thought came so clearly, as if someone else had whispered it in my ear.

There was a moment of quiet in the midst of madness in which I could do — what? Not curse them — Esseilte had cursed Drustan, and now she fawned on him. I must act so they could never use me again! Images of vengeance welled through my awareness, drowned thought and bore it away.

Presently a group of the men pushed through the door to fetch another cask, and I let them carry me with them out into the dark.

Even in the wind and the rain, it took less than an hour to ride to Bannhedos from the farm. Men scattered before me as I rode through the gate of the dun. Soaked to the skin, with the cider still rioting in my brain, I must have looked like the Morrigan in her rage. And perhaps She was present, for I was surely the black raven that night: the woman with the twisted mouth, frenzy, drunkenness, the millstone that grinds out the fates of heroes and gods. . . .

Still sitting my pony, I waited in the courtyard for them to summon the king. Torches bloomed in the doorway. In that place where I was then, neither the fact of his physical presence, or the shock in his face as he saw me, had power to move me at all.

"Branwen, what is it? Has ill come to the queen?" He came out to me, heedless of the rain. I glimpsed the white, ferrety face of Karasek among the others at the door.

"Ill . . . ?" I laughed harshly. "You might say so, if that includes black dishonor! If you have distrusted my guardianship before, believe me now — for two weeks your wife and your nephew have been living together at Nans Yann. Come with me now and you may take them. . . ."

For a moment I saw in Marc'h's face the shock of adjustment to a pain he had thought over and done, and a weariness at the prospect of facing it now, when his future wavered in the bal-

ance. He looked as if for the past month he had been riding
without rest and talking without sleep. Then his features hardened. He could not refuse to act — not when they had all
heard — not when the accusation came from me. But as we rode
out through the gates again, I could see the question in his eyes.

Why you? Why now? Branwen, why?

Light blazed from the doors of the farmhouse as we rode down
the road. Even if it had not still been raining, no one could have
heard us over the shouts, the laughter, the voices upraised in
song. After the darkness and the intermittent rush and the hush
of the storm it came as a shock to the senses, almost an insult,
that folk should be so merry and warm when we were chilled in
body and soul.

I slid off my pony — I had ridden her with only a halter and a
blanket, and she could find her own way to the barn — and
splashed across the yard to the door.

"Blessed Brigid, Branwen — where have you been?" Esseilte
exclaimed as I came in. I did not answer her, and perhaps my
face still held something of strangeness, for stillness spread
around me like a contagion, so that when the king stepped
through the doorway no one was moving in the room.

Marc'h stood on the threshhold like a spirit who must be in-
vited to pass in, his swordblade gleaming in the lamplight. His
dark gaze moved over the crowded tables littered with the remains of pork and apple pies smothered in cream, with crushed
berries and heels of bread and rinds of cheese, with cider in
mugs and spilled on the tables and dripping onto the floor. His
eyes passed over faces still flushed from drinking and song, eyes
widening as the more sober among them began to understand
what was going on . . . and moved inevitably to the seat of
honor in the middle of the longest table, where Drustan sat with
his harp on his knee and Esseilte nestled in the curve of his arm.

I blinked as a mallet began beating at my temples, and bit my
lip as I realized that it was my own heart's pounding that was
stabbing my head with pain.

"The feast is over," said the king. "All of you, get out of here,
now!" His voice stung even the most drunken into movement. I
think that if Drustan had called on them to defend him they
might have rallied to him, but he said no word. Only he gave his
harp to Esseilte and from its hooks on the wall he lifted down his

sword. The movement dislodged the beribboned corn-neck, which fell unheeded to the floor.

Wyn Vedras started to protest, even so, but one look from his lord silenced him, and he collected his wife and children and pushed them toward the door. Like the first trickle in a breaking dam, that got the rest of them going — stumbling and swearing, some of them, but all of them in a swirl of motion toward the door.

I saw Keihirdyn trying to slip out among them and touched Marc'h's arm.

"Keep that one — it is his doing that Drustan is here!"

The king recognized the lord of Barsa then and gestured with his sword. Keihirdyn edged back into a corner, still breathing rather quickly and glaring at me.

And then they were all outside. I could hear a gabble of voices that rose as the rain hit them and fell as they saw that the yard was full of armed men, and finally faded away.

Mevennus Maglos came in with Karasek behind him.

"My lord, the farm-folk have gone." He moved to one side of the door.

Karasek slammed it shut and took his place on the other, smiling. "The house is surrounded. Don't think you will escape this time, Drustan!"

"Oh, have you brought a straw rope to bind me?" Drustan laughed, a strangely lighthearted sound against the tension in that room. I winced. I had meant the rope of straw and all it implied for Keihirdyn.

I saw Keihirdyn pressing against the wall as if he wanted it to swallow him. Esseilte's face was whiter than the linen that bound her hair. But Drustan was smiling. Why was he smiling? The answer came to me, *Because he does not care. . . .*

Perhaps Esseilte realized it too, for she touched Drustan's arm, and whispered. His eyes were still on the king, but he cocked his head to listen.

"Ah, but my love, though you might swear not to see me again, I don't think he would believe you. I don't think *I* would believe you, for as long as we are both alive the link that binds us will draw us together, and perhaps even after . . ."

Esseilte leaned back against the rough stones, hands against her breast as if her heart were some frightened beast that she had caged there. For a moment her gaze went inward, then she took a careful breath and looked up at him.

"If you call me, I will find a way to come to you. . . ."

Drustan looked back at the king, eyebrows lifting in inquiry.

"It was all true, then —" Marc'h spoke finally. "All the accusations from the beginning. All those comedies the two of you played for me were lies. . . ." His voice tolled like a bell, throbbing with dissonant overtones of pain. It was the voice a king uses as he pronounces judgment. Drustan quivered as if he would have spoken, but the king was continuing.

"The opposition of my enemies I understand, even the treacheries of men who wait to jump until they see which way the tree will fall. The enemy attacks my body, and the traitor my government, but neither of them has the power to wound my soul. But to you, Drustan, I opened my heart. You were closer than brother, favored like . . . a child. I had no secrets from you, Drustan! How could I believe that you would live such a lie?" His voice was shaking and he had to swallow before he could continue.

"And you, Esseilte. Our marriage was a dynastic alliance, and for that perhaps you owed me no more than an appearance of fidelity. But when we came together we were joined in the sight of the Old Powers. You swore then to be my queen in spirit as well as in the sight of men, and to spend your life for this land. We could have restored the kingdom of Artor together, if you had been true . . . you must account to greater powers than me for that treachery!"

Esseilte's eyes widened, and for the first time she looked at me. For a moment I met her wondering gaze, then pain slashed behind my eyes and I hid my face in my hands.

"I have seen death all around me, these past two years," I heard the king say. "I have killed until my arm was weary, seen terrible things and ordered them done to people whose only crime was to oppose my rule. The two of you have betrayed me in all the deepest intimacies of the spirit. Why should I spare you?"

"Marc'h! You must listen to me!" Drustan cried. He was going to tell him, I thought then. He would tell him the whole contorted story, and then at last the king would understand.

"Enough! I have listened to you too long!" the king roared.

It was what I had said earlier. . . . What might Drustan have said to *me*, if I had given him time to explain?

"Call in the men to take him," said Maglos heavily. "And bring him before the chieftains for trial."

"I should have done that a year ago," Marc'h growled. "There is no time for it now. We are at war. But he shall have his judgment —" He turned to Drustan again. "A warrior's judging, at the edge of the sword."

"So be it." Drustan brought up his blade in salute. "Who is your champion?"

"*You* were my champion," answered the king grimly. "I will have to defend my own honor now. . . . Karasek, go tell the men to form the square. Mevennus Maglos, light torches and bring them outside."

Karasek grimaced, saw Keihirdyn half-hidden in the corner, and gripped his arm. "I want you where I can keep an eye on you! Come with me!" He went out and Maglos followed him with the torches.

Marc'h gestured to Drustan to go after them, and held out his hand to Esseilte.

"You shall come too, Tiernissa, and see what you have done!"

But it was I who did it! an inner voice babbled frantically. *I was the one who brought you down!* I sank back against the wall.

Waves of darkness rolled over me. The pain in my head was striking now in great hammer blows. I wanted to scream, but a stifled whimper was all that would come.

In my rage to strike back at Keihirdyn, I had betrayed Drustan, to whom I had made no promises, but in betraying him, I had struck also at Esseilte, to whom my life was bound. And beyond that, I saw now that I had betrayed Marc'h, to whom I had sworn the deepest oaths of all.

The clangor of steel on steel startled me back to awareness. I forced myself upright, snatched a carving knife from the shelf, and stumbled to the door. The rain had settled to a drizzle that made the torches snap and fizzle, casting an uncertain light across the muddy pools in the yard and the two men who circled there. They showed me also the white shape of Esseilte, held upright in Mevennus's arms, and Keihirdyn, bound.

It was clear from the way the fighters moved that during the past year both men had become accustomed to fighting with shields. Again and again, one or the other would shift his left side away and move his sword out in front as he remembered that it must serve to defend as well as attack the other. But what struck me most was how difficult it was to tell them apart, there in the rain. They were much of a height, and similar in build, and with their hair sodden to an equal darkness, even the shape of the skull was the same.

But while Marc'h moved with a settled power that was daunting, Drustan had a fluid grace that shifted him out from under the king's blows with apparent ease. I tensed as the king's sword flicked out in a feint to the right that drew Drustan's blade after it, then wheeled overhead and struck like a thunderbolt where Drustan's shoulder had been. Water sprayed in a glittering arc as Drustan slid out from under, then he recovered and leaped away.

"He's not fighting," murmured someone nearby. I bit my lip, realizing that it was true. Drustan was using all his skill to defend only, while the king came after him with grim efficiency. Marc'h struck again; Drustan's sword flared upward. The two blades rasped together, for a moment held, and then Drustan twisted under and out, and the sudden release of pressure sent the king off-balance and sprawling in the mud.

He rolled and came up in a crouch, still holding onto his sword. Drops of water leaped from the blade as he used its momentum to help bring him upright. Drustan stood watching him, breathing hard.

"You bastard!" snarled Marc'h. "Are you playing with me?" He drove in anew with a flurry of furious blows. Metal clashed and clanged, and this time it was Drustan who went down, rolling over and over in the mud before he could gain his feet again.

The constant trampling had churned the ground to batter. Both the men were feeling it now, fighting to lift their feet and sliding when they came down. The rain was coming down harder. One of the torches went out, and two of the others were sputtering.

"Stand, damn you, stand still!" yelled the king. He lunged as the younger man began to turn, and slipped, the shock throwing his arm wide. The tip of his sword scraped through the mud. Drustan's blade swooped toward the king's unprotected breast.

"Sweet Lady, stop, oh *stop*!" It was I who had screamed.

But as Drustan continued to turn, he pulled back his lifting sword so that it barely scored the front of Marc'h's riding leathers. The king recovered with a gut-wrenching effort, brought his own weapon up after it, and thrust through the great muscle of Drustan's chest beneath the arm. The blade jerked free. Marc'h fell back on one knee.

Esseilte gasped and collapsed against Mevennus as Drustan swayed and the sword slipped from his hand. Then the last torch went out.

The pain lifted from my skull and in that moment of blessed release my mind became preternaturally clear. Men stumbled through the darkness, shouting, but I slipped past them to Keihirdyn and sawed through his bonds.

"You have one chance to save yourself before I slit your throat," I hissed in his ear. "Get Drustan away — carry him if you must down to the river where we saw that boat. You can hire a ship in the harbor to take you home." I grabbed his hand and yanked him after me, found Drustan staggering toward the white blur of Esseilte's gown and thrust him into Keihirdyn's arms.

"Go, now! And if you abandon him, Keihirdyn, I myself will hunt you down and carve out your heart!" Something in my voice must have convinced him, for he grabbed Drustan and dragged him away.

I dashed for the stables then, jerked tethers loose, and pulled two of the horses after me into the yard. Pricked rumps sent them both bucking and trumpeting forward.

"The horses!" I cried. "They've taken the horses. After them!"

Someone had got another torch lit, and the red light stabbed my eyes. I dropped the knife and moved toward Esseilte.

"She's fainted," said Mevennus. "Help me get her inside."

The yard was a chaos as men ran for their horses or crowded around the king. I gripped Esseilte's arm and let the men drag both of us back toward the farmhouse. The dark tide was rising around me once more, and I thought that if I was lucky, in a moment I would lose consciousness as well.

Twenty-three

STORMS

Even in fine weather, at Durocornovium you were always aware
of the sound of the sea. There was the endless shush and shurr
of waves against the rocky shore and the hollow boom as they
ran up into the caves in the cove. There was the chuckle and
rush of the burn, adding its own music as it hurried down to
gossip with the sea. But when the skies grew stormy, the wind
whipped the waves against the brown cliffs like snarling hounds
that leaped against the land and savaged the stones.

In summer it had been exhilarating. As autumn drew on and it
continued to rain, it was a penance to live there. But I found it
hard to care.

After the fight at Nans Yann, neither Esseilte nor I had the
strength to make decisions. But the king had left orders for us to
be placed in the care of the monks at Lan Juliot (and, I supposed, in the custody of the garrison there) and so, as the days
drew toward the equinox, we came to dwell on this lump of rock
whose link with the land was slowly being gnawed away by the
hungry sea.

The monks made us as comfortable as they could in a small
building set into the slope above the cove. It was the warmest
place in the monastery, for a firing chamber built in the Roman
manner next to us sent hot air through rock-cut channels beneath our floor. Below it was the open chamber where in fair
weather the monks did their copying. In foul weather they used
our room, and the monastery library was still shelved along one

359

wall, but as the abbot pointed out, hospitality was also the work of God, and in any case, the weather, even in this wet September, was nowhere near what the monks called cold.

I spent much of my time prowling the springy turf that covered the wind-swept top of the island. Some of the monks had built their cells there, facing the sea — little boxes of stone just long enough for them to sleep in, or to murmur their prayers. I could not pray to the suffering God they served, and the Lady seemed to have abandoned me, but after a time the great, empty peace of the place began to work in me, and bring a measure of stillness to my soul.

Esseilte stayed in our room, reading sometimes, or working at her embroidery, or gazing into the flame of the oil lamp with eyes that did not see.

At the equinox, the storms grew more furious, and I was forced to stay inside. I lay on my bed, watching light and shadow chase each other across the rough beams of the ceiling, listening to Esseilte turn the pages of her book in the intervals between the crashing of the waves. A stray draft sent cool air past my face and I heard her cough.

"Are you still having trouble with your chest?"

"Not really, just a tightness sometimes," she said in the same even voice which she used whenever she spoke to me now. "It is not important."

I raised myself on one elbow to look at her. She lay wrapped in furs and supported by pillows, with the thick folds of a monk's robe of undyed wool over her own gown, but she still looked cold.

"What kind of a tightness? Does it make you dizzy? Is there pain?" Unbidden, memory began to turn the pages of Mairenn's spell book, reviewing her recipes and those I had added to it.

"Why should that matter to you? Don't fuss so."

"Esseilte!" The rawhide strapping of the bed creaked as I sat up fully. Her glance was veiled. "I have served you since I was born!"

"Have you?" She lifted her head, but her eyes still gave nothing away. "I used to think so, but I wonder now. . . ."

"Do you! Do you wonder who has kept your clothes in order and governed your household all these years?" Sudden as a fire in a dry wood, indignation burned through me. "Do you wonder who nursed you through all your illnesses? Do you wonder who makes sure this room is always heated, and the food is prepared to your taste?"

"And who does it all with eyes cast up to heaven like one of Ruadan's martyrs, waiting for the pat on the head, the praise, the sympathy! Who graciously heals the sick and babbles of visions, pretending not to see how simple folk look at her as she goes by? Saint Branwen the Unappreciated," Esseilte's voice shook, "puffed like an adder with pride!"

"Pride?" I gasped. "What pride could I have, except in the work of my hands? You have never taken up a piece of work that you could not put down the moment you chose! Everything you have was given to you. Everything I have I had to earn. You were born to pride of place and beauty, to silks, to gold, to the honor of men's eyes. I was born to stand in your shadow — can you blame me for seeking just a little sun?"

"Until you thought you *were* the sun!" she cried. "Who gave you the right to play God, Branwen? Who gave you the right to destroy the pattern of our lives?"

The building shook as another gust came howling in from the sea. My answer fell into silence as the wind died.

"You did . . ."

Esseilte stared at me.

"On the boat, it was your decision to drink the potion, but you forced the responsibility for it onto me. It was you who decided that Drustan should play Diarmuid to your Grainne, but the labor that allowed you to do it fell on me — the lies, the deceptions, the sleepless nights on guard while you and Drustan took your pleasure . . ." I drew breath, shaking, but Esseilte never moved. My temples were beginning to ache with a memory of pain.

"And I did it — it never occurred to me to choose not to — until I began to see how your deceptions were destroying Marc'h. If you blame me for loving him, remember that came of your choice too, Esseilte! And still I protected you, until I saw you and Drustan sit and smile while Keihirdyn raped my body and my soul!" I felt the bile rising in my throat.

"And then I saw that those had all been my decisions too, and I would no more. . . ." I carefully unclenched my fists from the sleeping furs.

"You didn't just say stop, Branwen." A pulse jumped in Esseilte's throat. "You tried to destroy us. I have never pretended to be a saint, but at least I have been consistent! How could I know what you were feeling? You never complained!"

"You never asked!" I spat at her.

"You were always so ready with advice, always taking things out of my hands and tidying them out of the way before I could learn what to do. You made me feel like an idiot, or a child. Only in Broceliande was I ever allowed to do anything real, and you put an end to that, too!"

"You were sick!" I leaped to my feet, glaring.

"What does that matter?" She took a careful breath. "I don't fear pain, or death even, if there is some reason to it all! The Morholt was your father, but you never understood him, Branwen. He died untimely, but while he was alive, he *lived*!"

"I never had a life, only a reflection!" I said bitterly.

"And so you stole mine from me!" came her reply. Her eyes blazed, but her hand had gone to her breast again and I could see that she was struggling to breathe.

My fingers had stiffened into claws. I ached to strike that look from her face, to obliterate the memory of these hurtful words, and knew that if I touched her she would die. I took one step toward her, then whirled and thrust through the door into the storm.

The wind struck as I emerged from the lee of the building. I staggered on the steps, then forced my way upward along the path. Even in the cove the waves recoiled in great fountains of spray. Out to sea the battle raged as though an army of gray mountains were at war. I pushed along, leaning into the wet wind, and dropped to my knees at the cliff-edge, when I could no longer stand.

A little farther, and I would go over. The mud and slick rock of the cliff would only speed my fall. Would I even notice the violence of the waters as they killed me? I wondered then. The chaos all around me still seemed less than the rage within. I crouched for a time unthinking, sharing the fury of sky and sea.

And then at last it began to falter. The wind no longer stung my face; there were moments of stillness; a little pale light glimmered from beneath the wings of the storm. I drew a deep breath and began to think again.

I was aware of a vague astonishment at the magnitude of the wounds Esseilte and I had given each other over the years. But there had also been love, hadn't there? Everything I had said was true, but I could see dimly that perhaps Esseilte had been speaking the truth as well. For all these years we had lived as close as shape to shadow. I knew her body better than my own. And yet I saw now that we had never really known each other at all.

Shivering, I got to my feet and stumbled back down the path.

Esseilte seemed to be sleeping when I came in. Her cheeks were marked by the glistening tracks of tears. But as the door closed her eyes opened and she sighed.

"Thank God. I was afraid the wind had blown you away!"

"No . . ." I began to strip off my wet clothes. The storm was over, but where could we go from here?

"Earlier . . . you said that Keihirdyn had dishonored you. What did you mean?"

I eyed her uncertainly, searching for any sign of hostility, but her brows were bent in a little frown, as if she really wanted to know. So I sat down on the bed, the dry stocking forgotten in my hand, and told her.

"But there was no love, Esseilte, no honor. It was more sordid than anything Meriadek ever said about Drustan and you. And Drustan had persuaded Keihirdyn to come to Kernow by promising that he could sleep with me. . . ."

Esseilte had gone completely white. Then the color flooded into her face again.

"I did not know! I cannot believe Drustan did either — I don't think that he could love me as he has and suspect such things of another man."

I shrugged, and tugged a linen shift over my head. "Perhaps not," I said quietly. "Or perhaps he was too concerned with his passion for you to wonder. I don't know. I was not sane."

"Oh, I understand madness." Her lips twisted. "Remember, I cursed Drustan. If the evil was not your fault, perhaps it was mine. Perhaps —"

She stopped. I finished belting my gown and saw her eyes clouded, her lips pressed tight in pain.

"Blessed Goddess," I breathed, hurrying across the room. I knelt beside the bed and took her left hand.

"No — that's the one that hurts," she whispered. After a moment she took a deep breath and her eyes focused on me. "It's all right now. It is like a hand that pushes against my chest. It never lasts for long."

But how often? I wondered. And how severe was the pain

while it was going on? And what if that hand should push too hard one day? Eyes stinging, I kissed her hand.

"Esseilte, sister, please don't leave me alone. . . ."

The weather continued to clear, but my emotions were still confused. And I worried about Esseilte, who grew no better as the month drew to a close. I thought a tincture of foxglove might help her, but I had none among my medicines. Then I remembered bunched herbs hanging above a flickering turf fire.

Ogrin's cell. . . .

I told the monks where I was going and commended Esseilte to their care. They were good men, and tolerant of human frailty, not like some who would not even look at a woman for fear of being defiled. But no one of them had the clarity of spirit that I had found in Ogrin.

Thus, with baskets filled with dried apples and grain for him, some salt, and little packets of herbs from my own store, I rode southward toward the moors. I breathed deep of air new-washed to autumn clarity, reining the pony around the puddles left by the storm. The water was brown, but it flashed bright as a kingfisher's wing when it reflected the morning sky. I told myself that I was going to Ogrin for advice, I was going to see if he had any foxglove laid by.

But deep within I knew better. Once before, he had healed my body. Now I needed healing for my soul.

It was four days of steady riding before I glimpsed the crag rising out of the tawny sweep of the moor. For a moment then I knew fear. I had simply assumed that Ogrin would be waiting where I had left him, like the folk of Faerie. But Ogrin was human like me, and I knew how I had changed. What if he had died or gone away? And then, like a signal, a thread of white began to uncoil against the sky, and before I could see details of the pale shape on the rock I knew who was waiting there.

The pony came to a stop at the foot of the crag, and after a few moments had passed, tugged the reins from my hands and began to crop the dry grass. Ogrin was clambering down the path, leaning on his staff. I thought his head a little barer, his gown a little more threadbare than it had been, but otherwise he seemed no different after all.

"Branwen—" He held out his hands to me and I slid down from the pony. All the way, I had been rehearsing what I would say to him, but as he smiled all words left me. I felt my face twisting, and as his strong hands gripped mine I collapsed to my knees before him, racked by sobs.

"I felt your coming, and your trouble —" said Ogrin when I had recovered enough to help him stable the pony in the shelter at the base of the rock and bring my baskets up the path to the hermitage. "Tell me. . . ."

I kept my eyes focused on the glowing coals. "I was betrayed, and in return I betrayed everyone I loved. . . ." I remembered what Esseilte had said to me. "I thought I was good, and I did evil! And now I am afraid that those I love will die and no one will need me ever again!" And that was more truth than I had intended to give him — more truth than I myself had known until then. I covered my face with my hands.

"My poor child." I felt the light touch of his hand upon my hair. "And what do you seek from me?"

"Absolution!" I exclaimed. But what I really wanted was for him to make the past four years go away so that I could start over again.

"I could give you a penance of prayer and forgive you in the name of the Holy Trinity. There are brethren of mine who have worn out their knees that way, seeking release from the bonds of the flesh and the world. And maybe for them such pains have merit. God knows there are times when awareness of my own unworthiness brings me to my knees with tears and groaning. . . ." He rubbed his hands back and forth on the worn cloth of his robe, remembering. "But you, I think, know already that self-denial can lead to more subtle sins."

"I tried so hard," I whispered. "I thought that I could make all right for everyone —"

"And did you labor out of love, or pride?" he asked then.

"I thought it was love. . . ." I hiccupped. "I thought that if I did enough, they would love me. . . ." Once more I saw Marc'h's face, rigid with pain, and Esseilte's angry eyes.

"And are you not worthy of love as you are?" he asked even more softly.

Not the chance-got daughter of a captive, not the servant fosterling! I began weeping again.

"I love you," he said then. "My God loves you. . . ." He put his arm around me and cradled my head against the rough wool that covered his bony chest. It was not a comfortable breast to lie on, but the peace that was in that man was like cool water on the fever of my pain.

"But I do not pray to your God," I said after a time. And that had not been my decision. It was the Lady, I thought, who had chosen me.

"Does that matter?"

"Abbot Ruadan would say so!" Incredibly, I wanted to smile. There was a little silence, then Ogrin sighed. I straightened and turned to look at him.

"I am a hermit not because I do not love my fellows, Branwen, but because I fear to be a scandal to them, and so I came out here to seek God in the wilderness. And though perhaps I am imperiling your soul and my own by saying so, it seems to me that He who is the Word cannot be bound by the names by which men try to limit Him."

"Or Her?" I asked.

"Perhaps, though that is beyond my theology." Ogrin's frown eased, and he began to smile. "Still, not even our Lord could become a man without taking flesh in the womb of a woman. Pray to the Mother of God, if you will. That should not offend even your Abbot Ruadan!"

"And what about those who have sinned against me?" I said, after a time.

"Their evils are not for your judging. Love them. Pray for them."

I did not understand it, for Ogrin had done no magic to take away my sins, but when I lay down on my pallet that night, I sank into a sleep that was as deep and comforting as any spell of the Sidhe, and I did not dream.

I woke like a child on a summer morning. As I dressed I realized that the headache that had haunted me ever since the fight at Nans Yann had finally gone away. A little porridge and some late berries were laid ready, but there was no sign of Ogrin. It was not until I went out that I saw him, sitting on the top of the crag. He looked as if he had slept as badly as I had slept well. He lifted his hand in blessing, but he did not speak, and wondering, I went down the path to see to my pony.

To the north I glimpsed the greener fields of a more settled country, but south and to either side the moor rolled away, dressed now in autumn colors — the garnet of heather stems and the rusty-purple of dying bracken, the dull gold of ripe grasses and bright gorse blossoms, all blended together by the pervasive thorny growth of furze. I tied a longer rope to the pony's halter, clambered onto her bare back, and let her find her own way through the gorse and out onto the moor.

We moved slowly from one bunch of grass to another. And after a time we came to a slope of good grassland, and I slid down. I looped the end of the rope around the base of a particularly tough-looking gorse-bush and lay down beside it. A light wind was pushing a few puffy clouds westward. A hunting hawk spiraled lower, decided we were not worth her interest, and slid away across the sky.

Laid thus between earth and heaven, I tried to pray. But my spirit remained stubbornly imprisoned by this form of flesh, which was not loved, if what Ogrin had told me was true, because I myself did not value it — no, not the flesh, or not entirely — but whatever I meant by *me*. But who was I?

My breathing slowed as consciousness quested within. For a time the spirit struggled, afraid that there would be nothing there to find. But if there was no answer, then nothing mattered, and I was lost already. I tensed, and forced myself to relax again, and of my own will finally, to let go.

There was a quiet place where I could rest, where I could stop the striving, and simply *be*. . . . *This is me* — I realized — *not Esseilte's servant or Keihirdyn's plaything, not even Marc'h's unacknowledged queen.* As at Modron's Well, I felt that this essential identity had existed long before the British captive bore her child; that I had wisdom that would serve me now, if only I could remember. But there was still something I needed. And in that inner stillness, words came to me —

"Mother! God-mother, my mother, or Mother of All! If You exist, then please speak to me now!"

I had, then, a sense of presence, as if something so great that its existence strained the bounds of reality had turned its attention my way. I strove to understand it, and felt a focusing, a descent to a plane in which my perceptions could clothe it in images my mind could understand.

Light from water refracted . . . a shimmer of brilliance took form. I saw the shape of a woman robed and veiled in starry blue like the depths of heaven on a summer night, or like deep ocean on a bright day when the ship is far from shore. And yet, despite the glimmering flow of Her draperies, She Herself was massive, more solid than anything I had ever seen before.

"Mother!" I called to Her. *"Help me!"* I held out my hands in an agony of need. Breathless, I waited, and She turned.

Light blazed from Her breast. I hid my eyes, and felt the splendor veiled. When I looked again, I saw that in the curve of one arm the Mother cradled a Child. With the other, She beckoned to me —

To approach that radiance . . .

To touch the hem of Her garment . . .

To lie upon Her breast and hear the world's pulse beat in Her heart. . . .

"Where have you been?" I pressed myself against that sweetness.

"I have been here since the Beginning; all that was created came from My womb. . . ."

"But I have not seen You!"

"Foolish child — you had only to look within!"

"I will never leave You, now that I have found You again!" I burrowed against Her breast, trying, perhaps, to re-enter Her bright darkness and forget all that the world had done to me.

"Truly? But what about those others that you love? They have wandered in shadow, like you. Will you not bear My love to them?"

"What is a mother's love?"

"To bear, to nurture, and then to set free. . . ."

As if they stood before me, I saw Esseilte, pale as bleached linen, but burning with an inner flame; I saw Drustan, hands outstretched in need; and I saw Marc'h, watching them with uncomprehending pain. And beyond him, I saw the land of Kernow, waiting to be renewed.

"I will go back," I answered, as I had once before, in the faerie ring. *"But I failed everyone before. What can I do?"*

"You must give birth to yourself, My daughter, before you can mother a child."

For the first time I really looked at the babe on Her other arm, who was at once the Child, and all children, and the King, and all mankind. And He stretched out one chubby hand to me and laughed.

Then I laughed too, and all creation laughed with me. I was still laughing when I opened my eyes and found my pony standing over me, butting at me reproachfully with her soft nose.

Ogrin had food waiting again when I came back that evening. But when he saw my face he only smiled, and did not try to speak to me. I ate, marveling at the smooth tang of the cheese, the texture of the bread, knowing the essence of each thing as a separate ecstasy. Sleep came easily, and when I woke I knew that I was healed.

In the morning I went down to water my pony, and then climbed the rock again. I had lost count of days, but when I saw the candles lit, and the portable altar balanced upon the heaped stones, I understood what day it must be. Ogrin had not told me to attend, but I pulled a shawl over my head and knelt there.

Ogrin came out of the cell with his missal in his hands, a silken stole adding an unwonted splendor to his garments, but I hardly noticed, for he went to the altar like a man going to his bride.

The familiar Latin words rolled forth, but I had never heard them spoken with such conviction. "Gloria in excelsis Deo, et in terra pax hominibus bonae voluntatis. Laudamus te, benedicimus te, adoramus te, glorificamus te. . . ." The life-light that shone around him grew brighter.

When the priest blessed the bread, I saw crossed lines of radiance in the air, and when he held his hands over it, light pulsed from his palms. Then he offered it to heaven, and the golden glow that filled the sky focused there. Ogrin was weeping; perhaps he saw his sacrificed King. But for one moment I seemed to see the radiant image of the Child.

And then the platter came to me, and I tasted union, and I understood that this, and the unity of flesh and spirit I had known in the Sacred Marriage, and the Mother and Child who had blessed me on the moor, were all part of the same Mystery.

When I returned to Lan Juliot, Gorwennol was there.

"Drustan is ill," said Esseilte in a still voice. "He has sent for me."

"It's that wound he took in the fight with the king," Gorwennol said to me. "My lord lost a lot of blood. But by the time Keihirdyn got him back to his island the wound-fever had gone down — Drustan's Isle, that is, near Plebs Marci, not Barsa, for even Keihirdyn knows better than to try to go there now. That was maybe three weeks ago. The sword only went through muscle, not into the chest after all. We thought he would get well."

I let my pack slide to the floor and sat down, feeling all of the strain of the long ride at once, or maybe it was only Gorwennol's news.

"Has the wound gone bad, then?" I tried to match Esseilte's calmness.

Gorwennol ran his hands through his graying hair and sighed. "It got all red and painful, then the flesh grew dark, draining stuff that stank so that Essylt" — he paused, flushing as he remembered whom he was talking to — "so that the lady could not bear to tend him anymore. . . ."

Esseilte and I traded glances, remembering the stench in the strangers' house at Temair when we battled for the life of the harper we had found in the sea.

"We've tried fomentations and cautery. It's like there's a poison in the flesh, that won't come out no matter what we do!" Gorwennol went on.

There had been no poison on the king's blade, but I had treated enough injuries to know that dirty wounds were more likely to mortify. I remembered the mud of the farmyard and shuddered.

"My lord was weakening, but still in his senses when he sent me to you, lady. He said that you and your mother's magic had cured him when he was this bad before. He said that if you cannot heal him, then there is no one on this earth who can —" His voice cracked, and he had to swallow before he could go on.

"'Tell her' — it's what he said to me — '*tell her that if she cannot come, or will not, still I love her, and I will wait for her in the Summer Land. . . .*'"

I looked at Esseilte, and the lamplight showed me the clean shape of the skull beneath the tight-drawn skin.

"But I will go to him," she said.

Gorwennol looked at her and saw what I had seen. He cleared his throat.

"Tiernissa, it has been a week, and he was very ill. He may be dead already —"

"No," she said in the same still voice. "If he had gone before me, I would know."

"It will be a week going back, or maybe more, because of the storms," Gorwennol went on doggedly. She nodded. Then they both looked at me.

After a moment I understood why. If I told Gorwennol that it would be death for Esseilte to undertake the voyage at this season, he would refuse to take her. Once more, the decision had fallen to me. I closed my eyes.

"*— To bear, to nurture, and then to set free. . . .*" I knew, also, what Esseilte was asking of me. But so soon? Did it have to be so soon?

"You will need the powder from the acorn mold—" I said aloud. "I have it with the other things, and I will copy out the spells . . ."

I saw Esseilte's eyes widen as she understood the gift that I was giving her—not only to let her go and to give her the medicines, but to stand aside and let her go alone.

When they had gone it began to rain, a steady, dismal downpour that matched my spirits. I knew I had made the right decision for Esseilte and Drustan, but I could find no joy in it. The second night it began to blow. Even atop the cliff I could taste salt-spray, and I shuddered as I lay awake, listening to the waves slam against the shore. It would be a ship-killing storm upon the sea.

I thought then, *If Esseilte is lost, Drustan will certainly die, and when both are gone, who will tell Marc'h how it was with them, so that he may at least understand the reason for all this pain?*

In the morning I dressed in every warm garment I owned, and went to beg from the abbot a better mount than my old pony. Then I set out to push it and myself across the width of Kernow to Bannhedos.

"And what storm-wind has blown you here, bird of ill-omen?" asked Karasek. I looked at him without speaking and moved stiffly toward the hearth in the middle of the hall, water from my sodden brat dripping behind me on the bracken that covered the floor. "A very bedraggled bird, I must say," he went on. "But perhaps she has brought us good news this time—is the Irish bitch dead, then, and you looking to the king to pension you?" The murmur of comment that had ceased at my appearance swelled once more. Someone laughed.

Crida came bustling out, stopped short as she saw me, then hurried to help me unpin the heavy wool. She gave it to a serving lad, with a flurry of instructions. I was marginally drier underneath, and soon Crida had wrapped a blanket around me and thrust a mug of steaming spiced wine into my hand.

"Don't mind the man," she said in a low voice. "With that tongue of his you could whet the whole war-band's swords!"

"I know. Where is the king?"

"Up there—" She pointed toward the loft and then spat. "With the Saxons! Is your poor lady gone, after all? I feared it—she did not look well."

"She lives—" I bit my lip. "I hope she lives, but I must speak with my lord."

Crida frowned. "Those heathen dogs can't talk without a horn of ale in their paws. They'll be wanting more soon, I suppose. I'll take it myself, dear, and tell him you have come."

Between the wine and the heat of the fire, I was almost asleep when I heard Marc'h's voice behind me. I dragged myself up from endless depths of exhaustion and turned. The hard look on his face softened as he took in my shadowed eyes and straggling hair, and he sighed.

"At least you have not come in hatred, this time. . . . What is it, Branwen, that you have half-killed yourself to ride here to say to me?"

I flushed, understanding only now how clearly he had read me. "Not in hatred, and so it is for your hearing only, Wor-Tiern." I glanced past him at the barely averted faces around us. Marc'h grimaced and motioned them away.

"Esseilte is ill, but she is not dead yet, unless this storm has drowned her in the sea—" I told him. "She is on her way to Drustan's Isle."

"And do you want me to go after her? For the love of God, why?" The king's voice had risen, and men looked around. He passed a shaking hand across his eyes.

"Let her go, Branwen! I should have done it long before. Even if I were as jealous as rumor makes me I could not go after her now. Things are moving to a final confrontation in Armorica, I must make sure of my allies, finish arranging for weapons and supplies, a host of other things, before I can leave here. . . ."

"Is there no one you can delegate to see to them? It is for your own sake that I think you should come . . ."

"Why?" His hand came down from his face and he stared at me. "My sorrow that I listened to you before, Branwen. Give me one reason why I should do so again!"

"For the same reason that Esseilte went, ill as she is now," I told him. "Because Drustan is dying from that last blow of your sword. . . ." There was a long silence.

"He would not fight me—he would not fight me and I was in a fury—" Marc'h whispered at last, his gaze fixing on the fretful flicker of the fire. "Oh, sweet Mary Mother, what have I done?"

But that I could not answer, nor make the decision that lay before him now. It had been pain enough for me to make my own. It seemed a very long time before he straightened and called for Mevennus Maglos, and began to give the orders that would allow us to go.

By the time we cleared the mouth of the Fawwyth and worked our way into the Channel the storm-clouds were fleeing eastward like the rags of a defeated army. The seas were still high, and the wind brisk enough to send spume blowing off the waves like froth from the neck of a sweated horse, but the king's longboat was built to ride them, and his crew the best in Kernow. I began to hope that we would not be too far behind Esseilte and Gorwennol, if they had reached Armorica.

Even so, it took nearly a week of hard sailing before we picked our way through the last of the black rocks and sighted Point Vanis and the coast of Cornovia. With a little shock I realized that I had passed most of the month of October in traveling. It must be hard on the Feast of Samhain by now. I remembered how the winds moaned among the shadowed mountains ahead of us. And at this season other things than wind would be whispering among the ancient stones. I shivered, remembering, and wished that this had happened at any other time of year.

We had come through the Rocks with the first light of morning, and a fair wind drove us down into the bay. It was just a little past noon when the oarsmen ran the ship up onto the stony strand of Drustan's Isle.

Other ships were tied there; one of them still unloading, tattered and bleached by hard weather till it looked like a ghost ship in the pallid sun. But my eyes were on the fort, where a palisade of new logs spiked above banks of stone. The gates were open, but the whole place seemed curiously still.

The men who had been working on the other boats looked, pointed, began to shout the king's name. I staggered as the solid ground heaved beneath me, then found my footing, and began to run. Just inside the gates I paused, panting. The new tower rose ahead. I could hear weeping from somewhere inside. More slowly now, I went toward it.

On the second level of the tower I found them.

I stood in the doorway, blinking. My nostrils flared at the stench of mortality as my exhausted mind tried to make sense of the scene. The only brightness came from the window. As I focused I saw there was a bed beside it in which a man lay still.

Someone was kneeling beside him, as silent as he. The weeping was coming from one of the other shadowed figures in the room.

Then I heard booted feet on the stairs. The room came to life as I stepped forward. Gorwennol's face sprang into focus, haggard in the harsh light from the window, and another, whom I recognized as Keihirdyn.

"The king!" came a cry from below. "Defend yourselves! The Wor-Tiern has come!"

Karasek shoved past me, sword rasping from sheath as he saw Keihirdyn move toward the weapons on the wall.

"Fight, will you? Oh no — you will not hide him from our justice a second time!"

Keihirdyn snarled like a trapped ferret and I saw I had misjudged him. When his own skin was at risk he could fight very well. Iron clanged. I dodged out of the way, making for the window. Karasek swung again, but perhaps his eyes were not yet entirely accustomed to the shadows, for his blow went wide. Keihirdyn grinned then and struck overhand, his blade taking Karasek just at the joining of the neck and shoulder where leather and linked rings did not protect him, and cleaving through muscle and bone.

Karasek's sword clattered across the floor and Keihirdyn jerked his own weapon free. And so he was standing above the body, blood dripping from his blade, when a flicker of steel brought my own gaze back to the door. A wheel of light rolled forward. Keihirdyn's sword was still lifting when the king cut him down.

And then everything settled to stillness again.

Now that I was closer, I could see that it was Esseilte who knelt beside the bed, the folds of the monk's robe lapping her like a shroud. Then I knew to whom the pale face within the curve of her arm must belong.

Marc'h stumbled forward to stand beside me. I understood at last why I had brought him here, for the cry that started in the depths of him grew until it shook the stones of the tower.

"Drustan! Oh my son, my son, my son!"

Twenty-four

SAMHAIN MORN

"Oh my beloved, the woman tells me that your ship has black sails . . ."
Marc'h looked up from the wax tablet in his hand. "This is not
Drustan's writing —"

"No," said the little priest who had been sitting in the corner.
"It is mine. Toward the end the lord Drustan became too weak
to hold a stylus, and also, he was in too much pain. I would have
stopped — it was not seemly — but he raved. . . ."

The man's mouth had a sour twist to it, and I felt the faintest
twinge of amusement. If Drustan's testament was a confession, it
was not addressed to the Christian god! The monk said that
Drustan had forced him to write it, but I wondered. Did he too
want to hear the story's end?

I could not tell if Esseilte was even listening. She still leaned
against the high bed with her head on Drustan's pillow, her gaze
fixed on his closed face, his wasted hand cradled against her
breast. The cold light from the window limned them both with
the same stark clarity, like figures in a monument. There was
something daunting in that stillness.

Shock, I thought. I had draped a cloak around her, but I did
not yet dare try to make her move. At least the bodies of Keihirdyn and Karasek had been taken from the room.

"Black sails — what does that mean?" asked the king.

"It was to be a signal, like in the old Greek tale of Theseus,"
Gorwennol answered for him. "Black sails if the queen would
not come. . . . But I bent on the white ones, so that he could

look out from this window and see!" He cast a venomous glance at the other Essylt's dark head.

She looked up at the words. Eyes still red and puffed with weeping shifted from one face to another, finding no sympathy anywhere. I could not see the beauty that Drustan had hoped might help him to forget his queen. Essylt Dornwenn was a little bony woman with a thick braid of black hair and eyes too like those of her brother Keihirdyn.

"You are looking at me as if I killed him! But Drustan was finished already — I thought that if he believed she had betrayed him he might at least end with a kind word for me! He was *my* husband, and he cheated me!" Her voice rose. "I had a right —"

"He was never yours!" My words crossed hers. "Hope might have given him strength to last until she could come with her medicines. . . ."

"He was better dying than saved by her witchery so that they could sin again!" Essylt said spitefully.

"Woman, your presence profanes the dead!" The king turned on her suddenly. "Go bury your brother. We have no use for you here!"

Essylt sat back as if he had hit her. For one moment longer she glared at us, and then, still sniffling, she ran from the room.

We stood silent, listening to the echo of her feet on the stairs.

"Shall I believe my heart or her words?" Marc'h's voice tightened as he began to read again. *"Oh my queen, perhaps this is the final testing . . . the only truth of my life has been my love for you, and even if you fail me, I will let nothing extinguish that pure flame."*

The sun was lower now, shining full through the window. It lent Drustan's cold face its light and glistened on the strings of the harp beside him. He lay as death had left him, hair tangled, body curved awkwardly against the pain.

"My heart tells me that you are coming, but my senses are leaving me, and I can trust nothing now. Why should you heal me, when I have brought you such pain? In all my life I have loved only you and my king. And my geas was that in serving one of you, I must betray the other.

"You have given me my death between you —" Marc'h's voice cracked. He put a hand over his eyes and handed the tablet to me.

I cleared my throat. *"I would have laid down my life to defend him, and he will need defenders in the days to come."* I swallowed, then went on. *"But I would rather have fallen asleep in your arms. This*

straw-death is not easy — the wound pains me more than the one the Morholt gave me, for it is nearer to the heart. But in all the stench and the struggle, the sweet curve of your breast still justifies the world. . . ."
I paused, suddenly aware of the weight of silence in the room.

"The ship lifts beneath me. It is bearing us to the Blessed Isles. You were wrong, Esseilte — the magic that we drank together was both death and love. . . ." The tablet slipped from my fingers and clattered on the floor.

"What more?" asked the king harshly.

"There is no more —" said the priest. "He stopped speaking, and then he smiled. And a little later, *she* came." He shrugged uncomfortably and nodded toward Esseilte. Marc'h let out a long, shuddering sigh, then turned to me.

"What magic, Branwen? What did he mean?"

I clasped my hands to still their trembling. "On the ship that brought us to Kernow — Esseilte thought to avenge her uncle with poison. . . ." I tried to untangle the interlace of emotions that had trapped us, to make him understand.

"But why didn't he tell me they were lovers?" Marc'h exclaimed when I had done. "I would —"

"You would have had to renounce the alliance. Esseilte's father needed it too much for her to risk that, and so did you."

"She bound Drustan with a geas of love, and I had bound him with a geas of loyalty!" the king groaned. "But he should have known that he could come to me. I gave him a home; if I could not have given him Léon, I would have made him my heir."

"Don't you understand?" I said. "The only kingdom that man ever wanted was the circle of Esseilte's white arms!"

There was a sound from the bed. The cloak slipped from Esseilte's shoulders as she bent, crooning, to straighten Drustan's limbs and smooth his hair.

"There, my love. Sleep now, sleep easy, and we will mourn you like a hero!" She pulled the coverlet up to his chest and patted it into place, then moved to the foot of the bed and stood looking down at him. I reached her side as she started to fumble with the cords that bound her braids and helped her to undo them, beginning to understand what she wanted, hoping that a release of grief would bring her back to us again.

"Take your place at the head of the bed —" I whispered to Marc'h.

Esseilte thrust her hands through the masses of her hair,

loosening it so that it fell about her shoulders in a golden shower.

"Let us be glad tonight, let us make all welcome tonight, let us be open-handed tonight, since we are sitting by the body of a king!" she cried suddenly.

"Ochone! Your blue eyes to be without sight, you that were friendly and generous and pursuing. Oh love! A pity it is he sent you to your death. You were a champion of the men of Eriu, their prop in the middle of the fight; you were the head of every battle; your ways were glad and pleasant. . . ."

She swayed, lifting her arms in the ritual gesture, and I realized that it was Grainne's lament for Diarmuid that was providing the words she needed now.

"Drustan was a warrior without equal," echoed Marc'h harshly. "A flame to fire the hearts of the war-host when our foes came upon us. Wise in council and fearless in the field of battle. . . ."

"It is sorrowful I am, without mirth, without light, but only sadness and grief and long dying," Esseilte's voice lifted in lament once more. "Your harp used to be sweet to me, it wakened my heart to gladness. Now my courage is fallen down, I not to hear you but to be always remembering your ways."

"He was a master of sweet music," I added, letting the sorrow of it take me. "A bard who knew all the histories of the heroes, and a hero who lived them." Gorwennol had stumbled to the other side of the bed to stand bowed with weeping, facing me.

"Sweet-tempered as a boy, and generous when grown — no man ever had a better master than the lord Drustan —" said Gorwennol.

"Och! My grief is going through me!" Esseilte wailed. "A thousand curses on the day when Grainne gave you her love, that put Finn of the princes from his wits; it is a sorrowful story your death is today. You were the man was best of the Fianna, beautiful Diarmuid, that women loved."

And that was surely true — all of it — as true for Drustan as it had been of Diarmuid of the curling black hair. I felt a sudden tremor, remembering how Esseilte had wanted to make her life into a hero-tale. Had she sought this ending, or had she only found herself trapped in a maze, too tormented to escape and determined to tread it blithely to the end?

"It is dark your dwelling place is under the sod, it is mournful and cold your bed is; it is pleasant your laugh was today; you were my happiness, Drustan. . . ." Esseilte's voice faded. She swayed, and I moved quickly. As I got my arm around her I saw that she knew me, and I tried to smile.

"There, love, it's over now. Rest now —"

"Oh yes, I will." She nodded, then looked back at the bed. "He is dead, Branwen, do you see? But I did go to him. Thank you for helping me."

"I would not have come after you, but Marc'h needed to be here . . ." I began, but she put her finger on my lips.

"Yes. I know. But I am glad that you followed me, Branwen. . . . In the storm, on the ship, I was afraid and wanted you." Her eyes met mine, wholly clear at last. "Grainne gave me the words for Drustan, but there are no tales to tell me what to say to you —"

I gripped her more tightly, not wanting to hear it, not now. She was like a bird to hold. I could feel her heartbeat fluttering wildly in her breast.

"Esseilte," I stammered, "Esseilte, love —"

"Truly . . . love. Forgive me. . . ."

But now, in this room at the heart of the maze, what was there to forgive? What was there to say except that through the tangle of all those other loves and loyalties there had run one bright thread that was my love for her and hers for me? And now that it lay in my hand, I felt it pulling free. Let us go on as we were, I thought wildly, with Esseilte using me, or abusing me, but here!

She caught her breath suddenly. Her pallor became bloodless. I saw the sudden beads of sweat pearling her skin.

"Is there pain?" The need of the moment suppressed all other thought as Esseilte nodded.

"Now . . . the sword . . . is in my heart also —"

"Let's get you to bed," I whispered. "Someone — help, quickly!"

Marc'h got to his feet, staring.

"Let me be —" Esseilte's gaze clouded, then refocused on the window. "Here . . . where I can see. . . ."

"See what? Oh, Esseilte —"

Her lips twisted. She gulped air, then seemed to grow easier.

"Drustan . . ." She nodded wisely. "He did wait . . . for me . . ."

"Then say farewell to him —" I murmured, holding her.

"The waters are rising . . . but he is holding out his hand.

Branwen . . . you must let me go—" She went rigid, and I felt
my own heart pierced by her pain.

Mother! my spirit cried. *Help me!* For a moment there was only
my own terror, and then, as on the moor, I felt that Other near
me.

*"My child—there is no loss. All is safe with Me, and I am always
here. . . ."*

There were no more words, but the Presence remained. Peace
replaced the fear. Esseilte's head lay on my shoulder. I pressed
my lips against her hair.

"Go in peace, my sister . . ." the words whispered through
me. "Love sets you free . . ."

A long sigh and a growing heaviness—I felt the spirit flow out
of her. . . .

And when there was only a dead weight in my arms, I let
Marc'h help me lift and lay her on the bed beside Drustan.

Marc'h went to his knees beside them, his face hidden by his
hands. But I straightened, seeking, with a new desperation, that
twist of perception that would let me *see*— For a moment I
swayed, dizzy with concentration, then I released my pent
breath, and in that moment without strain, looked at the window.

There was a dazzle of sunlight on the sea. But within that
brightness, it seemed to me I saw two forms of light, that gradually, as I watched them, merged until there was only one.

Whipped by the sea-wind, the flames stabbed at the black
shroud of the sky. The logs were piled high and drenched with
oil. Once the king had given the orders, men had been quick to
gather the wood for the pyre. Karasek and Keihirdyn had been
buried already. It was fearful enough to offer spirits hospitality.
No man of Armorica would willingly share his home with the
bodies of the dead on Samhain Eve.

The fire burned fiercely, sending up a great pall of smoke as it
bit through bark still wet from the storm. Only now and again,
when the wind shifted, could I glimpse the two bodies that had
been laid there to burn as once they had burned within each
other's arms.

But I did not need to see. It was I who had cleansed and
arrayed them, covered the straw mattress with new linen and
laid them there, breast to breast, with Esseilte's head on Drustan's shoulder where it belonged. Drustan's sword lay at his side

and his harp at his feet, and Marc'h had spread his cloak over them for a coverlet.

"May the earth release you, the wind of heaven lift you, the holy fire free you, and the waves bear you westward to the Blessed Land . . ." Words came to me that were not my own.

"So be it—" answered Marc'h and Gorwennol. Silent, we watched the flames clear from smoky orange to a pure gold.

"I will not give Drustan to the earth of Armorica," the king said heavily at last. "This land never accepted him in life. Take what is left of them back to Kernow, Branwen, and set up a stone to proclaim that the Lady Esseilte and the son of Cunomorus lie there. . . ."

"Your son by Gwenneth, Riwal's daughter." I looked up at Marc'h's profile, the planes of nose and jaw and the high brow molded like bronze in the light of the fire. "But why did you not let it be known? She was dead, and her father was your enemy."

"Riwal knew," Marc'h said harshly. "It was one reason why he hated me. I kept the secret because the price of Budic's friendship was to conceal from the world that I had betrayed his daughter and cuckolded his son! It is not a thing I am proud of. But I was young, and poor Gwenneth was very lovely, while Meliau and Budicca were both of them cheerful solid souls with no enchantment in them at all."

He sighed, and looked out across restless waves that whispered their own secrets to the wind. Across the bay, other lights twinkled back at us from an invisible shore. On the hills, the balefires were burning, and candles in every window showed the spirits the way home. But on this night the people stayed within doors. Tonight the spirit in everything was waking. Only Gorwennol had remained with Marc'h and me to watch beside the pyre.

"Old Budic was a fair man, but he had eyes in the walls," Marc'h went on. "Somehow he found out I had been Gwenneth's lover, and when I got the two children to Ker-haes for safety after she died and Meliau was killed, he forbade me to claim the younger one as my own. What he offered in exchange was his patronage for my son by Budicca. Drustan was sent into hiding in the care of Gorwennol, and I never saw him again until he was nearly grown. . . ."

He turned back to gaze into the flames. The fire had caught solidly in the larger logs. It blazed up as the wind caught it, so that for a moment we saw the shapes of our beloved shimmering through a veil of flame. The wind blew ever harder, and the fire roared hungrily. I heard a sudden jangle and crack of splitting wood and knew it for the sound that Drustan's harp made as it, too, died.

"I loved him, even before I knew who he was, but the right time to tell him so somehow never came. . . . If I had loved him more, perhaps he would have loved *her* less."

"You and Drustan were estranged by the secrets kept, and Esseilte and I were set at odds, at the last, by secrets shared —" I shivered and pulled the heavy cloak tighter around me, for though the heat of the fire seared my face, the wind off the ocean was very cold.

"Today all the secrets are being bared . . ." Marc'h answered bitterly. "The only offering we can make to the dead is the truth of their lives. I wonder if they care?"

"The truth of their lives, and of ours. Perhaps that is the gift they give in return."

The wind was backing, sweeping the flames aside. The pyre had already sunk in toward the center; the logs surrounding it formed a latticework of flame. There was hardly anything there, now, to show that here had been a fair woman, here a valorous man. How quickly the pyre had transformed what had been the source of so much love, and so much pain!

"It is some comfort to know why I always felt that taking Esseilte was like trying to embrace the wind — she never was mine to hold," Marc'h said then. "But it does not explain all!" Suddenly he turned on me.

I felt my heart falter and then begin its heavy beat again.

"If Esseilte became Drustan's lover on the ship, how could she have spent that night in the circle with me? The woman I lay with was a maiden. Surely in that place, on that night, I knew the truth of her, and what happened between us was real!" His voice shook.

"You knew the queen, but not the woman," I whispered.

"Branwen!" His low voice vibrated in my bones. "Look at me!" His hands gripped my shoulders and my hair whipped on the wind as I turned to him.

"It was real, my king," I answered, weeping. "The woman whose maidenhead you had in the circle of stones was me. . . ."

"This is the truth?" He forced up my chin so that I had to meet his eyes.

"Shall I tell you the track of the Dragon Power? From the

Maiden Circle to the Rock in the Sea; from the Rock to the
serpent stone; from the stone to the shrine, and onward to the
Tor and the circle of great Stones. . . ." I caught my breath on a
sob, for there were no human words for the emotions that shook
me now.

The king's hands vised my shoulders and I welcomed the
pain.

"Who . . . are . . . you?"

His words were lost in the roaring of the sea, of the wind, of
the flames. And it was they who used my voice to reply.

"I am the White Raven of Logres . . . I am the Queen of the
Hidden Realm . . . I am the Brigantia of Kernow . . ."

Marc'h's hands dropped from my shoulders.

"All this time —" he said in a still voice.

I nodded, trembling as the power that had flooded through me
drained away.

"I did what I could, but it was so little — Marc'h, I did try to
fulfill my vow!"

I felt the tears coming again and turned my head, but it was
the king's hand that wiped them away, and the king's arm that
drew me close, shielding me from the wind. For a time then we
were silent, but he stroked my back as one might gentle a frightened horse or soothe a child. And then I felt his breath stir my
hair.

"But why? You owed me nothing, Branwen — why?"

Perhaps truth is the gift the dead return. . . . If Esseilte could find
words for it, so could I. I stared into the red heart of her pyre.

"Because I love you."

The last bright log cracked loudly, and the coals collapsed into
a glowing heap upon the sand.

"Aethelbert of Kent will be bringing over his Frisians by mid-
November —" Boards creaked as Marc'h took a restless stride
toward the shuttered window. "He is very young, but an active
leader. I fear he will go far. There is a solidity to those Saxons
that is very disturbing. If they learn to combine before we do,
Artor's peace cannot endure."

The last of the rushlights was guttering, sending the king's
shadow flickering crazily this way and that as he paced the floor.

"Then why make them your allies?"

Still clothed, I lay on the bed on the other side of the room.
Marc'h had assumed that I would sleep with him when we re-

turned from watching the pyre. I had not objected. The passage of so much emotion had left me curiously empty. Perhaps tomorrow the reality of loss would penetrate and I would raise the keen for Esseilte. But not now. There were things that needed saying, but I could not force myself to seek for words. Easier to sit and talk of something neutral, like the war.

"Perhaps the barbarians will all kill each other —" Marc'h shrugged. "If they do not, it may prove useful to have at least one pack of the Saxon wolves on my side. Assuming, of course, that any of us survive. . . ." He poured a little spiced wine from the earthenware flagon that had been heating over the brazier into a mug, drained it, and set it down.

A little flutter in my belly informed me that the conversation had suddenly become personal again.

"The danger is great, then?" I asked carefully.

"It is," he sighed. "I never believed that Chlotar would be so damned persistent, but he cannot forgive his son for opposing him. I never thought the men of Domnonia would be so loyal to Iudual. And what I said about Drustan's value in battle was true. I will need him . . . I will need him so badly, and he will not be there!"

"Why not go home then? Must you continue this war? Leave these stiff-necked Britons to their fate and come back to Kernow!" I was babbling, I knew it, and somehow I was not surprised by what I saw in his face when he turned.

"I cannot desert men who have risked life and home because they believed in my cause. Chramn is waiting for me in Ker-haes with his family. I failed Drustan — I will not fail them. After — if there is an after — we will see. . . ."

Marc'h came suddenly to the bed, face twisting as he looked down at me. "Guard my land, Branwen, if I cannot! If I fall in battle, promise me that you will watch over Kernow!"

"How?" I raised myself on one arm. "My sovereignty is only in the Hidden Realm!"

"I will marry you legally as soon as it can be arranged —" Straw crackled as he sat down, then stretched himself full-length on the bed as if the energy that had upheld him had gone out with the candle flame. From the darkness I heard his whisper, "Oh God, I am so very tired. . . ."

Legally — a formality only — said his tone. How much he was assuming, as if the ritual that had bound us had made a marriage; as if my admission of love had been a consent to everything. But Marc'h had never said that he loved me. Was there any love left in him? Or was there only kingship and power?

If we could have built steadily from that first night in the stone circle, love might have grown between us. But what was there now? My belief that I had no choices had brought me in the end to weep with Marc'h beside a dying fire. I knew that my next choice must be made wisely, for it would be final. What was I willing to give? What did I require?

Marc'h rolled over and drew me to him. After a moment, shyly, I put my arms around him, and felt the weight of his head against my breast.

"I am too weary even to make love to you. . . ." he said to me, and then, when I thought he slept, "You should have lain with me when I asked you, in Ker-haes. . . ."

"Perhaps. Then, I could not see it that way . . ."

Marc'h did not answer. His breathing had deepened, and I knew that he was asleep now. I pulled the blanket up over us and held him closer, glad of his warmth against me. But I did not sleep. In the darkness, other senses were sharpened. I was painfully aware of the steady whisper of his breathing, and the irregular sighing of the waves against the shore. I tried to think, but questions flickered through my memory in bewildering profusion.

How could I sit by Marc'h's side and reign as his queen? In Ker-haes, I had feared to steal Esseilte's honors, but now her husband lay in my arms. *I cannot do it*, I thought, *even now when I have seen her bones*. To take her place would confirm her loss. That was my pain.

Marc'h lay unmanned by the loss of his son, and what spell could heal him?

And who could stop the malicious tongues that would be wagging when what had happened here was known? Then I thought of the boy, Dewi. He would never be Drustan's peer as a harper, but he was already fascinated by his story. Perhaps he would make a tale of it, and that would be the kind of memorial Esseilte had always wanted, after all.

Where are you now, my sister? Do you and your lover roam the hills of Armorica in the Lord of Death's dark train, or have you found a brighter path?

I grew still, listening to the sea. It must be a little after midnight, I thought then, and from the sound I knew the tide was turning. It seemed to me that I heard a distant murmur, like the sound of a great host approaching, or the sound that used to drift up to Temair on the wind from the Samhain Fair.

Carefully I eased away from the king, who did not wake, though he muttered a little and reached out for me. I padded across the room and pulled open the shutter. This chamber was above the one in which Drustan had died, and like his, its window faced out across the bay. The stars were hidden and the fires had faded, and so I heard and felt, rather than saw, what flowed down from the mountains and moors and pastures toward the sea.

Clearly I heard the slap of waves against a ship's hull, the splash as an anchor was raised. I recognized the groan of lines as invisible sails were run up the masts, the crackle of canvas that ceased as they were trimmed, giving way to a slow, regular creak of timber and cloth as the wind filled them and the ship began to stand out to sea. But the sounds seemed unnaturally loud, as if the boat were closer than it possibly could be, or as if it were larger than any vessel I had ever seen.

I felt the fine hairs rising on my neck and arms, and fought an impulse to slam the shutters and hide in Marc'h's arms. Was it death to look upon that ship? The people of Armorica thought so. But perhaps it would not be so for me, who had danced with the folk of the Hidden Realm. . . . And I knew that the answer to at least some of my questioning waited out there on the dark waves.

On Samhain, the doorways open between the worlds, and they who have eyes may see. . . .

I let my pent breath out on a long sigh. Racked by grief at Esseilte's passing, I had only managed to attain that deeper perception for a moment. Now I tried to release nerves tensed against pain, to allow the alteration in awareness that would let me walk at once in both worlds.

This too is something I have done many times before.

The tremor that was not a shiver ran through my body; I felt as if I were sinking, and yet my feet remained firmly planted on the floor. And opening my eyes, I saw the luminous outlines of a great ship moving gently seaward. Pale forms crowded the rail, gazing back at the land they were leaving. But I saw two that did not look back. They stood in the prow of the ship, arms around each other's waists, and all their being strained toward the open sea.

And though I myself remained in the tower room, my vision

grew longer and clearer, following the boat past Point Vanis to Inis-Sun, the holy isle, where the spirits began to shift away to other realms. But the pair that I was watching sailed onward. As its passengers departed, the boat diminished until it was only a coracle, but still it sped swiftly. I stood watching it until the sea grew nacreous with the first glimmerings of dawn.

Mist laid silver veils upon the waters, and prow to stern, the coracle began to disappear.

"Not yet," I whispered. "Oh, let me see —"

And then the sun rose behind me and pierced the mists with great golden rays. I saw a far green country with groves of fruited trees and singing birds; through meadows of green turf flowed crystal streams. And I saw Esseilte and Drustan step out of the coracle onto that shining shore.

"Branwen —"

The room was a-shimmer with a faint, rosy light. All my limbs tingled as I breathed in that glow, as if I had just awakened from sleep. The king was stirring, and I went to him.

"I know where is a distant isle, for miles around, sea-horses glimmer —" Marc'h whispered. "Drustan used to sing that. I thought I saw that island in my dreams, just now. . . ."

"I saw it too," I answered him. "Drustan and Esseilte were walking there. In Eriu they say that when the Sons of Mil conquered the land, the Children of Danu were dispersed before them. Many of them went into the faerie hills. But some fared onward over the sea to the Blessed Isles. I think that those we loved have found their way there at last." I bent to kiss him on the brow.

"It is dawn, my lord, and we are free —"

I understood suddenly what was needful. As Marc'h had awakened me in the circle of stones, now I must reawaken him. His initiation had made me queen, but we could not be mated unless I could restore his power. Somehow I had to heal the pain-racked man who had lain impotent in my arms, and make him king once more.

I brushed the tangle of graying hair from his forehead and smoothed the lines that grief had graven into his brow. Where fingers had gone, lips could follow, moving from forehead to eyelids, down gaunted cheeks to lips that lost their tightness as I kissed them, teasing until he sought my mouth like a thirsty man in a barren land.

"Your eyes are the eyes of the eagle," I whispered. "And your neck is a mighty tower. Honey is in your mouth, my lord — let me taste the sweetness of it, so — "

The power that was filling me had warmed me, and I pulled off my own salt-stiff woolen gown and the shift as well. The chill of the early morning was like a blessing on my glowing skin.

Beside the bed were a basin and ewer. I soaked a cloth and cleansed Marc'h's face and throat, unlaced his tunic and under-tunic and got him out of them, and began to bathe his chest and shoulders, following the cloth with my lips and kissing each new scar.

"Your breast is the breast of the white stallion, and the muscles of it smooth and shining underneath my hands. . . ."

Marc'h was lying very still, but as my mouth touched his nipples he started, and his hands closed on my arms.

"Branwen, I don't know — " His eyes were blurred, as if he were still struggling up from the wells of sleep. I sank down across him with my breasts pressing his chest, and kissed his mouth to silence again.

"But I do," I told him. "Look at me, Marc'h of Kernow, and tell me who I am!"

"Branwen . . ." he began, then his eyes focused. I could see him settling inwardly, gathering himself to meet the challenge he saw in mine. "You are my Lady and my Queen. . . ." He let out his breath again, his gaze now fully aware, accepting my right to claim him this way.

— Fully aware, and a little wondering, as if he had not suspected I knew the things I was doing to him now. I let my breasts brush his, then bent again to tease at his nipples with teeth and tongue, shivering as I felt them stiffen and my own hardened in sympathy. Some of those things, Keihirdyn had taught me. Oddly, I found that to perform in love the acts that I had learned under compulsion was healing me as surely as it brought new life to the king.

Light was growing in the room, and where I touched Marc'h it seemed to me that his skin was glowing. Last night he had been old, but now the wasteland of his body was reviving, skin becoming smooth and supple, muscles hardening, face losing lines that had been carved there by pain.

Slowly I unlaced his braes and pulled them off him.

"Your legs are strong columns, my love, the powerful legs of the stag that leaps through the forest. . . ." I kissed his toes, then began to move upward, kneading the corded muscles of calves and thighs. As I brushed past, his manhood quivered, and I smiled.

From head to foot I blessed the king's body, cleansing him, adoring him, restoring him, invoking the God in him as he had once invoked the Goddess into me. Every inch of him I claimed with the words of my mouth and the softness of my lips and the delicate sure pressure of my hands and the sweet sliding friction of skin on skin. I loved him until his hands clenched in the blankets and he moaned.

"Your manhood is the Staff of the Lord of Life, the Scepter of Sovereignty, the Rod of Power . . ."

When I stretched my length beside the king at last he was quivering like a bent bow. He set his hand upon my breast, and the power I had awakened in him began to flow through my own flesh in waves of silken fire.

"Branwen . . ." he said in a shaken voice. "Will you give me a child? The sovereignty should have passed to Drustan, but he chose another path. You have made me feel as if I could conquer the empire, but one day I must go to reign with Artor in the Hidden Realm. Will you bear a child to succeed me in Kernow?"

I blinked, seeing once more the Great Mother with her Son, and it seemed to me that She smiled.

"Here is the Cauldron of Life, my lord—" I moved his hand.

He covered me like a stallion rearing, a king stag leaping, an eagle spreading mighty wings. And I opened myself to receive his power.

Like lightning from the storm, radiance flared between us, building until at last the heavens opened and released the healing rain. In that moment, I knew Marc'h completely, his entire identity imprinted in my spirit, as mine was in his.

That explosion in the flesh set me free. I spun outward in an ascending spiral, every circle embracing at once more that was *him*, and *me*. I perceived the tower room, and Marc'h's body still entwined with mine. I saw the mountains of Armorica, misty with dawn, and the sea, and the land of Kernow curving out from the body of Britain like a horn, and Eriu. I knew the immensity of the turning world and all that was in it, but all that was encompassed by my awareness was only one manifestation of a Presence which the glory of my joining with Marc'h had enabled me to perceive—

Who are You?
Light bloomed around us.

"*I am the lover and I am that which is loved; no man pours out his strength for woman, nor does woman open herself to receive his seed without Me.*

"*I am that which gives birth and that which is born; no child turns in trust to its mother, nor does mother spend her life for her child, without Me.*

"*I am the thing that dies and that which is eternal; without Me, no body is released to the elements, and no spirit rejoins the One.*

"*I have many names and many faces; and every one of My children is dear to Me. Seek Me in the sea and sky and forest, and they shall bless thee. Seek Me in the faces of thy lover and thy sister and thy child, and they shall adore Me in thine.*

"*I am the Cauldron of Creation, as I am its Crown, and they who serve Me shall be sovereigns in all the worlds. . . .*"

Then the storm began to pass.

When eternity had ended, Marc'h and I lay linked in the stillness of the dawning, watching as the world was reborn.

Afterword

HISTORY OR LEGEND?

On the road to Fowey in Cornwall stands a seven-foot stone inscribed with these words:

DRUSTANUS HIC IACIT
CVNOMORI FILIUS
(Here lies Drustanus
The son of Conomorus)

In 1538, the priest John Leland recorded a third line, now illegible. This lost line of the inscription read: **CUM DOMINA OVSILLA** *(With the Lady Ousilla).*

Like Arthur's gravestone at Glastonbury, the memorial stone suggests a historical origin for one of the great legends of Europe, and it is rather more convincing, for while the monks of Glastonbury have been accused of political or economic motives for promoting their abbey as the site of Arthur's tomb, until our times the "Tristan Stone" was simply a memorial set up by a Dumnonian prince for his son.

Wrmonoc's ninth-century redaction of an earlier life of St. Paul Aurelian (St. Pol of Léon) states that King Marcus of Villa Bannhedos, on the Fowey, was also known as Conomorus. But the second name did not survive in Cornish folklore, and it was not until scholars began to examine early Breton ecclesiastical records that Conomorus and Drustanus were identified with

391

Marc'h and Tristan. Certainly in the Middle Ages no one would have had a motive for adding Iseult's name to the stone.

Saints' lives, place-names, and folktales attest that Marc'h was well-known in the sixth century as a ruler in Cornwall and in Brittany. In the medieval stories, Tristan's father was called Rivalin. Historically, the lord of northern Brittany in the mid-sixth century was Riwal, who was noted for having killed his daughter and son-in-law (Meliau, son of Budic of Quimper), and who pursued their son Melor and killed him also. Before Melor was killed, however, he took refuge with Conomorus, lord of Carhaix. It seemed to me that all these facts could be reconciled if Drustan had been a second son of Riwal's daughter, sired secretly by Conomorus.

Dumnonia, or Cornwall, was traditionally the territory of Arthur's heir, Constantine, and so Marcus would have considered himself the heir of Arthur too. When the events in this story must have taken place, men would have been alive who as children had seen King Arthur, though his deeds were already becoming legends. The tale of Tristan is therefore a legitimate part of the Matter of Britain, though not quite in the way described by the twelfth-century Norman poets who were the first to write the story down, or by Gottfried von Strassburg or Thomas, who gave it definitive form, or by Malory.

Ireland, Cornwall, Wales, and Brittany were the last Celtic strongholds in a world which was changing drastically as the Teutonic tribes that had swept across Europe began to settle in. The Peace of Arthur lasted through the first half of the sixth century, during which the Saxons remained quietly digesting their conquests, but in the British territories the internal disorders that followed Arthur's death at Camlann (probably in 515) stimulated the third, and largest, emigration of British into Armorica. In the sixth century the princes of Britain dashed back and forth across the Channel much as the Normans were to do in the eleventh, fighting over lands and lordships in both the greater Britain and the lesser.

During the same period, Ireland was enjoying an era of peace and unity whose equal it is still trying to attain. Iseult was said to be the daughter of the king of Ireland. If so, her father would have been Diarmait MacCearbhaill the last undisputed High King of Eriu, who reigned in Tara approximately from 548 to 563. Sixth-century Eriu was a period of remarkable cultural riches, the time of Columba, of Brendan the Navigator, and of the flowering of Irish monasticism.

Marc'h Conomor, Drustan, and Esseilte can all therefore be placed at the crossroads where history becomes legend — guardians, and perhaps victims, of the Celtic heritage. The year 560, in which my story ends, was a watershed between the age of Arthur and the early Middle Ages.

Conomorus's final battle, which took place in December 560, ended in disaster. His forces landed at the Île Tristan in the bay of Douarnenez (Drustan's Isle), and met the enemy near Morlaix. Marc'h was wounded and trampled in the rout, his body taken back to Castle Dor (Bannhedos) for burial. Prince Chramn was burned to death when he went back to try and rescue his family. A son of Marc'h is said to have been an ally of Waroc of Vannes in later years, and I choose to identify him with the second Budic, who eventually became lord of Kemper.

The year 560 was a bad year for Ireland as well. Curnan of Connachta killed the son of a steward at the Samhain Fair and sought sanctuary with Columba. When Diarmait arrested and executed him, the enraged Columba raised the northern Ui Néill against him and destroyed his strength in the battle of Cuil Dremhni the following year. It was in penance for his role in instigating this bloody battle that Columba went into exile from Ireland, eventually becoming the saint of Iona.

In the 570's the Saxons began to move once more, conquering the south of Britain to the Tamar, the west to Wales, and the north to the Scottish border. We do not know the names of those who followed Marc'h as rulers of Kernow. But even after the Saxons had overwhelmed the rest of the south, *somebody* managed to unite the Dumnonians well enough to hold off the English advance, and Kernow remained independent until the ninth century.

It is at least possible that the princes who led that resistance were the descendants of Marc'h and Branwen. . . .

When I began to do the research for this book I became convinced that King Marc'h and Drustan had indeed lived. The story of the lost final line of the inscription on the Tristan Stone (which I discovered by chance when the book was nearly done and I had already concluded that Esseilte *must* have been buried with Drustan) suggests strongly that Esseilte was real also. If so, she would have been served by Branwen, or someone like her.

I first attempted to retell the Tristan story in college, when for reasons I no longer remember I submitted to my professor of medieval French literature a summary of the story, in French rhymed couplets, illuminated. Although my version would give Thomas or Beroul no competition, it must have provided a welcome change from badly typed student essays. At any rate, I got an "A"!

In that version, I stuck to the traditional lines of the story. But in college one studies love as an unofficial part of the curriculum. I wondered what it would be like to live with one of the world's great love affairs — especially for those who had to cope with the consequences. Looking at the story, it seemed to me that without Branwen's help the whole thing would have been impossible, for in every crisis of the story it is Branwen who picks up the pieces without ever receiving any of the rewards. What convinced me finally to try and tell this tale was my curiosity about Branwen herself. History and literature abound in great lovers, but how often in either does one see this kind of loyalty?

And then Marc'h came into the story and carried Branwen away, and what had been a minor plot device in the medieval tale became the pivot of mine. Suddenly it was no longer merely a story about a pair of lovers, but about the meaning of sovereignty.

The main events of Marc'h's later career are well documented (most accessibly in John Morris's comprehensive book *The Age of Arthur*). The legend of Tristan and Iseult is the culminating version of a major theme of Celtic literature — the story of the woman who claims a young hero as her lover when she has been married to an older man. If such a story became attached to real people, then it must have resonated in some way with the actual events of their lives. In this book I have attempted to put history and legend together, and to try and show *how* such things might have happened to these people, in this setting, at this moment in history.

But where, then, is the fantasy? I have always found the real world to be as strange and wonderful as any work of the imagination. For me, the inner world is as real as the outer, and the events that take place in the realm of archetype and legend give meaning to what happens in the fields we know. It is for the reader to decide how much is fantasy, and what is real. . . .

MAGIC AND RELIGION

Considering the wealth of folk custom which survived to the nineteenth century in the British Isles, it is reasonable to assume that in the sixth century the pagan agricultural festivals could have still been celebrated quite openly, although some of their meaning may have begun to blur. To quote Morris: "Christianity [in the sixth century] was still the religion of kings and lords and townsmen, and nothing suggests that anything but the name had touched the bulk of the rural population before the coming of the monks" (p. 372).

Though all the Celtic countries were by this time officially Christian, people would have continued to use their herb-lore, household charms, and everyday magics. The old mythologies were evolving into the lore of Faerie. The Church, especially the Celtic Church, was still attempting to ease the transition by allowing the people to retain those practices and sanctuaries that were at the heart of their spirituality, and preaching the love of the God of Nature instead of hellfire. Perhaps the early priests perceived the two religions as being complementary rather than competitive. In any case, for several centuries people had the benefit of the harmony of the Old Religion and the compassion of Christianity.

However, the sixth century also saw the first of those clashes between Church and State which haunted the Middle Ages and which, in different forms, are still a problem today. The king was traditionally responsible for his realm's spiritual welfare as well as for its temporal safety. In addition to defending his people from human enemies he had to mediate between men and the supernatural realm. Both spiritual and temporal powers were diminished when king and priest forgot the earth from which they came.

The Celts lived in a world in which power radiated from the standing stones, healing came from the sacred wells, and the Old Powers — from the mischievous Cornish piskies to the Sidhe — were still active in the spiritual ecology. Whether these beings existed independently or were projected images is not important for an understanding of the story — what matters is that the people of that time thought they were real.

One of the best examples of Christian use of traditional material is the figure of Brigit, the fifth-century abbess of Kildare who somehow acquired the qualities of the goddess of the Tuatha Dé Danann who preceded her, who herself was the Irish version of the great Celtic goddess Brigantia, who left her name in sites from Spain to Scotland. More holy wells in the British Isles still bear her name than that of any other. It has been suggested that St. Brigit was originally a priestess of Brigantia (who was believed to exercise Her powers) who converted to Christianity with her entire community.

The Celtic year revolved around the great festivals which became the basis of the Christian liturgical calendar. In this book, several of these festivals take on a particular significance.

Samhain

The first of November was the end of harvest and the beginning of winter, and for the Celts (who dated the opening of their festivals from the eve of the night before), the beginning of the new year as well. This is the festival whose original meaning has been most widely retained — in All Saints' and All Souls' Days, and modern Hallowe'en — the feast in honor of the dead.

In Ireland, Samhain was the time of the royal fair at Tara, when all fires were made anew. The pattern of the procession was still remembered into medieval times. Everywhere, lamps or candles showed the spirits the way home. In Brittany, this feast took on a more somber character than elsewhere, and the lord Ankou was believed to ferry the souls of the departed across the sea to the Île du Sein or points beyond.

Midwinter and the Dragon

The Winter Solstice was less important than the four cross-quarter festivals. However, the Celts, like every other people, appear to have celebrated the moment in which the light is reborn.

In the book, I have dealt with the dragon-killing episode in the Tristan legend by drawing on Celtic dragon mythology, and extrapolating backward from the St. George and the Dragon mummers' plays which became a British Christmas tradition. The St. George play as such was imported from England, but Irish tradition also abounds in dragon-lore, and there is a carving of a man spearing a dragon on one of the stones at the mound of Lowth. The kind of ceremony I have described may never have been held at Newgrange, but its components are drawn from tradition, and its structure is valid, based on my knowledge of ritual.

Irish dragons are associated with water, and Newgrange was built in a curve of the Boyne. The ceremony in the story is based on archetypal relationships between dragons, water, and watershed-goddesses, Irish folklore regarding the tumuli of Newgrange, and geomantic theories of "dragon-power" associated with underground water systems and ley lines as conduits of spiritual energy.

The hypothesis that the earth (or at least the British Isles!) contains an energy network comparable to the energy meridians used in acupuncture is also the basis for the Great Marriage sequence in Chapter Twelve. The lines of force are called leys, first named and described by Alfred Watkins in the nineteenth century.

A major British ley runs down the spine of southwestern Britain, linking St. Michael's Mount with Glastonbury and passing through a number of sites dedicated to St. Michael or other dragon-killing saints in between. If this line is extended just a little farther, it passes close to the circle called the Merry Maidens near the Lamorna Valley.

Beltane

Beltane is the first of May, the beginning of summer. It is traditionally a festival which honors the strengthening sun and invokes fertility for crops and animals through a variety of symbolic acts, including bringing in greenery, dancing around the Maypole, and crowning a May King and Queen.

The May Day celebrations of modern Padstow are famous in the world of folklore. In 1984 I was privileged to observe what is certainly the best surviving example of a Beltane ceremony. The words of the May song have evolved through the centuries. Those used today may be no older than the Middle Ages, but the spirit of the song is undoubtedly the same, and a version of the modern words is certainly more appropriate than anything I could invent for the purpose. Most May songs are variants on the same tune, which suggests an original of considerable antiquity. Today, the ceremonies consist of a night sing on May Eve, followed by the morning procession around the town with the "Oss" and its attendants, sung to the accompaniment of accordion and drums with slightly different words. The Padstow Hobby Horse procession is one of the last survivals of the animal processions which were once found all over Europe.

Other May customs suggest the significance of this festival in promoting the fertility of Nature. Examples of sacred ceremonies for the same purpose involving kings and representatives of the Goddess are found from Mesopotamia to Africa. Ireland in particular had a very explicit rite for uniting the king with the symbol of sovereignty.

Harvest

Traditionally, the festival of Lammas, or Lughnasa, that begins August, was the start of harvest-tide (balancing Imbolc, the Feast of Brigit at the beginning of February). At this time the cattle were brought down from their summer pastures, and the harvesting of the corn (emmer wheat or spelt, rye, and barley) began.

The harvest rituals of Old Europe have been well-documented, and are astonishingly similar from country to country. The basic principles of deification of the last sheaf and sacrifice or mock-sacrifice to ensure fertility seem to be universal wherever grain is grown. Elements of the complete ritual were preserved in peasant communities in Britain and on the Continent through the nineteenth century. The custom of "crying the neck" is specific to Cornwall and Devon. Harvest songs are also common, especially drinking songs in praise of the barley from which men make beer.

LANGUAGE

The Celtic tribes reached the British Isles in a series of migrations, the last of which took place in approximately the second century B.C.E. Though all of these tribes spoke Celtic languages, their speech falls into two major branches, "P" and "Q" Celtic — or Goidelic and Brythonic. Goidelic became modern Irish and Scots (after the northern Irish or Scotti gave their name to Alba in the fourth century A.D.) while Brythonic developed into modern Welsh, Cornish, and Breton. The major evolution of Brythonic took place during the sixth century, and it took an additional century or so for the spelling to settle down. For the people in this story, language, like everything else in their lives, was undergoing rapid change.

For the sake of comprehensibility and consistency, I have chosen spellings and word-forms which reflect the pronunciation which eventually dominated in Brittany. To avoid confusion, the hard "c" sound has in most cases been represented by "k". Spellings of personal names have been treated in the same way. *Esseilte* is my attempt to convey the probable Irish pronunciation of the name whose original form was *Adsiltia,* "she who must be gazed upon." The Latin rendering of this name was *Ousilla.* In medieval Welsh it because *Essylt,* and in the European languages *Iseult, Ysol,* or *Isolde.*

The medieval French name *Tristan* developed out of the Pictish *Drust* or *Drustan,* probably for the sake of the word-play on *"trist"* — "sad." On the Tristan Stone it is given as *Drustanus.* In the medieval Welsh triads it is *Drystan.* The Latin name of the king was *Marcus Cunomorus.* The hard "c" of the Latin softened as a Celtic termination, and the medieval form of the name is variously spelled *March, Mark,* or *Margh. Marc'h* is probably as close as we can come to it. Branwen is the only one of the major actors in this story whose name has remained the same from our earliest sources. It means "white raven," and belonged to the ill-fated sister of Bran of Britain before it was ever given to Iseult's cousin and friend.

LITERATURE

Critics and literary historians have a tendency to identify motifs in stories with a kind of implicit "ah ha!" — to say the Grail story is just another quest for a magic vessel, for instance, as if that somehow explained its significance. What they miss is the depth of significance which each new use of a motif adds to the whole. To the people of an intact culture, each storyteller's variations would be enriched by being presented in the context of all that had gone before. A people's stories carry an immense weight of cultural values and models of behavior. Even today, psychiatry helps people to understand their problems by relating them to mythology. Celtic culture is exceptionally rich in stories which have retained their archetypal content. I have tried to demonstrate some of the ways in which, for good or ill, awareness of being part of such a cultural tradition might influence people's lives.

Educated people of the sixth century lived in an environment that was rich in song and story. Because the conversion of the Irish to Christianity was voluntary and gradual, their heroic literature was not lost. It is thought that Irish Druids entered the Church in considerable numbers, and continued many of their traditional educational practices. Certainly the Irish were the first European people to write down their national literature in their own language. The tales of Grainne and Diarmuid, of Deirdre and Naoisi, and of the Voyage of Bran which are featured prominently in the story come from the Irish heroic cycles.

In Britain, also, the basic motifs of the tales that took final form in the *Mabinogion* would have already been known. The stories of Branwen, and Culhwch and Olwen, as told by Drustan, are simplified versions of the later tales. The lament for Gerontius is taken from a ninth-century rescension of what is probably a sixth-century original.

In Brittany, the emigrants were laying the groundwork for a lively literature of their own. Many of the tales which were later retold by Marie de France, such as that of Graelent (Gradlon) and Guigemar (Winomarc'h), combine sixth-century Breton names and older motifs. Another rich source of songs and tales is the *Barzaz Breizh*, a collection made by the Vicomte de Villemarqué in the nineteenth century. Although doubt has been cast by Alexei Kondratiev and others on the antiquity of some of his selections, the songs (even in my translation) are certainly more authentic than anything I might have invented for Drustan to sing!

I have assumed that Drustan, as a trained bard who had traveled widely, would be familiar with all of these literatures, along with the classical material which was part of the education of a gentleman in the late Roman Empire. Where Drustan does not retell them in prose, I have recast translations into verse which suggests the forms of early medieval Irish, Welsh, or Breton prosody. These forms also provide the structure for the original lyrics Drustan sings, the lament for the Morholt, and (with the exception of the Padstow Night and May Day songs, which are very slightly adapted from the versions still used today), the ritual songs. The prayer to Brigid in Chapter Three and Ogrin's blessing in Chapter Thirteen are slightly adapted from material in the *Carmina Gadelica*, a collection of traditional poems and songs from the Scottish highlands. And I could not resist adapting the sailor's song from Act One of Wagner's *Tristan* in Chapter Eleven.

Sources

The following are only some of the most useful books in the towering piles of volumes which surrounded me while I was working on this tale —

J. F. Campbell: *The Celtic Dragon Myth*. Newcastle Publishing, 1981.

Tom Peete Cross and Clark Harris Slover, eds.: *Ancient Irish Tales*. Barnes & Noble, 1936.

Daphne Du Maurier: *Vanishing Cornwall*. Penguin, 1972.

Walter Evans-Wentz: *The Fairy Faith in Celtic Countries*. University Books, 1966; originally published 1911.

Sir James Frazer: *The Golden Bough*. MacMillan, 1935.

A. K. Hamilton Jenkin: *Cornish Homes and Customs*. J. M. Dent, London, 1934.

Lloyd Laing: *The Archaeology of Late Celtic Britain and Ireland*. Methuen, 1975.

Ruth P. M. Lehmann, trans. & ed.: *Early Irish Verse*. University of Texas Press, 1982.

Gwenc'hlan le Scouezec: *Guide de la Bretagne Mysterieuse*. Tchou, Paris, 1966.

Patrick Logan: *The Holy Wells of Ireland*. Colin Smythe Ltd., Buckinghamshire, 1980.

J. Loth: *L'Émigration Bretonne en Armorique*. Rennes: Imprimerie E. Baraise, 1883.

André de Mandach: "Le Triangle Marc-Iseult-Tristan: Un Drame de Double Inceste," *Etudes Celtiques*, 1986.

Marie de France: *Lais*. Ed. A. Ewert, Oxford, 1944.

Caitlin Matthews: *Mabon and the Mysteries of Britain*. Arkana, 1987.

John Michell: *The New View over Atlantis*. Harper & Row, 1983.

John Morris: *The Age of Arthur*. Scribner's, 1973.

Paul Newman: *The Hills of the Dragon*. Kingsmead Press, Bath, 1979.

Alwyn and Brinley Rees: *Celtic Heritage*. Thames & Hudson, 1961.

Gottfried von Strassburg: *Tristan*. Penguin, 1960.

—and a motley collection of booklets from Donald Rawe's Lodenek Press in Padstow on such varied subjects as Cornish hurling, wrestling, names, the Padstow May ceremony, and the like.

— DIANA L. PAXSON
Lammas, 1987

PEOPLE IN THE STORY

CAPITALS = major characters
Small letters = minor characters
italics = characters invented or named for this story
° = historical personages
°° = figures from legend
( ) = historical or legendary characters who are mentioned but do not appear on stage

IRISH

BRANWEN°°, daughter of the Morholt by a British captive and cousin to Esseilte. Her name means "the white raven."

ESSEILTE (OUSILLA)°, daughter of Diarmait Mac-Cearbhaill, High King of Eriu and his queen, Mairenn. Her name means "the desired one who is regarded with pleasure."

DIARMAIT MacCEARBHAILL°, High King of Eriu from 548 to 563

MAIRENN°, of Mumu, his queen, mother of Esseilte

the MORHOLT°°, Champion of Eriu, brother of Queen Mairenn

(Aed MacAillel°, Prince of the Ulaid)

Aillel of Dal Raida, a warrior at Temair

(Aillel°°, King of Connachta, Medbh's husband)

(Ainmere°, King of the Ulaid)

403

(Aoife and Scathach°°, warrior queens who trained Cuchulain)

(Amergin°°, the Bard of the Sons of Mil)

Amergin MacAlam°, Archpoet/Ard-Filidh of Eriu

(Brigid°, Abbess of Cíll Dara)

Brigid°°, goddess of healing, poetry, and smithcraft

(Boann°°, mother of Oengus, wife of Nechtain and/or of the Dagda, goddess of the river Boinne)

(Bran son of Febal°°, who voyaged to the Blessed Isles)

Brendan°, the Voyager, later St. Brendan

(Ciaran°, Abbot of Clonmacnoise)

Columba°, Abbot of Derry, etc. (born Prince of the Ulaid, later St. Columba of Iona)

(Conleth°, Abbot of Cíll Dara)

(Conchobar°°, King of the Ulaid, Cuchulain's lord, Deirdre's master)

(Corcc°, King of Cashel, fifth century)

(Cormac MacArt°, High King, 218–256)

Crimthan MacFergus, a warrior at Temair

(Cuchulain°°, the supreme hero of Ulster)

Curnan°, Prince of Connachta, royal hostage

(the Dagda°°, the "Good God" of fertility)

(Diancecht°°, the Physician of the Tuatha Dé Danann)

(Diarmuid O'Duibne°° of the Fianna, lover of Grainne)

(Deirdre°° the fair, beloved of Naoisi)

(En°° son of Ethaman, poet and historian of the Tuatha Dé Danann)

Donal MacForgaill, one of the Morholt's followers

Domnall MacLeite, a trader and agent of King Diarmait

Eithne, Princess of Mumu, visiting Temair

Fedelm, a nun of Cíll Dara

(Ferdiad MacIdaid°°, who killed the dragon, loved Finnabair, and was killed by his friend Cuchulain)

Fergus MacCiaran, one of the Morholt's followers

Fergus MacGabran, Prince of West Midhe and Champion of Eriu

(Finn MacCumhail**, the great war-leader who was supposed to marry Grainne)

(Princess Finnabair**, daughter of Medbh)

(Finnian*, Abbot of Moville, whose book Columba copied)

(Fintan MacBócra**, architect of Temair)

Firtai Iugalach, a warrior at Temair

Gabran, King of West Midhe

(Grainne**, daughter of Cormac, who eloped with Diarmuid)

Leborcham, the woman-satirist

(Loegaire**, High King, 428–463)

(Lugh Samildanach**, god of all crafts)

(Matholwch**, King of Eriu in the second branch of the *Mabinogion*)

(Medbh**, the great warrior Queen of Connachta)

Messach, nurse to Esseilte and Branwen

(Miach**, son of Diancecht, from whose body the healing herbs grew)

(the Morrigu**, daughter of Ernmas, also called the Morrigan, goddess of battle)

Muadan MacDaire, warrior of Eriu

(Mughain*, Diarmait's second queen)

Muiredach* King of South Leinster

(Naoisi**, son of Usnach, who eloped with Deirdre)

(Nath*, High King, 405–428)

(Niall* of the Nine Hostages, High King, 379–405, ancestor of the Ui Néill)

(Niamh**, of the Sidhe, who carried Oisin to the Land of Promise)

(Oengus Og**, of the Sidhe, lord of the Brugh na Boinne)

(Ruadan*, Abbot of Clonmacnoise, Diarmait's enemy)

Sionach, Cairenn, Brecc, Esseilte's Irish handmaidens

(Slaine** son of Partholon, of the first inhabitants of Eriu)

(Ternoc the seafarer*)

(Tuathal* of West Midhe, Diarmait's predecessor)

BRITISH

DRUSTAN° of Léon (also called Dughan the harper), supposed son of Meliau of Léon and Gwenneth daughter of Riwal, natural son of Marcus Cunomorus of Ker-haes

ESSYLT DORNWENN°° (of the white hands) of Barsa, whom Drustan married

GORWENNOL°°, Drustan's tutor and companion

KARASEK of Nans Dreyn, Drustan's enemy

KEIHIRDYN°° of Barsa, brother of Essylt Dornwenn

MARCUS CUNOMORUS° (Marc'h, the Horse King), King of Kernow and Mach-Tiern of Ker-haes in Armorica (527?–560)

MERIADEK°°, steward of Bannhedos, Karasek's ally

MEVENNUS MAGLOS, a lord of Kernow and envoy to Eriu

OGRIN°°, the hermit of Goss Moor

(Artor/Arthur° of Britain, Dux Bellorum, High King, 475–515)

(Auroc°, Mach-Tiern of Léon)

Beli map Branek, a lord of Kernow

(Bran°°, High King of Britain in the second branch of the *Mabinogion*)

(Branwen°°, sister of Bran in the second branch of the *Mabinogion*)

Bretowennus, lord of Penryn

Brigantia°°, territorial and tribal goddess of Britain

the Bucca°°, Cornish analogue of Pan, Puck, and the Horned God

(Budic° of Kemper, Meliau's father, Marc'h's ally)

(Budic II° of Kemper, Marc'h's son by Budic I's daughter)

(*Budicca*°, Budic's daughter and Marc'h's first wife)

Crida, housekeeper of Bannhedos

(Culhwch°°, a hero of the *Mabinogion*)

(Deroc° of Domnonia, son of Riwal)

Dinan, a friend of Drustan's

Fragan Tawr, a warrior

(Gildas°, chronicler of the kings who followed Arthur)

Captain Gorgi of the *Flower o' the Broom*

(Gradlon°° of Ys, "Gradlon Mor")

(Gradlon/Graelent°°, the lover)

(*Gwenneth*° daughter of Riwal, Drustan's mother)

Hadron Hardhand, a friend of Drustan's

Iestyn, one of Marc'h's men

(Iudual°, son of Jonas of Dol)

(Jonas°, mach-tiern of Dol, killed by Cunomorus)

Ladek, a messenger

(Macliavus°, mach-tiern of Venetorum, Marc'h's ally)

(Meliau°, mach-tiern of Léon, son of Budic)

(Melor° of Léon, son of Meliau murdered by Riwal, later St. Melor)

(Morgaine°°, sister of Artor and Queen of the Inner Realm)

(Olwen°°, beloved of Culhwch)

Paul Aurelian-Paulus Aurelianus°, Abbot (later St. Pol of Léon)

(Pritella° daughter of Auroc, wife of Jonas of Dol)

Perran of Dynas Ban and his wife *Kew*

Rigan of Tregor, an ally of the King

Riwal/Pompeius Regalis°, mach-tiern of Domnonia, Drustan's grandfather

(Samson°, Abbot of Dol, enemy of Cunomorus, later St. Samson)

Theodoric° son of Budic, later King of Glevissig

(Tremor°, later St. Tremeur of Carhaix, Marc'h's son by Tryphyna)

(Tryphyna°°, Marc'h's second wife)

(Unhintic°, sister of Urien of Rheged, wife of Theodoric)

(Urien° King of Rheged, 560?–590)

(Vitalinus/Vortigern°, Wor-Tiern of Britain)

(Winomarc'h/Guigemar°°, a legendary warrior of Léon)

Winwalo°, son of Fracan (later St. Guenolé)

Withgy, Marc'h's horsemaster

Wydhyel map Ladek, a lord of Kernow

(Yspadadden°°, chief giant, Olwen's father)

Yvan, a youth of Marc'h's household

SAXONS

(Aethelbert° of Kent, King of the Jutes and Frisians)

FRANKS

CHRAMN°, son of Chlotar, Merovingian prince, ally of Cunomorus

(Arnegund°, Chlotar's third wife, Chilperic's mother)

(Childebert°, King of Paris, Chramn's uncle)

(Chilperic°, Chlotar's last son)

(Chlotar°, King of Soissons and later King of the Franks, Chramn's father)

PLACES IN THE STORY

ERIU (Ireland)

Places

Atha Cliath = Dublin

the Bearbra = the Barrow

the Boinne = the Boyne

Brugh na Boinne = Newgrange tumuli

Inber Colptha = Drogheda Bay

Abbey of Cíll Dara = St. Brigid's abbey on the Curragh, in Leinster

Temair = the hill of Tara

Tobar Bhride = the well of Brigid at Mullengar

Territories

Connachta = Connaught

Laigin = Leinster

Midhe = Meath

Mumu = Munster

the Ulaid = Ulster

409

BRITAIN

Settlements or fortresses

Bannhedos = Castle Dor
Belerion = Penwith
Dynas Ban = Castle an Dinas
the Fawwyth = the Fowey
the Heyle = Hayle estuary
Ker-Esk = (Roman, Isca Dumnoniorum) Exeter
Kerrek Los = St. Michael's Mount
Lan Juliot/Dyn Tagell = (Roman, Durocornovium) Tintagel
Lan Wedenek = Padstow
Lys Hornek (hill fort in Penzance)
Modron's Well = Madron Well (near Penzance)
Nans Yann = Lantyan farm
Ogrin's rock = Roche Rock
Porth Ia = St. Ives
Portcaster = Roman fort at Portsmouth Harbor
Porth Mawr = Whitesands Bay
Sabrina Sea = Bristol Channel
Welnans = Golant

Territories

Clyde = SW Scotland
Demetia = Dyfed
Dyfneint = Devon
Dumnonia = Cornwall and Devon
Glevissig = Glamorgan
Gododdin = SE Scotland
Gwent = Caerwent
Gwynedd/Venedotia = N Wales
Kernow = Cornwall
Powys = (Roman, Pagenses) north central Wales
Rheged = mostly Lancashire and Dumfriesshire

ARMORICA (Brittany) and GAUL

Settlements or fortresses

Barsa = Île du Bas

Dol = (Adala Dolum) Dol

Drustan's Isle = Île Tristan

Geso = (Roman Gesocribate) Brest

Inis-Sun = Île de Sein

Kemper = (the confluent, Roman Civitas Aquilonia) Quimper

Ker-haes = (the fortress of Ahes, Roman Vorgium) Carhaix

Lan Brioc = St. Brieuc

Lan Paul near Barsa = (Roman Castra Legionum) St. Pol de Léon

Lutetia (Lutetia Parisorum) = Paris

Namnet = (Roman Portus Namnetum) Nantes

Plebs Marci = district of Ploumarc'h in present-day Douarnenez

Pt. Vanis = Pt. du Van

Redon = (Roman Condate Redonum) Rennes

Tregor = Tregeur

Venetorum = (Roman Dartoritum Venetorum) Vannes

Territories

Broceliande = (Pagus trans Sylvam, Breton Brokilon, Porhoet) forest of Paimpont

Cornovia = (the country of the Cornovii) Cornouailles

Domnonia = (the land of the Dumnonii), present-day Côtes du Nord (Bro Brioc, Bro Trecor, Bro Malo, Bro Dol)

Léon and Achm (medieval Lyonesse)

Neustria = Frankish district including Armorica

Uhelgoat = "the High Wood" (the forest of Huelgoat)

Venetia = (the country of the Veneti) the Vannetais

Diana L. Paxson grew up in Pacific Palisades, California, and majored in English at Mills College. She earned her M.A. in Comparative Literature at the University of California at Berkeley, specializing in the medieval period. While in graduate school she started the Society for Creative Anachronism, an international organization dedicated to recreating medieval arts and activities.

Ms. Paxson has written numerous short stories for magazines and original anthologies (including *Thieves' World, Darkover,* and *Witchworld*). Her novels span the centuries, from the historical *(White Mare, Red Stallion)* to the contemporary *(Brisingamen* and *The Paradise Tree)* to the far-future (her Westria series). *The White Raven* is her first retelling of the great Celtic epics.

In addition to her writing, Ms. Paxson has served as an officer in the Society for Creative Anachronism, worked for ten years at Far West Laboratory for Educational Research and Development, and in her spare time composes for and plays the Celtic harp.